Jojo's French Escape

Lorraine Wilson

One More Chapter
a division of HarperCollins*Publishers*
The News Building
1 London Bridge Street
London SE1 9GF

www.harpercollins.co.uk

This paperback edition 2020

First published in Great Britain in ebook format by
HarperCollins*Publishers* 2020

A catalogue record for this book
is available from the British Library

Ebook ISBN: 978-0-00-836311-6
B Format Paperback ISBN: 978-0-00-836312-3

This novel is entirely a work of fiction.
The names, characters and incidents portrayed in it are
the work of the author's imagination. Any resemblance to
actual persons, living or dead, events or localities is
entirely coincidental.

Set in Birka by Palimpsest Book Production Ltd, Falkirk
Stirlingshire

Printed and bound in Great Britain by CPI Group (UK) Ltd,
Croydon CR0 4YY

To Anna Bell, John Prentice and Flump (aka The Artful Dodger). I'll be forever grateful for the encouragement and inspiration provided by writer friends and cheeky puppies!

Chapter 1

'New beginnings are often disguised as painful endings'

Lao Tzu

From annabelgrant@thestickybun.co.uk
To joannagrant@thestickybun.co.uk
Subject: Heads up
Hi JoJo,
Hope you're okay? It's been a while since we heard from you. Mum's been worrying. I know you said you've been much better lately, and you're happily settled in France but you feel so far away and after what happened last year it's difficult not to be a bit concerned when you go quiet. Just humour me and stay in touch, okay?

I only ask because I love you, you know that, right?

Anyway, I need to give you a heads up about something. Two somethings in fact, I want you to be forewarned so you have some time to think.

Something number one: Have you decided what to do about the café? Because if you're going to stay in France maybe you should think about selling? I'm happy to keep looking after it for a bit longer but I was thinking that maybe I'd like to go traveling, at some point anyway. I know how much The Sticky Bun means to you but if you're not coming back . . . Your call.

Something number two: we had some people from the television company turn up on the doorstep. They said they'd tried to get in touch with you, but you weren't answering your phone or email. They were talking about doing a special 'one year on' piece for Sex in the Suburbs @Nite, it's a companion panel show to the main Sex in the Suburbs series . . . well, you know the kind of thing they want. Where is Joanna Grant now? And does she still hold a grudge? Maybe they were planning to give you a surprise on-air reunion with Aiden and Sally and hoping you'd punch Aiden? Who knows.

Actually, I'm hoping you'll punch Aiden. On or off air, I'm not fussy.

Dad told them to fuck off. Can you believe it? After all the grief he's given us over the years for bad language? Anyway, I thought you should know. Just in case they try to ambush you.

Stay safe okay sis? And please send me a reply soon.

Miss you lovely. Sending hugs.

Annabel

xx

P.S. I love the photo you sent me with Pickwick sitting on your shoulder. Who knew a miniature Yorkshire terrier could do a parrot impression. Poppy's dogs are so cute, I'd love to meet them. Send me some more pics when you get a chance. Peanut's dancing on YouTube is hilarious and Treacle sounds really sweet, I'm glad he's not so timid now and getting over his pre-rescue traumas.

'*You 'know, I'm sure it's her, it's definitely JoJo . . .'*

'No, really? So she's like a waitress now then?'

I do my best to block out the voices and sit tall in my chair at the kitchen table. There's a tightness in my chest. It's just anxiety, I know.

Just. Ha!

I try to keep in mind how far I've come in the past year. I knew that a new summer season would bring its challenges and I'm determined to hold on to all the progress I've made since last year.

Last summer I would've been hiding in my room or the loo having a full-on panic attack, not just a few anxious twinges. It would be fair to say that when I first arrived in France I was in pieces but after a year of Poppy's non-judgemental, easy-going company and the peace of living in a rural community that couldn't care less about English reality TV I'm finally feeling more like myself again. I love running the guesthouse, and the fresh air and outdoor lifestyle have been great for me. Discovering the French markets has been amazing and inspiring, both in terms of the fresh produce for cooking inspiration and the antique *brocante* markets for interior design ideas. Gradually I've clawed and climbed my way out of the dark hole I landed in last year.

And I'm not going to let a few people gossiping push me back down again.

It's taken a while to put the pieces back together again, like an emotional jigsaw puzzle that's more or less finished. Some pieces have the edges knocked off and there are a few holes where I've lost pieces of myself, but I am mostly together again.

Mostly.

And I plan to stay that way.

'I read she had a breakdown and checked into the Priory . . .'

Do they realise their voices are carrying from the terrace into the kitchen?

Days like today are just a little wobble. Hearing the English guests whispering, speculating, wondering if it's really me . . . it knocks me. But like a Weeble I'm determined to wobble back into place. I won't let it keep me down for long.

I do the yoga breathing Poppy taught me and it works well, the tightness in my chest lessening. Ha! Take that, anxiety! Who's in charge now? So the guests want to talk about me. So what? I absorb the peace of the kitchen, of cosy hot chocolates with Poppy, of glasses of wine on the kitchen table or out on the terrace while I plan menus and compile to-do lists and Poppy sketches in her journal.

I pick at the frayed edge of my denim shorts. I spent last summer shrouded and sweltering in baggy clothes and baseball caps. This summer I'm looking forward to wearing cute summer dresses and pretty tops. I'm finally emerging from my shell again and I'm done apologising for being me.

I think about Annabel's email and the *Sex in the Suburbs* people wanting me to do a panel show and have to suppress the urge to laugh hysterically. As if!

A large furry muzzle appears on my knee. First impressions suggest the muzzle is attached to a giant shaggy rug but on closer examination it's possible to see a pair of eyes amidst the fur. They belong to one of Les Coquelicots' most important residents, Barney, who is a crossbreed griffon/beagle/hearthrug. I can attest to the fact that he makes a lovely foot warmer and footstool in winter. In summer, not so much. We'll have to think about giving him a fur cut soon, before the really hot weather hits us.

He rests his head on my lap and leans the rest of his shaggy body against me, his pale, milky eyes reflecting his blindness, a disability he's adapted to with amazing ease. Putting his head on my lap and leaning in is Barney's version of a hug and I reciprocate, reaching out to sink my hand through curly, thick fur until it meets dog.

On my other side another important Les Coquelicots resident, Pickwick, puts his front paws up on my shin and taps me, asking to be picked up. As he is a miniature Yorkshire terrier he can barely reach my knees but like Barney he doesn't let anything hold him back, not even the crooked front legs he was born with. Peanut and Treacle, the Chihuahuas, are even smaller still and are undoubtedly out the front with Poppy and the guests, dancing about on their hind legs, looking cute and begging for as much food as they can get their paws on. Barney and Pickwick tend to keep me company in the kitchen though, when Poppy goes to Leo's.

I definitely have a special bond with them. Barney because he virtually lives in the kitchen, determined everyone remembers that since his rescue he's now an indoor dog and shouldn't be left out at night. Pickwick because I've taken to dog-napping him to sleep on my bed at night and I talk to him a lot. In my defence he does talk back, making odd pigeon-like noises that sound exactly like he's chattering away, making his point. Poppy has the Chihuahuas – well, and she has Leo too now and soon she'll have Leo's dog Maxi as a permanent addition to the pack – but my bed is pretty empty so having a tiny Yorkie curled up on my feet or occasionally on the top of my head on the pillow is good company.

Poppy says that Barney and Pickwick only stay in the kitchen because I sneak them extra treats. I like to think it's more than that though. Felix, our cat at home, would be horrified – I've become a dog person.

Dogs are great though. They just listen and don't pass judgment. They continue to offer their unconditional love and support no matter what.

If only people were the same.

If you imagine the stupidest thing you've ever done and multiply it by a hundred, even then you probably won't come close to the appalling, stupid decision that got me into this mess. I do hope not anyway. I wouldn't wish that kind of humiliation on anyone.

My self-preservation instinct compelled me to run. I got as far as the South of France, where lack of funds and the kindness of strangers made me decide to stop running and start hiding. And where better to hide than a tiny, welcoming village in the heart of the Languedoc countryside? I left the happy, body-confident, outgoing JoJo, the Joanna Grant everyone knew from the telly, behind me in England and reinvented myself as 'just Joanna', a reserved, itinerant worker and cook with a love of baseball hats and baggy clothes.

Recently though I've been feeling like it might be okay to be JoJo again.

I'm not sure at what point my hideaway became my home. Initially I couldn't see how to get over it, given the drama and scandal were on the internet for ever, a replay available at the tap of the screen or click of the mouse. But I took things one normal, non-disastrous day by normal, non-disastrous day, and each day the world didn't end I breathed a little easier. My mind became filled with other, nicer preoccupations but every so often something happens, like tonight, and it hurts, like I'm knocking against thorns hooked deep beneath my skin.

Sitting in the kitchen is calming me. It's the heart of my friend Poppy's guesthouse, Les Coquelicots – a *chambre d'hôtes* in the village of St Quentin sur Aude and the scene of many a consoling late night hot chocolate over the past year. Not just for me either – Poppy had her own stuff to deal with last year when her boyfriend Pete dumped her by text the day she signed the purchase papers for the house, announcing he wouldn't be moving to France with her after all. The fact that she got over it and is now in a relationship with Leo, the lovely village vet, gives me hope that maybe one day I'll find that too. Okay, that seems like a stretch now, but that I'd even be contemplating it would have seemed inconceivable last year. So . . . maybe.

I put the kettle on to make a cup of tea. Les Coquelicots isn't just a home, it's been a safe haven, a second chance and a place to hide from the world, all while still technically working and paying my way, wrapped up in one. Helping Poppy renovate the house and turn it into a profitable business has saved me from going completely insane. Without something to keep my hands and brain busy I would have rerun what happened last year over and over on an endless loop until I . . . No, I don't want to think about what I might have done if I hadn't met Poppy, if she hadn't given me a chance, if she hadn't, well, saved me, I suppose. It sounds melodramatic but it happens to be true.

I pop my cup of tea onto the stripped pine table that I found for Poppy at a local *brocante* market and rest my forehead on my arms, inhaling the faint aroma of beeswax polish as I calm my breathing and block out the conversation from the terrace. I hear Poppy's voice outside, back from Leo's and greeting the guests. I'm reassured she'll steer the conversation elsewhere. People often make the mistake of thinking she's soft but there's a core of steel running through her when the people, or for that matter the dogs, she cares about are threatened.

I sip my tea and resist the urge to go out on the terrace and put the story straight, to correct all the lies. It wouldn't do any good and would just make things worse but I'm only human and the urge to defend myself is one I've yet to master. It's not fair but it is what it is. I know I'm not to blame. I've done nothing wrong. I've nothing to be ashamed of.

I repeat the mantra in my head and eventually the urge to wade in and explain myself subsides. I've been telling myself the exact same thing every day and I do believe it.

Mostly.

There are questions I'm not sure I'll ever get answers to. Like if I've done nothing to be ashamed of then why do I feel so ashamed? And why do so many people on the internet believe I should be ashamed of myself and want to tell me so in great detail? Head belief and heart belief seem to be two very different things.

I bend down to scoop up Pickwick and let him perch on my shoulder, parrot style as he likes it. I think I'm starting to understand how eccentric misfits end up the way they are. I mean, I've been using a Yorkshire terrier who thinks he's a parrot–pigeon hybrid as a counsellor, for pity's sake, talking away to him about everything that happened.

Well, it helps and at least I know he's never going to sell my secrets to the tabloids. I don't believe he'd betray me even for a lorry full of dog treats. Whereas my cat would so sell me out for his favourite salmon treats.

By the time the meal is over I've sent Annabel a short reply and some dog photos and I've cheered myself up enough to put a smile on my face for Poppy. I remove Pickwick from where he ended up falling asleep, curled up on my chest, and together Poppy and I clear the plates and wipe the table down.

'Fancy a hot chocolate?' I stack the dishwasher with the dirty plates and ignore the half hopeful, half plaintive expressions on the dogs' faces. I know they aren't hungry because I fed them myself earlier but they are skilled little actors.

'Yes please.' Poppy yawns and stretches, apparently oblivious that Peanut and Treacle have abandoned their attempt to break into the dishwasher and are trying to scale her like she's a climbing frame. 'Just don't expect any small talk, I'm completely out of it.'

'No problem, I used all mine up on Barney and Pickwick anyway.' I get the milk out of the fridge and find a clean milk saucepan. Good hot chocolate can't be done in the microwave; the milk needs to be heated slowly and the cocoa powder added gradually. We use a Swiss brand of hot chocolate powder that comes in milk, white and dark flavours and has added B vitamins that make it good for us. That's our story anyway and we're sticking to it.

Poppy yawns widely and sinks down into a chair.

'Did it go okay up at the Château earlier?' I ask. 'Was there a lot of wedding planning talk?'

'Oodles of it,' Poppy replies glumly, absent-mindedly fiddling with her engagement ring.

'Happiest day of your life, remember?' I tease.

'Only if you don't have two different lots of relatives to keep happy who both want – no, both expect – different things.'

'You could just elope?'

'Then I wouldn't be making anyone happy. There's a difference between upsetting a few relatives and pissing everyone off.'

'So, upset the few then. If you can't win don't try.' I whisk the chocolate powder into the hot milk until it becomes frothy.

'I know that's sound advice, but this is my mum we're talking about.' She laughs. 'Choosing to get married in France so Leo's dad doesn't have to travel has been a little contentious, as you know. But anyway, enough about me, I had a nice evening, ignore me, I'm just a bit tired. How are you? You seem . . . off.'

She tilts her head and examines me. She has an uncanny ability to pick up other people's emotions, which can be annoying at times, when you're trying to pretend everything is okay, for instance. But I know it's only because she cares.

'The guests were talking about me.' I lower my voice. 'They recognised me.'

'Oh,' Poppy frowns. 'Nothing too . . .'

'No, nothing too . . .' I leave the possibility blank too, deliberately. 'It's only going to get worse over the summer. We've lots of bookings from English guests and I'm not going to hide away like last year. I'll just have to, you know, deal.'

'Not all of them will have heard of you.'

'No,' I concede. 'If they were marooned on a remote island with no wifi last summer they might have missed the story of "disgraced TV star Joanna Grant". Yes, seriously, you know, it's like my official moniker or something. It appears no journalist or blogger can write the words Joanna Grant without adding the word "disgraced".'

'Well, I hadn't heard of you,' Poppy replies mildly.

'Which is just one of the reasons why I love you.' I pass

her a mug of hot chocolate. 'But you've got to admit you're not exactly typical . . . You don't even have a TV here.'

'Oh, I just haven't got round to it yet,' Poppy replies vaguely. 'I must admit I've never quite understood why you are the one who is disgraced when you did nothing wrong. It was all down to him.'

Him. Yes. It was my ex-boyfriend, reality TV star Aiden, who filmed us having sex without my knowledge. It was Aiden who was responsible for getting the video online, and this just after I had to absorb the shock of finding out, live on TV, that he was cheating on me with my best friend Sally. Apparently, the close-ups of my tear-streaked face were prime-time entertainment. My life became a soap opera.

Or rather a very public melodrama. Maybe now it's obvious why I prefer the company of dogs to humans? I sit down and drink my hot chocolate sitting next to Poppy in companionable silence. I kind of love her obliviousness. It gives me hope and reminds me there is another kind of world out there, it's just up to me to find it.

Why Aiden behaved the way he did I'll never know. I used to think about it. I had plenty of sleepless nights thinking about it, wondering if it was because he fell in love with her, or I wasn't making him happy. Maybe I just wasn't enough for him? As for turning our sex life into a sordid sex tape . . . well, I don't think I'll ever understand that.

My sister Annabel's theory is that he's a selfish prick

who can't keep it in his trousers, or, and this one gets my bet, he did it to make better telly and keep the spotlight on him and doesn't care about Sally any more than he ever cared about me. The only love Aiden knows involves the use of a mirror or a TV camera.

As it is, I'll never know what was going on in his head because I can't trust him to tell me the truth. He is the one still on TV, the star of *Sex in the Suburbs*, loving the limelight and basking in seemingly endless adulation while I'm the one . . . disgraced. He was seen as just a bit of a lad. I was seen as a . . . well, as a slut, to put it bluntly. That was how the narrative went online. You've got to love double standards, haven't you?

Ha! Either that or delete all your social media accounts.

Although deleting all the links to my social media accounts on my phone feels a bit like sticking my head in the sand, ostrich-like. That world is still out there but for me it's a dangerous place to visit. The temptation to engage is too strong, the desire to defend myself, to set the record straight, to persuade the people who think they know me that they're wrong . . . It's mental quicksand and I avoid it at all costs.

The cost of my mistake has been that I've had to leave behind my family, my home and my business. And I've lost my ex-boyfriend and my ex-best friend. I don't know what our guests think of me, but I can bet I've heard it all before and probably a million times worse. People don't generally troll face to face, not when they can look into your eyes and see that you're a human being, just like them. But they come out in force online, hiding in the anonymity of the internet. Aiden fans actually told me I should kill myself. That was the point when Dad disabled the house wifi and took my phone away 'for my own good'.

'Are you ever tempted to just say to people, "Yes, I'm *that* Joanna," and set the record straight?'

'Of course, but honestly it's better not to engage. I want to leave all that behind me and how can I if I have to keep rehashing it?'

'I suppose.' Poppy bites her lip. 'Do you want me to say something to them?'

'God no, I'm okay, Poppy, honestly I am. Please don't worry about me,' I implore her.

The thing is, I've probably even thought some of the comments myself. Some people seem to think that anyone who ends up on reality TV knew what they were signing up for and deserves whatever they get, regardless of how vile it is. If you're on television you've agreed to be public property, entertainment with no holds barred.

I never signed up to be vilified and hounded out of my life, home and business. I didn't know what I was doing. I didn't have a frickin' clue what I was doing. I signed a piece of paper allowing a production company to use my café in a new upcoming reality show. It would be great PR for my business, they said. I wouldn't have to be in it at all if I didn't want to be.

And yes, I read the contract. Twice. I didn't understand it all though. My dad read the contract too, but he is a painter and decorator, he doesn't speak legalese.

I was so naive.

Stupid might be a better word.

We both read it another time, together, and still declared ourselves baffled. The people seemed nice enough and they said the contract was standard so . . .

Like I said, I was stupid and I've paid for that signature a million times over. I had misgivings when the working title of the show was changed to *Sex in Suburbia*. I was determined to stay out of it. I didn't want to be famous, I just wanted to cook and make my café as successful as possible.

Then I met Aiden. Gorgeous, charming Aiden who was so bloody sexy I would've done anything for him. I can see now that he manipulated me. At the time though I was operating in a haze of powerful hormones and mesmerised by Aiden's charisma.

I was stupid and flattered and I fell in love. It was all too easy to say yes to a date with Aiden and agree to let it be filmed. When he asked me out he was so charming. He charmed the pants off me.

Literally.

Unfortunately, he also charmed the pants off of Sally, my best friend and waitress at The Sticky Bun. I found out while being filmed watching the episode in which I told Aiden I loved him. God it makes me cringe to remember that. I actually told him I loved him, and his response had been 'I know'. As sozzled as I was on hormones and lust, I knew that wasn't a good sign.

While I was watching that episode, he and Sally 'popped by', as though anyone ever does anything spontaneous on reality TV, and simply had to tell me what they'd done because they felt so terrible about it. They didn't want to hurt me, but they were in love. I think Sally said something about destiny but I'd kind of blanked out by then.

They didn't feel terrible enough to tell me in private first though.

If only Aiden could've let me lick my wounds in private after that. I could accept that what had been love for me was only sex for him, but I couldn't accept what he did next. As soon as the media lost interest and ratings began to drop, he made sure a video he'd secretly shot of us having sex found its way onto the internet. It was . . . explicit. I've never been one for sex under the covers with the lights off, though if I ever have sex again I might change my mind about that. Somehow, I think insisting all electronic devices be left in another room might spoil the mood or display a lack of trust or something.

To add insult to injury they had the right to keep on filming in the café because I'd signed that bloody piece of paper.

Stupid.

'You're really okay?' Poppy's voice breaks into my thoughts.

'Yes, sorry, I'm a bit tired. I'm off to bed once I've finished my chocolate and finished clearing up.'

I stroke Barney's soft ears and find it therapeutic. I have so much here in St Quentin sur Aude that I love. This is my new life. I'm not doing any 'Joanna Grant, one year on' special shows. I can't believe they had the nerve to doorstep my parents about it. Good old Dad, telling them where to go.

When the press found me last year, I considered doing an interview to get them off my back but in the end one European royal's love life became more interesting. I got a reprieve, thank God, because I couldn't bear it if I had to leave St Quentin.

Annabel's right, I need to think about selling the café because my life is here now. Barney's contented sigh pulls me out of my head, and I focus on stroking his soft furry head and caressing his big floppy ear. Only one of his ears flops; the other sticks up for reasons best known to himself and his mixed-breed gene pool. I love him and all the animals here. Things could be much worse.

'You know that it's this weekend the chef friend of Leo's is coming, yes?' Poppy scoops the two Chihuahuas up onto her lap and finds room for Pickwick on her shoulder while scratching Barney's other ear. She says having multiple dogs has made her good at multitasking.

'No.' I frown. 'What chef friend of Leo's? I didn't even know he had a chef friend. He's coming for the weekend or for longer?'

I am extremely fond of Poppy but sometimes her vague attitude to details can be a tad . . . challenging.

'Didn't I say? Sorry.' She pulls a face. 'He's coming for a few months, having some time out in the South of France. But the big news is he's going to help us get The Barn off the ground. He has a good reputation apparently so his influence will be really useful.'

'I thought we'd decided it wasn't doable to get the restaurant up and running for this season with all the delays we've had with the renovations and paperwork, so we were going to leave it until autumn?'

'Maybe you weren't there when Leo was talking about it?' Poppy asks. 'No, it's no good, I can't remember when we talked about it. The thing is this friend of Leo's can come now so it makes sense to use him. Leo met him during his time in Paris. I guess if you weren't there when Leo and I talked about it I was probably supposed to tell you. Sorry.'

I bite back my irritation. Poppy is rubbing her forehead and I can see how tired she is.

'So, this chef friend, he's staying here in Les Coquelicots then?' I ask, as calmly as I can.

When the idea of turning the large barn behind the guesthouse into a restaurant was first suggested I was dubious but then we went on field trip visits to similar ventures, mostly on farms that had taken the initiative to diversify. Some barn restaurants were so rustic they didn't even have electricity, all the food being brought through from the farmhouse kitchen. Others were more sophisticated with white linen tablecloths and crystal glassware but one thing they all had in common was great food made from local, fresh ingredients. It made sense to capitalise on the extra visitors to the Château's art gallery and wine tasting tours. I've been excited about having a new project to manage.

I was really looking forward to working on the menu and getting the restaurant up and running but with all the delays from the builders time has been running out and I'm crazy busy now we are entering the main season for the guesthouse. I don't have time and I need help but even so . . . I feel a bit like I'm being sidelined.

'Yes, we've got space for the first week. I checked and blocked it out on the calendar. I thought maybe after that he could have my room for a bit? I can always stay at Leo's if we're strapped for space.' Poppy grimaces. 'I'm really sorry this is the first you've heard about it. We're not trying to take anything away from you. We thought you could use some help. You already do so much.'

'I suppose it would be too much on my own,' I admit. 'It's just a bit of a mental adjustment, his coming and being in the house. You know how anti-social I am.'

'I don't know, you seem to be getting more sociable. You even came to the village party.'

'I suppose.' It's true. I have gradually been testing the waters, dipping my toe in, paddling in the shallows. I've even made friends with Sophie, who works in the notaire's office, and Angeline, who is Leo's partner in the vet practice. Though they were Poppy's friends first really.

'Don't worry, I'm sure he's very nice.'

'Of course.' I roll my eyes. 'Chefs are known for being good-natured and friendly.'

I smile to soften the sarcasm but I'm already uneasy . . . My world is cosy and safe and I don't want anyone upsetting the balance. It would be great to have the opportunity to learn from a professional chef but what if he's a misogynist who has no interest in the ideas of a female amateur chef? What, horror of horrors, if he tries to take over my kitchen as well as the Barn project?

'You never know, you might hit it off, after you've both worked in the same industry.' There's a glint in Poppy's eye as she smiles. Her comment is so predictable. She's been trying to pair me off with virtually every single male we come across from the widowed farmer in the next village to the author with a holiday home in St Quentin. Anyone in close proximity of marriageable age basically, the bar isn't set particularly high.

'Noooo. No way. Stop right there, Poppy. I'm okay single. Maybe one day I'll meet someone great and start dating again but there's no rush and I'm not looking yet. I don't need a man in my life to be happy.'

Pickwick lets out a high-pitched woof.

'Sorry, Pickwick,' I add. 'Male canines excepted.' I get up and head back to the dishwasher to finish the last bits of clearing up.

'It could be great. He likes cooking, you like cooking . . .'

'And we're going to have to work together, at least for a while.' I pause, biting my lip. 'I've already had one relationship ruin my workplace. You know I had to leave my café behind. I love what I have here and would never do anything that might jeopardise that.'

Poppy gives me a sceptical look but doesn't say the obvious. That I'd be scared to date again. Getting close to anyone again is going to be scary. That's true but I really do mean what I say about not letting a relationship ruin something I care about again. Annabel's email about the café is weighing heavy on my mind.

Starting a relationship again would be hard enough without it having the capacity to affect my work too. I'll always remember that gut-wrenching moment when I realised Aiden and Sally had betrayed me. It was like being in a lift that suddenly plunged downwards: there was a physical, inward lurch and then emotional free-fall . . .

Climbing back up again has taken so long. If, and it's a big if, I meet someone I think is worth the risk I'll be a lot more careful with my heart.

I sigh and shove the cutlery down into the tray with a loud clunk. I feel the need to make amends with Poppy. My desire to protect the status quo is a selfish one. She just wants to make sure The Barn is a success. I do too.

'It's an exciting project. I loved that trendy barn restaurant you took me to up in the Black Mountains. It would be great if we can create something similar.' I try to inject enthusiasm into my voice and to swallow my emotions back under control. 'Anyway what do you know about him, this chef? He's French, yes?'

'He was working in Paris when he and Leo met but he's not French. I think Leo said he'd been in London for the past few years. He's called Callum something. Callum O'Connor, that's it.'

I stop, dropping a plate into place in the dishwasher rack with a loud thunk.

'Not *the* Callum O'Connor. The celebrity chef? Haven't you heard of *Callum O'Connor's Cook Off*? Or his *Kitchen Cook Off* show?' I stare at her blank expression incredulously.

'Hmm, dunno, I've never heard of the show or of him. Leo might have said he was on television, I can't remember,' Poppy replies distractedly while texting on her phone. I've lost her.

'Honestly, Poppy.' I sigh, trying to rein in my growing agitation.

'What?' Poppy looks up from her phone, expression blank.

I take a deep breath. I'm tempted to ask how on earth she hasn't heard of one of the most famous TV shows in the UK but then we are talking about Poppy. I was living with her for months before she found out who I was and even then it was only because somebody told her.

'Never mind. Why on earth would *he* want to come here? I don't understand.'

'Why, what's wrong with here?' Poppy raises an eyebrow. 'I seem to remember he wanted some peace and quiet. Leo said he was taking some time out. You can ask him when he gets here.'

She doesn't say what we're both thinking, that I came here for some peace and quiet, to get away from scandal. I'm sure Callum isn't coming here for the same reasons as me though; I haven't seen any scandalous news about him online. Not that I really keep up with the news now I'm here. I've been too busy.

'Hmm.' I finish stacking the dishwasher and set it going, trying to hide my agitation.

'What's wrong?' Poppy asks gently. It seems after all this time of living together I can't hide my feelings from her.

'He'll know who I am.' I wrap my arms around my body and lean back against the kitchen counter. A French male chef was going to be bad enough but an Irish celebrity chef from London is much, much worse. Even worse, he's a celebrity chef I've always liked and respected. I care about his opinion.

Poppy's forehead crinkles. 'I thought you were feeling much better nowadays, about meeting new people I mean?'

I don't know how to explain that although I'm feeling better and happier about socialising, having my home disrupted by someone from the very world I ran away from feels way out of my comfort zone. I doubt I'm even on his radar . . . Regardless, I can't say what I'm feeling because Poppy will worry.

'It's a bit different, Poppy, but don't worry, I'm sure it'll work out fine.' I shrug. 'It's just whenever I meet someone new, well . . . I can't help wondering if they've seen the sex tape.'

I wonder if Callum O' Connor has seen it. Uncomfortable emotions prickle at my skin. Embarrassment tinged with shame.

I know Poppy hasn't watched it. If she had she might understand why ditching the bland, oversized T-shirts and leggings I hid in last year is such a big deal. Wearing clothes that are pretty, colourful or revealing, anything that might draw somebody's eye to me, is taking a lot of courage. I might be ready to engage fully with my new life here, to start being JoJo again, but that doesn't mean I assume it's going to be easy.

Considering that when the sex tape video hit the internet I took to my room and hid under my duvet, I know I've come a long way. I remember Mum saying quite tartly that it was a bit too late to be covering myself up now, wasn't it? Like locking the stable door after the horse has bolted. There's nothing like a bit of support from family.

'You've got nothing to be ashamed of.' Poppy places a hand on my elbow. For her distractedness she can be very perceptive sometimes. 'You know if anyone ever gives you any grief we'll set the dogs on them, celebrity chef or not.'

I look down at the two tiny Chihuahuas, one miniature Yorkie and the blind ex-hunting dog who happens to be a total softy. My mouth quirks involuntarily into a smile at the idea of them defending me, though I'm sure they'd all give it a good go. The Chihuahuas in particular are utterly fearless. Barney is the only one who might be capable of actually defending me but all anyone has to do is give him a biscuit, scratch him behind his ears and he'll roll over to have his tummy tickled.

'I'm sure that won't be necessary, Poppy.' I smile. 'Actually I've always wanted to learn from a professional chef so you're right, this could be a good thing.'

I turn my back to her to put our mugs into the sink and decide I'll make sure it's a good thing. It's supposed to be healthy to step out of your comfort zone and I've got to get used to facing the outside world again. Les Coquelicots has been my refuge and while I'm worried about Callum O'Connor rocking my lifeboat I have to admit I'm the teensiest bit excited about meeting him. Okay, maybe more than a teeny, tiny bit excited.

I've always liked cookery shows from the how-to variety to competition and reality shows. I used to watch them with Gran, cup of tea and piece of freshly baked cake in hand. Of all the celebrity chefs Callum O'Connor is undoubtedly the hottest.

But that has nothing to do with why I'm starting to feel a little bit excited about meeting him. That'll be because I'm interested to learn from a professional chef. It has nothing to do with his piercing blue eyes and alpha male personality.

Honest.

Last time I worked alongside a fanciable celeb it ended in emotional carnage. I've been there, done that and got the sex tape to show for it. I won't make the same mistake again.

Chapter 2

'I hope you live a life you're proud of. If you find you're not, I hope you have the strength to start over all over again'

F. Scott Fitzgerald

From sallyvickers89@gmail.com
To joannagrant@thestickybun.co.uk
Subject: Time to Move On
Come on JoJo, you can't ignore me for ever. Can't we be grown up about what happened and put it all behind us? I understand you're jealous that I was the one who got to be with Aiden in the end, but we all need to move on.

I would like the three of us to meet up, to sit down and have a civilised chat, like adults. Talking of which you need to tell your sister Annabel to grow up and stop yelling insults at us. It's very undignified and her language is atrocious.

All the best,
Sally

From annabelgrant@thestickybun.co.uk
To joannagrant@thestickybun.co.uk
Subject: Miss you
I miss you lovely. Are you ever coming home? Dad said to let you know there's been an offer on the café and will you get in touch with him? I hope you will. He misses you too, you know, and I think you're going to have to get some documents witnessed, to do with the sale?

Maybe I'll have to come over to France to see you if you haven't got time to come to me. I could bring the papers with me. Your very own personal courier!

Lots of love and xxxx
Annabel

I've read Sally's email five times and I'm still boiling inside. She wants me to be grown up about it? Why can't they just leave me alone? I'm so angry I want to throw something or yell, but I can't without Poppy hearing, and she'd be upset for me. It's like she actually feels what I'm feeling and then I end up having to comfort her and it's all messed up frankly.

I wish I could go for a run – that usually helps me cope with overwhelming emotions – but I haven't time. Callum O'Connor is arriving any minute now and this really isn't the emotional state I want to be in when he does. Why do Aiden and Sally want to see me? It can't really be because they want to have an 'adult' conversation. As if. With anyone else I'd think they want my forgiveness to make themselves feel better. Maybe Sally does, a bit. I'd like to think there's a little bit of guilt or regret in there given we were friends, we saw each other every day, danced together, drank together and cried together. I can imagine how Aiden manipulated her. He's good at that.

He certainly doesn't care about my forgiveness. He's completely amoral. When the empathy gene was being handed out he didn't get in the queue. I really think he believes life is one big Aiden show, and everyone around him is just a bit-part actor in the drama of his life.

I think it's much more likely they want to create more drama out of this somehow. I always used to joke that Sally was a drama queen. Hearing her exaggerated tales used to be funny. Until I became a victim of her rewriting of events. Well, she can send as many emails as she likes, I'm not going back to talk to them or do some stupid spin-off show. *Joanna Grant, One Year On.*

I look in the mirror and stare at the beautiful turquoise sundress Poppy bought me from the market at Mirepoix. I smooth the fabric down over my hips. I love it. It's knee-length so not too revealing but it's pretty figure-hugging. Having larger than average breasts can make some dresses look almost indecent. I don't think I've got a vest top that would go underneath it though. Most of my wardrobe is still in England at my parents' house. I stare critically at the cleavage-hugging bodice and try to tug it up a bit. Sod it, I'm wearing it. I can't meet Callum O'Connor in ripped denim shorts and a T-shirt. He practically oozes Gaelic charm from every pore and he's pretty damned sexy.

But that's not the reason I'm determined to look nice. It's for my own benefit. I shouldn't have to hide under baggy clothes. I've got nothing to be ashamed of.

So there. I address my reflection in the mirror.

At least I think I know my motives. It's so confusing being me nowadays. I overthink stuff, I know I do. It comes from spending too much time alone and not really sharing things with anyone, except Poppy. I'm not sure I recognise the woman looking back at me in the mirror. My face is thinner and tanned and my long, light blonde hair has turned a shade of white blonde in the sunshine. I've regained the weight I lost in the early months. That's the effect of French patisserie combined with weak will power for you. I look healthy though, just different from the old me.

Maybe if I don't recognise myself then Callum O'Connor won't either. I'm 'Just Joanna' who helps in the guesthouse. No one special. Move along, nothing to see here and all that.

I run a hand over the beautiful turquoise cotton fabric that skims the curve of my hips and an unwanted image of the sex tape video comes to my mind. It's forever burned into the hard disk of my memory banks, the image replay of me putting on a show for Aiden. He used to like watching me strip and touching myself. It's why it looks like I'm staring right into the video camera. It's why most people think I was complicit. That I did it to extend my fifteen minutes of fame.

It's why most people seem to think I got exactly what I deserved.

I was, in fact, staring directly at Aiden who was leaning back against his desk, just to the right of his open laptop. The laptop that was recording footage of me. I didn't think anything of the laptop at the time. I mean, who would? It was always on his desk and usually open.

I know, because I've been told, that it goes on to show me enthusiastically giving my narcissistic boyfriend a blow job and then getting fucked by him, doggy style. He always did have a high opinion of his bottom.

I say I've been told because I couldn't bring myself to watch the rest of it. Annabel watched it for me and told me what was in it. I had to know. Quite why I'm a slut for having sex with my boyfriend in the privacy of a bedroom I don't know. Maybe my 'sin' was to enjoy it. I like sex and I miss it but the humiliation was far too high a price to pay for a sex life.

It's why, despite wanting to look attractive today, I don't have any designs on Callum. Dating someone you're working with is never a good idea but dating someone whose celebrity would put me straight back into the firing line would just be suicidal.

I won't ever let myself be humiliated like that again.

I try again to hike up the neckline of the dress but to no avail. It's like the dress is saying, 'You have boobs. Live with it!'

Fine, the dress wins the argument. I have boobs and I

refuse to be ashamed of them. I head downstairs, Pickwick, Peanut and Treacle following at my heels like my own personal entourage. I feel slightly sick. I'm excited to meet Callum but I'm also nervous. I've built myself a safe life here. I don't want anyone upsetting the balance just as I'm finding my feet again.

By the time I get outside Leo's jeep is pulling up, back from the airport, and both Leo and Callum are getting out of the car. The dogs desert me instantly and converge on Callum, mutt-mobbing him. Even Barney trots out of the kitchen and heads towards the group, picking up on the excited woofs of the others. Callum picks up Pickwick and is cuddling him. He certainly gets full marks so far. Poppy really ought to get a sign made for the guesthouse: 'Must love dogs'. It's a bit of a house rule around here.

'I'm glad you changed your mind and decided to come after all.' Poppy greets Callum by kissing both his cheeks, French style, while Leo grabs Callum's bags from the boot. 'I think you'll like it here.'

I hadn't realised that Callum coming was ever under any doubt. I wish I didn't have mixed feelings about him being here, but I suppose it's natural. I just need to rise above them and be brave, new life and all that.

'Cal, this is Joanna,' Leo introduces me. I fold my arms across my chest, suddenly self-conscious about the amount of cleavage my extrovert dress is showing.

'Yes, I know, I recognise you from *Sex in the Suburbs*. My twin sister is a fan of the show. I thought you normally preferred to be called JoJo, or was that just on TV?' Callum is smiling politely and he looks friendly but there's something cool in the way he's appraising me that unnerves me.

I know he can be tough, I've been watching downloads of *Callum O'Connor's Kitchen Cook Off* on my iPad ever since Poppy said he was coming. In that series he goes into restaurants and tells the head chef everything they're getting wrong. To be fair he does then help them to make improvements before they go on to compete with other restaurants, but he can be pretty . . . intense. It didn't help any anxiety I felt about cooking this evening. I thought maybe it was hyped up for the camera, to create conflict, but there's something in his expression now that unnerves me.

'You can call me JoJo if you like.' I smile at him, hoping to encourage a thaw. 'Should I call you Cal?'

I instantly feel like I've been over-friendly, like I'm coming across as a fan girl he needs to fend off. The brief pause before he answers surely confirms it. Or it's even worse, maybe he's seen the sex tape. I hug my arms even tighter around me and do my best to avoid direct eye contact. He really does have the most piercing blue eyes; the camera didn't lie about that. He also has the kind of penetrating gaze that makes me feel like he can see absolutely everything.

'Sure, no problem.' Cal flashes me the same polite smile as we make our way into the kitchen and then he turns to greet Poppy. I can't help noticing she gets treated to a genuine, wide smile that makes his eyes crinkle just a little bit.

Hmm.

'We're going up to the Château to see my parents before dinner,' Leo says. 'Would you like to join us?'

'No, I'll stay with the dogs,' I say quickly, even though we all know Barney is happy to snooze in his basket and the little ones are always welcome up at the Château.

'I think I'll stay here too, Leo, in case Joanna needs a hand with dinner.' Poppy stands close to me. I know she's worried about me from the frown lines on her forehead. 'We'll see you later, okay?'

Once Callum and Leo have gone I let out a sigh. I hadn't even realised I was holding my breath, nor how tense I was. It's the first time I've met anyone from the celeb scene since I moved here. The fact he says he's seen *Sex in the Suburbs* makes it so much worse. He probably watched my life implode. I was naive to hope he might arrive without any preconceived ideas or prejudice about me.

I bite my lip and try to swallow down my irritation. Then I turn to Poppy and make sure there's a smile on my face for her benefit.

'You're going to help with dinner?' I ask, raising an eyebrow. Poppy isn't exactly known for her culinary skills and is basically happy to leave the kitchen as my domain.

'Well, I can make you a cup of tea if you'd like one?' Poppy asks. 'I just didn't feel right about going off and leaving you on your own.'

'I'm fine, Poppy, honestly, you don't need to worry about me. I'll have that tea though, thanks,' I say, sitting down at the table and getting out my phone so I can run through my checklist for dinner. I'm determined it will be perfect.

'And maybe a tiny bit of chocolate?' Poppy heads for the kettle. 'After all our mothers aren't here to tell us we'll ruin our dinner.'

I think my consumption of chocolate is probably low down on my mother's list of the things she worries about with me. I've heard plenty about Poppy's mother though and can appreciate Poppy might have had to move to another country to escape the constant criticism, or at least keep it at a distance.

'Go on then. I'm always happy to be plied with tea and chocolate. You're very good to me. Can I marry you?' I ask and smile when Poppy giggles.

'I would but I'm already marrying Leo.' She turns from the kettle, leaning back against the counter while it boils, and faces me. 'Should I be calling you JoJo? Is that what you prefer to be called?'

I look up from my list, considering my answer.

'I don't know. My family and friends call me JoJo but I've got used to being called Joanna. Honestly I don't mind. You can call me what you like, it's no biggie.'

I left JoJo behind in England and thought I was happy to see the back of her, to reinvent myself. But I'm in a better place now so maybe I could be JoJo again. Odd that

Callum 'Cal' O'Connor should be the one to reintroduce my nickname.

'Did it go okay, do you think?' I frown down at my list. Have I played it too safe? Maybe I should be trying something more complicated for dinner but I'd rather cook something I'm confident about and do it well. I'm feeding Cal, not trying to win his approval.

Yeah right. I grimace inwardly.

'Of course. It was fine, nothing to worry about,' Poppy says firmly.

'I wasn't a bit . . . you know?'

'Absolutely not.' She places a bag of Maltesers next to my phone.

She must've got them in specially, which is so sweet of her. She knows they're my favourite.

'And you look gorgeous in that dress,' she adds.

'Hmm.' I glance down at my cleavage. 'Maybe I'll go and get changed.'

'Absolutely not.' Poppy snatches the bag of Maltesers and holds it out of my reach. 'And anyway, if you change now it will look like you dressed up specially to meet him.'

'Which I did.' I roll my eyes. 'You made me.'

I don't add that I didn't need too much persuading. I was hardly going to meet the cool celebrity chef wearing my old leggings and bobbly cardigan.

'Yes, but you don't want him to know you dressed up for him. Play it cool.'

'Poppy, I'm not playing it any way. I told you I'm not

interested in a relationship, I'm just interested to meet a professional chef.' My cheeks heat up as I remember Cal's intense blue eyes and that penetrating gaze. If anyone is playing it cool it's him, only I suspect he's not pretending. I'm a little bit disappointed about how meeting him went. He thinks I'm just another fan girl, which I kind of am, a little bit, but that's as far as it goes. 'So, no attempts at matchmaking, okay?'

'I s'pose.' Poppy nervously chews her lip as she places two mugs of tea on the table and lets me have the chocolate back. 'Actually, there is something else I wanted to talk to you about, while Leo isn't around.'

'Oh?' I pop a Malteser in my mouth.

'You know I want another dog?'

Ah, so that's it. She's clearly been looking at rescue websites again.

'You always want another dog.' I laugh, relaxing as I realise the subject is moving on from Cal.

'Well, I could do with some help, to, you know, support my position.' Her eyes are wide and hopeful. 'I'm not asking much, just a little discreet lobbying perhaps.'

'In other words, you want me to help you gang up on Leo to persuade him to give in?'

'Something like that.' Poppy chews her lip again. 'You see, there's this puppy.'

Her grin is half pleading, half rueful and I can't help grinning back.

'And I suppose this puppy is exceptionally cute? Yes, of

course, ask a silly question.' I roll my eyes. 'What's his story then?'

'He was abandoned when he was only four months old, poor little thing.' Poppy's eyes flash with uncharacteristic anger.

'You really think Leo will say no?' I ask. 'You could dig your heels in. Say there's always room for a little one . . . ask for him to be your wedding present?'

'I can try. I mean we'll be a five dog household once we're living together full time and six isn't really that much more than five.' Poppy shrugs. 'I can't bear to leave him in rescue, he's a sweet little thing. I can't stop thinking about him. Maybe if I can't, you could possibly . . .'

'You know I would love to but . . . well, it doesn't seem fair to the dog, given I don't know when I'll have my own home again or where I'll end up. Say I had to get a full-time job somewhere and had to leave the dog at home or try to afford dog day care. It doesn't seem right when I'm not settled.'

'You've got a home, here with me.' Poppy uses her no-nonsense tone. 'It's your home for as long as you want it to be. And I promise there will always be a job for you here. With The Barn opening we're going to have more work than ever.'

I wish I could be sure of her words, but I don't even know where Poppy and Leo are going to be living after their wedding. I don't think they even know yet. The last time I asked Poppy she replied vaguely that they hadn't talked about it yet. They're not going to want me hanging around if they choose to live here instead of in Leo's barn conversion. And there's the fact they've brought Callum O'Connor in. Who knows how he's going to upset the status quo? I have a feeling I can't shake that things are going to change now he's here.

Thinking about what all the changes might mean for me makes my stomach clench. Until I arrived in France and found St Quentin sur Aude I didn't even know I wanted this. No one in my family has ever lived abroad but now I've got a taste for life in France I can't imagine going back to England. Despite what I said to Poppy this does feel like home. The truth is, now I've got a lovely home with people I care about and a job I really enjoy in this sunny corner of rural France, I'm terrified of losing it.

I think about all the things I've come to love – my early morning runs around the lake, drinking wine on the terrace, watching the sun set behind the mountains, putting dance music on and dancing with Poppy and the Chihuahuas, shopping at the markets and cycling past field after field of sunflowers in the summer, revelling in the feel of warm sunshine and fresh country air on my skin.

Not to mention that the French really couldn't care less who I am, something I'm wholeheartedly appreciative of.

'Thanks, Poppy. What you said means a lot to me.' I force a smile. I know she means it now, but things change and maybe Leo won't want me around once they're married. Has she even asked him? Knowing Poppy, probably not. I don't want Leo to feel like I come as part of a job lot with the house, like a resident elderly aunt no one can face putting in a home.

'I really do mean it, you know.' She stares at me thoughtfully in the uncanny way she has sometimes of seeming to read my mind. 'You know you can trust me, don't you?'

'What's not to trust?' I reply honestly. Poppy has well and truly earned my trust over the past year. Her total lack of interest in all things celebrity has been pretty refreshing too.

Pickwick is tapping determinedly at my leg again, asking for a cuddle. I reach down to scoop him up, easily forgiving him for succumbing to Callum O'Connor's charm. His little pink tongue is sticking out as usual and he's looking particularly cute. I plant a soft kiss on the top of his head. I love him but at the back of my mind there's the reminder that he isn't really my dog, he's Poppy's. Wouldn't it be nice to have a bond with my own dog too? The seed Poppy has planted has already taken root and I think she knows it. I'm already wondering about the puppy and worrying that he might be feeling sad in the dogs' home, wondering why his humans have disappeared.

Arghh, she's got me, well and truly hooked me.

I try to focus on making sure dinner is as perfect as I can get it. I haven't planned anything pretentious or showy because I didn't want it to look like I was out to impress the celebrity chef. Even though I kind of do. Who wouldn't? Hopefully my grilled goat's cheese and cherry tomatoes on brioche French toast, spinach and ricotta risotto and individual strawberry tarts will do the trick.

We eat out on the terrace. It's a beautiful temperature for outdoor dining. Poppy and I have decorated the table with wild flowers from the meadow and Leo provides the wine from the Château cellar. I'm hoping Cal will comment on the food but as we eat he and Leo spend the time catching up about their time together in Paris. Cal entertains us with stories about harsh training conditions with verbal abuse often reinforced by a bit of physical abuse in the form of flying saucepans or fists.

'So why are chefs seen as so bad-tempered?' Poppy asks.

'It's a high-pressured environment. It's the chef's reputation at stake so if an underling messes something up or isn't mindful of presentation they are effectively ruining the reputation of the chef. Also, most chefs really care about producing good food that will be appreciated and take pride in it. I know I do.' Cal's eyes gleam and he leans forward towards Poppy. There's something of the animation, the passion he displays in his television shows, evident in his features and hand gestures. 'If you've busted a gut in a hot kitchen getting a dish perfect and then someone lets it get cold or drops it you can imagine why tempers flare.'

'Yes, it would be like someone smudging one of my illustrations.' Poppy nods thoughtfully.

I can't help wondering, with all this talk about producing food that will be appreciated, if he might say something about my risotto but beyond a polite thank you when I served him he hasn't said a word directly to me. I wasn't imagining the slight coolness to his attitude towards me. It's not there when he talks to Poppy and I can't help feeling miffed. I should be used to being prejudged by people, but it still annoys me just as much as it ever did. I might be ready to start over and face the world again but I'm not sure the world is necessarily amenable to giving me the fresh start I want.

I wish I could say that I don't care what Cal thinks, that his opinion doesn't matter, but the fact is I do care. I serve the dessert, trying my best to keep my feelings undetectable. Poppy obviously picks something up because she gives me a big thumbs-up and raves about the strawberry tartlet. If she's hoping Cal might take the hint and praise me it doesn't work but I do appreciate her making the effort.

Pickwick is under the table, rubbing himself against my legs like he thinks he's a cat. I'm sure it's his way of offering support, not just him making his presence known in case there's any spare food going.

Feeling awkward I decide to turn the conversation away from food.

'How is *Only Dogs and Donkeys at Christmas* coming along?' I turn to Poppy and try to give her all my attention but a part of me is still hyper-aware of Cal. I'm wearing another of the sundresses Poppy found for me at the market in Mirepoix. It's red with a tiny floral print, feminine but also a little bit sexy.

Now I feel like the girl who tried too hard which is doubly annoying because I'm not out to snare Cal but to learn from him, something I hoped would develop naturally and easily given we're going to be working together.

Hmm. That fantasy is dissolving fast, leaving a bitter taste in my mouth that no amount of strawberry tartlet can fix. I guess my hope that the labels I was given last year had worn off was a vain one. It's like Cal has already decided I'm not worth getting to know, like he decided that before he even met me.

You don't know me.

I feel like interrupting his conversation with Leo to tell him so but just about manage to restrain myself, clearing the plates and heading inside to make coffee instead. Quite how people come to the conclusion they know who I am from the heavily edited highlights on *Sex in the Suburbs* or a sex tape filmed without my consent, I don't know. I deposit the plates in the dishwasher rather more heavily than I should but the thunk of crockery and clatter of cutlery is strangely satisfying and one way of expressing my irritation without mortally offending Leo's friend.

'He obviously hated my cooking.' I frown morosely at the clearing up waiting to be done, the dishes that need soaking before they can go in the dishwasher and the few obstinate items that insist on remaining in a previous century and want to be washed up by hand.

'Why on earth do you think he hated it?' Poppy helps with loading the dishwasher.

'When I asked him if everything was okay he said the meal was "fine, thanks".' I scowl at the detritus in the kitchen, and all the effort it represents. All that work dismissed in one sentence and by someone who knows what he's talking about, that's what really bites.

'You're upset because he said the meal was fine?' Poppy laughs. 'Seriously?'

'Yes, seriously.' I sigh. 'He didn't even do me the courtesy of a proper critique. I'd rather be told what was wrong than be dismissed and damned with faint praise.'

'So, you're annoyed he didn't praise you and you're also annoyed he didn't criticise you?' Poppy frowns and stares at me, biting her lip thoughtfully.

'I know it sounds a bit loopy when you put it like that, but you haven't seen his programmes.' I squirt washing-up liquid into the sink and turn the hot tap. I prefer to get all cleared up before I sit down to relax in the evening. Leo and Cal are still outside, lingering over the coffee. I can't escape the nagging sensation that they are talking about me but that's pure paranoia and I try to ignore it. 'In his programmes he comes down quite hard on the amateur chefs, and he's even more forceful about it in the shows where he's going into restaurants. The point is it's always constructive criticism, aimed at helping them to be better chefs. The fact he didn't bother with me makes me feel . . . well, not great. But it's okay, really. I'll get over it.'

I swallow down my disappointment and try to hide just how upset I am from Poppy. She'd only want to fix things and that could be truly excruciating. I imagine Cal's disdain if he was forced to take my cooking seriously and my jaw tightens. I know I'm just an amateur but so are all the people on his shows. Poppy's passion is her art; my creativity has always been channelled into cooking and baking.

'Perhaps when he's not working he just keeps his opinions to himself?' Poppy suggests. 'He could just be trying to be polite.'

'Because his real opinion would offend me so much?' I ask.

Poppy looks stricken. 'I didn't mean that . . . I . . .'

'You're okay, Poppy, I know you're just trying to cheer me up,' I say. 'Anyway, enough about Callum O'Connor. How about we have hot chocolate once we're cleared up?'

'If you do your white hot chocolate with salted caramel swirls I'll do the rest of this clearing up,' Poppy offers.

'Okay, it's a deal. Shall I do a dog count? They've been in and out begging all evening. Shall I make sure everyone's back in?' I offer.

'Good idea, remember to check the cushion covers.'

Treacle took to using the cushion covers as sleeping bags last winter, climbing in and sleeping on top of the cushions. As he is so tiny he's not actually visible once in place and, as Poppy discovered one particularly fraught night when she woke me to tell me he was missing, you actually have to pat all the cushions to find him.

Pickwick and Treacle are on the sofa in the living room together and Maxi and Barney are both squashed onto one dog bed in the kitchen. Peanut, however, is missing. She's got into the habit of playing hide and seek lately, only she doesn't ask us if we want to play first, which can be a cause of anxiety. I don't tell Poppy as she'll only stress, I'll look in all her favourite hiding places first. At just over two kilograms she's the smallest dog in the pack, the tiniest dog I've ever seen, in fact, and that means she can hide in the smallest of places.

I check under the sofas, one of her favourite haunts, and a place to hide treats from the other dogs who can't fit underneath. I'm determined to let go of my bad mood. So what if Cal doesn't take me seriously? We are going to have to work together and I'm determined he'll come to appreciate my worth. I'll just have to prove myself. I know I shouldn't have to and I don't have to but I'm determined to get praise from Cal's lips if it bloomin' well kills me.

I check the log pile, another of the dogs' favourite places to play. I hear the faint tinkle of metal dog tags in a bush over by the terrace, approach quietly and kneel down to peer into the gap beneath the foliage. Cal and Leo are talking so I don't want to call for Peanut and have to engage in conversation with Cal again. In my current odd mood, I might embarrass myself by insisting he tell me what was wrong with my risotto.

Peanut's eyes gleam in the darkness. I stretch out but can't actually reach her. Without equipment to cut away the branches or a way of shrinking myself, Alice in

Wonderland style, I'm going to have to rely on her deciding to cooperate with me.

I tap the ground in front of me, frowning at her. She stares back, implacable. I try to look friendly instead of cross and tap my lap instead, the signal all the dogs know as an offer for a cuddle.

She remains unmoved. 'Is that all you've got?' her expression seems to say. It's half battle of wills and half game.

'What's this?' I whisper very quietly, pretending to fiddle with my pocket, as though just about to fish out one of her favourite duck treats.

She tilts her head, contemptuous of my bluff, the insult to her intelligence. It always works with Pickwick but then he is very stomach-orientated.

There's a root digging into my bare knee and I am tempted to speak a little more sharply to her but then Leo and Cal would come and find me hiding in a hedge like a stalker.

That's not going to happen.

I swivel round and turn my back on Peanut, pretending to ignore her. She's bound to crack first. She loves her comforts, particularly going under Poppy's duvet at night with her favourite weasel toy. She'll crack first.

Or I'll be spending tonight under the stars.

I find myself tuning into Leo and Cal's conversation.

'She represents everything I hate about celebrity culture, everything I came to France to get away from,' Cal says.

Is he . . . is he talking about me? My heart pounds and

I feel very hot all of a sudden. Everything he hates? But he doesn't even know me.

'JoJo really isn't like that,' Leo protests. 'She's a total star. Poppy wouldn't know what to do without her. Without JoJo she really would've struggled to get Les Coquelicots up and running.'

'Really. That surprises me,' Cal says and adds something in a lower tone I can't make out.

'God no, there's no way she knew she was being filmed. She's really not like that. She's not some fame-seeking celebrity-chaser, you're perfectly safe . . .' Leo defends me. 'Do you really think I'd saddle you with someone like that? When you get to know her properly, you'll see I'm right about her. At least give her a chance.'

There's a pause. My fingers dig into my legs and I burn with humiliation and anger. My chest is painfully tight until I remember to breathe. Peanut has crawled out of her hole and climbed onto my lap, snuggling into me. I know she senses I'm upset, she always does. For all her cheekiness she's an affectionate, sensitive little creature.

'I suppose I trust your judgement,' Cal says, breaking the silence. 'You can't blame me for being careful. JoJo got famous dating a celebrity. I told you about the problems I had with Daria, my last girlfriend?'

'What happened?'

'All she cared about was going to parties and clubs where there'd be photo ops and she could see other famous people and be seen.' Cal's voice is scornful, but I can't help wondering if he's more hurt than he's letting on. After all I've dated someone like that myself. 'She really had me fooled and she's part of the reason I wanted to take some time out. I need some time away from that scene, so I can work out what I really want from life.'

'Well, it's good news for us you're taking that time here. Any help you can give us we're very grateful for and of course you can stay as long as you like.'

My jaw clenches and I grind my teeth a little, seething silently. As long as he likes?

Peanut tilts her head back and looks up at me, her serious little eyes seeming to communicate vast depths of wisdom and knowledge. That or she's telling me it's past her bedtime and asking me why we're faffing about.

'It's probably just as well things are over with Daria,' Cal muses. 'Given I'm not sure exactly how long I'm going to be here. In my experience long-distance relationships don't work, it just ends up being an incredibly slow and drawn-out break-up. Well, I've got other things on my mind at the moment, more important things. Did I tell you my twin sister Caitlin is pregnant? I can't believe I'm going to be an uncle.'

Leo and Cal lapse into a lament for the days of their youth and are now talking about a mutual friend from their time in Paris together. I tune out. My heart is pounding and I realise just how awful it would be to be found eavesdropping, especially after *that* conversation, and decide to creep away while the going is good. My knee throbs painfully where I've been kneeling on the root and I bite my lip to prevent any vocalisation of the pain giving me away. There are plenty of other things I'd like to vocalise to Cal's face. I have a hundred scathing but poised retorts swirling around in my head, as well as some not so poised insults. So Cal is worried I might be after him? Or rather after the reflected glory of his fame?

As if.

After all I'm 'everything he came to the south of France to get away from'. After that remark I'm not even sure I can be polite to him, never mind wanting to be intimately involved with him.

You don't know me.

How many times has that thought echoed in my mind over the past year? Enough that it stirs me up, disturbing the emotional silt I've been successfully keeping well below the surface since I moved here.

What about the fact that I came here to get away from the world Cal belongs to? He is the one disturbing my peace, not the other way round.

I was here first.

That childish argument almost makes me smile at my own belligerence but I'm too upset. I had hopes of a professional working relationship with a man I admire and want to learn from. I set out this evening to impress him and I failed. Big time.

Suddenly I'm really, really tired. I feel a familiar pressure behind my eyelids and squeeze my eyes tight shut. I refuse to let that man make me cry. He doesn't know me, so his opinions mean nothing.

But still they niggle and prick at me to the extent that I have to lie to Poppy and tell her I have a migraine.

I can't tell her what I overheard. She'd fret and it might cause problems between her and Leo. After all he's Leo's friend and I'm her friend. Maybe this will seem less terrible after a good night's sleep. Most things do.

Except I don't get a good night's sleep. I get a terrible one, unable to switch off the repeated conversation going around and around in my mind. I think of all the things I'd like to say and that leads me to older feelings, to the anger I never expressed to Aiden and Sally. I swallowed it all down then, like I'm trying to do now, and my body isn't happy.

I'm still feeling grumpy when I'm unloading the dishwasher the next morning. Cal, on the other hand, is making an effort and I really wish he wouldn't. It's too late now I know what he thinks of me. He's rolling round on the floor with Barney in a way I would have found adorable only yesterday. In a way I'm glad I overheard him because now, if I feel my hormones fluttering and quivering in response to his very manly pheromones, all I have to do is recall what he said about me and the temptation is easy to turn down.

'He's a great dog.' Cal gets up off the floor and sits at the kitchen table. 'They all are, super cute.'

Humph. I narrow my eyes at him suspiciously, feeling

like channelling my inner Miss Piggy. She wouldn't have put up with any nonsense from Cal.

He rubs the stubble on his chin thoughtfully. 'Do you know where I can get a razor around here? I left mine at home.'

'There's a supermarket outside Mirepoix,' I say. Yesterday I would have offered to drive him, but I really wouldn't want to inflict my company on him.

Never mind my inner Miss Piggy, my inner bitch is out and dealing with the situation just fine.

'You know, Barney's old owners were going to have him put down because he's getting on a bit and has gone blind,' I add and reach down to stroke his huge floppy ears when he ambles over in response to hearing his name. 'But you know, he's the happiest dog I've ever met. Just goes to show you shouldn't make assumptions, doesn't it? It's why labelling people . . . or dogs . . . isn't very kind. Don't you agree?'

I don't meet Cal's eyes. I'm not interested in confronting him for Leo and Poppy's sake. I focus on Barney instead, stroking him and appearing casual.

'Yes, I suppose you're right,' Cal replies at last and I glance over at him. He's studying me quizzically. The coolness of yesterday isn't there in his eyes. He's looking at me, not through me. Maybe he decided to give me a chance after Leo stood up for me. That's all good except I'm not sure I want one any more.

My good manners battle with my bruised pride and sleep-deprived mind and reluctantly I relent.

'I'm going to the supermarket later. I can pick up a razor for you if you tell me what brand you want. Or you could come with me, but I've got an awful lot to get and you'd be hanging around for ages so . . .'

'I don't mind hanging around.' Cal smiles and I'm sure there's a glimmer of humour in his eyes; they sort of crinkle at the edges, like he's someone who smiles and laughs a lot. Like he's taking pleasure in disconcerting me.

Okay, so the truth is he is so bloody sexy my hormones are swooning all over the place. I fancy him but I'd rather die than admit that now. No way am I going to give Cal the satisfaction of saying he was right, that I'm some kind of career celebrity girlfriend, looking for my next meal ticket.

Our eyes lock and my cheeks feel warm.

I do my best to ignore the flipping sensation in my stomach. He came to France to get away from 'people like me'. I have to remember that; I can't get swept away. And I came to France to get away from people who think they know me, who make judgements based on lies and prejudice, so this . . . this cheek-burning, stomach-churning hormone-induced head-fuckery is going to have to stop.

I bite my lip and Cal's gaze fixes on my slightly parted lips. Time seems to slow down, neither of us speaking. Even the dogs are silent, watching us solemnly.

Then the kitchen door opens and Leo and Poppy arrive, dispelling the weird tension between Cal and me, plunging me into confusion.

Later I'm throwing Pickwick's ball for him in the garden while the Chihuahuas and Barney sunbathe. The grass is long and needs cutting but I haven't had time to get round to it yet. As a result Pickwick is bouncing along like he's on springs, for reasons best known to himself, and he does look very cute, which is why I can't resist him when he brings the ball back to me and looks adorably hopeful again and again and again . . .

'You'll be doing that all day.' Poppy joins us and flops down onto the grass next to Barney. 'He's got you wrapped around his paw.'

Pickwick then drops the ball at Poppy's feet and proceeds to take it in turns who he gives it to.

'He's got both of us wrapped around his paw,' I comment.

'True. Well, they love you like you're one of the pack, so until you get your own dog you know you're welcome to borrow my little horrors any time you want, yes?' Poppy says, watching the Chihuahuas mutt-mobbing me, her lips quirking into a smile. 'In fact, I'm kind of counting on it given the gallery work, finishing my next book and arranging a wedding . . . I'm not sure how I'm going to get everything done. My to-do list is humongous and it never seems to shrink.'

I'm amazed she's left it a full twenty-four hours before bringing the subject of me rescuing a dog up again.

'That's why I'm here. I'm your spare pair of hands,' I say. I've been selfish, focusing on how unsettled I feel by Callum O'Connor's presence in the house. It's time to stop thinking about myself and be what Poppy needs me to be. 'Why don't we relabel it and call it your "do it" list? Much more positive. We could use an app to sync the list to our phones and split the tasks between us. If we're sharing the list, it means we both stay accountable.'

We both know I mean *she* stays accountable and I'm being kind in not saying it. Creative and lovely Poppy may be but organised and practical she isn't.

'Thanks, you're a star.' Poppy gives me a quick squeeze of a hug and turns abruptly away, bending down to pick up Pickwick's ball.

I swear I see unshed tears in her eyes. I thought she was taking on too much and I've tried to say so but Poppy was adamant she could do it all. I'm not sure she would've listened to me or Leo, however we approached it, she's been so fired up about her new projects.

After she's thrown the ball again for Pickwick and he's gone bounding off she turns back to me.

'You really are a star, you know,' she says seriously, a tiny frown line in between her eyes. 'And I don't think I'm the only person around here who thinks so – you know, there was a definite frisson in the kitchen earlier. I'm sure he fancies you. We didn't interrupt anything, did we?'

'No, he definitely doesn't fancy me and no, you absolutely didn't interrupt anything.' I snort. 'Trust me, you're way off base there. Besides we only just met.'

I wrap my arms protectively around my body. I've had no end of people who think they know me because they've seen me on television or, worse, online. The ones who feel the need to tell me about it usually either hate me or think they're in love with me, rarely anything in between. The ones who supposedly 'love' me have seen my naked emotion on the TV show or my naked body in the sex tape, or both, and imagine themselves in love with a version of me that only exists in their head.

'Really? That's odd. Hmmm,' she muses. 'You know, I'm rarely wrong when it comes to picking up those kinds of vibes between other people. I read about this scientific study that says it only takes us three seconds before we decide if we're attracted to someone. So the length of time you've known each other really doesn't mean anything—'

'Stop,' I cut her off before she has me and Cal married in her head. 'I mean no, don't go there, please, Poppy. I really think you're wrong in this case.'

I think about what Poppy said, the three-second factoid. If I were a pre-Aiden version of JoJo, meeting Cal for the first time, would I or wouldn't I? The answer is obvious: of course I would. He is exactly my type. Which is exactly why I'm not going there.

I'm sure Poppy thinks I'm protesting too much and secretly I'm dying for a man to come along and sweep me off my feet, but she couldn't be more wrong. The whole sweeping thing is overrated. I'd rather keep both my feet firmly planted on the ground.

I'm never going to let a man unbalance me like that again.

Poppy bites her lip and then drops down onto the grass next to the Chihuahuas. I sit down next to her, recognising the look on her face. There's something she wants to talk about. I do my best to ignore the flutter of alarm deep inside me.

'You know, I've been thinking . . .'

'Uh huh?' I eye her with wary caution, wondering if we're still on Callum, or me adopting a dog, or whether she has a brand new topic on her mind.

'I've been thinking about how you can move on,' she says.

Move on? The flutter is instantly upgraded and my stomach twists in a sharp response. I try to control my breathing.

'But I thought you said this was my home . . . Have you spoken to Leo since we talked, is that it?' I keep my voice as calm as I can but even so all the dogs stop what they're doing and watch me, ears pricked and eyes curious.

Poppy frowns, her face a mask of incomprehension.

'Of course this is your home.' She pats me on the arm. 'What's wrong, why are you upset?'

'You said move on . . . like you want me to leave here.'

'I meant metaphorically, of course,' Poppy says, looking at me like I'm nuts for misunderstanding her.

'So . . .?' I steady my breathing again, reassured I'm not about to be turfed out with nowhere to go except the one place I can't.

'I was thinking maybe you should look up what other

people who've been victims of sex tapes have done, how they've moved on,' she suggests, her tone becoming more confident as she gets going. 'I'm sure some of them must have found it empowering, eventually.'

I hate to burst her bubble and I know she's only trying to help but I have to be honest with her. Nothing else will stop her once she's got an idea in her head.

'The thing is, Poppy, except for those who've actually made the tape themselves and sold it for cash, it seems to pretty much universally lead to a desire to die.'

Peanut must hear the catch in my voice because she gets up from where she's sunbathing and comes over to me, hopping back onto my lap and rubbing her head against my chest like she's a cat. Actually, all of Poppy's dogs seem to think they're other species. They also do good impressions of parrots, meerkats and even baby kangaroos.

I stroke Peanut's head. She's the tiniest fully grown dog I've ever seen but she has the biggest heart.

'Seriously?' Poppy deflates and frowns, scooping Treacle up onto her lap, absentmindedly stroking him and not noticing that Pickwick has come back and has dropped his ball by her feet.

'Yep, I tried researching it a while back to see if anyone else's story gave me hope.' I sigh. 'Apart from a few celebrities who went on to put it behind them and become even more successful it was pretty much doom and gloom. After the fourth suicide I stopped reading.'

'Oh, Joanna.' Poppy plops Treacle onto my lap, clearly deciding that this is a two-Chihuahua kind of situation.

Pickwick also brings me his ball, so I'm inundated with cute.

As if sweet pupsters can make things better. Though actually they kind of do. There's plenty of room on my lap for both the Chihuahuas and they stare up at me, concern shining in their big eyes as I stroke them both, trying to reassure them that I'm okay, it's okay, everything's okay.

They've both got a history of abuse in their past and they can get anxious, Treacle in particular. I stroke his head and he settles down contentedly next to Peanut, a big smile on his face. He's one of the few dogs I've met who really does smile.

'Even the celebs who went on to recover admitted there were times when they wanted to die too,' I say quietly, looking down at Treacle and Peanut as I stroke them and not meeting Poppy's eye.

'But you're . . . okay, yes? You know you can always talk to me if . . . well . . .'

'Yes, I know, thanks, and I'm fine,' I say.

'Because for all the people who couldn't cope there must have been plenty of others who have coped. It's just that you're not going to find those stories online.' Poppy eyes me hopefully.

'Yes, I'm sure you're right.' I tell her what she needs to hear.

It's partly true. Though I can't imagine anyone taking

it completely in their stride. They might look okay on the outside but I'm sure they've had their moments. I've long abandoned the myth that most people are coasting along the surface of life. I've been under water and I've seen the frantic thrashing. A lot of people have 'stuff' that they just don't talk about.

I am fine though, certainly getting there. There are lots of days when I can almost forget anything bad happened, when the sun is shining and I'm browsing in the market with no one recognising me. I love cooking here and doing up the accommodation, and helping Poppy set the guest-house up has been a lot of fun. Having a project to occupy my mind really helped. Poppy is always saying how much I've helped her. She really doesn't get just how much she's helped me.

I'm not going to mention all the nights I woke at two or three in the morning and lay awake until the first note of birdsong provided a soundtrack to the soft light of dawn. On those days I would get up and go for a run as soon as there was enough light.

Running has helped. I'll never tire of watching the sunrise reflected in the surface of the lake, or marvelling at how still the world is at dawn. There can be movement all around me from nature but there's a particular type of stillness that the absence of other humans creates and I love it.

In the early days here in France it was the only way to stop the anxiety from eating me up. Running takes me out of my head somehow, away from the thoughts that do me no good at all and could drive me mad if I let them. Poppy loathes running and has made it plain she thinks I'm nuts for being a runner, but then she always loses herself in her artwork when she's stressed. I guess we all have our way of coping with things.

'You're okay really?' Poppy breaks into my thoughts, her gaze searching.

'Yes, I am. Maybe not all the time but I'm certainly getting there,' I reply more truthfully.

Pickwick has given up trying to get Poppy's attention. When actually putting his ball on her foot doesn't work, he brings it to me again instead. I can't resist his hopeful little face and throw the ball for him, watching him bouncing through the grass undaunted, his optimism undiminished by the fact he's lost the ball. I know he'll keep looking until he finds it too.

I wish I had that kind of bounce. People talk about bouncing back, and hey, you know, that sounds fantastic to me, but they hardly ever talk about how you do it.

'Didn't your friends in England help you at all?' she asks.

'Well, Sally was my best friend. We were in each other's pockets ever since the first year of primary school. Maybe that was partly the problem: we were friends simply because we were put together and we both liked the colour pink.' I shrug. 'I can't help feeling we can never really know someone else, not really. We might think we do but . . . Anyway, I don't want to talk about Sally.'

We both watch Pickwick trotting around, leaving no clump of grass unexamined until he finally finds his ball and seizes it triumphantly. I turn my face up to the sun and wish life could be as simple as this all the time. Poppy, the dogs, the garden . . . But Poppy is getting married, Callum O'Connor is in residence and I don't know what happens next.

'What about your other friends?' Poppy sounds hopeful and I hate to disappoint her.

'You remember that thing I said about not really knowing people? Ex-boyfriends and friends sold their stories about me and their photos of me. Most of the stories weren't true and I honestly didn't see that coming either.'

I stare down at Treacle where my fingers are buried in his sandy, soft fur. Peanut has turned to rest her tiny muzzle on my chest, her eyes tiny pools of concern. I manage to give her a small reassuring smile, albeit wobbly. Poppy and I don't usually talk about this kind of stuff but I don't mind opening up now. Not to Poppy anyway.

Those months after the first blow last year felt like a rapidly growing snowball, gathering up one betrayal after another as it hurtled out of control and became an avalanche, capable of sweeping my whole life away.

Okay, maybe not my whole life. I don't want to be overly dramatic about it and I know some people lose absolutely everything in life in terrible ways, including losing the roofs over their heads. I wasn't homeless and I had food.

Also, my family remained reliable. They couldn't look me in the eye, but they stood by me all the same. To be fair, my sister Annabel was great about it all and she understood when I just had to get away. I think she would've come with me except I needed her to cover for me at the café. At the time it was 'just until things blow over'. Except that moment never seemed to arrive.

'They can't have been very good friends then.' Poppy wrinkles her nose as though unable to comprehend selling out a friend for cash. It's one of the many reasons I love her.

'I suppose not.' I shrug and meet Poppy's eye, trying to give her the same reassuring smile I gave Peanut. 'I'm okay, Poppy, honestly. It's behind me now. I've got a new life here and new friends, both human and furry. I'm happy being single too. The absolute last thing I want is for you to matchmake for me. I know that's hard for you to understand in your current loved-up state.'

She has the zeal of a new believer since she fell in love with Leo. Her matchmaking is probably just a symptom of getting engaged. It seems wedding planning has only increased her desire to see everybody paired off and as happy as she is. I overheard her asking Leo about Angeline's love life the other day.

Or maybe she's feeling it too, that the wedding will mark the end of the time we've spent together, just the two of us. Our safe little hideaway where we both licked our respective wounds, painted walls and drank hot chocolate is changing. Maybe she's worried about me. That seems much more like her than an assumption that a man is all we need to make everything better.

She doesn't reply and I glance over at her. She's staring into the distance and hasn't seen Pickwick drop his ball at her feet again.

'Sorry, Poppy, I didn't mean it. I appreciate you trying to help, really I do.'

I shift up next to her on the grass and rest my head on her shoulder, awkwardly giving her a half hug. Only awkward because the Chihuahuas insist on being in the middle of it and the logistics are difficult.

'Is it too early for a drink, do you suppose?' Poppy asks, finally noticing Pickwick and throwing his ball for him again.

'Definitely not too early but I'll have to wait until later, I've got a supermarket shop to do.' I rub at my temples.

'Have you still not got rid of your migraine from last night?' Poppy asks, solicitously. 'I can do the supermarket shop today if you like?'

'Have you got time? I might be all right if I take more meds.' My offer is half-hearted though. I am starting to get familiar stabbing pains behind one of my eyes. I don't mention I'm supposed to be giving Cal a lift. I really wasn't looking forward to having to make polite conversation for the duration, pretending I don't know what he really thinks of me. Holding my tongue for Poppy and Leo's sake is going to be hard but I'll try. I owe them that much.

It's all my own fault that I really do have a migraine coming on now, karma for saying I had one last night, or maybe it's my body giving me an out. I throw the ball that has just landed on my foot.

'Don't be silly, it's fine,' Poppy says, as I knew she would. 'Why don't you go and take your meds and lie down? If you're okay this evening we'll have that drink.'

'Okay.' My sleep-deprived mind readily accepts. We get to our feet, both watching Pickwick as he heads off into the grass that's taller than he is in places, utterly undaunted and relentlessly optimistic. Bounce, bounce, bounce . . .

It's all my own fault that I really do have a [illegible] [illegible] [illegible] [illegible] for [illegible] had the last night, [illegible] [illegible] [illegible] [illegible] [illegible]. I [illegible] [illegible] [illegible] has just landed on [illegible].

'Don't be silly,' [illegible] says, as [illegible] she [illegible]. 'Why don't you go and take your [illegible] and lie down? [illegible] [illegible] this evening [illegible] than [illegible].'

[illegible] [illegible] [illegible] [illegible] [illegible] the [illegible]. [illegible], both watching [illegible] as he [illegible] into the grass that is taller than [illegible] in places [illegible] [illegible] and [illegible] [illegible] bring, because [illegible].

Chapter 3

'If all you can do is crawl, start crawling'

Rumi

From callum@callum'scook-off.com
To caitlino'connor85@hotmail.com
Subject: You were right
So I'm still reeling from our Skype convo!!! I cannot believe I'm going to be an uncle! Life suddenly got real. I guess Mam's already putting you under loads of pressure to move back to Ireland already?

I can only assume your mother-to-be status has conferred extra wisdom on you because you were right – I really did need to take some time out to get my head straight. Well either that or you've been right all along that being five minutes older than me does make you that much wiser!

Seriously though, coming to the south of France was a really good idea. I'm already feeling less stressed. It's fun helping Leo set up the château restaurant and I'm loving being in France again. I'd forgotten how much I enjoy planning the perfect menu, getting back to creating great food, instead of having to focus on creating good TV.

Talking of TV you'll never guess who else is working here, staying in the same house in fact . . . All I'll say is that there's a link to one of your favourite shows. Do you want to try to guess? I would tell you but I know you'll be insufferable after the 'wiser than me' comment so I have to make you suffer a little.

Take care of yourself Caitlin and say hi to Mike from me.

'Joanna . . .' Poppy's tone is half optimism, half entreaty. She sits down at the kitchen table and I wonder what the topic is today. I do hope she's not going to give me grief about avoiding Cal. I've become rather skilled at it, if I do say so myself. The great thing about having a guest-house to run is that there is always housework or laundry or shopping to be done. Whenever it looks like Cal might be about to engage me in conversation or the others try to get me to join in with an outing I simply pluck a task from the household or wedding 'do-it' list I share with Poppy and claim it's urgent.

In spite of the list being on Poppy's phone she hasn't got to grips with it yet, so she doesn't have the ammunition to refute my claims.

I avoid being alone with him at all costs. The odd moment between us in the kitchen that first morning showed me how dangerous it could be. There's chemistry between us, that's undeniable, but chemistry can be potentially explosive. I've already blown my life up once for a man. I don't intend making the same mistake twice.

The dogs mill around us, sticking their noses in the air hopefully and then retreating beneath the table with a collective canine sigh once they realise I'm only preparing salad. Even Peanut, who gets more excited about apples than chicken and is the only dog I know who will eat broccoli without the added inducements of gravy or cheese, draws a firm line at eating lettuce.

'Poppy . . .' I mimic her tone and grin to show her I'm just teasing.

I put down my knife and stop chopping cucumber for a minute to get up and fetch the dogs a duck strip treat each. It took all of thirty seconds for that disappointed dog sigh to work on me. Yes, they've got me wrapped around their little paws. It took them no time at all to train me up into a half decent dog-servant.

'You know Leo's being stubborn about me getting another rescue dog?'

'Hmm,' I reply noncommittally. Personally, I can see Leo's point that five dogs is enough for one household, particularly when they're having a game of indoor chase or starting a howling competition with the other village dogs, and I happen to be one of their biggest fans. I think I know where this is going. She's failed to persuade Leo so she's going to have another try with me.

'I suppose I can see his point . . . maybe,' she adds grudgingly. 'Anyway, I was thinking, if we do end up living at Leo's instead of here at Les Coquelicots then that would leave you isolated. I know we wouldn't be that far away but even so I think you could do with a dog to keep you company, and it would be good for protection, you know? Apparently, dogs are the best burglar deterrent there is.'

'Maybe,' I reply cautiously and move to sit down next to her. 'You know how much I like dogs and I'd love to own one but I'm still not sure it'd be right to do it until I'm settled.'

'You *are* settled.' Poppy tilts her chin up. 'I keep trying to tell you to consider Les Coquelicots your home too. I mean it. Quite apart from the fact you're part of the pack now, from a totally selfish point of view, how on earth would I ever manage without you?'

Her smile is disarming, I can tell she really means it and I feel my resolve melting.

'So, we're still talking about that puppy you can't stop thinking about, are we? Go on then, show me. Is he cute?' I obediently take the bait and I hold my hand out for her phone.

'One of the cutest things you'll ever see, I promise.' Poppy hands over her iPhone to me, beaming. 'I just know you're going to fall in love with him.'

On the screen is a cute little sandy-coloured puppy who

looks a lot like a Chihuahua but without the typical apple- or fox-shaped head that Treacle and Peanut have. He has one ear sticking up and one ear dangling down, a long swishy tail and white socks on his front paws, one higher than the other as though he needs to be told to pull his socks up. He has a cheeky glint in his eye and still looks very young. He'll be trouble, I know. It'll be extra work because I'll have to train him on top of everything else . . . but . . . I want him.

'He has ears like Barney's,' I say and hand the phone back to Poppy. Barney hears his name and looks up hopefully, so I give his head a scratch. 'Poppy, only you could suggest a Chihuahua puppy as a guard dog for me.'

I have an image of the puppy defending me against a scary burglar and get an attack of the giggles.

Poppy catches the giggles from me like they're infectious and struggles to keep a straight face to do the rest of her pitch.

'Seriously, Chihuahuas make great watchdogs, they're alert to any noise or intruders and the racket they make is a deterrent to burglars.' She nods solemnly but the corners of her mouth twitch. 'Think how much fuss Peanut and Treacle make when the postman comes. Anyway I think this puppy is a mixed-breed puppy, not pure chihuahua. Maybe that's why he was abandoned. I reckon he's either a Golden Chihuatriever or a Labrahuahua.'

'A what now?'

'A cross between a Chihuahua and a Golden Retriever or a cross between a Chihuahua and a Labrador.'

'Seriously?' I narrow my eyes at her.

'Really, I'm not winding you up.' Poppy laughs. 'They are real breeds, go ahead and google them if you don't believe me.'

'Hmm.' I suspect she's messing with me. She does sometimes and she always manages to get me because it's so unexpected. I get out my phone to look them up. 'What do you know, you're right. How is that even possible?'

We both snort with laughter.

'Artificial insemination maybe?' Poppy suggests once she's stopped giggling. 'However it's done the results are really cute.'

I have to agree that the Chihuatriever puppies closely resemble the rescue pup Poppy wants me to adopt. My reluctance is for show, a kind of token protest at being manipulated, but she had me as soon as she showed me his photo and we both know it.

'They are, and okay, you've persuaded me. If you're sure we've both got a home here I'd love to adopt him.'

'Of course.' Poppy gets out of her chair and throws her arms around me, hugging me hard. Peanut somehow manages to jump onto my lap and wriggle up in between us, planting tiny Chihuahua licks on both our faces. If there's a cuddle going on she has to be in the middle of it. Her tiny size makes it easy to use the smallest of gaps to insinuate herself into any hug.

I manage to extract myself before all the rest of the dogs mob us.

'So, who do I contact then? What do we do next?'

In spite of my reservations I feel . . . happy at the thought of getting the puppy. It shocks me because I haven't felt happy for so long, I've just been stuck in survival mode. Something stirs inside me, something soft and loving.

I've been suppressing a lot of my personality and desires since I ran away. It was the only way I could find to shrink down and hide, to make sure I didn't attract any attention. Here, at home with Poppy, I've been able to be myself a bit but even then it's like I've used a dimmer switch on myself and turned down my brightness as well as pressing my mute button.

I've only been a shadow, a mere ghost of myself. Annabel wouldn't recognise me. The thought makes me uncomfortable but I'm not sure why. I'm still not ready to attract attention or connect properly with the outside world. But a puppy . . . I can manage to love a puppy and the thought makes me happy.

I take a side look at Poppy. Did she engineer this? She's made it like I'm helping her out and helping the puppy out so why do I get the feeling she's actually trying to help me, in one of her roundabout creative ways? The smile on her face is certainly satisfied. Whether she meant to or not makes no difference to the outcome.

I'm taking a first step and it's furry.

The next afternoon I'm finishing the laundry and thinking about having an early night, bingeing on a Netflix box set on my iPad, given I've got an evening off. I don't need to prepare any meals as the only guests staying tonight are a couple of German hikers who are meeting up with friends in Mirepoix.

'You have to come with us, JoJo.' Poppy's voice behind me startles me so much I almost bang my head on the cupboard above the washing machine.

'Come where?' I ask suspiciously. I know she badly wants me to get on with Cal. I'm sure she still harbours the ridiculous notion that he likes me. Okay, so he's been polite and friendly, with none of the coolness I saw in him that first night. I'd even go so far as to say he's physically attracted to me but that doesn't mean he has any respect for me. I can't forget what he said about me to Leo and I don't want to tell Poppy because she'll be upset for me and it will make everything awkward. I know Leo hasn't told her because she's fiercely loyal and isn't one to hide her feelings.

It's fine. I'm dealing with it.

'Carcassonne. There's a medieval fête on today. It goes on into the evening.' Poppy takes half of the wet towels out of my hands and we walk together to the washing line to peg them out. 'We thought we'd get a meal out, maybe even go to the Hotel de la Cité for cocktails afterwards. What do you think?'

She knows my weaknesses. I've always wanted to go to the Cité when there's an enactment on. I have a bizarre desire to see knights on horses and . . . oh well, okay, maybe it's just the knights I'm really interested in. I might not be a history buff like Poppy but that doesn't mean I'm immune to the magic of Carcassonne. The Cité is such an otherworldly place – just stepping onto the drawbridge and entering the walled city beyond its battlements feels like walking into another time.

I think the whole knight thing is in my genes. One of Mum's favourite films is *Robin Hood: Prince of Thieves* and she had a thing for Kevin Costner when she was younger. As a result, I saw the film more times than I can remember when I was growing up. Ever since I told her that parts of the film were shot here at the old Cité in Carcassonne she's been saying she must come and visit. I assume she means to see me as well as the walled city . . . I'm not entirely sure what the bigger draw is. It's not like we've been getting on brilliantly since everything blew up last year.

Maybe that's why it's even more important than ever for me to get some photos of knights on horseback set against the backdrop of the Cité battlements. She'd love to see them, and it would give us something . . . neutral to talk about.

'By "we" you mean . . .?'

'Well, the two of us and Leo and Cal, of course,' Poppy says, handing me the peg bag. 'And the little dogs, of course. We can carry them if it's really busy or if they get funny about the horses. You can carry Pickwick if you like.'

At least she doesn't press me about why I've been avoiding Cal or go on about him being perfect for me with 'his love of cooking and all'. Maybe she has given up on matchmaking and this is just one of her usual attempts to get me to venture out into the real world. It is very underhanded of her to use Pickwick as a lure to get me come along.

'It's fine, I want to go. You can stop doing the hard sell.' I smile to show I'm grateful to her for including me in the plans. 'I'll get some photos for Mum, she'll love that.'

'Ah, the Kevin Costner thing.' Poppy's face relaxes into a smile.

It'll be fun. It will be fun. I repeat the thought like a mantra in my head. And I'll just have to dress up in armour myself, but of the psychological kind, designed to repel charm and raw sex appeal – both of which Cal possesses in abundant quantities.

Chapter 4

'They always say time changes things, but you actually have to change them yourself'

Andy Warhol

From sallyvickers89@gmail.com
To joannagrant@thestickybun.co.uk
Subject: Coming to see you
Okay JoJo, as you won't reply to my emails and you've blocked both me and Aiden on your phone (which is just rude of you and totally unnecessary) I guess we'll just have to come and see you in person.

From annabelgrant@thestickybun.co.uk
To joannagrant@thestickybun.co.uk
Subject: Coming to see you
Hey big sister, you sounded really down in your last email. You are okay, aren't you? I'm really worried about you . . . What's all this about things changing at the

guesthouse and a new chef arriving??? I'm confused, I thought you did all the cooking for the guests? You always sounded so settled there, I hoped it was going to be the new start you needed. I can't believe they want to push you out. From what you've said in your emails it doesn't sound very likely. I'm not surprised you're feeling a bit insecure but I'm sure the wedding isn't really going to change everything. Have you tried talking to Poppy and her fiancé about it?

You know I'm sure I could get someone to cover at the café and make it out for a short visit. I'd really love to see you, I miss you!

The flights look a bit pricey during the school holidays and I was going to surprise you in September but if you need me before then don't worry about the cost, Dad said he could lend me some money.

Let me know soon so I can start making arrangements.

Oh, I almost forgot, what's all this about you planning to get a puppy? Have you got any photos of him yet?

Hugs,
Annabel
xx

As always, the first sight of the mediaeval Cité of Carcassonne on the Languedoc skyline takes my breath away. It's a fairytale castle crossed with a fortified, walled city with cobbled streets and an actual drawbridge.

It can't fail to impress a twenty-first-century tourist so I can't imagine how awe-inspiring it must have looked to the mediaeval traveller.

We walk up to the drawbridge and cross into the walled city. As soon as they step onto the unfamiliar cobbled surface Peanut and Treacle get cold paws and refuse to walk even though they've been here before. Poppy scoops up Treacle and Peanut nestles comfortably on Cal's shoulder like the tiny monkey/parrot dog she is, snuggling into his neck with a satisfied smile on her face. She is such a little tart, that dog, incredibly sweet but always after any fuss going and keen to win over any new visitors.

Pickwick is happy to keep trotting along on the ground, even pulling a little on his lead in an attempt to overtake some slow-moving tourists in front of us. I can't help wondering how long it will be before I'm walking my own dog, hopefully not long if everything goes okay. It also occurs to me to wonder when I stopped feeling like a tourist and started feeling like a resident.

Pickwick is a little trouper, not bothered at all by the horses, knights or archers. The knights bear a red Cathar cross on the white tabards they wear over their armour. I stop for a minute and pass Pickwick's lead to Poppy so I can take some photos on my phone for Mum.

There's a general party atmosphere on the cobbled streets and Cal appears to be enjoying himself. Not that I'm watching him.

Much.

Unfortunately, on one of the rare occasions that I happen to be watching him he turns back and catches me. Damn.

With a smile he hangs back and falls into step with me.

'So, do you come into Carcassonne often?' Cal asks, fixing his piercing gaze on me.

I shrug. 'Not much, I'm pretty busy at the guesthouse. We are quieter over winter but then so is everything else. There's not much like this going on then.'

'That's a shame,' Cal replies. 'It's a shame to spend so much time shut away in the guesthouse when you have the whole of France on your doorstep.'

What the . . .? Talk about a quick switch from small talk to the Inquisition. What business is it of Cal's? My jaw tightens and any party atmosphere in me is extinguished. Just as I'd been thawing a little, he reminds me of his habit of making assumptions.

'Well, we're out and about now,' I say, biting back a more snarky reply.

A group of teenage girls ahead catch my eye. They are staring our way, nudging each other and giggling. My stomach tightens and I feel my jaw clench as we approach. I'm sure they're staring at Cal, they must be. He is far more famous than me. But there's something sneering in the way they are watching that doesn't match up with a fan girl attitude.

Crap.

Why did I let my vanity override my common sense? 'Because of Cal,' my truthful self answers and I wish she'd shut up. I spent far too long fussing over what to wear this evening, wanting to look nice but not like I'd made lots of effort. Although of course it did take lots of effort to look effortlessly nice. I sigh. My mind is a very complicated place these days.

'Slag,' one of the girls says with a broad south London accent and a few of the others giggle. Just my luck to come across an English tour group.

I try not to flinch, to make my face a blank mask but I'm not sure I succeed.

I don't care, I don't care, I don't care . . . My mantra isn't too successful either because it isn't true. I do bloody care and I hate bullies. The injustice of it makes me want to march over and have it out with her but before I know it her friends will be filming the whole thing on their mobile phones and the whole thing will blow up.

I feel Cal's warm hand slip into my free hand and the gesture is so unexpected it makes me start. He squeezes my hand and the astonishing show of support makes hot tears spring to my eyes. I blink them away fiercely and once we have left the group behind us, I withdraw my hand. It feels too nice. I could easily get used to it and let the gesture seduce me into wanting it to mean more than it does.

My hand is tingling. I was right about the sexual chemistry between us. It's hard not to think about how more sexual contact might feel.

'I know what it's like, JoJo.' Cal's tone is quieter now.

I reluctantly slow my pace. I'd been about to stalk ahead, and poor little Pickwick's paws were moving awfully fast to keep up with me. I turn and look up, meeting Cal's intense gaze.

He knows what it's like? I should be grateful to him but I'm simmering with an anger disproportionate to anything Cal could possibly deserve from me, particularly given he's showing me unforeseen support this evening. Maybe this is the downside to hiding away from the world and being unable to express any anger: anyone you do meet is then fair game for some misdirected anger. Never engaging, never expressing anger and having to push it all down means I have an unhealthy cocktail of repressed emotions raging inside me, desperate to find an outlet. Anger at the girl who labelled me a slag stirs the mix and I can't repress an irritable surge, my radar locking on Cal's piercing blue eyes. As if he, TV cookery's golden boy, could possibly know what it's like . . .

'What, you mean you've also been publicly dumped on television, unwittingly had a sex tape made of you and then had it distributed on the internet for the world and your gran to see?'

Cal doesn't flinch.

'I mean I know what it's like to get knocked down and to have to pick yourself back up again. I know it's really hard.' His tone is serious.

I meet his gaze. His blue eyes, usually dancing with amusement as though contemplating a private joke, are solemn. I look away again quickly, unnerved by the sudden flash of connection I feel.

'What happened?' I ask, feeling considerably less prickly. I'm not so self-centred that I believe I'm the only one who has ever felt the way I do. I know some people have had far worse things happen in their life and coped much better than me. Still, I'm fairly sure Cal doesn't know exactly what it's like. Betrayal live on TV and then via a leaked sex tape is a pretty unique set of circumstances.

'I opened a restaurant with a friend in Dublin. This was before I moved to London. I left a lot of the business side of things to him – that was his area of expertise. I didn't realise he was borrowing money from the business to fund his gambling habit until it was too late. The restaurant folded and it wasn't anything to do with its popularity or the quality of the cuisine.'

'Oh, I didn't realise, I'm sorry,' I say. I'm aware that my armour is slipping a little, that Cal has found a chink in it.

'Not many people know about it. It was a tough time and I'll admit there was a temptation to give in to feeling sorry for myself or to beat myself up for not noticing the signs.' Cal shrugs. 'These things happen. People will screw you over in life, but you can't let their actions beat you or define you. Lots of successful people in life have had terrible setbacks and failures but they don't let that be the end of the story, just a stepping-stone to another one.'

My hand tightens around Pickwick's lead and I look

down at the cobbles. Is that what he thinks I'm doing? Feeling sorry for myself, choosing to be a victim? How else was I supposed to handle it? I don't remember asking for his opinion. Whatever happened to polite small talk? Not that I'm a fan of sticking to talking about things that don't matter but honestly . . . It feels like Cal is still making assumptions about me without bothering to find out the truth from me. This is just as bad as complete strangers assuming they know me because they've seen a highly edited micro-second of my life.

My cheeks grow hot and I keep my eyes fixed on the cobbles in front of me as we walk. I'm not a victim. I didn't choose this and I don't feel sorry for myself. Well, maybe sometimes, a little bit but . . . Bah, this is exactly why I need to get out more. I have entire conversations in my head and drive myself . . .

'Watch out, JoJo.'

Cal puts out an arm to pull both me and Pickwick against the wall as a procession of horseback riders and men with flaming torches pass us by. His hand remains on my lower back and he stands partly shielding me from the procession. My body registers his touch and the nearness of his body with a powerful jolt of erotic electricity. My body flushes with yet more heat.

They seem to take forever to pass us, but I don't step away from Cal, I can't. It's been so long since I felt anything like this, so long since my body had any kind of reaction to anyone. I'm sure he's aware of it. Of course, he is, he's an attractive man, fully aware of his power over women.

Unfortunately for him this woman knows that sexual chemistry isn't everything. Also the things he said to Leo about the kind of woman he assumed I was . . . Can I ever forgive him?

'Who was it that said that a life without passion is a slow way to freeze to death?' Cal's words sound casual, but they're spoken close to my ear, ostensibly to be heard over the noise of the crowd around us but I'm positive he's aware of the effect of his warm breath on my nerve endings.

I know without a doubt he isn't talking about passion for a career or for life in general but the kind of passion that got me into trouble in the first place. It's too much, his presuming to know me. We've barely spoken and yet he's challenging me this evening like this is some sort of intervention.

I'd be more indignant about his presumption if he didn't happen to be right, damn him. Being right doesn't make him any less annoying. His words are too perceptive and I daren't meet his eye. I can't risk betraying that his words resonate with me.

Once the riders are past, I pull away, annoyed with my body for responding to Cal with such abandon. Didn't it get the memo my mind sent out regarding the policy change? A celebrity hookup is absolutely out of the question for several reasons: firstly I can't risk the attention and secondly I don't want to give Cal the satisfaction of thinking he was right about me all along.

I bite my lip and ignore Cal, lengthening my stride to make sure I catch up with Poppy and Leo before anything else can be said. I really don't know why Cal is so bothered about engaging with me. I thought he'd dismissed me. That was the first night though, and a private conversation. Maybe he's doubting his assessment of me?

Well, I don't care. I can't do this, not with him. Yes, I want to move on, and I'd like to date again, I miss physical affection but someone easier, less annoying and definitely not a celebrity.

I manage to thwart all his attempts to get me on my own by sticking next to Poppy and Leo. It's not easy to do given the steady flow of foot traffic and it gets me some annoyed looks from tourists trying to come in the opposite direction. Poppy frowns the first time I refuse to fall back and walk next to Cal and then, when it happens again, she rolls her eyes at me, fully aware of what I'm doing.

When I do glance over my shoulder it's to see Cal smiling at me. He doesn't seem offended exactly. Instead he seems to find me funny, an attitude that needles me far more than it should.

We take refuge from the crowds in the leafy courtyard garden of a restaurant within the walls of the Cité. It's an oasis from the noise and bustle we left just a few steps away when we stepped through a stone archway. Large church candles nestle in alcoves and niches in the old stone walls. White fairy lights are strewn across the leafy green boughs of the trees that are dotted around the garden, amidst the tables.

'I'd love something like this theme for our wedding reception,' Poppy says wistfully, looking up at the boughs.

'Candles in the wall alcoves in the barn would be easy enough to do. It might be a good permanent look for the restaurant's decor,' I suggest, relieved to have something else to focus on.

Pickwick taps my knee with his paw; it's his signal to request, or rather demand, cuddles. I scoop him onto my lap. Peanut appears to be surgically attached to Cal; she's totally into him and has no shame in showing it. I almost feel a teensy bit jealous of her. Treacle is on Poppy's lap. Leo is the only one of us who is dog-free and that's only because Max, his Pyrenean mountain dog, and Barney, the blind rescue dog, are both not great with crowds.

'White lights on the beams maybe?' I add. 'And for the wedding I have seen saplings used, or elaborate branch arrangements in the middle of tables. Just a thought, but if we can't do the saplings and we want to keep it simple we could open up all the doors to the barn and have the party half outside in the field with lights and white lanterns strung up in the trees. It needn't be complicated.'

'And this is why I love having you as my right-hand woman.' Poppy beams. 'If I was planning the wedding on my own I'd get brain freeze over the length of my to-do list. Sorry, I mean my do-it list. You've got great style, JoJo, and you're so practical too.'

I shift uncomfortably in my seat. I'm not sure if she's trying to reassure me or up-sell me to Cal. Maybe it's just reassurance – she did promise not to matchmake and I think I got through to her . . . I hope so anyway.

It's the first time she's used my nickname that I can remember. I think this must be Cal's effect creeping in.

It's okay though. I think I'm happy to be JoJo again. Joanna was pretty unhappy. If I can get back to being JoJo, then maybe I can get back to being my old self again.

I'm not sure if it's that easy though. I think what happened has changed me. I used to trust easily and love freely. I can't imagine being like that again but maybe it's a good thing.

'Leo told me how indispensable JoJo has been to you both. That's why I think she'd be great at helping me with The Barn,' Cal announces.

'Oh, but really, I'm not . . . I mean I haven't . . . How could I possibly help you? I just help with the guests' meals. It's nothing . . .' I stare down at my menu, flustered. Spending more time with Callum O'Connor is the last thing I need right now.

'She's being modest, Cal,' Poppy scoffs. 'She runs the whole thing virtually single-handedly and she's been doing all of the admin since I took on the art gallery and extra freelance work. Plus, she's had the experience of running her own business back in England as well as knowing how things are done here.'

I'm cringing. I love Poppy lots and appreciate she's my

best cheerleader but I really, really wish she'd shut up right now. I don't want to be 'sold' to Cal. Quite the opposite.

'Yes, I know, Leo said,' Cal replies.

I can feel his gaze on me like it's tangible. I'm far too hot. I stand up abruptly and push my chair back.

'Just off to find the loos.' I hand Pickwick to Leo.

'You know she would've gone to catering college but her mum had an accident and so she had to stay home to help.'

I don't think I'm meant to hear Poppy's words, but they reach me because I have to loop back on myself to get inside the cool interior of the restaurant. I really wish I could block the words out and my cheeks burn. I would never, ever compare my skills to Cal's or my café to his restaurant and I'm mortified he might think I have delusions of adequacy. He's a trained professional and I'm just an amateur who likes to bake.

If it weren't for the fact I'm wildly attracted to him and he seems determined to needle me I'd love the chance to work and learn alongside a professional chef. But it's too risky. I may have been keeping the lesson of Aiden well at the forefront of my mind but my body refuses to behave. Today isn't the first time that an unexpected brush of Cal's fingers has set my nerve endings tingling. If I can't stop the inappropriate sexual electricity from darting through me, I need to play it safe and keep my distance as much as possible. Even if he were a regular guy it wouldn't be safe; I'm just not ready. But he's not a regular guy, he's a celebrity, so it's far, far too risky.

Thankfully the subject has changed by the time I get back to the table. I resist the urge to tell Cal that Poppy has been up-selling me because she's a good friend and really it's not true. I would but my saying anything is only going to start Poppy off again.

I sit back and listen to the conversation, observing Cal. I'm dying to discover he's vapid and self-obsessed but unfortunately for my libido he's not. He's intelligent and interested in Poppy and Leo, asking lots of questions about the St Quentin vineyard, the village veterinary practice and Poppy's books and art.

Why does he have to make it so hard for me to hate him? If he was a self-centred name-dropper it would be so much easier to ignore the chemistry humming through my body. The subject turns naturally back to The Barn.

'My vision for The Barn is really good quality food on a small scale so there's time to pay real attention to detail.' Cal's eyes light up and I can see he has real passion for the project, I can also see the charisma that makes him television material.

Maybe he was talking about a more general passion earlier? But I remember his warm breath on my neck and the hand that lingered on my lower back for just a second too long to make it casual.

'From what I've seen around here there are plenty of restaurants providing fast-turnaround dishes for tourists. We need to cater to the more discerning diner, who would rather have one amazing meal out as opposed to two average meals,' Cal adds.

'Yes, and that should appeal to residents as well as tourists. Of course, we're hoping to draw in those tourists who stop at the Vineyard for wine tasting.' Leo seems almost as enthusiastic as Cal.

'The art gallery might bring in more traffic too,' Poppy says. 'We have some amazing local artists on board.'

I don't contribute. In fact, I try to be as invisible as possible, talking quietly to Pickwick, who is back on my lap, and using toilet breaks for the dogs as an excuse to get away from the table whenever Cal tries to turn the conversation to me.

His words about a life lived without passion have taken root in my mind and I don't want him to see how unsettled I am. I hate that he was right, right about that anyway. I hadn't noticed just how cold and numb my life has become while I've been stuck in survival mode.

Cold and lonely.

Once I've thought the word 'lonely' it looms large. I read that loneliness can take as many years off your life as smoking or being obese. I don't know how true that is, but I've heard similar things about stress so maybe it's true.

I'm not lonely because no one cares about me – Poppy couldn't be a better friend to me – but I just feel . . . disconnected. It's not my life that's the problem so much as me. Usually I'd say I'm a fairly passionate person. It's my heart that's grown cold. I've become detached. I'm sleepwalking through life and Callum O'Connor is the only one who has noticed. Or maybe he's just the only one who has called me on it.

Deep in thought, I've barely tasted the confit de canard I chose for my main course. I try to pay more attention to the tarte tatin I ordered for dessert as it's one of my favourite dishes. I take a bite of warm apple, puff pastry and vanilla ice cream and make myself savour it. It's not often I get cooked for, certainly not once we're into the summer season, and as much as I enjoy cooking it is nice to have a night off.

I glance over at Cal. I may have surreptitiously been watching him. Sneaking peeks when I think he's not looking at me. He really is bloody gorgeous with his piercing blue eyes, wild black hair and a smile that does things to me . . . complicated, sexy things . . . This might be harder than I thought.

At that moment his piercing eyes lock onto me. I know then, in the flash of exchange that passes between us, that he has noticed every glance. Maybe I haven't been as surreptitious as I thought. I think someone might have been refilling my wine glass while I've not been looking. He sees me, sees far more of me than I want him to. Of course, he knows I'm attracted to him.

I think he probably even knows about the illicit sex fantasies filling my mind. Something tells me he's having them too.

I break eye contact and look away, down at my plate. He may think he knows what happens next but he's wrong. Everyone knows how this goes. Girl fancies boy. Girl plays hard to get and protests just a little bit too hard. Girl inevitably falls into bed with boy and admits what everyone knew from the start – that she likes the boy.

That is not what's going to happen here, for a very good reason. Willingly volunteer to be trashed in the gossip columns again? Not likely. I ran away to France for a reason and I'm not going to forget it for a pair of brilliant blue eyes and some Irish charm.

So, he may have a point. I might well be sleepwalking through life but that's my choice. I never asked him to wake me up or challenge me, intervention style. He's going to have to find another fuckbuddy while he's here. People always assume I'm easy, because of the sex tape, but, much as I enjoy sex, I've only ever had sex within a monogamous relationship. Well, *I've* been monogamous, at least. I don't think I could do sex without emotion, I'm too much of a romantic. Well, I used to be anyway.

I won't be the one to scratch Cal's itch to keep him from getting bored, during the short time he's here. It won't be long before he goes back to London and forgets all about me.

'I can teach you how to make that if you like?' Cal interrupts my thoughts.

I imagine the two of us in the guesthouse kitchen, plenty of accidental arm brushes and opportunity for deep and meaningful conversation.

A flush creeps up my neck and onto my cheeks.

'Sorry?' I ask politely, armour back in place.

'Tarte tatin. I can teach you how to make one that's a world away from the one you're eating.'

I'm torn. Of course, I'd love to learn from a professional chef, but I really can't . . . I can't risk it given the chemistry between us.

I always regretted not being able to take up my place at catering college. Mum suffered horrible injuries in a hit-and-run accident and needed someone at home with her. Dad was working away. My sister Annabel was still at school, so I had to step up . . . I don't regret putting family first or being there for Mum. I just wish I hadn't had to let go of my ambitions at the same time but that's life. It's the kind of thing that happens to lots of people who just quietly get on with what needs to be done.

'I'm not sure we'll have time, but thank you, I appreciate the offer,' I say. 'What with opening up The Barn, preparing for the wedding and keeping the guesthouse running through its busiest season.'

'Oh, I'm sure we can make time.' Cal shrugs, laidback and unconcerned by all the hard work ahead of us this summer.

'Okay,' I reply, fully expecting he'll forget all about it. I'm certainly not planning to remind him.

One-on-one time with Cal is to be avoided as much as possible if I'm going to stay safe. Alone is safe, that's a given.

Alone is also lonely.

I try to ignore that thought and stroke Pickwick instead. Maybe I should stick to dogs.

Chapter 5

'Learn from yesterday, live for today, hope for tomorrow'

Albert Einstein

From callum@callum'scook-off.com
To caitlino'connor85@hotmail.com
Subject: It's true!
No, I'm not kidding you. It's really JoJo from Sex in the Suburbs, she's living and working here. At first, I thought we really wouldn't get on. After all you know how I feel about reality TV, and after the way Daria behaved I was a little jaded, I'll admit.

As a result, I may have been too quick to judge. I fully admit it's one of my failings but at least I do admit it when I get it wrong. She's interesting. I think I might really like her and I really don't think she cares about being famous anymore. It's a shame she lives in France.

You know how I feel about long-distance relationships, they almost never work out.

So I guess I'll just have to hold back and remember why I'm here, to plan what I want from my future, not to get distracted by what could only ever be a holiday romance.

I do care about her though and I'd like to help her. I think she was treated really badly. It's interesting that she was one of your favourites from the show.

How are things with you anyway? Are you still feeling sick? Have you tried adding stem ginger to your diet? I've heard it helps.

Btw do you still follow Sex in the Suburbs? What's this Aiden character like?

'I am glad we're not going to the actual rescue centre.' Poppy swivels in the driving seat and checks the in-car sat nav. We've pulled up so we can program in the address of the woman who's fostering my puppy. My puppy, that sounds good.

We've taken her car so I can look after him on the way back if I need to. I've got him a little car harness to attach to a seat belt. It was the smallest I could get but I think it might still be too big.

'Because you'd want to bring them all home with you?'

'Maybe not all.' She shrugs. 'Just as many as I could fit into the car.'

'Leo would kill you,' I reply but we both know that isn't true. 'Okay, maybe not actually kill you but . . .'

'He'd give me a lecture about it not being my responsibility to save every abused and abandoned animal in Europe, make me rehome them all and make a donation to the charity . . .' Poppy pauses reflectively. 'Maybe it would be worth it.'

'You have far too much going on at the moment,' I say. 'You should be stressing about flowers or your wedding guest list like any normal bride-to-be.'

'Mmm . . . It will all work out, I'm sure,' she says, biting her lip, a sure sign she's feeling a bit stressed. 'Leo says things are done on a different scale here in France – it's more low-key and relaxed so I shouldn't plan everything the way we would in England.'

Thanks, Leo. I send him an annoyed telepathic signal.

'I've researched the differences between French and English weddings and I'm not sure he's right about not planning. I'd say it's a good thing I'm helping you.' I roll my eyes. 'If I left it up to you and Leo, God knows what would happen on the day. In fact, God will be the only one in the know. Talking about flowers we really do need to sit down and go over our "do-it" list. It's time to get organised . . .'

'I know I'm really lucky to have you helping. Oh, actually, about the flowers – I had an idea.' Poppy follows the sat nav's instructions to turn off down a country lane that looks more like a rough farmer's track than a road to me.

'Oh really? So what idea was that?' I try to keep my voice neutral. I've been the sounding board for a few wacky wedding ideas so far and have managed to successfully keep her on track for a more traditional wedding, in line with what she and Leo originally said they wanted. Also, hopefully, a wedding that will keep both sets of parents happy too and honour both French and English traditions.

'I saw this story online about a bride who didn't have flowers at her wedding. She had her bridesmaids carry rescue puppies down the aisle instead. Guests were called on to donate to the charity to help pay for foster care and in most cases they even found the pups new homes,' she says. 'After all our dogs will be at the wedding so what's the problem with adding a few more to the mix?'

'Your mum would have kittens.' I'm sure Poppy is imagining cute little puppies who stay quiet and are well behaved for the wedding and reception. I'm imagining lots of incontinent puppies weeing on the bridesmaids' dresses.

'Well, we could have kittens as well, I suppose,' she replies a little doubtfully. 'But with Peanut's cat-chasing tendencies it might not be a good idea.'

'No . . . I meant . . .'

'I know what you meant.' Poppy's face creases into a laugh. 'Got you.'

'So . . . it's a joke?'

'About the kittens, yes,' she says.

'Okay, good.' I relax a little.

'But I'm serious about the puppies,' she adds.

Before I can question her any further the car announces that we have arrived at our destination.

I've already decided to call my puppy Flump. He's being fostered by a woman who already has three dogs of her own and three additional foster dogs so he's going to be used to other dogs at least. Just as well given he's being introduced to our pack later. He's had his vaccinations so we're good to go. From what I've read about introducing new dogs to existing dogs the fact he is so much younger than the others will help – they shouldn't feel threatened.

When the creamy bundle of fur comes hurtling into the room, a stuffed duck in his mouth, I think I've been converted to the idea of love at first sight.

The toy isn't his, apparently, we work out after a bit of translation. He likes to take the other dogs' favourite toys to get them to chase him. Mad chases seem to be his favourite thing. Well, along with cuddles and duck strip chews. He's on my lap in seconds, chomping on the chew I've given him, duck toy abandoned on the floor. His fur is so soft, and his big eyes take me in solemnly, trustingly. It's then that I feel it, the crack in the ice, the surge of warm love for him rising up inside me. It's up to me now, to protect him and be worthy of his trust. Even after the chew is finished, he stays on my lap, looking up at me, just waiting. Like he's saying, 'Come on then, let's go home.' Poppy has been taking care of the paperwork for me, so I just have to sign my name. And just like that I'm now a dog owner.

And maybe it's just my imagination but I don't feel quite so alone.

I'm still feeling a bit off about Cal being in the house. He's altered the dynamic somehow, like he's changed the energy of the house. It's not necessarily a bad thing but for me all change is scary. St Quentin is my safe place and Cal has invaded it.

I'm sure he's perfectly nice but he's a charmer and I've had my fill of charming men. So what if my body experiences a little . . . frisson when he is near? My mind is in control and it's staying that way. I'm learning from my mistakes. I need to be more careful about who I trust, and I can't trust my body to make the best choices for me.

I step into the shower and squeeze out some shampoo to rub into my scalp. There wasn't time to wash my hair earlier and it's annoying me. The warm water cascades down over my shoulders and over my breasts.

Sex with Cal would be lovely. I try to squash that thought down, to not imagine what it would be like if he joined me in the shower.

I have to suppress those instincts; they're only going to lead me into trouble again. I've always been a sexual person, happy in my body and aware of my sexual energy. I can't help but feel that in suppressing my sexual energy I'm also losing a vital part of myself.

There are some exceptions to the rule of not trusting anyone. Poppy, for example. Poppy is . . . well, Poppy is Poppy and you can't help but trust her. I can't imagine her ever betraying me or being bitchy, and honestly, I owe her so much for taking me in and giving me something to concentrate on. It's not exaggerating to say I was drowning and she threw me a lifeline, pulling me up into her lifeboat. I was in a dark place when she found me. I honestly don't know what might have happened to me if I hadn't stopped in St Quentin that day I met her.

I step out of the shower and after towelling my hair dry a little I wrap the towel around myself. Flump jumps up from where he's been curled up on the bath mat and leaps into the air, clamping his jaws around the hem of the towel, trying to tug it away from me. He obviously thinks this is a brand-new game, like trying to tug my socks away from me before I put them on – that's another of his new favourite pastimes.

'Hey, let go, squirt. That's not a toy.' I tug firmly back, put my clothes in the washing basket and head out, planning to scoot quickly back to my room before anyone can see me. 'Come on, let's go – no, not that way.'

Instead of slipping quickly to my room I'm forced to follow Flump, who is woofing delightedly. I turn the corner and bump into Cal, also wearing a towel although his is lower, around his waist. I try not to stare at his chest but really, it's quite lovely, and the thought of what it would be like to press my bare breasts up against his firm, hairy chest flits into my mind before I have time to bat it away. I've always been appreciative of a hairy chest. There's just something so . . . manly about it.

Bad hormones. Down, girl. Engage your brain. I give myself a mental slap and try to focus on a spot just over his shoulder. Big mistake. I forgot to keep my eye on Flump, being distracted by manly chests and X-rated thoughts.

'Hey,' Cal exclaims.

I look down. Flump is tugging the hem of Cal's towel and manages to pull it free from the knot round his waist.

'Oh, crap, I am so sorry. No, Flump, it's not a tuggy toy.' My cheeks flush with heat as I drop to the floor and attempt to disengage Flump. Unfortunately, he sees my intervention as part of the game of tug of war. For a small puppy he's surprisingly strong and determined.

I can't believe this is happening. I'd suspect a set-up if it hadn't been my puppy who led me into it and is causing the problem. I'm trying very hard not to look at the triangle of hair snaking down to Cal's groin. Despite Cal's best efforts there's a lot more on show now than a hairy chest. My cheeks burn even hotter as I realise I'm kneeling down in front of Cal in a rather, um, suggestive position. I'm just level with . . . oh, double crap. I squeeze my eyes shut and firmly reject the thoughts trying to break through. It's been a while since I felt turned on. A long while. And now Cal is doing it just by being there. And by accidentally flashing me, I suppose. Hmm.

Hot with embarrassment and mortification, I finally get

Flump's jaws open by sliding a finger gently into his mouth at the point where his jaws meet.

'I'm so, so sorry,' I squeak in Cal's direction and hold Flump firmly against my chest, using him to cover up the glimpse of cleavage my towel seems determined to put on show. I scuttle quickly back in the direction of my room but not before I've caught the highly amused gleam in Cal's eyes. There was something else in his expression too, something darker and more intense. I'm struck by the certainty that he knows what I was thinking about the position I was kneeling in and he was thinking it too. The atmosphere was certainly charged.

I'm feeling far too hot and edgy, unsettled. I make it into my room, finally able to relax my firm hold on Flump and sigh in relief. Oh, fuckity fuck. That was . . . I need a drink. Next time I go to the bathroom I'll wear my big towelling robe, even if it is getting too hot for it. We're only in May yet we've had several days where the temperature exceeded thirty degrees. They're forecasting a heat wave.

I think I've got my very own heat wave going on as well.

It's definitely going to be a hot summer. One way or another.

I sit on the bed and brush out my damp hair while Flump beats up his toy squirrel, providing a soundtrack of adorable squeaky growls and woofs. I can't help wondering, since when did I scuttle away from sexy, half-dressed men, acting like a timid mouse?

Since I got humiliated, trolled and slut-shamed for the

whole world to see. The answer resounds loud and clear in my mind.

This isn't me. Why have I let them change me? Why am I letting them win?

The thoughts unsettle me but as I get dressed they have to compete with other thoughts of the X-rated, raunchy kind. Being so turned on after so long feeling nothing sexually is a shock of seismic proportions.

I knew Cal staying in the house would make waves and rock my nice safe lifeboat. I wish I didn't want two totally opposing things. It's just not possible to be safe and at the same time take a chance on Cal. My body and mind are now officially at war and I don't know what to do about it.

The next morning I'm trying to sort out bedding when I realise Flump has disappeared again. To him the guest-house and grounds are one giant playground and he resents having his movements restricted. I have a sneaking suspicion I know where he might be, and my stomach does a weird flip when I think about checking to see. It appears Flump and I aren't on the same page regarding avoiding Cal. If anything, Flump seems to adore Cal and seeks him out at every opportunity, which is . . . awkward, to say the least. In fact Flump seems to adore everyone, human and canine alike, and gets on well with all the other dogs, and even if Pickwick is a little bit sniffy about having to share my attention now, he does seem to recognise Flump is a pup and cuts him a bit of slack.

I'm thinking of giving Flump the nickname Houdini as he's become very adept at getting through closed doors and escaping. He's always quick to dart away if he hears Cal's voice. He loves attaching himself to the bottom of Cal's jeans, hitching a ride along the floor. Cal takes it all in good humour instead of getting annoyed. He seems very fond of my puppy, and all the guesthouse's canine contingent, something which makes it even harder not to like him.

I make my way to Cal's room reluctantly, wondering if Flump has stolen something of his again. A squeaky puppy woof from behind the half open door confirms my suspicions. He seems to be able to open doors, I haven't worked out how yet. If he wasn't destined to be a pet dog he would make a good criminal mastermind instead, especially as he looks so innocent and sweet. He is definitely the cheekiest dog I've ever met.

I peer around the door to find Cal trying to catch Flump as he darts around the room. Flump is winning and seems to think being chased is a great game. Cal is certainly encouraging this opinion by laughing uproariously.

'I am so sorry.' I stare at the black object in Flump's mouth. 'What has he stolen this time?'

'My wallet.' Cal rolls his eyes. 'Is he stealing to order now?'

He makes a lunge for him and Flump leaps easily to one side.

'Oh, God, I'm so sorry.' I have a feeling I should record

that sentence and just hit replay every time he gets into trouble. 'Flump, come here. Come here right now.'

My words make no impression on him, even though he came back every time when we were doing recall training in the garden the other day. He fixes a reproachful eye on me, as if to tell me he can't play the recall game right now because he's playing the chasing game.

'Maybe you should call him the Artful Dodger? He'd make a good burglar. I have to say I admire his cheek.' Cal echoes my earlier thoughts. 'I've lost count of how many things he's stolen from me. I don't know how he's opening my door, I've definitely been keeping it closed. It does seem that my stuff has a certain fascination for him. Up until now it's mostly been socks . . . and towels of course.'

I glance at Cal. His face has split into a wide grin and his eyes aren't so much dancing as doing an Irish jig. My cheeks flush, my stock response to Cal nowadays. It seems my body is determined to betray me. Cal raises both his eyebrows and I can't help it, my mouth mirrors his grin.

A thumping noise from the bed gets our attention. Flump sits on top of Cal's duvet, wagging his tail so hard it's banging on the bed. Either he's pleased that his furry matchmaking skills seem to be working or he's excitedly waiting to bolt if the chase resumes. I'm considering an undignified launch towards the bed when he decides to race towards me to show me his bounty. He drops it on my feet and his happy face seems to be saying, 'Look, Mum, look what I found. Let's go and buy dog treats.'

I pick it up and give it a wipe on my jeans before sheepishly handing it back to Cal.

'I'm so sorry,' I repeat, wondering if it would be rude of me to suggest he gets a lock to put on his door. 'I can go and get some baby wipes and give it a proper clean if you like?'

'It's fine, JoJo. Stop stressing and quit apologising while you're at it.' Cal laughs and takes the wallet back from me. His fingers brush mine and I shiver; the sexual electricity that pulses through me is scorching. If that's what touching his fingers feels like I can't help wondering what having the rest of him touching me, pressed up against me, skin on skin, might feel like.

Now I can't meet his eye, still possessed by the notion that sometimes he seems able to read my thoughts. The sense of connection is uncanny. Is it possible for only one person to feel this kind of sexual chemistry in isolation? Surely not.

I risk a glance at him. He's ruffling Flump's ears and talking nonsense to him.

'Why is it that one of your ears sticks up while the other one dangles down?' he asks Flump solemnly, kneeling down so he's eye to eye with him.

Flump replies by licking Cal's nose.

I smile. 'Barney's do the same. I think it must be a secret club thing.'

'The Sticky-Up Ear Club?' Cal suggests.

Did Poppy tell him that was what we'd jokingly called

it? It would be an odd thing to share with him. Either he really does read my mind or we just happen to think alike.

'Yes, how did you know?'

'Your puppy is rubbish at keeping secrets. He talks in his sleep,' Cal says solemnly, then grins at me again. His grin is warm, disarming and conspiratorial, drawing me in.

I'm mirroring his grin. It's virtually impossible not to respond to Cal when he smiles at me like this. It's like being bathed in warm sunshine. There are definite cracks forming in the ice around my heart.

I like Cal even more that he can talk nonsense like this. It's been so long since I had the luxury of being silly and talking with Cal is . . . well, it's fun. But it's dangerous too, my mind issues a warning. Remember why letting Cal get close is still a really bad idea.

Getting close to Cal is only going to draw attention to me. Invisible is the only way to avoid more pain. The familiar thoughts chill me, halting the brief thaw and damping down my momentary happiness. But I want Cal and opting for invisible feels like forgetting who I am. The inner battle confuses me, and I wrap my arms around my body. I've got to keep in mind Cal is a celebrity and the associated risk of exposure. My stomach lurches when I think about being in the public eye again and everyone dredging up the old stories. It seems my body and mind are in total agreement on that issue at least.

I wish I knew how to deal with this, that I could talk

about how I'm feeling about all this, not just the JoJo story-lite version. Not sharing makes me feel more alone but I can't share with Poppy, I don't want to worry her. She'd want to fix me and I don't want her feeling responsible for my happiness on top of everything else she's worrying about.

If not Poppy then who else could I talk to? Not Annabel – I've already caused her enough worry, it doesn't seem fair to add to it.

Could I talk to Cal? The idea of talking to him doesn't feel so ridiculous any more. I have the feeling he'd cope well with anything I had to say and talking to him as a friend needn't lead to anything else. It's not like I have many more options. Though I can hardly confide in Cal about my growing attraction to him.

I feel stuck, like a car trapped in a muddy rut. I'm revving the engine but I'm going nowhere. I desperately want a push but I'm not sure how to ask for one.

My thoughts turn back to Cal. I'm so aware of him my skin is prickling and my senses are on high alert. I'm aware he's standing close to me, our bodies virtually touching, and his scrutiny of me feels almost palpable. I ignore the urge to open up to him; I need to know him better before I can give in to my instinct to trust him. I bite my lip, the thought sobering me up as I bend down to pick up Flump.

'We'd better get on. We've got beds to make up, haven't we, Flump?'

Cal places a hand on my elbow as I turn to leave. My

pulse instantly accelerates. I turn and regard him with a mixture of anticipation and trepidation. If he makes a move on me do I really have the resolve to stop him and say no?

'JoJo, I'd really like you to work with me on the Barn project. You've done a fantastic job here at the guesthouse. Poppy and Leo rave about you. No, really they do.'

He keeps hold of my arm as I smile awkwardly, not sure how to respond to the compliment and thrown by my disappointment that he isn't asking me out.

'You know the area, you shop the markets, you're familiar with French bureaucratic red tape and you've got great organisational skills. I'd be mad not to ask for your help.' He raises an eyebrow. 'How about it? To start with, maybe you could show me around a bit? Help me get a feel for the area?'

The combination of the word 'feel' and the continued touch of Cal's hand on my arm is distracting me and wrecking my ability to stay detached.

'Um, yes, well probably. I am quite busy . . . We'll see. I'll have to ask Poppy.' A flush creeps up my neck. Why am I gabbling? 'I'd better get on now. Sorry again about the thieving.'

Time to beat a hasty retreat before more words tumble haphazardly out of my mouth. I hesitate at the doorway, think about waving but thankfully veto the impulse before my hand moves. It's just as well I'm carrying Flump because otherwise I'm not sure I'd know what to do with my hands.

What has happened to me?

I try to quell the urge to say 'yes', to let myself be swayed by the thought of spending more time with Cal. I must keep myself safe at all costs and remember what happened with Aiden, as if I'm likely to forget. Out in the hallway I snuggle my face down into Flump's soft puppy fur and sigh.

If anything like that ever happened again, I'd just die. I can't ever let myself be that vulnerable again.

Chapter 6

'Have the courage to follow your heart and intuition. They somehow know what you truly want to become'

Steve Jobs

From annabelgrant@thestickybun.co.uk
To joannagrant@thestickybun.co.uk
Subject: Seriously???
You have Callum O' Connor staying at Les Coquelicots? He's the chef you were talking about? Is he really as hot as he looks on TV? Please tell me he is, and he isn't one of these celebs who are shorter and less inspiring in real life. This is soooo exciting. I've heard he's a bit of a player though. Okay, not so much heard as I've read about him in the gossip mags. Sorry, I know how much you hate them, and I know they get things wrong all the time, I know that because of what they wrote about you.

Still, promise me you'll be careful, yes? If you were

to become 'linked' with him that would plunge you back into the media spotlight and I just couldn't bear to see you devastated again sis. I know you say there's nothing going on with the two of you but for someone who isn't interested you spend a lot of time talking about him. You've got to admit he's definitely your type.

Just sayin'!

Love and hugs,
Annabel xx

I'm in the garden when I read the email from Annabel on my phone and I'm feeling annoyed at her presumption that I'm automatically going to make the same mistakes again. Surely I haven't been going on about Cal that much? Thank goodness I didn't tell her about the whole towel-slippage incident. I haven't told anyone but that doesn't mean I haven't rerun what happened in my mind a few times and possibly imagined a different ending . . . But that's where it ends. Some fantasies are just better staying as fantasies.

I glance up to check on Flump only to see him slip through a narrow gap in the gate where the gatepost has come slightly away from the stone pillar. The gate that leads to the track that leads to the road. Panic courses through me.

'Flump,' I call after him, trying to keep my voice normal, as though nothing is wrong. I run as fast as I can, even though I'm utterly torn between racing and tackling him or hanging back because I don't want him to think it's a race and speed up.

'Come here, sweetie,' I coax, or at least I try to, but Flump is far too excited at being out on his own and off lead to listen to me. We've been doing recall training, but he always seems to know when I haven't got a treat and guess what? Right now, I haven't got a treat.

He halts for a moment by the hedge, like he's considering coming back but then he sticks his nose in the air as though catching an interesting scent and he dashes off again. Everything is a game to him and this is fun.

I hear the car accelerating along the road far too fast and feel sick to my bones. No, no, no.

Not Flump.

This can't be happening.

I see Cal at the end of the drive, he's walking back to the house and I yell to him. He's closer to Flump than I am. I know I can't get there in time and the sick feeling intensifies. My hopes temporarily rally when Flump runs close to Cal whose arms are wide and his stance low in an attempt to block him, but the attempt fails and Flump slips through, streaking onwards towards the road. It's getting dark and I'm terrified the driver won't see him. This can't be happening, it can't . . . Please God, don't let Flump be hurt.

I race up the track as fast as I can, hellbent on stopping the car, even if it means running in front of it. I had no idea it was possible to love a dog this much or that the fear of him being hurt would be so intense.

Cal beats me to it, running into the middle of the single

track road and holding his hand up to stop the oncoming car. In that split second of terror, a moment so horrifying I'll never forget it, I swear my heart stops beating. It may only be a split second but it seems to last an eternity.

Thankfully, with a screech of brakes the car stops too.

I race behind Cal and swoop in to grab Flump and clutch him to my chest, dimly aware of Cal both thanking the driver for stopping and apologising to him.

I wait for Cal at the top of the track and he puts his arm around both me and Flump and guides me back down the track to the guesthouse. His arm stays around me the whole time, all the way back to the house, and I have to admit I like it there. We have the kitchen to ourselves tonight as Poppy is over at Leo's with Peanut, Treacle and Pickwick but Barney is still here and comes to greet us, tail wagging madly, as if it's been days, not just minutes, since we were last here. Being blind makes it hard for him to adapt to new environments and Poppy says he seems happier here in his own home where he's not going to walk into an unexpected sofa or wall.

I collapse into a chair, still clasping Flump to me. His fur is damp with my tears. I'm not sure I can ever let him go.

Without asking Cal puts the kettle on and makes me a tea which he places on the table in front of me.

'Drink your tea. It's okay, you can put him down now.' With a tenderness I didn't know he possessed, Cal prises my fingers away from Flump and puts him down on the floor where he immediately races off to wrestle with Barney.

Flump isn't affected by his recent adventure and also not bothered by the fact that Barney is at least six times his size. Barney seems to enjoy playing with Flump and is incredibly gentle with him.

I watch them, clasping the mug in both hands, letting the warmth seep into my cold fingers. After a couple of sips, I feel less numb.

'Cal, I don't know how to thank you.' I look down at my tea. 'I don't think I could've got there in time. If it wasn't for you then he . . . he . . .'

'Shh, hey, it's okay. He didn't. It's okay.'

'I think there's something wrong with the gate mechanism, it doesn't seem to want to stay closed properly.'

'If you like I'll take a look at it to see what's wrong,' Cal offers. 'If you just show me where you keep your tools.'

'It's my fault, I thought there was something wrong with the gate the other day and I meant to say something. If anything had happened to Flump, I never would've forgiven myself.'

Cal takes the mug from me and puts it on the table. Then he bends over my chair and wraps me into a hug. The comfort of it is deliciously sweet. It's a hug I've been craving for a while. I really need this, and not just now in this situation. It's a basic human need I've been ignoring for a while – to feel the comfort of another human being, to establish and experience a real connection. To be touched.

I'm dizzy with relief that Flump is okay and my guard

is lowered but even so, I can't deny a hunger for more of this.

For more of Cal.

Peace seeps into me with the hug, stress easing out of my taut muscles. Gradually the horror of what might have happened to my lovely, vibrant puppy fades from my mind. Flump's okay and I owe it to Cal.

Does this mean I have to forgive him for the things he said to Leo when he first arrived? There's a definite thaw inside me towards Cal. My anger has mostly dissipated and I'm not sure I want to freeze him out any more. Maybe there's another option that won't mean I have to abandon caution. We could be friends. Friends hug, don't they?

I'd like to be friends who hug.

I definitely want lots of hugging.

Crap, I think I might be enjoying this hug a bit too much. With a sigh I disengage, forcing myself to pull back. We'll have to go easy on the hugging. I pick up my mug and drink the rest of the tea.

'I don't know how to thank you.'

'I do.' Cal holds my gaze. There's a definite gleam in his eye.

He's not talking about . . . Surely not.

'Um, what?'

I'm no longer feeling cold and numb, in fact it's the reverse: I'm rather hot and my skin feels super sensitised.

'Get more involved with the Barn project. It'll be more fun with you helping.'

I'm not sure whether I'm disappointed or not, that he wasn't suggesting what I thought. 'Okay, I can do that.'

'I've got one more request.' Cal sits down in the chair next to mine and angles it towards me. His eyes are dancing their usual Irish jig. He takes the empty mug from my hands and his fingers brush mine in a way that doesn't seem accidental. The atmosphere feels charged with anticipation and attraction that weave a web of connection between us.

Is he playing with me?

'Oh?' I meant my tone to be polite and perhaps a little cool but instead I come across as nervous, even to my own ears.

'Maybe you could take some time off and show me the area? I know you said you'd think about it and I get the feeling you'd like to spend time with me but . . .' He shrugs. 'You'd rather make up excuses and tidy up your linen cupboard or scrub floors that are already clean than do something you'd actually like to do? Do you want to explain that to me?'

I don't think he needs me to explain it to him at all but making me say it, making me vocalise my fear of getting hurt, would mean admitting I really like him. Or at least that I think I have the potential to really like him, enough that he could have the power to hurt me. I'm not ready to do that. I can forgive him for the things he said but forgetting is going to be harder, and wouldn't admitting I like him just play right into his hands and prove him right?

I bite my lip, I'm so torn. Part of me thinks I need to confess that I overheard that conversation so we can somehow put it behind us but, well, I just can't face it. I do like him but not because he's a celebrity. In fact, I like him despite him being a celebrity but is he ever really going to believe that?

'I could spare some time to show you round, if that's what you'd like.' I pull both my hands back onto my lap and ignore the second half of his question.

Elephant in the room? What elephant?

'Okay, thanks, JoJo, I'd appreciate that.' He smiles and shakes his head a little.

Maybe he's sharing a joke with the elephant.

Yep, it's official. I'm losing it.

Poppy needs to spend some extended time at the gallery to organise a display so I'm looking after all the dogs the next day. All except Maxi who goes to work with Leo.

I'm getting ready to take them out and wondering if I can really manage all five or if I should do it in two runs when Cal comes down from his room.

'I'll help you,' he offers, taking Barney and Pickwick's leads from me. 'I could use some fresh air and sunshine, a nice break from paperwork and planning.'

The offer is not phrased as a question. I can hardly turn him down when I clearly do need help. I don't think he'll let me get away a second time with not answering his question about why I'm avoiding him, so I give in. It seems the easier option.

We head off down the track to the lake, sun warm on our bare legs and arms. I'm living in shorts and T-shirts now the days are heating up. Poppy says she hasn't seen me in leggings once since Cal arrived but that is purely coincidental.

Probably.

Flump hurtles off after Peanut and Treacle while Pickwick and Barney trot along at our heels. Cal's good with the dogs, I can't help noticing. They all seem to like him a lot and supposedly dogs are good judges of character.

It's warm but not too hot, with a slight breeze ruffling the leaves in the trees and sending ripples across the surface of the lake.

'So what made you go into TV rather than, say, stick with running your own restaurant?' I ask.

'Because I don't think you should ever just stick with something because you're comfortable with it. I believe you need to continually challenge yourself if you're going to make the most of this life.' Cal looks at me, his eyes serious. 'You can't be free in your comfort zone. And if you're living in survival mode you're stuck, you're not growing at all. Who wants to get to the end of their life just to say, "Well, hey, I survived"? Not me.'

I stare out at the lake, watching reflected light dancing on the surface of the water. I'm not sure if he's just talking generally or if the words are aimed at me. They could certainly be made for me right now.

I've got two choices. I can dial the conversation back down to small talk and spend the rest of Cal's stay with us deflecting him when he talks about anything that matters . . . Or I could actually talk to him. Open up to him and be honest. There's a novel idea.

'So . . . how do you stop being stuck then?' I ask cautiously.

'You have to embrace uncertainty.' Cal's eyes seem to pierce through my defences, penetrating me, seeing the fear and pain I try to hide from people.

'Hmm.' Embracing uncertainty doesn't sound too appealing to me at the moment. It certainly doesn't sound safe but . . . he's right. I am stuck. I'm certainly not living life to the full. I feel like I've spent too much time in stasis. Maybe this, Cal's words, is what I need to hear right now.

'If you're never prepared to be wrong, to fail and to risk making mistakes, you'll never do anything really worth doing,' Cal adds.

I want to protest that it really isn't that easy. I don't want to get drawn into this discussion but the thoughts that ricochet around my head insist on expression.

'What if you do make a mistake and it all goes horribly wrong?' I blurt out, not meeting his gaze. I'm thinking about the post Aiden fallout, an example of 'horribly wrong' on a nuclear level.

'Then you pick yourself up, you learn from it and you approach your next goal.' Cal's words are unequivocal, but his voice is gentle, like he's sensing my mood. 'You can't be a slave to needing to know how things will turn out before you act. How can anyone learn or grow or create anything wonderful if they're hobbled by fear?

'I've read that humans fear loss far more than we value gain. Overcoming that bias is one of the most important things we can learn.'

His words resonate with me. I chew my lip. I'd love to be dynamic like Cal but I'm not feeling brave. In fact, the fear knotting me up is so visceral I don't know if I can overcome it. Not without help anyway and asking for that help would involve reaching out properly and opening up all the darkness inside me for someone else to see. Can I really do that?

Maybe, possibly . . . Cal's words are sinking into me, being absorbed by my cells as seeds of hope being sown, taking root. I used to be a risk-taker.

Even if I discount everything that happened as a result of taking a risk with Aiden and the television show, the last time before that when I took a risk was when I bought The Sticky Bun and built my own business. I poured my heart into that café, trying out hundreds of recipes and decorating the place myself, staying up to midnight each night for a week to get it finished.

Yes, it's now in the loss column because I can never go back there and I'm going to have to face selling it. That bridge has been well and truly dowsed with petrol and burnt to a crisp. But the gain column also has plenty written in it. There were moments of intense satisfaction, of joy, of feeling supremely fulfilled and proud of myself for making it work. Those moments haven't been invalidated simply because I've moved on to another stage in my life and they won't be invalidated by my selling the café.

Maybe it is time to take a risk again, to come out from the bed I've been hiding under for the past year. If I don't, the other option I have is to stay stuck and lonely with only the dust mites for company. Oh, and all the little dogs who can fit under the bed. They'll keep me company.

That's not me any more though. I am so over drifting through life like the ghost of the woman I used to be. I know now why I've been avoiding contact from my family and trying to dissuade Annabel from visiting. It's because I can't lie to them, and I know they'll be able to see just how different I am from the JoJo they know.

We sit down on a grassy mound where the riverbank converges with the lakeshore. There's an intricate network of exposed tree roots stretching down from the grassy bank to the river, looking like very complex drinking straws. The deeply rooted, majestic trees stretch up above us to the cloudless blue sky. Where we are sitting is a suntrap and the trees provide a welcome dappled shade beneath their silvery green dancing boughs.

Cal catches my eye, as I look up into the branches overhead.

'It's a beautiful sight, isn't it?' He peers up with me. 'Have you heard of the Japanese healing tradition of Shinrin-yoku?

It means the sense of well-being that comes simply from being in woods or a forest. Forest bathing is actually part of preventative therapies in Japanese medicine.'

'No, I hadn't heard that, but I really like the sound of it.' I lean back against a rock so I can stare up into silvery green boughs and relax. I'm sure it's psychological but I feel like the trees are having an effect on me already. I like talking to Cal, I realise. It's been so long since I felt challenged or truly engaged in a conversation.

'I have more interesting tree facts for you, if you like?' Cal's tone is playful.

'Sure.' I grin. 'Hit me with your scintillating tree facts.'

'I didn't promise they'd be scintillating.' Cal laughs.

'Hit me with your moderately interesting tree facts then.'

'Okay, did you know that tree parents live together with their offspring in communities? They support them as they grow and share nutrients with those who are sick or struggling. Because of their interactions, trees in a group are protected and live to a good age whereas solitary trees have a tough time and in most cases die earlier than those in a group.'

'Really? I've never thought about it. If I had I might have assumed they'd be competing for resources.' I turn my head to him. 'Okay, so that is kind of interesting.'

'Really, it's true. Scout's honour and everything.' Cal's mouth twitches at the corner. 'There have been lots of scientific studies in recent years that show trees are more social and intelligent than we previously thought. They even communicate by sending electrical signals to each other; they warn each other of approaching danger. Those underground connections,' He gestures to the roots exposed at the side of the bank. 'They are like a wood-wide-web. They warn about drought or disease or insect attacks and other trees alter their behaviour when they receive the messages. As well as slow pulsing electrical signals they communicate using pheromones and scent signals.'

'So that's basically geek speak for saying trees talk to each other?'

'Yes, geek speak, otherwise known as scientific evidence.' Cal's tone is teasing. 'There's also something known as the Backster Effect. Backster was one of the leading experts on the polygraph for the CIA and he did experiments to see if hooking plants up to the polygraph machine produced any results. Nothing happened until he decided to get some matches to burn one of the leaves at which point the plant reacted and the polygraph picked it up. It wasn't a fluke; he did the experiment over and over again. But I'm digressing. The important point in all this is how interconnected everything is.'

'I guess. That is just freaky about the polygraph. I'm not sure what to think about trees communicating. Though I did always love the idea of trees talking to each other in stories. Perhaps Tolkien and Enid Blyton were ahead of their time?'

'*The Hobbit* and the *Magic Faraway Tree* series? I loved

those too.' Cal grins and I see the echo of the cheeky boy he used to be. The cheeky boy he still is, sometimes.

As the dogs splash around in the river Pickwick decides to grab one of the tree roots and starts tugging, undaunted by the fact it's as wide as his muzzle.

'Pickwick, that isn't a stick, you muppet.' I roll my eyes.

'And that tree is going to tell on you to all his tree friends.' Cal laughed. 'Perhaps we'd better make our escape before they start pelting us with dead branches.'

On the walk back I can't shake the feeling that something inside me is changing. I like the idea of us all being interconnected. Maybe it's time I put down roots. It's got to beat hiding under the bed forever. I'm sure there's a lesson here about needing to reach out and connect.

I don't want to be that lone tree, unsupported and disconnected.

It's hard to define exactly what I'm feeling. Stirred up is probably the best way to describe it. I need time to process these new ideas. I feel the pull of Cal's charisma and the charm that seeks to pull me along in his wake. He casually links an arm through mine, and I start at the shock of desire that runs through me at the skin-on-skin contact.

It's not holding hands but it's certainly something. I don't know if I'm relieved or disappointed when I have to take my arm back so I can put Flump on a lead. I'm not sure how it's possible to feel such contradictory reactions simultaneously. Yet I do. My body might feel bereft but my mind is glad of the distraction, of having to make sure Flump doesn't take himself for a much longer walk.

Everything is happening a little bit too quickly for me. Cal's passionate ideas and powerful sexual chemistry could easily sweep me away. I need to be totally sure if I'm going to let myself get closer to Cal. I'm fairly sure from the signals he's giving me that he's up for a whole lot more than linking arms but what exactly? What does he want from me?

Until I know that, until I can be really sure that his opinion of me has changed there can't be any more than that.

Chapter 7

'In nature we never see anything isolated, but everything in connection with something else'

Johann Wolfgang von Goethe

As the days grow hotter, we see the first of the sunflowers appear in the fields surrounding St Quentin. The plans and paperwork for The Barn are progressing at the usual laidback French speed, which almost threatens Cal's positivity until he decides to 'just go with it' and 'kick back a bit'. The 'do-it' list I share with Poppy for the wedding gets variously renamed the 'do-I-have-to-do-it?' list, the 'we-must-get-on-and-do-it' list and now the 'just-do-it!' list. Though sometimes we add a swear word or two between 'just' and 'do', if we're having a bad day.

I'm up early, even though I haven't any guest breakfasts to get, because I'd rather Flump hurtled around the garden like a furry nutcase before it gets hot. He throws himself into everything with such joyful abandon that it can't fail to put a smile on my face. He is so innocently, unequivocally happy. It's like he has effortlessly prised open a crack in my heart and for the first time in ages I feel pure love and an un-complicated joy. What I feel for Cal, the cautious seedling hope that has been tentatively growing during our evening walks to the lake, is far more complicated and deeper.

One advantage of not being on duty in the kitchen is that I am still in my nightshirt. It looks like it might be a T-shirt dress though, so it does for Flump's morning walks. As we are still toilet training I don't exactly have time to hang about getting dressed and doing my hair and make-up.

Flump is now bounding about chasing a butterfly with such a comical look on his face that I laugh out loud. It's a definite change in me. I can't remember the last time I laughed properly, not just a polite smile at someone else's joke, not before Flump and Cal came onto the scene anyway.

Loving animals is so much easier than loving humans. Maybe I should just be like Angeline and end up surrounded by lots of rescue animals. She seems pretty happy. I take a quick look at my phone and look again at the text message that came in from Annabel last night. I really must reply. Or add it to my 'do-it-or-else' list.

I don't want to hassle you JoJo but you're going to need to decide if you're going to take the offer for the café.

Great. Do I accept the offer so that it's all over and done with, even though it's a low one? I rub my forehead, feeling a tension headache starting there. Then I look up and notice that Flump is nowhere to be seen. Ever since he ran out onto the road that time I've been plagued by panic when he disappears. Even though it's usually only for a few minutes and it's only to hide behind a bush or under the sofa, somewhere I hadn't even known he could fit.

We've been training and he thinks recall is a good game. Unfortunately, he also thinks hide and seek is an even better game, for which I blame Peanut.

'Flump, Flump, come here.' I pace around the garden trying hard not to feel fraught. Logically I know he won't have gone far. In this direction, behind the house, there are only fields and a neighbour's garden, no roads really to worry about.

But still, he's too much of a puppy to go missing. If he did get further afield he has no road or traffic sense yet. He doesn't know to be careful of cows . . . What if there are cows in calf in the fields? Panic grips my chest and I'm finding it hard to breathe. I pace the perimeter of the garden, peering through hedges and fencing, becoming frantic when I can't find any hole he could have escaped through or see a flash of creamy tail amidst any of the dense foliage.

'Flump, Flumperooni, come here right now,' I shout, resorting to one of his nicknames.

'What's wrong?'

I turn around to find Cal has joined me. I'm so relieved to see him I could cry. Cal always seems to be there when I need him nowadays. I'll process that thought later. Right now, I need to focus.

'It's Flump, he's gone. He was just here.' I point at a spot by the hedge. 'And now I can't . . .'

Embarrassingly my voice wobbles.

'Shh.' Cal takes hold of my elbows and something about the firm gesture and the calm eyes that meet mine helps stop my panic spiralling. 'Let's listen for him.'

I nod and we creep up to the hedge.

'Call him now and then stay quiet,' he says in a low voice.

'Flumper, come here, Flumperooni.'

I ignore Cal's eyeroll at the nickname and join him in listening.

I can hear the faint tinkle of Flump's tags knocking together. I part the branches of the pine tree, trying to penetrate its darkness and notice that the wire at the bottom of the fence has been pushed up a little, perhaps by a fox or cat on its nocturnal rounds. I continue to push through, ignoring the branches scratching at my bare legs and also ignoring Cal's suggestion that I wait.

Just as I am trying to squeeze through the bush and to swing my leg over the wire, I feel my nightdress tear and my leg snag on the same thorns. Fantastic.

Cal whistles for Flump and the little dog races happily

towards the fence, ducks underneath it and hurtles towards Cal, ignoring me completely. I grind my teeth and try to pull free from the bush only to discover that I am well and truly stuck.

Oh, bloody hell.

'Do you need some help there?' Cal asks, peering in at me with Flump in his arms. They are both wearing identical WTF expressions, as though my behaviour is inexplicable.

'I'm fine,' I huff and try to disengage myself, to no effect except for another tear in my favourite nightdress. 'All right, maybe I'm not okay. Can you help me?'

My request for help is tinged with an irritation that rationally I realise Cal doesn't deserve, given he's helping me yet again. Maybe that's where my irrationality creeps in. Yet again Cal gets it right and I'm the one stuck in the thorny bush. There are real-life comparisons that could be drawn from this, I'm aware. And I've no doubt Cal is aware too.

There's another, much more basic reason why I'm reluctant to let Cal help me and that's because I don't wear underwear under my nightdress. In hot weather it's much more comfortable and it's not like I ever bump into anyone when I'm doing Flump's early morning toilet run. Not usually, anyway.

I can't think of a way to mention the fact without making the situation even more mortifying.

'Sure, no problem.' Cal seems to be enjoying my

predicament, or maybe he's just enjoying the fact that I'm asking for help and having to rely on him. His fingers are gentle as they unhook the thorns from my dress, one by one. 'Have you heard that spending just twenty minutes in contact with nature lowers your stress hormones?'

'Ha ha, is that so?' I grit my teeth and wince when he unhooks a thorn from my thigh. His fingers travel higher up and I go rigid.

'Sorry,' he says. 'I'll try to be more gentle with the next one.'

I don't bother to explain that I'm tense for another reason altogether. Instead I close my eyes and just hope he doesn't notice.

Cal seems to enjoy the experience of extracting me from the hedge far more than I do. Although all the accidental touching and brushing up against me is definitely having an effect of a very distracting nature. His hands linger on my body once I'm out and he runs his eyes over me.

Flump is at Cal's feet, also scrutinising me, head tilted as he tries to puzzle out why I'm making such a meal out of hopping through the hedge.

'That thing about stress hormones?' I try to divert attention from the growing sexual tension.

'What about them?'

'I'm no scientist but I think the stress hormone effect might be negated if the trees are actually attacking you.'

I look down at the torn hem of my nightdress and the trickle of blood running down the back of my leg.

'Hey, it was self-defence,' he says, a definite twinkle in his eye. 'You just launched yourself at the hedge, no introductions, what do you expect?'

'Hmm.' I attempt a withering glare, but it seems to glance right off of Cal's sunny mood.

'You could do with cleaning those scratches. Would you like me to help? I have first-aid training because of working in kitchens.' Callum attempts a more solemn expression and I can't help but smile back at him. It's hard to stay cross with him for long.

I'm aware one of the scratches on my chest is near one of my breasts and imagine his fingers gently caressing me. His touch, while disengaging me from the thorns, was surprisingly tender. I have no doubt that some of the touching was not accidental but it's not like I didn't enjoy it.

I enjoyed it too much, that's the problem. I've just about got used to our chats and have been kidding myself I can keep Cal in the friend zone.

'I'll be okay, thank you.' I pick Flump up, concerned he might run after Cal instead of coming with me. That would be mortifying. 'And thanks for helping me get Flump back, yet again. I really appreciate it.'

I am genuinely thankful for his help with Flump, who seems utterly determined to get himself into as many precarious situations as possible, just to keep me on my toes. Having someone else with me definitely helped to keep my panic in check.

'At least let me put antiseptic cream on those scratches. Did you know you've got a nasty one here?' Cal lightly touches the back of my neck and I shiver.

'I'm sure I can manage.' I stare down at the top of Flump's head, aware my voice lacks conviction and that my skin is flushing pink at the thought of Cal touching me again. Yes, I might be sore and look like someone has been using me as a pincushion but evidently my body is still capable of arousal.

'Don't be an eejit.' Cal deliberately thickens his Irish brogue to make me smile. 'You can't even see half the scratches, let alone reach them. I promise it will all be above board. Flump can be your chaperone if you like?'

I laugh and roll my eyes. 'You're the eejit, Cal.'

'That is the worst Irish accent I've ever heard.'

'It was deliberately bad. I was being ironic, obviously.' I grin. 'Okay, I'll confess, I totally wasn't, I'm just really crap at accents.'

'Definitely a little eejit.' Cal puts an arm around me as we head back to the house.

'Ow.'

'Sorry.' He moves his arm. 'I'll make it up to you. I always wanted to be a doctor.'

'Really?'

'Yes, I always have been fascinated by science, and how things work. Plus, I used to enjoy playing the game

Operation. Do you happen to have a funny bone that needs removing? Because I'm pretty handy with a pair of tweezers.'

'Ha ha. No, I'm good, thank you.' I giggle. 'See, my funny bone is intact and working!'

I realise I've laughed more since Cal arrived at Les Coquelicots than in the whole of the rest of the year put together. It reminds me of who I used to be, makes me feel more myself somehow. It feels . . . nice. Nicer than nice. Resisting Cal is getting more and more difficult. I'm finding it hard to remember why it's worth protecting myself. This is one risk that is looking pretty attractive from where I'm standing.

'You're a good girl, are you?' Cal's eyes are teasing.

'Hardly,' I say and think desperately of how to change the subject before the rest of me turns as pink as my neck. 'So, why didn't you study medicine then?'

'Let's say my dedication to study didn't match my enthusiasm.' Cal shrugs. 'I'm an intellectual butterfly, flitting from subject to subject as something new grabs my interest. So many things to discover, places to go, girls to kiss . . . you know.'

I bite my lip, losing my battle with the flush that has spread to my cheeks. There's no way he hasn't noticed. My body may as well be signalling my interest with a neon sign.

The silence stretches between us, comfortable but charged, crackling with sexual electricity. I abandon my attempts to defuse it or damp it down and decide to enjoy it instead. It's been a long time since I felt like this.

'I think I can imagine,' I reply eventually and open the back door to Les Coquelicots, putting Flump down on the floor.

'If you sit down at the kitchen table I'll go and get the antiseptic cream and some wipes,' Cal offers, briefly touching my elbow before he heads off upstairs to the bathroom where we keep most of my first-aid supplies.

I can feel the anticipation coiling inside me, a mixture of fear, emotional desire and physical attraction bubbling up and spilling over. I fiddle with my torn nightdress hem and nibble anxiously at my lower lip.

When he comes back with the first-aid box and gently pulls the top of my nightdress down at the back so he can use alcohol wipes on the scratches, I can't help starting a little at the contact.

'Sorry, did that hurt?'

'Um, yes, a little bit.'

Sure, that would be why I jumped. Absolutely nothing to do with Cal touching my neck. I've always found my neck is particularly sensitive to male attention but that's not a piece of information I'm about to volunteer willingly.

When his fingers gently brush away strands of hair on my neck that have come loose from my ponytail I inhale sharply, and my pulse quickens.

I glance round at Cal and catch a knowing gleam in his eyes, a warm, teasing light that is more playful than predatory. My skin flushes. I can't help my body responding to him. His fingers linger on the pulse point on my neck.

'Did you know the heart beats on average one hundred thousand times a day? That's thirty-five million times a year.'

'How can you possibly remember that?' I ask.

'I like trivia. Like I said, I'm particularly interested in anything science-based.' He disposes of the first lot of alcohol wipes in the kitchen bin and grabs some more. 'I used to read a lot of *How to. . .* and *Science for Boys* type books as a child and I still read widely on topics that interest me.'

He picks up the cream and I tilt my head forward to make it easier for him to apply it. I notice the scratch on my chest and wonder if he's seen it. The thought of the hands that are so tenderly ministering to my back slipping around to do the same to my chest makes my heart rate pick up. I think my heart will be beating a lot more than one hundred thousand times today, thanks to Cal.

'So, any more interesting facts about the heart to share?' I ask in an effort to distract myself from the thrumming of my own.

He leans over me to dab at the scratch on my chest. His lips are close to my right ear and I can't help silently begging for his mouth to close the gap. Maybe he picks up my signal because I swear his lips oh so gently brush against my earlobe and a not so gentle shock of sexual electricity courses through me.

His fingers trace down from my collarbone to my heart where he places the palm of his hand over my nightdress. He moves slowly, giving me the opportunity to stop him at any time. I can't bring myself to stop him. My skin prickles deliciously to his touch. It feels almost unbearably intimate. There is no way to hide the rapid thrumming of my heartbeat now. No hiding how turned on I am by him.

'The heart is the most powerful source of electromagnetic energy in the body. The field actually extends way beyond the surface of our bodies. There's even evidence that our hearts emit complicated signals, like they are transmitting information. These signals can be picked up by other people, subconsciously of course. So, if you ever get a bad vibe from someone, you're probably basing it on more than just a subjective feeling.'

'Seriously?'

'Yes, our hearts are talking to each other.'

'Like the trees?'

'Like the trees. There's always a lot more going on beneath the surface than we think.'

My heart is doing a bit more than talking at the moment: more like it's doing the conga at a booze-heavy office party. I get up and twist around, leaning back against the kitchen table as I tentatively place my own hand over Cal's heart, and he replaces his on mine.

'We can even influence each other's heart rates.' Cal's eyes are dark now, almost indigo blue as his gaze locks on mine.

Now that isn't news to me. Cal has been influencing my heart rate since the moment I met him. I don't think I've ever met someone so vibrant or so interested in the world around him. Aiden had charisma of a sort, but it quickly became apparent that the only planet he was interested in was the planet Aiden.

Cal's energy stirs me, makes me want to know more, to experience more and to start looking outwards, to the world around me, instead of the inward, centred life I've been living since I went into hiding.

I'm holding my breath, wondering whether he's going to kiss me, how far he plans to take this. It could just be a flirtation. I'm sure that for some men flirting is like breathing, instinctual and unthinking. For others maybe they like to know that they can still attract a woman; they don't really plan to take it much further than flirty banter and enjoyment of sexual tension. As for Cal? I have no idea what he really wants from me.

For that matter I don't know what I want. I want him to kiss me, of course I do . . . But mixed in with the genuine desire and magnetic attraction is a lingering anxiety that nags at me like an unrelenting toothache. It can't be calmed by desire or soothed by anything except trust. Can I trust Cal? It's far too soon to tell. My body says yes but my body has been wrong before.

I want him, I really do, but I'm unclear about his motives. Does he just want to be able to say he fucked the girl from the sex tape when he goes back to his real life?

Also, there's one hell of a difference between coming out of hiding to live a relatively quiet life and switching a great big spotlight on myself by dating another celebrity.

I stay paralysed by conflicting desire and indecision.

Instead of leaning in for a kiss Cal's fingers skim under the hem of my nightdress, lifting it up a little. My breath hitches again and my body tingles in a most delicious way, my skin prickling with anticipation. This is pretty forward for a next move.

But instead of lifting it up high enough to display my lack of underwear he takes his other hand from my chest and grabs another antiseptic wipe to clean up the nasty scratch on my thigh.

From the twitch of his lips I'm guessing he knew exactly what I was thinking and that he might already know I'm not wearing anything underneath. He then trails a finger up my body, over the hem of my nightdress and over my hip, taking me totally by surprise when he goes in for a tickle.

I giggle. God help me, Cal has turned me into a giggler! Then I wriggle away, half relieved, half disappointed. Clearly, he's not going to take this further until he gets a full green light from me, rather than a light that keeps flickering from green to amber and back again.

'Just checking your funny-bone response, to see if it needs removing with tweezers.' He grins. 'As I recall from my highly educational game of Operation it's located just about here.'

He reaches out and tickles me again before I can get away and I squirm. I can't even remember the last time I was tickled. It's fun. I'm having fun. My mind dimly recognises the unusual concept.

That Cal decided to make me laugh rather than trying to get into my pants make me like him all the more.

Can I trust him? Only time can tell me the answer to that. My impatient, horny hormones are going to have to take a number and get in line.

Chapter 8

'And suddenly you know: It's time to start something new & trust the magic of beginnings'

Meister Eckhart

One week later Cal persuades me to leave Flump at home so we can go on a field trip he promises is necessary research but sounds suspiciously like a dinner date. The setting for Château Abbeye de Camon couldn't be more idyllic. The pretty, rural village of Camon is surrounded by forest and fields of sunflowers.

'I can't believe we're eating somewhere that's over a thousand years old.' I peer out of the car window at my first sign of the Château.

'I've heard great things about the food here,' Cal says, pulling Leo's jeep up onto the gravel driveway inside the Château's grounds. 'It's deliberately kept to a small scale so the chef can pay attention to detail and create something special. It's the kind of vibe I'd like to get going for The Barn.'

Cal proposed this meal out as a research trip given we're still waiting for the contractors to finish the electrics and plumbing at the barn before we can go any further. It all sounds very plausible, but I have to say it's really starting to feel like a date. He's looking really handsome in a pale blue shirt that seems to make his eyes even more piercing than usual. I'll admit I dressed up too, wearing a dress that shows off my cleavage instead of hiding it. I also put on perfume and a little light make-up.

I even shaved my legs. Not because I'm going to have sex with Cal tonight. I'm not. It's just . . . in case.

Like the pretty lingerie set I'm wearing is just to make myself feel nice.

Oh, who am I kidding? I know I probably, really, absolutely shouldn't sleep with him, but I so want to. Over the past week the sexual tension between us has been mounting until I'm practically fit to combust. It's like Cal has laid the fire but he won't strike a match until I say so. I'm starting to think it's a deliberate strategy, to get me going to the point where I practically beg him. He wants it to be my choice and he wants me to be ready. All the accidental touches and lingering glances that pass between us haven't helped one bit. Not to mention the intense way he has of focusing on me as though I were the most fascinating person he's ever met . . . I'm sure he looks at everyone like that but God, it's working. Our conversations during our evening walks have helped me get to know him better, to understand his passion, his keen intelligence and a mind that's always asking questions.

Combined with just the right amount of alpha cheekiness and I'm a goner.

I sigh.

'Are you okay, JoJo?'

I nod as Cal takes my arm and we enter a long corridor. The floor and walls are made of ancient stone. I catch glimpses of centuries-old tapestries and wide-open fireplaces in the rooms we pass. It's been beautifully renovated and yet still retains the peaceful feel of an old abbey.

The dining room is small, with an intimate feel. There are stiff white tablecloths and a candle alight on each table, glinting off the gold gilt picture frames and candlesticks. There are murals on the walls depicting a Château Camon from centuries ago.

'Poppy would love it here,' I say. 'She's a real history nut. I'll have to get Leo to bring her. I think she's a bit frazzled at the moment with all the extra work she's taken on with the gallery and the wedding planning. A lot of the stress is coming from her mum. She keeps sending her all these passive-aggressive emails.'

'All women are passive-aggressive,' Cal replies solemnly.

'They are not.' I swat his arm.

'True, some are just aggressive.' He grins and I roll my eyes at him, not deigning to answer a remark made just to wind me up.

'But you're helping with the wedding, aren't you?' Cal asks, handing me a menu. 'More than just the reception at The Barn, I mean.'

'Assuming we manage to get The Barn up and running in time, you mean?' I raise an eyebrow. The contractor delays and the discovery of a burst pipe underground have put everything behind schedule.

'Should I touch wood or cross myself?'

'Cross yourself,' I say. 'After all, this is an old abbey.'

He crosses himself.

'Cal!'

'What? You told me to, and I am an Irish Catholic, it's part of my muscle memory. Anyway, the arrangements for the wedding – all going okay?'

'Um, sort of,' I reply distractedly and refuse to let my mind run over all the unchecked items in my 'do-it' list.

I cast my eyes down the menu. There's Roquefort soufflé to start with, then asparagus soup with a deep-fried risotto ball, scallops, lamb and then a trio of desserts or cheese-board.

'This looks seriously yummy.' I put the menu back down on the table.

'Would you like to help me plan the menu for the reception?'

I look up to find Cal's blue eyes fixed on me. Always so intense . . . so sexy . . . My mind goes blank for a minute. Well, not blank exactly . . . I have to chase out thoughts of what it would be like to have those piercing eyes on me during sex, while he's inside me.

What did he ask me? Oh, the reception, yes . . .

'Um . . . yes, of course. That would be fun.'

'They rely on you a lot, Leo and Poppy.'

'I don't mind. I love being here in France and without Poppy . . .' I shrug. 'God knows where I would have ended up.'

'But you used to own your own business, your own café, didn't you?' He is still intensely focused on me. 'Don't you miss it?'

I fight the urge to look away, back down at the menu. I feel like I can't hide anything from him, that when he looks into my eyes, he can see everything.

'I don't miss it as much as I thought I would. I'm still cooking, and I love living here in the south of France – the beautiful countryside, the mountains, the markets, the gorgeous sunshine . . .'

'So what are you doing with your café then?' Cal asks. I should have learnt by now that he's not one to take the easy conversational path.

Some of the warm glow I've been feeling dissipates and I examine the menu again. At that moment I'm saved by the waitress bringing out the Roquefort soufflé along with a basket of soft, freshly baked rolls.

'Well?' Cal presses, once we're alone again. He's as tenacious as a terrier, a bit like Pickwick with a stick; he refuses to drop things.

'I'm selling it,' I say eventually, trying not to think about all the hard work I put into that place, sometimes working almost twenty-hour days when we were at our busiest and short-staffed.

'That's a shame. How do you feel about that?'

I mentally roll my eyes. At least I *think* I just thought the eye roll, maybe I actually did it. Oops.

'I'm . . . a little sad,' I admit eventually. 'But I can't go back. That's my old life and this is my new one.'

I watch as he digests this along with a piece of bread roll.

'Maybe you could invest in Les Coquelicots or The Barn once you've sold?' Cal suggests, taking a spoonful of the soufflé, examining it critically and then giving it a nod of approval. 'That's good.'

I take a spoonful myself. It's more than good, it's pure fluffy perfection. I usually find the taste of Roquefort overpowering but the flavour in this is just right, not too strong at all.

'I haven't really thought about that.' I chew a mouthful of bread roll and swallow. 'Do you think it's something Poppy and Leo might be interested in?'

'It doesn't hurt to ask,' he says. 'You're already practically running the guesthouse. Wouldn't it be nice to have something you know is yours again, even if only partly?'

'Yes, it would be nice,' I reply thoughtfully.

Much as he can annoy me – after all, people who are always right can be a real pain – let's face it, Cal is definitely right about this. It's what's missing for me. I know Poppy says I can stay forever but actually owning a share of the business would help me feel more secure, help me to believe St Quentin really is my home and not just a lovely daydream or extended holiday.

'You know I'm right.' Cal smiles then, half cheeky, half smug.

'Sure, but do you have to be insufferable with it?' I ask, but I'm smiling to take the sting out of my words.

Cal's smile just widens. As usual he's Teflon-coated when it comes to my irritable attempts to keep him at arm's length. And as usual his good humour has the effect of diffusing any bad mood on my part.

He's good for me. The thought flits through my mind and not for the first time I wonder if I'm letting Aiden ruin yet more of my life by making me distrust and keep at arm's length a lovely, if slightly annoying at times, man who is interesting, funny and sexy as hell.

Have I been dressing up my fear of getting hurt as wise caution, protecting me?

If I'm honest I know the answer to both those questions. The issue of him being a celebrity is another matter, but I put that to the back of my mind. Surely my nice new lingerie set deserves to be seen by someone other than myself tonight?

The asparagus soup is equally delicious and accompanied by a deep-fried risotto ball containing a little smoked haddock.

'I think I could eat a whole plate of these risotto balls,' I comment, changing the subject, confident I can deflect Cal with the subject of food.

'They're good, aren't they?' He smiles as though he cooked them himself, instead of just finding the restaurant.

The scallops and lamb are equally delicious but for me the best course is the trio of desserts. One is a fritter with delicious jam in the middle, the second a crème brûlée and the third a cheesecake.

'Those were quite the most delicious desserts I've ever tasted,' I exclaim once I've finished.

'Ah, but you haven't let me cook for you yet,' Cal says, teasingly.

'That's only because I've either been doing meals for guests or we've gone out to eat,' I protest. 'I know you're here to help Leo out, but I assumed it was also supposed to be a break for you. I could hardly expect you to cook for everyone – that's not time off for you.'

'I enjoy cooking. It's never cooking I need time off from,' Cal says enigmatically.

'Oh, so what did you want time off from?' I decide to be direct and ask. It's not like Cal ever holds back on my account.

'People mostly.' Cal looks at me as though considering whether to confide more. 'You know I would love to cook for you sometime, if you'd be willing to let me take your kitchen over. You can be my taste tester for menu options.'

'I'd love to do that and of course you can use the kitchen – it's not mine anyway.' I take a sip of coffee, aware I'm not sure how much wine I've had exactly and might need it to balance things out a bit.

'I've never seen Poppy cook anything.' Cal smiles wryly.

'That's best for everyone concerned.' I laugh. 'I'm not

being mean: she'd be the first to admit it. But then lots of people can cook, to my level I mean, not to your level of expertise, obviously. Where was I? Oh yes, Poppy, she's really talented. She can paint and the children's stories she creates are really lovely.'

'Don't do yourself down, we all have valuable skills. Yes, I've seen Poppy's art and it's lovely, but has it ever occurred to you that she's been able to take on more artistically because she's had you around to help her?'

'I'm not sure about that . . .'

'Well, I am, and I know because she told me herself.' Cal's grin is back.

'I walked straight into that one, didn't I?' I smile ruefully.

'Somehow I knew you would.'

'Did you now?' I take another sip of coffee and try to think of something to take the conversation away from me. 'So, I suppose what we can do for Poppy and Leo's reception is going to be limited by the size of the guest list?'

'Definitely,' Cal agrees. 'Anything that has to be timed perfectly is difficult on a large scale. The kitchen at The Barn is going to be more equipped for a smaller scale catering, like this.'

He gestures around the dining room. 'This is what I see as the vision for The Barn. Small scale, intimate dining for people prepared to pay the price for good quality ingredients and attention to detail.'

'So this meal tonight really was about research then?' I

raise an eyebrow. I think the wine is making me braver. Or my hormones. Probably a combination of the two.

'Why, did you think this was part of a master plan to have my wicked way with you?' He's smiling but his eyes are inscrutable.

He is obviously far better at deflecting than I am. Hmm.

'Maybe . . . So was it?'

'Maybe.' Cal's grin widens.

We're interrupted by the waitress, ready to refill our cups. While she's pouring more coffee, I catch Cal looking at me thoughtfully, a knowing gleam in his eye making me feel decidedly hot, in spite of the cool air inside the thick Abbey walls.

'What are you thinking about?' I ask once we're finally alone again. I'm sure I already know but for once it would be nice to hear him actually say it.

'An entirely different kind of tasting menu.' He quirks an eyebrow, the gleam in his eyes intensifying.

'I don't think you're allowed to have those kinds of thoughts in a monastery.'

I hold Cal's gaze in a way I probably wouldn't have, back at the guesthouse. Maybe it's the great food and wine relaxing me, or the absence of housework, chores and demanding dogs asking for cuddles and treats.

Or maybe I'm just horny as hell after a year with no sex and my recent exposure to all the lingering looks, accidental touches and pure sex appeal that are Callum O'Connor. What I'm still not sure about is why he's interested in me. Is it just because I've been knocking him back and that makes me a challenge? He assumed I'd be an easy conquest because . . . well, frankly everyone does. Everyone who doesn't know me.

The assumption by some that a woman who knows she likes sex is a slut has always annoyed me. It's such a messed-up attitude to something that should be celebrated – a lovely way to connect with another human being and to make each other feel wonderful. At best it's heavenly . . .

I glance at the thick stone walls and bite my lip. Now I'm the one having sacrilegious thoughts.

'What are *you* thinking about?' Cal's gaze is fixed on my mouth. I know he didn't miss me biting my lip.

'Oh, tasting menus, of course,' I say airily, trying to ignore the blush that creeps across my cheeks as an extremely erotic tasting image comes to mind.

I can't believe how easily Cal gets me blushing. I'm turning into Poppy. I don't usually blush. I'm the cool, calm and collected one out of the two of us. Although that is frankly not too hard.

It must be the sex drought doing this to me. Oh, sod it. Maybe it's time for a deluge.

Cal has spotted the blush. Of course he has. The corners of his lips quirk as though he's trying to repress an unseemly grin of triumph.

The haste with which he asks for and pays the bill is definitely unseemly though. He takes my arm as we walk out. The corridor is quiet, the lighting throwing flickering shadows onto the walls and stone floor, the chill air of the courtyard drifting through.

I shiver, partly from cold and partly from something a great deal less chilly. Cal rubs the length of my arm, his palm warm against my bare flesh as he pulls me against him. It's a seemingly innocuous gesture but one that sends a sharp erotic charge through my body.

Something is still bothering me though. I've never been completely able to get Cal's conversation with Leo out of my mind.

'What are you thinking?' Cal asks softly.

'The thing is . . .' I hesitate but it's no good. I have to tell him and get it out there. 'Look, I overheard you talking to Leo the first night you got here . . . about me. I wasn't deliberately eavesdropping, just looking for Peanut, who was playing one of her hide and seek games, you know.'

My heart is beating hard and I wrap my arms around my body in a very basic attempt to protect myself.

'Ah, I did wonder.' Cal pulls a rueful face. 'Sorry, I was being a dick. I was in a weird place, there was some stuff going on that I was trying to get away from, and you being here, well, that sort of made it difficult.'

'I know the feeling.' I reply dryly, looking pointedly at him.

We both smile and it breaks the tension.

I wonder if he's going to elaborate on the 'stuff' but he doesn't add anything else.

'What made you wonder?' I ask.

'Well, you were friendly when I arrived but after that first day I'd keep catching you glowering at me.'

'I do not glower,' I exclaim indignantly.

'You so do, but it's kind of cute,' Cal whispers and reaches out to stroke my cheek, stopping just short of my mouth and making me tingle all over.

'Hmm . . .'

'You're doing it now.'

I stick my tongue out at him.

'Can you forgive me?' he asks seriously, eyes dark as they lock on mine.

I think about him slipping his hand into mine when the English girls were taunting me, how lovely he's been with Flump, how tenderly he unhooked me from the hedge, but most of all how he has been there for me, encouraging me and really seeing me. I haven't felt 'seen' for a long time. I didn't want to be but now I think maybe I do.

'Sure.' I smile. 'I forgive you.'

I feel a layer of tension between us dissolve and the warmth of a new understanding reached.

On the journey home my mind is too active though and I can't help overthinking everything. Does Cal's apology mean he believes that I wasn't complicit in the sex tape Aiden made of me? I hate how much it matters that he believes me, but it really does. So many people have judged me and refuse to believe the truth but if Cal is still one of them that would really hurt. I don't want to bring it up. If Cal and I are heading where I think we're heading I don't want either of us to be thinking about Aiden or that . . . video.

Sally always used to say you couldn't trust what a man said before sex, that they'd say anything if it got them laid. I can't believe that about Cal though. He's certainly not shy about speaking his mind. He's too direct to be trying to dupe me, I'm sure.

Am I being naive? And why on earth am I thinking about Sally? I glance across at Cal and feel desire pulsing inside me, rushing through my blood. I am so, so tired of being careful. I want to throw caution to the winds and follow my instinct.

When the car is stopped at a junction Cal reaches over and gently strokes my thigh. We don't speak but the energy between us is taut, thick with anticipation, and I know for sure I'm not the only one feeling it.

Back at the guesthouse I'm reunited with an ecstatic Flump, who is torn between jumping and licking me and doing mad, celebratory laps around the house. The other dogs soon join in the chasing and by the time I've extracted myself from the scrum Poppy and Leo are leaving with Maxi, Peanut, Treacle and Pickwick in tow.

It's unusual for Poppy to leave without chatting to me first. I wonder if Leo hustled her out at a signal from Cal.

'So, is this where you try to seduce me then? After plying me with wine and good food?' I lean back against the kitchen counter, trying to look relaxed and wishing I felt the bravado I'm trying to act.

'Is that an admission you'd like me to seduce you then?' Cal's mouth quirks into a smile that is a touch self-satisfied.

I nibble at my lower lip, feeling outwardly frozen and inwardly torn between desire and fear. I want to say yes, I'd very much like that but . . . I'm aware I'm standing at the edge of something. I'm at a tipping point, still not totally decided on whether I want to be tipped or not. It would be so easy to cling to the familiar and not run the risk of falling. It would be safe.

I look down at my shoes. Hasn't life got to be about more than just feeling safe? Desire pulses through me. I want this. I want him. I really do. But I need to remember there's a very good reason why I've been trying to keep my distance from Cal. I never wanted to feel this swept away again – and on a scale of being swept away, if Aiden was a one, Cal is one hundred.

Which means Cal could badly hurt me.

'JoJo?' Cal takes my hand and gently squeezes. I look up and meet his gaze. When I do the anxieties fade away and desire emerges into sharp, all-consuming focus.

With his other hand he tenderly strokes the side of my face.

I expected a lot of things from Cal, but his tenderness disarms me totally. Passion flares inside me in response. How can such a simple touch feel so incredibly sexual and intimate?

Cal's intense gaze is still locked on mine and I realise he is waiting for an answer, a definite, unequivocal green light.

'Yes,' I whisper, answering his question and ignoring the urge to second-guess myself.

Want morphs into necessity. I need this.

Cal presses in closer and his lips meet mine. The kiss is gentle at first, tender and soft as he teases my lips and my tongue. It feels incredibly intimate, like we're sharing a breath, locked in our own little bubble.

It's also incredibly seductive, slowly arousing me. My fears recede, warmth spreading through me. It's been a long time since anyone kissed me like this. Actually, I don't think I've ever been kissed like this. His lips travel down and along my jaw line, his stubble lightly grazing my skin.

I let out a breathy sigh and press against him as he kisses my neck. His hands slide up beneath the hem of my dress, one hand cupping my bottom while the other skims my knickers, pressing lightly between my legs. An involuntary low moan escapes my lips.

I'd forgotten the joy of exploring another body and of being explored. I undo his shirt buttons and slip my hand inside, my fingers discovering hard muscle and finding his heartbeat. My investigation halts when he pushes my knickers to one side and strokes the wetness between my folds up over my clit. I gasp and lean against him. I'm very wet already, almost embarrassingly so, and his fingers slip up inside me easily. I'm still steadying myself against him when he brings his fingers up to my mouth and spreads the wetness over my lips. He then dips his head and takes his time licking along my lips before plunging his tongue into my mouth, hungrily claiming me with a passionate kiss.

I love that he can be both tender and passionate. I love his depth. I love . . . this. God, do I love this.

By now I'm glad of the kitchen counter behind me and Callum's body holding me up because my legs feel embarrassingly foal-like – liable to give way at any moment. He pulls back briefly and stares into my eyes. His eyes seem darker now, midnight blue, with dark pools that glitter with intensity.

I stare back, feeling magnetised and drawn in.

Swept away . . .

I swat at the niggling fears buzzing at the back of my mind like flies butting up against a fly screen. I'll be fine, I can be careful. I won't get sucked in. It's just sex.

And whatever happens I will never, ever have sex near an open laptop or anything with the capacity for video so . . . I'm fine. It's fine.

My body is silently begging for more than touching. If Cal doesn't take the lead soon the begging might have to become vocal. I call a truce between desire and the fluttering anxiety – this is sex, not love.

It's only sex. I can enjoy it while protecting myself. I just need to hold some of myself back this time, not be so naive.

I think I've probably well and truly left my naïveté behind me, somewhere between home and the Channel Tunnel terminal in Folkestone.

'You okay?' he asks quietly.

I nod.

'I had imagined a different kind of . . . tasting but this . . . um . . . works.' My cheeks feel very hot. All of me is very hot now I think about it.

Callum laughs, breaking the intensity of the moment and the locked gaze.

'Oh, that wasn't the tasting. That was just the *amuse-bouche* before the tasting.' Callum grins.

'*Amuse-bouche*?' I snort with laughter.

'Yes, it's a small taste of what's to come, served before a starter. It literally means to amuse . . .'

'The mouth, yes, I know what it is,' I say. 'Well it's certainly worked. You've whetted my appetite. What else have you got on the menu then?'

'Would you like my head between your thighs for starters?'

My sex throbs a response.

'God, yes,' I blurt.

He takes me by the hand, leading me out of the kitchen. 'Your room or mine?'

'Mine,' I say quickly. As part of my self-protective strategy my room is the safer choice: definitely no laptops or devices with webcams that could possibly be activated remotely. I would never have known that was a thing, were it not for my special interest.

First, we have to evict Flump from my bed and put him outside. From the look he gives me he isn't impressed.

Then Cal and I are kissing again, and I can't think about anything. I can only feel. It feels so good to be touched again. I really have missed this, the human contact and the sense of connection. I want his hands everywhere. All of me craves his fingers, his mouth and . . .

I reach between us and press my palm against Cal's growing erection, feeling it stiffen through his jeans at my touch. Then I open the remaining buttons of his shirt and pull it open, stroking the hard muscle and the dark hair that snakes down into his waistband.

Cal guides me back towards the bed and when the back of my thighs hit the mattress he pushes me down, gently but firmly persuading me to lie down. He tugs me back down towards him a little so that my bottom is close to the edge of the bed. Then he pushes my dress up to my waist and spreads my legs wide so his mouth can get better access from his position down on the floor.

I expect him to strip me, but he takes his time stroking me through the lacy fabric of my knickers. The increasingly damp lacy fabric. He increases the pressure until I'm squirming and desperate to feel his fingers inside me again. It feels like an age before he pulls down my knickers, edging them down over my thighs.

I exhale loudly when he parts my legs even further, stretching me wide open.

When he slides two fingers inside me and scissors them to open me up my exhalation becomes a sigh of pure pleasure.

I catch a glimpse of Cal's reflection in the mirror opposite the bed and see that he is absolutely intent on what he's doing, focused on my sex like it's the most fascinating thing he's seen in ages. When he curls his fingers back so that they hook my G-spot I almost buck off of the bed. I'm not sure I've ever been this responsive. Is this just my body being pathetically grateful to experience human touch after so long?

Or something more?

I prop myself up on my elbows so I can look into Callum's blue eyes and I'm startled by the jolt of connection I feel. It's unexpected, this emotional connection. Exposing myself emotionally as well as physically wasn't part of the plan.

I close my eyes and let feeling obliterate thought as Cal's thumb circles lightly over my clit at the same time as he manually manipulates my G-spot. I'm lost in sensation, my breathing fast and shallow, getting closer and closer, when all of a sudden he withdraws his hand. I prop myself back up again and open my eyes to stare at him questioningly.

He smiles wickedly. He's teasing me and enjoying it. I narrow my eyes in response.

'This, JoJo, is what I meant by a tasting menu.' He lowers himself back down so his head is between my thighs. 'And I don't plan to rush it. I like to savour what I taste. This is just the starter.'

With one hand on each thigh, stretching me wide, he

lowers his mouth to my clit and sucks me hard, making me buck and moan. He alternates gentle pressure with firm – licking, kissing and tasting me everywhere. I have to say I feel . . . well, savoured, I suppose, does cover it. Just as I can feel my climax mounting he takes one hand off of my thigh and slips his fingers inside me again, fingering my G-spot at the same time as he teases my clit with his tongue.

Fuck. I jerk off the bed so hard when I climax that I seriously worry I might've broken Callum's nose with my pelvis. Is that even possible? I lie panting, rocked by the scale of the seismic orgasm. When I raise my head and look up at him I'm relieved to see an absence of blood. Phew, that would've been an awkward injury to describe to a doctor. Never mind what the internet would have had to say about it . . .

That thought makes me want to giggle hysterically but luckily I'm too mellow for hysteria and I've recovered myself by the time Cal strips off his clothes and climbs onto the bed next to me. His erection presses against my hip as he takes off the rest of my clothes and fondles my breasts with that surprising tenderness again. He stares with fascination at my hardening nipples and although I'm still recovering from my climax his focused attention is sending my libido through the roof again.

His erection twitches against my hip again and I reach out to stroke it. I want to give him as much pleasure as he's given me. When I crawl down to take his cock in my mouth a flash of memory distracts me, the part of the sex tape that showed me giving Aiden a blow job. I try to focus but part of me wants to look over my shoulder to triple check there's no strategically placed phone filming me even though this is my room and I know there can't be . . .

As if he senses my mental distraction Cal reaches down and threads his fingers in my hair, stroking it in a way that makes me melt and sets my scalp tingling. It definitely gets me focused again. His touch draws me back into the moment and I focus on giving Cal pleasure, swirling my tongue around the head of his cock and taking his shaft deep into my mouth. His moans tell me I'm doing something right. I'd forgotten the deep satisfaction of giving this kind of pleasure. I focus on his breathing and shut out the voices of the internet trolls who made me feel dirty, who said I didn't deserve to live. The only voices that matter at the present moment are mine and Cal's. The World Wide Web has shrunk down to the here and now, to the two of us.

The present moment is all there is and I lose myself in it, in the sensation and the feeling and the joy of connection that I've missed so much.

Only now do I realise how much I've been missing it. Of course, I knew I was lonely but I thought I was okay. Okay-ish.

Now that Callum and I are touching each other in the most intimate way possible I realise just how disconnected I've been. I've always been a toucher, a hugger, tactile and easy with my affections. I've always loved easily and freely.

Too freely.

In hiding away from the world I've suppressed a vital, affectionate part of my personality. Allowing it expression again feels joyful and emancipating but also terrifying. Well, I'm feeling the fear and doing it anyway, like Mum's fridge magnet tells me to. I focus on Cal, on his taste, on the sounds he makes and the feel of his cock as it slides between my lips. I focus on the tenderness he's shown me, on all the times he's been there to help me out, on all the positive seeds of thought he's been sowing in my mind on our daily walks.

And on the core of strength I sense in him that makes me want to lean against him and let him protect me, just for a little bit. I know, I know, I'm a big girl and should be able to protect myself and all that but sometimes it's just nice to know that somebody competent has your back. Because I'm so, so tired of having to be strong alone in this amazing, terrifying world. Holding everything inside has been exhausting. Can I really just let go?

I feel Cal's eyes on me and look up to see him watching me. I don't stop but take him in deeper, continuing to mimic the clench of my sex with my mouth while I cup and play with his balls.

He strokes my hair back from my face and the intense, tender expression in his eyes draws me in again. As our gazes lock the background chatter in my head fades away and I feel a kind of peaceful contentment, so mellow I feel like I'm a cat stretching out in a patch of sunshine. Just basking. Just being.

For the first time in ages I don't have memories from the past or fears for the future rolling in my mind like a constant ticker-tape. I'm actually in the present moment and it's good.

I taste salty pre-cum on my tongue and lap harder, swallowing when he comes, all the while locking eyes with him and never once breaking my gaze. After a year of self-imposed isolation the intimacy of the moment blows me away.

I crawl up the bed and lie next to Callum. He lies on his side and gently strokes my face, my hair, my back . . . The caresses reveal more of Callum's gentle side. That he can be both intensely commanding and supremely tender is threatening my ability to hold myself back from him emotionally.

But I have to, have to . . . need to do things differently this time. Even if all I want to do is crawl into Cal's arms and stay there forever. I quite fancy the idea of attaching myself to him like a baby koala and refusing to let go.

I smile at the ridiculous image and Cal reaches out to touch my lips.

'Where did you disappear to?' he asks.

'Uh . . . I . . .' I consider pretending I've no idea what he means but I'd be lying, and he knows it. It feels wrong to lie to him after the intimacies we've just shared. I hesitate and consider how to explain without ruining this moment. 'It's hard to shut out everything that happened to me. You're the first since . . . you know . . . it all happened.'

'You're talking about the show?'

'Well, yes, partly. I ended up getting lots of vile trolls on social media because of the show but it was after the . . . the tape . . . it got really bad – you know, the tape Aiden leaked?'

He nods and it's an effort to maintain eye contact. I'm tempted to bury my face against his chest. To hide from him. I manage not to pull away but it's far from comfortable looking into Cal's piercing blue eyes. As always, it's like he sees far more than I'm consciously allowing and that feels . . . disconcerting.

'I suppose when you've been slut-shamed you're bound to feel a bit funny about sex,' I say. 'It's . . . awkward.'

Fuck. Am I really talking about myself in the third person? And awkward doesn't even cover it but the achingly painful places inside me feel too grubby to air, especially in this special space we've created in this room. Talk about ruining the mood.

What if he runs a mile when he sees just how dark some of my thoughts are? And they are. I'm talking an abyss, black hole type of dark.

'Why do you feel ashamed when it was Aiden who acted like a prick?' Callum's piercing stare is unwavering, not giving me any wiggle room.

Shame. My biggest enemy, even worse than fear. Its thorns have hooked me, got under my skin, and it clings to me despite all my attempts to wriggle free.

'I just do.' I shrug. 'I know in my head all I did was

have sex with my boyfriend and . . . enjoy it. Somehow that makes me a slut. People don't believe I didn't know I was being filmed so I just got what I deserved but I really didn't. Didn't know I was being filmed I mean.'

I know I'm gabbling but I can't help it. After so much containment the words seem to want to spill out.

'Your ex is the one who should be ashamed,' Callum says firmly. 'Please tell me you know that, JoJo.'

I stare at him intently, looking for a sign he's just telling me what I want to hear. Looking for any evidence that he doesn't believe his own words. I don't think he's playing me.

'But Aiden *isn't* ashamed. Not even remotely.' I laugh bitterly. I will never, ever be okay with the logic of the sexual double standard that has Aiden as a bit of a lad and me as a slut.

'So, why on earth are you carrying his shame?' Callum strokes my face again with that devastating combination of tenderness and unrelenting challenge that undoes me. I swallow hard and suppress the urge to cry. I just about manage but I still can't speak.

'Come here and have a cuddle.' Callum's expression softens and he pulls me into his arms. 'You're lovely, JoJo, and you've got nothing to be ashamed of. Nothing. Okay?'

'Okay,' I mutter into his chest and melt into the embrace, enjoying the sensation of being held, of letting go of the weight I've been carrying, just for a few minutes.

I think he knows I don't believe it. Not at an intrinsic heart-knowledge level.

As if he reads my mind he pulls me up from the bed and over to the floor in front of the full-length mirror. He sits with his legs wide open and gets me to sit in between his legs, my back to him.

'Open your eyes, JoJo.'

Cal's commanding tone gets me obeying instantly.

He strokes my lower lip. I watch him, watch myself, watching him . . .

'Nothing . . .'

He strokes down my neck to my breasts, caressing them with soft sensual circles.

'To . . .'

Both hands reach down to my abdomen, continuing to stroke.

'Be . . .'

His hands reach the top crease of my thighs and he parts them, hooking each leg over his so I'm fully exposed to the mirror, both of us watching.

'Ashamed . . .'

He strokes my sex tenderly, playing with my clit, dipping first one finger inside me and then two.

'Of . . .'

I struggle to keep my eyes open as he brings me to my second climax. My sex contracts around his fingers and I watch myself . . . watching him . . . watching me come.

'You're beautiful, JoJo,' he says, planting a kiss on top of my head. 'You're sexy and there is nothing wrong with that. Don't you ever let anyone make you feel ashamed of your sexuality again.'

I lean my head back against his chest and smile. He really does sound quite commanding, quite stern.

'You're pretty sexy yourself, you know,' I say, wriggling my bottom back against him. 'Are we ready for the next course yet? Ah, yes, I can feel you are.'

Back on the bed Cal enters me for the first time and I welcome him, uncoiling and opening. I draw him in, deeper and harder, enjoying the weight of him on top of me, between my thighs, revelling in the unique energy we create together. It's not just sensation, it's both a release and a connection. It's joy.

Cal hooks both my legs over his shoulders and now the penetration is deep, so much deeper and harder. Sweat beads on our skin and by the time Cal climaxes inside me we're both breathless and spent.

We are still for a moment, Cal still inside me. Still one.

That was . . .

I have no words left and crawl gratefully into Cal's embrace. He puts an arm around me and hooks one of my ankles over his so I'm lying half on top of him.

It seems I needed this, for Cal to unhook thorns of a different kind. To disentangle me. I used to think strength meant having to do everything ourselves, to be independent and above all things to cope. I'm wondering now if real strength lies in asking for help, in letting a gentle pair of hands help to set us free. It's not weak to be afraid and it's not weak to ask for help if we get stuck.

As we cuddle and I hear Cal's breathing deepen into sleep I'm remembering what he said to me about nature, how interconnected we all are and how the lone trees who don't get to share resources suffer.

I really don't want to be a lone tree any more.

I nestle my head against Cal's chest, comforted by the steady thrum of his heartbeat.

Just sex . . . Yeah, right.

Chapter 9

'I learned that courage was not the absence of fear, but the triumph over it. The brave man is not he who does not feel afraid, but he who conquers that fear'

Nelson Mandela

From callum@callum'scook-off.com
To caitlino'connor85@hotmail.com
Subject: Trouble
Hi sis, I hope you're okay and my little nephew to-be isn't giving you too much trouble? Is he still kicking at night?

So it seems working out what I want to do next in life is a little more complicated than I expected. I feel pulled in several directions and my agent obviously has very strong views but honestly, I'm still not sure what to do next.

Also, a slight, teeny tiny complication – I may just

have fallen for an ex-reality star. Yes, you know who. I know, after the way I slagged off Sex in the Suburbs it's kind of ironic that I'm willingly taking a step into that world. If the press find out. Which of course they will at some point and it'll be some kind of sordid love triangle or whatever. Meh. You're laughing, aren't you?

I don't know, it's hard. She's special but she's been really badly hurt, I don't want to put her through any more crap, but I feel drawn to her in a way I can't explain logically. It's thrown everything up in the air for me to be honest.

Planning the Barn restaurant has been great though, it's reminded me of the good old days when I cared more about substance than style. Part of me is feeling tempted . . . but we'll see. I'll let you know when things are a bit clearer for me.

Take good care of yourself Caitlin and say Hi to Mike.

From annabelgrant@thestickybun.co.uk
To joannagrant@thestickybun.co.uk
Subject: Thought you ought to know
Hi JoJo, how's things? I know you don't keep up with any celebrity stuff nowadays so you might not have heard the news? Anyway, I thought you should know – Sex in Surburbia is doing a summer special not a million miles away from where you're staying. It can't be a coincidence surely? I'm wondering if that's why Sally asked to meet up with you all along? I bet the

sneaky cow wants to manipulate some drama or other and plans to have a reporter or five on speed dial.

So, if you were thinking of meeting them please don't FFS! Not that I thought you would but sometimes you're too nice for your own good sis. Seeing the best in people and giving them the benefit of the doubt makes you a good person but it also leaves you wide open for getting shafted and I couldn't bear to see anything like that happen to you again.

Are you sure I can't come out and see you? I could bring out the café sale documents to sign rather than getting them couriered. Also I could be around to give that cow-breath Sally a good bitch slap if she tries anything. Or Aiden for that matter, and you know exactly where I'd like to hit him ;-)

Hugs xx

After I've read Annabel's email my jaw is rigid, and my hands tighten their grip on my mobile phone. I try to contain my fury that of all the places in the world to film a summer special they are coming to my special place. This part of France is my safe hideaway, it's protected and kept me safe and now it's being invaded.

Also I'm angry that they've spoiled my post-sex high. I was feeling lovely before I read that email, floating on a serene cloud of blissed-out hormones. Happy. That's it.

But now that feels tainted. Like I'm never going to get away from my past. I close my eyes tight and breathe deeply, trying to recover some of the bliss I felt earlier, lying in Cal's arms.

Is it just a coincidence or is someone behind this, orchestrating yet more drama, yet more misery to sell to viewers? Of course, it can't be pure coincidence, France is a big place and Languedoc isn't as well known as Provence or the Cote d'Azur.

Well, I won't be talking to anyone from the show. As if! So I've nothing to worry about then. But still a gnawing anxiety is squirming in the pit of my stomach and a low-frequency anger pulses through me. Cal is right. It's really time I moved on from all this. I need there to be more to me than 'the disgraced TV star'. I'm tired of always playing it safe.

Is it too risky to carry on my affair with Cal if there are going to be reporters hanging around? It is an affair, isn't it? I know it can never go anywhere; it's a holiday fling and Cal will be going back to London at the end of the summer. My home is here now, and his television career is in London and I already know what he thinks about long-distance relationships. Didn't I hear him tell Leo he wasn't prepared to go there, that it was too much trouble?

I don't think I can bear to miss a single minute of it because of fear. The sex with Cal is amazing and my body constantly craves more affection, more Cal and more sex.

I won't let Sally or Aiden or anyone from the press spoil this for me.

I put the email to the back of my mind, where it festers,

and go in search of Cal as soon as I've finished making up all the beds that need to be done.

I find him in his room. I have no reservations about sex here instead of my room. My dormant sex drive has gone through the roof since we first had sex and I'll admit I'm insatiable.

'Hey you.' Cal greets me with a wide smile and closes his laptop. It's a sign of how happy I am that I don't even cast it a second look. Well, barely, anyway. Of course, he's not trying to hide anything, why would he be? He's probably guessed I'm worried about webcams and is closing it out of consideration.

'Hey you, fancy some sex?' My own smile mirrors his.

'Yes, please. Can I order off menu? I had no idea it was part of the service here. Just think what I've been missing these past weeks.'

I swat him on the arm and he pulls me down onto his lap. Our lips meet for a tentative, searching, increasingly passionate kiss. Humour recedes and need, hunger and roaring desire surge up inside me, blasting through my flimsy 'safety' barriers and leaving me achingly vulnerable. I've never felt this passionately attracted to someone before and it's, well . . . scary. That he can have this much power over my body leaves me at his mercy.

Need pushes even these fears away. Cal kisses me back with an intensity that matches my own. Maybe he needs me, needs this as much as I do.

Please let him need me too. Soon our hands are

exploring, up beneath T-shirts. I stroke Cal's chest, feeling his rapid pulsing heartbeat beneath my fingertips. Cal cups one of my breasts through my lacy bra and my nipple hardens instantly. His other hand slides beneath my bottom, squeezing in a way that leaves me wet between my legs.

I move, swinging one of my legs over to straddle him, the soft fabric of my skirt riding up so that I can press down on his growing erection.

'I want you,' I whisper in his ear.

He slips a hand up beneath my skirt and inside my knickers, his fingers slipping easily inside my wet folds.

'So you do.' He smiles wolfishly. 'Now there's a coincidence, I happen to want you too.'

I rub his erection through his jeans, and he groans, standing up, carrying me to the edge of the desk we had moved into his room so he could work. He then manoeuvres me round so he's behind me, hands running down over my breasts, lifting my T-shirt up over my head and unhooking my bra so he can touch me more freely.

His erection presses into my bottom.

He manoeuvres me so I'm bent over the desk and flips my skirt up around my waist. My bare breasts are pressed against the desk and my face too, on one side. Cal makes me wait, teasing me through my knickers before pulling them down.

His thighs edge my knees apart as his fingers work their usual magic, caressing my clit before dipping inside to massage my G-spot. Then he caresses both spots at once and the resulting wave of pleasure leaves me gasping.

'You are so good at that, I swear you have magic fingers.'

'So you only want my fingers . . . You don't want this?' He rubs just the head of his cock up and down my wet slit, making me moan.

'Yes, I do, please,' I beg. 'I want you inside me.'

'Okay then, if you insist.' He enters me in one long thrust. The angle is satisfyingly deep and he's rubbing in all the right places. The pulsing pleasure feels primal, visceral and urgent. I need him as much as he needs me.

It's like he's set me free to enjoy sex again. No need for internal angsting or overthinking absolutely everything. It's good to experience sex without the angst again.

'Later I'm going to take it long and slow. My mouth is going to explore every inch of your body. I'm going to make love to you and savour every minute. But right now you've got me so turned on it's going to be a hard, fast fuck, okay?' Cal's voice as he leans over me is ragged and slightly breathless. His lips tickle my neck as he speaks and I shiver, whether from the words or the nerve endings he's touching I don't know.

'Okay,' I gasp as he pulls almost all the way out and then slams into me. He wasn't kidding about the fast, hard fuck but then I might have admitted to him I liked it this way.

I think I love it this way. The emotional, intimate sex we had was so powerful that I've been feeling a little raw, emotionally speaking. This hard fuck is the perfect antidote for that. Okay, it might leave me a little raw in . . . other ways but I actually kind of like that too . . . I like to feel where Cal has fucked me.

I like this feeling, of every inch of him filling every inch of me. Of being explored and possessed in this raw, physical way. Of giving myself to him.

I feel exposed and to some extent vulnerable but only in the hands of a man who by his own admission is turned on by giving me pleasure.

I like being able to own my sexuality again.

When I climax I come so hard it's just as well the desk is there to muffle my cries. He comes inside me almost immediately, while I'm still clenching and convulsing around him in the aftershock of possibly the most powerful orgasm I've ever experienced. I relish the weight of his body on top of me and the primal satisfaction of a man coming inside me. I've always found it a good feeling but with Cal it's so much more.

When he pulls me into his arms on his bed I feel as close to satisfied as I've ever felt. Not sated exactly because I'm not sure I could ever get enough of Cal, but more joyful, peaceful and positive than I can ever remember feeling. I know it's partly a hormonal euphoric high but I'm sure this is more than that.

There's no way I can kid myself that this is a meaningless fling to get me back in the game, a tentative test to see if I can engage with the real world again.

I've had plenty of 'just sex' and there is no 'just' about sex with Cal. There's a strong sense that I'm in the right place. That here in Cal's arms is the best place in the world to be. Dangerous, powerful emotions. I wasn't supposed to fall in love. This was supposed to be a pleasant connection, some satisfying sex, something to make me feel alive again but . . . well, nothing heavy.

I've lost control of the situation fast. I'm worried the 'L' word will escape my lips. It's far too soon. I'll have to make sure I don't blurt it out but it's true. I do.

I love him, I love him, I love Cal and I can't undo it. I hold him close and for the first time in years I pray, to God, to the Universe, to anyone listening, that this doesn't end badly.

Disgraced former *Sex in the Suburbs* star Joanna Grant has been spotted with celebrity chef Callum O'Connor in the South of France, in the tourist city of Carcassonne. According to onlookers the couple were walking hand in hand and were definitely behaving like an item. At one point they stopped for a passionate kiss (see photo above).

So it seems Joanna's assertion she was leaving the celebrity life behind forever has turned out to be a little short lived. Is this her way of making a come-back? Or perhaps the real question we should be asking is whether she's using Callum O'Connor or he's using her. Rumour has it Callum recently signed a book deal so the publicity sure isn't going to hurt him.

When asked for a comment Joanna's ex-co-star and ex-boyfriend Aiden said 'I'm glad to hear Joanna's finally moved on. I've always felt bad that she didn't want to stay friends.'

I feel sick when I scan the webpage Poppy's friend Michelle sent her. Is this Aiden and Sally's doing? Or someone from the show, leaking a story to remind the world who I am so they remember when the main story comes out about my tearful 'reunion' with Aiden and Sally in a few weeks?

To add insult to injury it's a really crappy photo of me. My hair looks like I've been pulled through a hedge backwards because Cal likes playing with my hair. Really likes playing with my hair, which is fine – I mean I love him playing with my hair – but it does make me look a little . . . deranged.

Cal looks gorgeous, of course. I remember how charming he was that day. He has a book deal? Seriously? I don't get why he wouldn't tell me about it if he wasn't hiding something. I remember him always closing his laptop around me. Is he being courteous or is it something more?

A nasty whispering fear suggests I've been spectacularly stupid again. I've been crazy enough to trust someone after all that happened with Aiden and I'm being punished for my naïveté. Really? I just can't believe all that stuff about me having nothing to be ashamed of any more was part of Cal's seduction strategy. Just so he can tell everyone he slept with the girl from the sex tape and sell some books off the back of it . . .

No. My head says it's simply not true. My heart agrees. It just can't be. Cal is not like that. I have a bond with him, I trust him. I know the kind of man he is and he isn't an Aiden.

He's still just a man though, flawed and complex like we all are. No one is either all good or all bad. Perhaps I've built him up into this wonderful fantasy man who doesn't actually exist except in my head.

The tiny, anxious niggle is rapidly turning into a rolling snowball of a panic attack, increasing momentum with every racing, fearful thought.

I fight to control my breath and push through the clamour of swirling, noisy emotions. The ticker-tape of doom is scrolling endlessly in my head again – breaking news: celebrity seeks publicity . . . disgraced sex tape celebrity has messy hair . . .

So. Not really breaking news then.

Sex with Cal means something more than just a physical connection, I'm sure of it.

Almost sure.

I seem to have lost non-angsty, definitely-not-overthinking JoJo and backslid, badly.

With Cal it meant something. Why am I listening to the crazy woman in my head? It still means something. Why should an online article get to decide my relationship status? There's no call to be thinking in the past tense. I hug myself, feeling cold, despite the building heat of the day.

What am I going to do if Aiden and Sally try to orchestrate something and send reporters to ambush me? What if he held back extra video footage, another sex tape, for just such an opportunity?

My stomach lurches and I think I might actually be sick.

Part of me wants to take Flump and run and hide again, find a hole somewhere to crawl into and shut the world out so no one can hurt me again.

I don't want to leave the life I've started for myself here in St Quentin. I'm happy here with Poppy and Leo and the other dogs. I'm happy here with Cal, for however long he's here. Not to mention I can't leave before Poppy's wedding: I'm virtually organising the whole thing for her now. I can't possibly leave her in the lurch.

I was just starting to feel like myself again – like it might be safe to be that girl again. Safe to reach out and touch someone. Safe to shine.

It still might be. A small voice of hope whispers and I hug myself closer, as though my flesh and blood arms can protect me from the world and all its hurt.

Cal at least deserves the chance to see the article and react. The book deal might be nothing, his non-disclosure easy to explain. I should know that more than most, how many facts are faction or even pure fiction.

He'll probably laugh it off, perhaps even make a joke about my hair. Or maybe he'll believe the ludicrous claim that I am 'using him' to reclaim lost fame, like the piece online says. Maybe he's already seen it.

I quicken my pace from the house to the barn, wanting to be wrong, hoping we aren't about to have our first fight.

He'd probably laughed off, perhaps [illegible]. I told about a [illegible] half? Or maybe he'd realised [illegible] that [illegible] lost time [illegible] say 'Maybe [illegible] already seen'?

I decided my pace from the house [illegible] to be wrong [illegible] though [illegible]

Chapter 10

'Life is 10 per cent what happens to you and 90 per cent how you react to it'

Charles R. Swindoll

I should wait to talk to Cal until I've calmed down, but I can't. The anxiety is so insistent. The niggles of doubt, urging caution in our relationship, were like flies buzzing against the fly screen. Now the fly screen is broken and I'm being attacked by a swarm.

I have to know the truth, have to confront him. I push damp strands of hair off my forehead. It's too hot to be rushing like this. The air is humid, the atmosphere fittingly heavy with that pre-storm feel we only seem to get in summer. The night will end in torrential rain and dramatic lightning. Poor Barney will be terrified, shaking with fear. Large as he is, he'll find a lap to jump on, a storm being the only time he tries to do that.

I've come to love this place, these people and the animals.

I thought Cal's arrival would threaten all of that. Maybe I was right after all?

I find him down at the barn. He isn't alone. He's supervising the commercial cooker installation, making sure everything has arrived that's supposed to have and Leo is there too. He's chatting to Cal when I approach but he must read my face correctly because he backs off to give us some space.

'What's up?' Cal smiles his usual warm smile and it's hard to stop my own mouth responding and mirroring him. 'JoJo?'

I realise I'm breathing really hard and try to calm it, to bring myself down. My arms are still wrapped tightly around my body. Like they offer any protection from an emotional onslaught. My whole body is rigid with tension, my jaw so tight it hurts. I open my mouth to speak but nothing comes out. Literally nothing.

Angry with myself I get my phone out and click the link to the online article again. I can't help glancing at that photo again. God, that hair, I really do look deranged.

I hand the phone over to Cal, not able to meet his enquiring gaze.

'Fuck,' Cal curses and takes hold of my arm, steering me out of the barn.

Once we're out of earshot and standing in the shade of a tree he turns me to face him.

'Talk to me, JoJo,' he says. 'Tell me what you're thinking.'

'I really thought you liked me. You must've thought I

was so stupid.' To my horror the last words I want to say aloud are out there, exposing my naked vulnerability. To make things worse, tears roll down my cheeks and I'm stifling a sob. Yes, I really should've waited to confront him.

'Stop that. Stop that right now.' Cal's tone is authoritative and his grip on my arms firm, not hurting me, not restraining me even; it's more like he's holding me up, keeping me from falling apart.

My body obeys him unquestioningly and some of the tension seeps out of my taut muscles. I look up and meet the piercing blue eyes I know so well. Inside I'm at war between the part of me that fears I've been duped and the part that trusts him implicitly because . . . well, just because; it's intuition, I suppose, my gut instinct. My breathing slows as our gazes lock and I feel connected to him again.

'I do like you, JoJo. I like you very much. How could you ever think otherwise just because of an online article? How many of those articles ever told the truth about you?' Cal's tone is incredulous.

I'm starting to feel vaguely ridiculous for overreacting. He's right. I should know more than anyone just how the press works and how facts never get in the way of a good story, especially a celebrity gossip story.

'I'm sorry, Cal,' I whisper and rest my head against his chest, inhaling his delicious familiar scent and reassured by his physical strength. I really must have it bad because even the scent of his sweat turns me on.

God, I'm lost. Please let this be real, please.

Cal strokes my hair, soothing me, easing the stress out of me with each caress. I don't care about the photo, I'm never going to ask him to stop playing with my hair.

'I am really sorry,' I apologise again and bury my face back into his chest because frankly it's a really nice place to be. I think I could stay like this forever, inhaling him and revelling in the sense of feeling protected. I know it can't last, I know it's an illusion to expect protection and anti-feminist to want it but still . . . God, it's nice.

I exhale and force myself to ask the question I really need the answer to.

'So what's this about a book deal?' I pull back a little and try to keep my tone light and free from suspicion.

'My agent has been talking to publishers, but as I haven't actually signed the contract yet I'm not allowed to talk about it.' Callum shrugs as though it's no big deal. 'Though I guess I can now, given the information is already out there. The publishers won't be happy. I think they wanted to time the press release with some book fair or other.'

He wouldn't use me. Of course, he wouldn't.

'So, a cookbook? Autobiography?'

'Cookbook with a little bit of a travel guide thrown in. A simple guide to French cooking with my impressions of the best markets in Occitanie. The importance of using good, fresh ingredients. Food porn pictures from French markets, you know the kind of thing.'

I watch his face. He's trying to play it down, but his eyes are gleaming. I think he's really into the idea of a book.

'Food porn?'

'For people who aren't actually going to cook – they're just going to look at the pictures and think about cooking. Or who knows, maybe I'll manage to get them excited enough to actually buy some ingredients and cook a meal from scratch. That's the hope anyway, to inspire people to cook.'

I really wish I could be happy for Cal but the words from the online article are still going around and around in my head in that familiar ticker-tape of doom. Well, I am sort of happy for him. It's great things are going well for him and he's enthused but . . .

'Why am I still disgraced?' I ask a small, quiet voice. 'That's what I don't get. All I did was have sex with my boyfriend in the privacy of a bedroom. I didn't even know I was being filmed. I really didn't. Oh, and I also got cheated on publicly, my heartbreak served up as entertainment. I never wanted to be a flipping reality TV star.'

I hope Callum will understand my reaction, that he'll get why seeing my name and my face, along with that 'disgraced' label, is so hard to bear. Will I be carrying that label around forever? Will they dredge it out every single time Cal is mentioned in the press? Celebrity chef Callum O'Connor is dating 'disgraced ex reality star Joanna Grant'. That kind of thing. So even if I stay away from cameras as much as possible and let Cal go to events on his own, I'm still going to be in the public eye.

Assuming I stay with Callum, assuming he wants me to . . . If we do stay together, we are going to be in the media spotlight, and I will be wearing that label forever.

I really don't know how I feel about that. Actually, that's not true. I know exactly what I feel and it's depressing the hell out of me.

This is what I ran away from and now it's come looking for me. If I stay with Cal I will never escape it, ever. And if I wanted to run, then who knows, maybe this time round I'd find it harder to be able to successfully disappear.

'I know, JoJo, I know.' Cal tightens his hold of me.

'Do you?' I ask.

'I can't know exactly what it's like to be you, but I know you, JoJo. Please let's make this our problem, not just your problem. I don't want you vanishing on me, whether that's running off to Italy or just disappearing into your head.'

Okay, he really does know me.

'*Our* problem?' I ask. 'I like the sound of that. And anyway I can't go to Italy.'

'Why not?'

'Flump hasn't got his pet passport yet.'

Cal laughs and hugs me hard.

'It'll be okay.' He pulls me up against him and as his lips find mine I feel like I'm being torn into two – the desire to disappear and stay hidden is warring with the desire to trust, to love, to embrace and hold onto how wonderful I feel when I am with him.

As the kisses become more urgent my heartbeat picks

up and I feel sexual energy roaring through me, powerful and urgent, demanding release. Like I've repressed that part of me for far too long and now that it's had a taste of freedom it's surging into life and protesting its captivity. I don't think I could kick it back into line if I tried.

I don't think I want to.

As if by mutual consent we are moving towards the house, both gripped by the same sense of urgent desire. At least I hope I am not the only one feeling it with such intensity. I glance sideways at Cal and catch a glimpse of his dark, dilated pupils. The firm grip of his hand holding mine also reassures me.

We go to my room as it is the nearest and as soon as the door is closed behind us we're kissing passionately, hands exploring and tugging impatiently at clothing as though we are both in a hurry to put our recent conversation behind us.

We lie naked on the bed, facing each other, eyes serious and bodies momentarily still, our clothes lying where they fell on the floor. It's as though we're savouring what's to come. Cal reaches out a hand and tenderly strokes my cheek. His finger traces a line along my jaw and down between my breasts. I revel in the sensation of his rougher skin trailing against my soft skin and super-sensitised nerve endings. I jerk when his finger dips into my belly button and over my abdomen.

My breathing is ragged by the time he slips first one and then a second finger inside me. I'm already wet for him when he scissors his fingers inside me, opening me up and stretching me. He watches where his fingers penetrate, and my reactions, as though I'm the most fascinating thing he's ever seen. As usual his fascination makes me feel sexy and attractive, confident in my body in a way I've not been for a very long time. I feel more myself again. A whole self and not merely the shell I've been presenting to the world.

He's good for me, he is. I should never have mistrusted him.

Should I?

I suppress my doubts and give myself over to the rising tide of desire, surrendering to the pleasure of being touched, to the sensations of needing and giving. My body's response to Cal is unequivocal. My body trusts him. I let go, let the powerful undercurrents wash over me, through me, carry me to climax and beyond.

I move round to stroke Cal's chest and down over his stomach and abdomen to his erection, finding pleasure in his sharp intake of breath and low groan. This age-old dance of sexual connection is one our bodies know the steps to without being taught. But with Cal . . . well, it's like upgrading from the awkward shuffle of teenagers at a school dance to a full-on dirty dance with two professional dancers. When he enters me, I wrap my legs around him, drawing him in deeper. I know when we take this slow it's delicious but today there's an urgency between us, like it's post-fight sex, driven by a desire to put all bad feeling behind us, and quickly.

That it wasn't really a fight is purely down to Cal. I reacted emotionally, from a place of fear. Outside the window there's a distant rumble of thunder. It's warm in the room, and our bodies are slick with perspiration. I focus on Cal, on the man between my thighs, in my heart, in my head . . . Wasn't I supposed to be holding part of myself back? Ha!

I fix my eyes on his as I pull him deeper into me with my heels and my hands, wanting him harder, needing him closer.

'Please, please don't let me be wrong about you. Please don't hurt me. I just couldn't bear it.' I beg Callum silently because saying no to him doesn't feel like an option any more. He's simply irresistible.

There's a shift deep inside of me, like a tipping point, not just an orgasm but a seismic shift of some kind. He's penetrating not just my body but the very heart of me. Our eyes lock and I feel the connection, soul to soul. Each thrust pushes away my resistance and erodes my barriers. It's both terrifying and exhilarating.

And I don't want it to stop.

Please, please let it be okay this time.

I'm not sure who I'm begging, the Universe, the God of my Sunday School childhood or maybe Cal himself.

When he holds me afterwards we're both quiet, as though we know something important just shifted for us. A crisis bypassed. It's raining now, torrential raindrops hitting the windowpanes. It might be turbulent outside but there's a stillness and a peace in the room. I know Cal probably needs to get back to the barn, but I don't get any sense he's only holding me because it's expected and he's itching to get away. He hooks my ankle with one of his feet and pulls it over his leg so that I'm where he wants me. Yes, I'd say he's definitely got me where he wants me. Stripped back, laid bare and his.

All the doubts and inner reservations in the world mean diddly squat because I'm transfixed, mesmerised by Cal. There's nothing on earth that could make me willingly throw this away. There's no playing this down or pretending I have any real control over the situation. I'm his. I'm in love.

And I'm lost.

Chapter 11

'When we deny the story, it defines us. When we own the story, we can write a brave new ending'

Brené Brown

Poppy's Daydream Blog

Hi, it's JoJo here, Poppy's housemate. She's really busy with preparations for her wedding so she's asked me to post a puppy update today! She said some of you wanted to know how things were going with the latest addition to our pack. So, here goes . . .

Things Flump has chewed so far:

My Kindle cover
His dog bed
My toothbrush
The electricity bill

A paperback copy of *Eat, Pray, Love* – I'd like to think he has an advanced sense of irony but really it was just the top book in the pile. He has 'eat' and 'love' covered already. He might want to learn to pray, if he's going to keep up this current stream of chewy robberies!

He steals pretty much anything he can get his paws on frankly. I'd forgotten what hard work puppies can be. I absolutely adore him but trying to stop him from killing himself by eating something poisonous, chewing electrical wires, leaping off of the sofa back to see if he can reach the desk or making a break for it to run towards the road is heart and panic attack inducing! I love him so much I can't bear the thought of anything happening to him.

He's definitely a cross breed as he's growing to be at least three times the size of Peanut and Treacle. The closest match I've found for him online is a Labrahuahua or a Golden Chihuatriever. Yes, they really are a thing. Who knew?

One of his ears sticks up all the time while the other dangles down. Like Barney's ears in fact. Barney is very gentle with Flump. They wrestle together and sit cuddled up with Flump using Barney as a sofa. I think they've formed a Sticky Up Ears club in solidarity. Dogs with uniformly positioned ears need not apply :-)

From annabelgrant@thestickybun.co.uk
To joannagrant@thestickybun.co.uk

Subject: Hi
Hi JoJo, how's it going?

I'm really glad to hear you say you're happy again and it all sounds really wonderful but . . . Well this is difficult, but I need to ask – are you one hundred per cent sure he's not using you? I'm sure you must've considered the fact that a high profile romance with you isn't exactly going to hurt his media profile?

Please don't get me wrong, I'm not saying I don't believe he could genuinely care about you – I think you're amazing – but anyone who doesn't love you to bits, just for you, doesn't deserve you at all IMHO.

Please don't hate me for asking the question. You're so far away and I can't help worrying. I'm afraid you're too close to the situation to be able to view his motives objectively. Remember you wouldn't listen to anyone who tried to warn you about Aiden, you were so sure.

I'm only asking you to think about this, properly think about this, because I love you and can't bear to see you get hurt again.

Love and xxxx

Poppy and I drive to Toulouse to go wedding dress shopping. I practically had to kidnap her to get her here, so strong is her dislike of clothes shopping. Typically, she has left it really late, convinced she will find something off-the-peg that won't need any alterations.

We park beneath the Place du Capitole and exit the car

park in the corner adjacent to the incredibly impressive Capitole building. The long, neo-classical facade dominates the vast square but the other three sides are lined with restaurants and shops.

'Maybe I could just get a nice dress that isn't a wedding dress?' Poppy suggests, eying the shops up with as much enthusiasm as any hermit forced into a city centre to shop. 'I still don't know why you wouldn't let me buy a dress off of the internet.'

'Seriously?' I loop my arm through hers, just in case she was thinking of making a break for it. 'Because you can't see it or touch it, never mind know if it is going to fit. For such an important occasion you just can't leave it to chance.'

'Mum wants me to wear her veil,' Poppy says glumly as we head to a bridal shop I've marked on the map on my phone.

'Have you ever thought of saying no?'

'To Mum?' Poppy looks horrified. 'I've tried a few times but somehow it always comes out as yes. I don't want to hurt her feelings.'

'But this is *your* wedding, Poppy.'

'Ha. I wish we could just elope, but we can't do that to Leo's parents. They are so looking forward to showing us off to the whole village. Oh, and apparently all the villagers expect to be invited in for an aperitif after the ceremony and would be incredibly offended not to be included.'

'I'm glad we haven't got to worry about that part of the proceedings. I know Madame Dubois will have it well in hand. I suppose it's hard because you've got French and English wedding traditions and the different expectations of your parents and his to consider.'

Poppy exhales loudly. 'Haven't I just?'

'Is it getting to you?'

I spot the shop we're looking for and head towards it. 'A bit.'

'Have you told Leo?'

She sighs. That's a no then.

'Why not?'

'He's got a lot going on at the moment and with his dad being so ill recently he's just focused on making it perfect for his parents. I don't think he's really thought about the culture clash. He doesn't understand why planning the wedding is stressful. I get the impression all the planning is a bit more low-key here. Or he's just being a bloke about it . . . I'm not sure which.' She chews her lip.

'Don't let yourself get so stressed out trying to keep everyone happy, Poppy,' I implore her. 'Come on, you love Leo and you're going to have a beautiful wedding reception at the Château. At least the groom came with the Château so you don't have to worry about venues.'

She manages a small smile.

I head for the shop entrance, but Poppy goes to look at the window display first, instead of going to the front door.

'That one. I want that dress.' She points at an elegant dress on the mannequin making up the main display. It's quite modern in style; it could almost be an evening dress. There is a little lace at the neckline and on the sleeves but apart from that it's a plain pearly silk. It gathers loosely at the waist with a silky tie instead of having a fitted bodice and it then flows down, pooling in a silky swirl at floor length.

'It's beautiful but it is literally the first dress you've seen. You haven't even set foot in the shop, never mind tried it on, and we still have appointments at two more places. Don't you think we should have a look around a bit first?'

'I want that one.' Poppy's tone is resolute.

'It does look lovely and I can see you in it actually.' I steer her to the doorway. 'But let's try a few others, just in case.'

Because Poppy has trouble saying no to everyone, including me and the shop owner, she does obediently try on six other dresses but we leave with the first dress that Poppy saw and cancel the other appointments. As luck would have it they had one in her size and it's a good fit. The hem is a little long and I have to talk Poppy out of doing the alterations herself, reminding her she has a book deadline before her wedding. Luckily, I persuade her that Madame Dubois would most likely be delighted to alter the hem for her. As she makes all her own clothes it's an easy favour to ask.

'So, are you happy?' I ask Poppy.

We are sipping ice-cold drinks, sitting at an outside table of one of the cafés overlooking the main square. Well, I'm sipping. She's mostly biting her lip and staring into the distance.

'Poppy?' I prompt her.

'Sorry, what?' She turns and looks at me, expression blank.

'Are you happy with your dress?'

'Oh, the dress, yes, it's perfect,' she replies absently.

'What's wrong then?'

'Mum's veil is really old-fashioned. It just won't go with the dress. I don't know what to do.' She stares at a bead of condensation running down the outside of her glass and traces its path with her finger.

I ponder for a moment before speaking.

'Okay, so don't do it over the phone or by Skype, do it by email where you can think about your words more carefully,' I suggest and take another sip of my fresh orange juice. It's a hot day and the cold drink is very welcome. 'How about saying that "the style of dress just won't work with the veil – sorry, Mum. Though I do like the thought of incorporating something of yours into the ceremony." How about that? Would that work, do you think?'

'Maybe.' Poppy's expression is a little more hopeful and she drinks her drink instead of playing with the glass. 'She can be very . . .'

'Persuasive?'

'Stubborn, manipulative and unable to see anyone else's point of view . . . was what I was going to say.' Poppy pulls a face.

'Okay, well, failing all diplomatic measures we could get Flump to run off with it on the day,' I suggest. 'All I need to do is put it within his reach, tell him not to touch it and he'll think running off with it is a great game and a way to get me to chase him.'

'That's true.' Poppy actually smiles this time. 'Great idea. Thanks, JoJo.'

'So, are we taking the mature and sensible solution or the cowardly one?'

'Fuck mature and sensible,' Poppy says, her grin reminding me why I like her so much.

'It seems having a puppy with a taste for larceny might actually come in handy. Who knew?'

'Ah, Flump is adorable. Don't worry about the stealing, I'm sure he'll grow out of it. Anyway, tell me, how are things with you, JoJo?' Poppy fixes her attention on me suddenly. 'Sorry I've been so self-obsessed lately.'

She hasn't. She is one of the most sensitive and least self-obsessed people I know but there's no point telling her so. She just gets anxious about things and when that happens it's like she gets lost in her own head. That's how she described it to me one time. I think it has something to do with her creativity.

'I am okay, thanks. You don't need to worry about me, just focus on your wedding and your deadline.'

I honestly don't want to add my worries to everything she already has on her mind.

'You and Cal seem . . . friendly,' she says, her mouth twitching.

'If that is a euphemism for shagging like rabbits then yes, we are friendly.' I laugh.

'So everything is . . . okay?'

'I suppose so.' I shrug. 'I mean the chemistry is off the scale.'

'So why only "suppose so"?'

'It's because it is off the scale that I'm worried.' I pause and decide how best to explain it. 'It scares me that I'll get swept away by it. Like I did with Aiden.'

'Is it the same as it was with Aiden though?'

'No, it's far more intense. It's more everything . . . That's what worries me. I don't feel in control and if it's more everything, that means I could be even more badly hurt than I was before.'

'In control isn't all it's cracked up to be, you know,' Poppy says. 'If I'd stayed in control I wouldn't have got together with Leo and be getting married soon.'

'And you wouldn't be worrying about veils either.'

'True but even with all the wedding stress you know I wouldn't change anything. I wouldn't do anything differently.'

'I know,' I say, and I know the conversation is purely academic because I wouldn't do anything differently either. Maybe I just needed to vent my anxiety, to get it out of my system. But as we drive home, I'm still plagued by a niggle, the niggle that says I've opened myself up to a whole world of hurt.

'I think Flump has lost one of his puppy teeth.' I get up off of my bedroom floor and hold it up to show Cal, who is still in my bed. Flump looks up with curiosity.

'What are you going to do? Put it under his dog-bed cushion for the puppy tooth fairy to find?' Cal jokes.

'What a sweet idea.' I laugh. 'He can wake up to find a duck strip dog treat in its place in the morning.'

'You're really going to do it, aren't you? You're nuts about that puppy.'

I shrug. 'Maybe. You've got to admit you're pretty fond of him too.'

'He's a little thief.'

'But such a cute one.'

Flump takes a flying leap onto the bed and sits on Cal's chest, staring solemnly down at him.

'Okay, he's cute, I'll give you that,' Cal says and as though he's understood every word Flump turns in a couple of circles and settles down on Cal to sleep. 'It looks like I'm stuck here. My services as a dog bed are required.'

Would it be so bad to be stuck here? I want to ask him but don't know how. Don't dare to is probably closer to the truth.

I climb into bed next to Cal and cuddle up, taking some comfort from the warmth of his body next to mine. It's been a couple of days since I talked to Poppy, but my niggles haven't gone away. In fact, they seem to be doing overtime at the moment, but I've looked at my calendar and suspect they're getting a fair bit of help from my not so friendly monthly hormones. I know from experience that this is not a great time of the month to pick a fight or start a serious discussion, no matter how much I might be itching to get Cal to declare exactly what his intentions towards me are.

There's nothing wrong with taking things slow. Nothing wrong with the fact Cal hasn't told me he loves me. I mean I haven't told him either and it's his actions, not his words, that matter, surely?

After five minutes of cuddling, Flump settling in between us, I crack and opt for the one thing I know will make things better.

'I really need some chocolate.'

'By chocolate I'm assuming you mean some of that highly processed sugar masquerading as chocolate I've seen you eating. Why don't I make you a nice chocolate dessert like a mousse or a chocolate cheesecake for later? That way I know you're getting good-quality ingredients.'

'No, I need chocolate. But thank you,' I say and mentally tell my hormones to cool it, he is only looking out for me and wants me to eat well. The hormones gnash their teeth a bit but agree to hold off savaging him for a while.

'Why do you *need* chocolate?' Cal looks bemused and my hormones do a little more teeth gnashing while I try to rein in my more irritable than usual temper. He doesn't deserve it. I probably ought to warn him about the savage hormones – it's only fair.

'Let's just say savage hormones are soothed when you feed them chocolate. It distracts them and stops them attacking,' I reply as patiently as I can. 'Science proves it's true.'

Cal pulls me into a hug and Flump manages to stick his head beneath Cal's armpit so he can be a part of it.

'Are you sure about that?' His lips quirk.

Damn, I'd hoped mentioning science would get him onside and appeal to his inner geek, but I might've known he'd expect me to reference the actual research.

'You don't believe me?' I ask, raising an eyebrow.

He merely raises an eyebrow back at me. I pretend to huff but don't pull away from the hug.

'Okay, so science actually says the darker and purer the chocolate the better, but my hormones happen to be very partial to Maltesers.' I eye him with mock seriousness. 'My hormones are so savage they have been known to mug an old lady for a Malteser. They also bite the heads off innocent males who get too close. The guilty ones too obviously.'

'Is that so?' The corners of Cal's mouth twitch as though he really wants to smile but is trying to suppress it, unsure just how hormonal I am. 'You know it is possible you are just a little low in magnesium. Have you tried—'

'Don't tell me to eat a sodding banana. I've had two bananas and a magnesium tablet already today. I really need chocolate.'

'Would you like me to go out and get you some?'

'Yes, please.'

'You know, if you wanted chocolate you should've just said so at the start of the conversation . . .' He grins wickedly and slips quickly out of bed before I can get to him.

Not that I was really going to swat him. He's going out

for chocolate for me, and that makes him a modern knight on horseback as far as I'm concerned.

Words are easy. Small, everyday actions speak louder.

I'd rather focus on the trees right in front of me than worry about the bigger picture of the wood I can't see. I have Cal here and now and I want to enjoy him without worrying about what might come next.

Chapter 12

'Being deeply loved by someone gives you strength, while loving someone deeply gives you courage'

Lao Tzu

From annabelgrant@thestickybun.co.uk
To joannagrant@thestickybun.co.uk
Subject: Twitter thing
So, there's this thing you need to see. I know you're not active on social media anymore but I think you should be aware of what's being said. I know I'd want to know . . .

@aidenholmes – I am truly sorry for @Jojogrant It's a real shame she never got over me but what can I say, I fell in love. I hope she'll find the maturity to sit down with us and talk. @sexinthesuburbs #sexinthe-suburbs

@sallyfletcher – @Jojogrant is my dearest friend. I deeply regret if she is upset with me and hope to

meet up with her very soon. @sexinthesuburbs #sexinthesuburbs

@sallyfletcher–Watch this space. South of France here we come. Hoping for a big reunion with my bestie @Jojogrant It's time to move on #bestiesforgive #reunion #sexinthesuburbssouthoffrancespecial #sexinthesuburbs

What a cow, eh?

Hugs,
Annabel
xx

From joannagrant@thestickybun.co.uk
To annabelgrant@thestickybun.co.uk
Subject: Twitter thing/WTF???
They're trying to make it sound like I'm the one in the wrong. Unbelievable. Though really, I shouldn't be surprised by anything now. What is this apologising on Twitter about anyway? They've never apologised to me. Not even once.

Oh, sod it. I'm going to do some cleaning and vent my anger on the bathrooms. As if I'd ever want to sit down with either of them.

Love xx

I attack the bathrooms with gusto, pouring bleach down plugholes and scrubbing at the showers, determined to eradicate every single smudge. My pre-menstrual hormones are not helping at all and as hard as I scrub, I can't expunge their words from my brain. Will I ever be free from bloody Aiden? Why can't he just leave me alone? I have no idea why they're trying to stir things up again. As for Sally, well she's definitely more beastie than bestie: #beastienotbestie – I wish I could tweet that. Except I'm definitely not going to. I've resisted the urge to fight back via social media for this long and they're not drawing me out now. I learnt long ago there is absolutely no point in engaging. The only thing to do is to ignore them, as hard as that may be. If I do that for long enough they'll go away.

Eventually I run out of energy and collapse on a chair in the kitchen. Flump jumps up onto my lap for a cuddle, snuggling his head against my chest, trusting, lovable and utterly adorable. I stroke his silky soft fur and feel some of the tension leaving my shoulders. The surge of love I feel for him lifts my mood. I want to talk to Cal about it but don't want to interrupt him and Leo again. There's a strong chance I might cry, what with my unhelpful hormones and all, and I don't want to look unbalanced. I try some of the yoga breathing Poppy taught me. Square breathing, I think she called it, though that might just be her name for it. I breathe in for a count of four, hold for a count of four, breathe out for a count of four, wait for four and then repeat the cycle.

After a couple of rounds of square breathing and stroking Flump I'm feeling a lot calmer. Not happy exactly but at least not actively homicidal any more, so that's an improvement.

The dogs all pile into the kitchen, barking excitedly, greeting Cal when he comes in as though they haven't seen him for months, rather than just a few hours.

'Cup of tea?' Cal has entered the room without my noticing.

'Not sure.' I bite my lip, looking down at Flump. My chest and throat are tight. I don't feel quite right, but I don't know how to ask for help.

'A walk then? Maybe you need a change of scene.' Cal places a hand on my back.

'Maybe . . . Okay then.' I think my nervous energy will be easier to cope with if I'm moving so I get up and grab Flump's lead.

Once we're outside on the path leading to the lake Cal reaches out and takes my free hand. I'm keeping Flump on the lead until we're well clear of Angeline's donkeys. I can do without any additional stress today.

I find comfort in his hand holding mine. In the hope that there is an 'us'. In the gut-wrenching longing for it not to be just me alone against the world any more.

'What's up?' he asks.

I pass him my phone to show him the screen grabs of the tweets. It's far easier than trying to tell him, given my tight throat and the tears threatening to fall. Cal reads them and then pulls me into a big hug. I rest my head on his chest and he strokes my hair. God, this feels nice. So, so lovely to be held and comforted. To feel connected again.

Something inside me shifts and the desire to cry passes.

Why do I care what they say when I have lovely Cal here next to me? I'm not going to let them get to me like this. Not any more.

'Have you ever read *The Power of Now*?' Cal asks as we walk to the lake.

'No, but I've heard of it I think.' I shrug. 'I don't really read self-help books. Sorry, no offence. They're more self-development books. I just think of most of it as common sense.'

'None taken.' Cal laughs. 'I think.'

Maybe I shouldn't have said 'no offence' then, but I'm really not in the best mood for making conversation.

'So, what's it about?' I ask lightly, feeling the need to make amends. 'You obviously think it's relevant for me or you wouldn't have brought it up.'

'Okay, in a nutshell it's basically saying the only time that exists for us is now.'

'Hmm.' I try to keep the scepticism out of my tone.

'What's already happened is past, it's no longer happening and what's going to happen is the future, it's not actually happening yet.' Cal pauses. 'What the author is getting at, I think, is that spending our energies, thoughts and emotions on either the past or the future isn't healthy for us. The only moment that really matters is right now. All you have to deal with right now is walking the dogs, so you don't need to worry, just enjoy it. Be here with me. Not back in that awful place with Aiden and Sally. Or in a future scenario being ambushed by paparazzi. That may never happen, and you don't need to deal with it now. I get that what happened was terrible, really horrible and I'm so sorry it happened to you, JoJo, but the thing to hold onto is that it's not happening right now – and those tweets: they're just words from people whose opinions you don't rate any more.'

'Okay, that kind of makes sense.' I consider Cal thoughtfully. 'What kind of self-centred, thoughtless celebrity are you anyway?'

He laughs. Thankfully he gets the joke. Aiden was forever worrying about what he looked like. I had to keep propping up his ego, which in retrospect was kind of exhausting. I can't remember the last time, or any time in fact, that Aiden discussed a book he'd read or expressed an interest in anything outside of his world. I like that Cal reads widely and is interested in the world around him. He's certainly opened my eyes and my mind. He has a profound effect on me.

I'd like to think I would've grown out of Aiden anyway, with or without what happened with Sally, but I honestly don't know. Sexual chemistry can be a bitch. We had a connection of sorts; it just wasn't a healthy one.

Sexual chemistry can also be heavenly. I glance at Cal and feel the familiar desire curling and unfurling inside me. If sexual chemistry is going to make a fool of me, I'd much rather it was over a man like Cal. I can't think of a worthier man to risk humiliating myself for. I've got to risk it. Cal is worth risking myself for. I'm sure of it.

Can I tell him I love him? Can I be the first to mention the L word? I look at him again but lose my nerve.

'What are you thinking?' Cal locks his gaze on mine, giving me that feeling he's staring into my soul again.

Tell him what I'm thinking? As if. Some thoughts are definitely not made to be shared. Not ever.

'Just what you said really.' I try to keep my tone upbeat and casual but I'm not sure I succeed. 'So you think I should let it go then? Just like that? Let them carry on spreading their version of the truth and who I am while I . . . I don't know, look at the flowers and commune with the trees?'

'No, I never said that,' Cal explains patiently. 'Just that it's been suggested that no one who spends their time living in the past or the future can ever really be at peace. I'm not talking about what's right or what's fair or even how you get to the place where you can let go and just be. Just because getting to a place of peace is hard doesn't mean we shouldn't try it.'

'Well, I suppose the other alternative, of hanging onto everything for ever, isn't that appealing either,' I admit. 'I have to let go.'

'Talking of letting go.' Cal sweeps me into a hug. I untangle Flump's lead and let him off to play in the lake; there's not really anywhere else for him to go. Then I put my arms around Cal's neck and we kiss like teenagers, only with a lot more skill. I'd forgotten how nice kissing could be. How it's possible to lose yourself, for the world around you to disappear as the kissing stirs other, deeper desires.

If I have to try living in the moment, I think I've found a wonderful way to practise . . .

The next day I go to Mirepoix market with Cal. Walking around the bustling market with him I think it's possibly the first time my heart has felt as sunny as the cloudless blue sky above. We're holding hands. In public. And I'm not freaking out. I'm not worrying about what the world is thinking about me or saying about me. Living in the moment is curiously liberating. I feel great and being with Cal is just so natural. We are constantly touching in some way, even if it's just a hand on an arm or holding hands. As though neither of us wants to break the physical connection, like we need to feel skin on skin. Being with him and not touching him just feels wrong.

Cal is enthusing about the quality of the fruit and vegetables and the artisan bread and cheese. I buy some juicy-looking peaches, dark red cherries, my favourite Pink Lady apples and some fresh viennoiserie and let Cal choose the rest. He doesn't need to sell me on the quality of the produce here at the market. I've been shopping here for a year and love it. Market day is the highlight of my week. I make another stop at a dried-fruit stall to buy dried strawberries and dried cherries, both utterly delicious, and then slip my arm through Cal's as he walks happily around the stalls, telling me his plans. He's going to cook for me over the next couple of days and test out some of the proposed menu for The Barn on me.

I'm not an idiot. I know I've got happy hormones whizzing around my brain courtesy of the extremely lovely sex we had just this morning but this feels like much more than a post-sex buzz, as though we've connected on more than just a physical level and there's a deep peace in that connection, a sigh expelled, coming home to rest after a long journey – that kind of feeling.

Not that I'd say so to Cal. I don't want to look like a stalkery bunny-boiler who's already secretly planning our wedding – because I'm not. I just feel blissfully, joyfully happy to know him, to like him and to know he likes me.

I haven't bothered with my hat and slouchy clothes today. Partly because I want to look my best for Cal but also because all that seems so unimportant right now. I've been hiding and living in my head for too long. Time to try living in the real world.

'Hey, what are you thinking about?' Cal pulls me closer as he examines the cheese on offer at one stall.

'Thinking it's time to stop thinking so much.' I shrug, embarrassed. It's been such an ingrained habit to keep everything to myself for so long. It's going to be hard to break.

'I agree.' Cal grins. 'There are so many much more exciting things we could be doing. Do you want to practice your mindfulness again?'

I told him about how easy I find it to live in the moment when we're kissing and he's been very obliging.

He leans in for a kiss and it quickly becomes more

passionate. I automatically lean into him. When we pull apart something catches my eye and I turn to see a couple of tourists in the crowd with their phones out, filming us.

I instantly turn away, burying my head against Cal's chest. My happiness trickles away as fast as a bath that someone has pulled the plug out of.

'Can we go, please?' I whisper imploringly. 'I want to go now.'

I'm practically tugging him to follow me. It's hard enough resisting the urge to run. It's so crowded though with tourists and buggies and dogs that running isn't really an option. Plus, do I really want to be filmed running away? For a moment I think Cal is going to argue but he must see the panic in my eyes because he quickly follows, his arm protectively around me.

'It'll be okay, JoJo.' Cal's voice is calm. He isn't rattled at all. But why would he be?

'It'll be okay for you. The press love you.' I try to keep the accusation out of my voice. It isn't his fault he's the darling of the TV cookery world. Or maybe it is. After all it's a role he's chosen, deliberately chosen, not accidentally fallen into.

Hot tears prick at my eyelids. It's all I can do to blink them back and focus on not crying. The thought of my crying being videoed and trending all over social media, of Aiden and Sally watching it, makes me stiffen my spine and clench my jaw. I will not give them the satisfaction of pretending to give a fuck.

'We were only kissing, JoJo. It's not the end of the world.' Cal's tone is gentle, like he's trying to calm me down, like I'm a nervous dog he thinks might bite him.

I don't reply because the thought of people watching me kissing Cal is freaking me out so much I can't breathe. This is more than a photo, people were actually filming me. The last video footage of me went viral and it *was* the end of my world. I lost a boyfriend, best friend, my business, my home, the respect of my family . . . I even had to leave my country behind. I can't bear the thought that today might signal the end of the world, and the new home, I've built here in France. And I was honestly thinking being spotted wasn't important any more? Just how delusional am I? I was just too wrapped up, too wrapped up in Cal to think straight.

I have no idea where I'll go if I have to leave France. The thought makes me even sicker and in spite of Cal's hand on my back I feel utterly alone.

When we get back to Les Coquelicots we go straight to Cal's room. My pulse is beating hard, the pain in my chest tightening, rising and choking me. Cal pulls me into a hug and although my limbs are stiff and initially unyielding, I melt, my body instinctively obeying his touch in spite of my turbulent emotions.

God, I love this, feeling the warmth of his body against mine, feeling my heart rate slow in time with his, that perfect moment when our energies somehow combine to create something new – something 'us'.

I feel like the perfection of this moment has been tarnished by the videos that have been made of us kissing, now fair game for public consumption. The 'us' I've been treasuring is now mass-market entertainment for all the people who forget that we're real people with feelings.

There's no reason why this should be worse than the photo they got of us in Carcassonne but this is Mirepoix, my local town, my back yard. I shop here and come here for coffee. Also, the fact that it's video means my brain can't help forging an emotional link to the other video . . .

I press my face into Cal's warm T-shirt, inhaling his scent as though trying to imprint it onto my memory. Am I afraid I have to remember it in case its presence in my life is fleeting, about to be snatched from me?

He strokes my hair as I attempt to calm down. As usual his presence does soothe me but not totally. I can sense the storm clouds amassing around us. This hug is the calm in the eye of the storm, one brief moment of peace to drink in so I can arm myself for what comes next.

I don't feel anywhere near ready for it. Fear has stripped me of all my new-found energy. I was supposed to be finding my strength, putting down roots, being brave.

But now I'm afraid that's nothing more than a fairytale illusion. I'm the frightened girl I was last summer again. There's been no growth, no change. I'm not brave.

Whatever was I thinking? Whatever did I let Cal persuade me into thinking?

'I can't be public property again, I can't do this.' I pull

my head back and look up at Cal. Is it so terrible to admit that a part of me wants to sink into his arms and let him take care of me. A feminist voice inside me squeaks an objection but I so, so long to melt into Cal's embrace, to let myself believe the lie that he can make this all okay for me, that he can make this go away. To let myself believe it just for a day, an hour, a minute . . .

I close my mind to the buts and the doubts and let Cal's hands slide over my body. I let the tide of heat rise inside me, pushing down the pain and the fear, for now anyway. For one evening, one night, I'll put my phone into airplane mode and stick my head in the sand, pretending I can actually turn off the internet. I'll believe for just one night that Cal can make this all go away.

'It's okay, you're okay. It'll be okay.' Cal soothes and holds me, and I so want to believe him, I do, but . . .

Soon my negative thoughts have been put on mute, along with my phone, and I'm simply experiencing the force of Cal's desire, the hardness of his erection pressing into me and the heat of my body's response to him.

The sex has an urgency, an increased passion to it, as though both of us are afraid that tonight will be about making memories. Or maybe it's just me, and Cal is simply reacting to my urgency, to the nip of my teeth on his neck, to the progress of my lips and tongue down his naked, hairy chest to where the hair snakes down to his cock, only briefly stopping at his nipples to suck and gently tug with my teeth.

I am so hungry for him I'm ravenous, I want to kiss and lick and taste him, all of him. I want him in me, on me . . .

There's a level of passion rising up inside me I didn't even know I was capable of. Unlocked by fear perhaps? I don't know but I'm lost in my appreciation of Cal's body, in his innate sexiness that has driven me wild and sent me reeling since I first met him. I'm not holding back any part of myself, not this time, not if it might be our last . . .

I relish the sensation of his hard erection against my soft, full breasts. Knowing he's reacting to me, that I'm giving him as much pleasure as he is to me, is intoxicating.

If relishing sex with a man I adore is wrong, if it makes me bad somehow, like so many internet trolls felt compelled to tell me, then I just don't care. This feels good, the very best kind of life-affirming good, and why on earth wouldn't I love something this good?

I've never felt as full of tenderness as I do right now, taking Cal's erection in my mouth. I'm moved by his trust in me and by the desire I have to give him the most pleasure I possibly can with a willing mouth and loving tongue.

He strokes my hair away from my face so that he can watch what I'm doing, and I know without a doubt that I love, love, love this man. More than I've ever loved anyone.

And the poignancy of the timing isn't lost on me, that now I'm finally sure of it, it's the one moment that I also know I might have to let him go, to lose all of this.

Because I can't go back to the way things were last summer.

'God, JoJo, I really love you,' Cal says, moaning his appreciation as his hands tangle in my hair, stroking my head.

I let some of my hair fall in front of my face and hope he doesn't notice the few stray tears that escape my eyes and roll down my cheeks. The true pain of loving, of loving deeply, and what the consequences could be hits me and leaves me reeling, even as he comes in my mouth and I swallow down every drop I can, wanting all of him.

I never knew loving could hurt this badly.

I wipe my eyes discreetly as Cal recovers his breathing. Sweat beads on our skin. I haven't come yet, but I know he'll take care of that once he's got his second wind. Anyway, tonight isn't about whose turn it is. It's not about getting off.

This is so much more than that. Just like I never realised what loving deeply meant, I never realised sex could be like this. That it could be more than just physical and also that it is both utterly and completely perfect when you're in love. Not technically perfect necessarily but perfect in a deeper, more meaningful, heart-warming way.

Right now, I'm experiencing a depth of intimacy that no magazine articles telling me how to give the perfect blowjob could possibly have prepared me for. I just wasn't prepared for this powerful, intimate expression of sexual love or this expansion of my heart into something achingly tender. It's a joy that's both fragile and transformative.

And once we've made love again and are lying entwined, limbs and sheets tangled . . . That's when the fear creeps in.

Chapter 13

'When you come out of the storm, you won't be the same person who walked in. That's what this storm's all about'

Haruki Murakami

From callum@callum'scook-off.com
To caitlino'connor85@hotmail.com
Subject: Here's a thing . . .
So, you know I'm always saying everything happens for a reason and that drives you mad because you don't agree, but . . . I really do believe it Cait. I think the right people are drawn into our lives at the right time. I thought at first that I was meant to help JoJo find her feet again and move on in her life and that perhaps she was meant to teach me about not being quick to judge and not being a snob about reality TV. Now I'm starting to think that she is the one helping me and teaching me stuff, helping me to evaluate what I really want in

life. She's helped me a lot while I've been thinking about how to move forward. Weird, huh? I thought I needed to shut myself away from people so I could think and make a decision, but I almost shut out the woman who had something to teach me.

Did you get caught up watching Sex in the Suburbs for me? What's your take on Aiden then?

Love to you and Bump/nephew-to-be!

'There's something I need to tell you, JoJo.' Cal strokes and plays with my hair while I cuddle up, trying to ignore all the pesky niggles that are like flies buzzing angrily at my mental fly screen again.

I feel sick, my chest instantly tight. How bad can it be though? He told me he loved me. Nothing else matters.

Except I know that's not true. The other things that matter are just on mute, along with my phone. I haven't been able to get to sleep and neither has Cal. It could be the warm night, or it could be we don't want to waste this time before the world bursts in again. I know I want to hold onto every minute.

'What is it? You're not going back to London, are you?' I ask and try to remember to breathe.

'No, it's, well . . . it's something I wanted you to hear directly from me, not just find out.'

'Please just tell me. This is torture.'

'I've been asked to take part in a special show being filmed here in a château near Carcassonne.'

I stiffen in his arms and squeeze my eyes shut.

'And?' I ask even though I know the answer.

'It's the *Sex in the Suburbs* Summer Special. I'm supposed to teach them to cook French cuisine.'

'How long have you known?' I try to keep my voice as calm as Cal's but it's difficult.

'It's a recent thing.'

Of course, it would be. Why didn't I listen to the niggles? Why didn't I see the signs?

'Why do they want you? Why not someone French?' I pull back from Cal and fold my arms protectively over my bare body, hugging myself. 'I thought you hated those kind of reality shows?'

In the dim light I see Cal shrug. 'They want me because I help bring in the ratings. And as for hating those kind of shows . . . well, maybe you've taught me not to be so judgemental.'

He's not being arrogant about the ratings, just telling the truth. He's hot.

He knows it.

I know it. God, do I know it.

The producers of *Sex in the Suburbs* know it too. They know his Gaelic charm and the piercing blue eyes that have women claiming control of the TV remote all over the UK.

But . . . But . . .

What if Annabel is right and this is a set-up? Isn't the timing of all this a bit too neat? Cal arrives and gets into my knickers and then he gets an invite to cook for my famous ex-boyfriend's television show. My famous ex-boyfriend and ex-best friend express a wish to have a showdown . . . sorry, I mean a reunion with me. Everyone gets a bit of extra publicity and everyone is happy.

Except for me. 'Disgraced Joanna Grant' whose story gets another airing along with those awful old pictures of me with puffy eyes and tear-stained cheeks, maybe even a still from the sex tape with a blurry patch covering my crotch and nipples, as if that makes showing it okay.

'I've been really stupid again, haven't I?' I don't recognise my voice, maybe because my throat is constricted. My eyes burn with unshed tears of humiliation. 'I never thought of myself as naive but clearly I'm a first-class idiot. It was all leading to this, wasn't it? Extra publicity for your book and for *Sex in the Suburbs*. Extra publicity for Aiden. Did you cook this up together? Ha! "Cook", do you see what I did there?'

'No. Stop it, JoJo. You're better than this.' Cal's tone is authoritative, commanding even. He takes hold of my shoulders and holds me firmly, waiting until I meet his eyes before he carries on. 'That simply isn't true so stop winding yourself up.'

I'm not convinced I am better than the dark emotion snaking through me, hissing and spitting and wanting to strike at a victim, any victim. But I feel the brakes being applied to my careering mood before I skid out of control and face the inevitable crash. My body and emotions succumb to his tone of authority, seemingly without question. I trust him at a cellular level. I meet Cal's arresting gaze and am rocked by its intensity, by the connection, by the reminder of who Cal is.

'Do you trust me, JoJo?'

There's a tension in Callum's grip that suggests he's anxious about the answer. That small, surprising evidence of his vulnerability touches and reassures me. If he didn't care about me then he wouldn't be bothered about my answer. Of course, it could be just that he's anxious his plan is in jeopardy but . . . I really don't think so. Momentary freak-out aside, I really do trust him. It really could just be that Aiden and *Sex in the Suburbs* are cashing in on my emerging relationship with Cal, looking to see what emotional drama can be squeezed out of this situation. I almost pity them.

Almost.

It's the trusting Cal that scares me so much. It's trusting people that gives them the power to hurt you. I thought I'd sworn off it as a bad habit, but bad habits are hard to shake and I am, it seems, an inherently trusting person. Even when presented with overwhelming evidence that it isn't a safe way to live. The fly screen in my mind is dark with buzzing flies but they haven't broken through yet.

'JoJo?' Cal interrupts my thoughts.

I remind myself he's looking for a simple yes or no, not the inner workings of my mind.

'Yes, yes, I do,' I say firmly and unflinchingly in an

attempt to make up for my slow response. 'Sorry, I was just thinking . . . well, it doesn't matter what I was thinking. It's just hard . . .'

Cal leans forward and kisses me lightly on the lips with just enough sensuality to set my body humming and wanting more.

'I can turn the gig down if you like. I haven't signed anything yet. Would you like me to?' Cal asks, pulling back to watch my expression.

'Your agent wouldn't like that.' I frown.

'It's not her decision.'

I know he's offering me a lot. The publicity from doing the special would help his career and will probably help publicise his *A Taste of French Cooking* book. I bet the publishers will get a book cover done and put up for pre-order to tie in with the show. That I'm tempted to take him up on the offer makes me feel guilty. I'd be hurting his career. I'd be thwarting a good chance of publicity for a project he actually cares about – his book. This is his career and if I'm any kind of friend I'll support him in that and want the best for him. Am I a friend with benefits or a girlfriend? He said he loved me but was that just sex talk?

Everyone knows that things said during sex can't really be relied on. Don't they?

Aargh. Great, so now I'm feeling needy as well as selfish for wanting to put myself before what's best for my friend/ maybe, probably boyfriend.

'It's fine, honestly it is. It'll be good for the book.' I force a smile. 'Just . . . you know, try to keep me out of it, if that's okay? I really don't want to have anything to do with the show or anyone associated with it, ever again.'

'Except for me, I hope?' Cal replies lightly.

'Yes, of course, except for you.' I roll my eyes and lightly swat his arm.

'Phew.' He exaggeratedly wipes his brow, but I swear I see a momentary micro-expression of real relief. I feel some genuine relief myself. The fact he even offered to give it up suggests my deepest paranoid fears of an evil conspiracy are completely unfounded. Then I think about Cal meeting Aiden, and Aiden and Sally staying in the area, and any feelings of relief slip through my fingers like wispy dandelion seeds blowing away in the wind.

'You know, there is another way to deal with all this.' Cal says.

'What?' I sink back down onto the bed and ask warily, my internal antenna clicking into action. Is this where I get to see Cal's endgame, his casual but very convenient suggestion of a plan that benefits him?

Stop it, JoJo, I scold myself. Cal offering to give it up wasn't a bluff.

'Confront Aiden and Sally, have it out with them, stand up for yourself instead of rolling over and playing dead.'

'You think that's what I'm doing here? Just rolling over and playing dead?' I narrow my eyes at him.

'Aren't you?'

'No,' I retort angrily. Cal says nothing and the silence irritates me into self-justification. 'Creating distance from my old life isn't the same as giving in.'

'If you say so.' He pulls a face and anger flares into life inside me.

'You don't know what it was like, you don't know. I had to get away.' I don't move away from Cal again, but my limbs are rigid and my jaw tight.

'Yes, you needed some distance, some time and privacy to heal, I get that.' Cal's tone is gentler now.

'But?'

'You've had that time. Now do you want to spend the rest of your life unhappy and hiding?' His gaze pierces me and his words sting.

'Of course I don't want to have to hide and I don't want to be unhappy,' I reply with irritation. 'It's not that simple.'

'Do you have to hide? I get that you needed to for a while but how long for? Will you still be hiding in the kitchen in a year's time? Five years' time? Ten years'? How long are you planning to stay a victim?'

'I . . . I don't know. I'm not.' I shake my head, totally furious, not sure why I was obsessing over whether Cal loves me or what I mean to him. Right now, I hate him. Hate him for asking these questions. Hate him for talking as though I have a choice. 'It's really not that simple.'

I get what he's doing. He's calling me a victim to annoy me, to annoy me into proving him wrong.

'It's your choice.' Cal shrugs. 'You can stay hidden and

never risk being hurt again. Good luck with that, by the way. I'm not sure life really works like that and there'll be a price you pay for hiding.'

Reluctantly I nod mutely. I know that's true. The price of loneliness, of disconnection from my family and friends and losing a sense of my place in the world, losing my sense of myself . . . they're all part of the price tag I've needed to pay to stay safe.

'Or do you face this head-on, now that it's not so raw?'

Not so raw? When he just rubbed salt in my wounds himself and saw me flinch?

But . . . I suppose it's sort of, a little bit true. Maybe. I'm not as devastated as I was even six months ago. I'm stronger than I was.

'Why does it matter? Why do you even care what I do?' The snake inside me is still spoiling for a fight.

'You matter, JoJo,' Cal says calmly, refusing to rise to the bait. 'You're important.'

'No, I'm not. Of course I don't matter. There are billions of humans. What does it matter if I decide to spend the rest of my life in hiding, under a rock? Or under a duvet, preferably. I'm insignificant.'

He pauses, regarding me thoughtfully.

'You've heard of the Butterfly Effect, yes?'

'What?' I frown. 'Yes, I think so. Something about if a butterfly flaps its wings it can affect weather systems on the other side of the world? Cause hurricanes and that sort of thing?'

'Pretty much. So, if a butterfly can have an impact rippling out to potentially affect world weather systems then what makes you think what you do doesn't cause ripples that matter too?'

'I hadn't really thought about it.'

'What you do causes ripples, whether you realise it or not. You can hide under a duvet for the rest of your life if that's what you really want, JoJo, but that has a ripple effect all of its own. Everyone matters. You matter. You matter to me.'

'I don't know if . . .' The words wither on my lips and I press my mouth and eyes shut, trying to hold the wave of emotion at bay. His words affect me, they stir and they shake me. And closed lips and eyelids are no barrier. I don't know about it not being raw. This feels pretty bloody raw to me. But Cal does have a point. I've been putting not just my phone but my whole life on mute for so long, and it has been taking its toll. I haven't felt like myself for so long.

'What don't you know?'

'I don't know if I can do it,' I reply bleakly, feeling wretched.

'What's the worst that can happen? Hasn't the worst already happened?'

'I suppose.'

'Well, I can't decide for you. It's your choice.' Cal sighs and reaches out for me. 'I just want you to be free, not living in fear and hiding as though you've got something to be ashamed of. Them coming here . . . well, maybe it's a sign it's time to do something, you know?'

I feel like I'm disappointing him but this . . . this is huge and it's not a decision I can make lightly. I can't do this just to please Cal.

If I do it for anyone, I'll be doing it for myself.

It's not like I'm heartbroken any more. Aiden isn't even in the same league as Cal, but I can't shake the feeling that the new life and new love I've been nurturing will be tainted somehow by Aiden and Sally. That they'll reach out through Cal to crush it and snatch me back into the dark vortex of their influence. They've sucked so much life out of me already. I very nearly lost myself. I might have . . . if Poppy hadn't taken me in.

'I don't want them ruining my life here.' I sigh into his chest. 'I feel like I'm just starting to get back on my feet again and they're swooping over me like the bloodsucking life-force vultures they really are.'

'So what you're saying is you're on the fence about how you feel about them?' Cal laughs and I join in, glad that some of the heavier tension dissipates with our laughter. I want to get back to the earlier intimacy of the evening. I want to make the most of our time.

'You know, I'm still not sure exactly why you do TV cookery shows,' I say, still trying to quell my earlier doubts about the convenient timing of everything.

'Because I love it. It's my passion.'

'TV?' I frown. He's never struck me as someone who wants to be famous for its own sake.

'No, the cooking.' He sighs. 'I must admit I'd hoped the

TV deal would give me a platform to share that passion, get people inspired to use good ingredients, buying locally. Everything we're trying to do at The Barn, basically. The concepts I hope will come across in the book.'

'But?'

'It's too much about appearances, the glamour of it, getting to know the "right" people.' He shrugs. 'I'm not so good at that side of it.'

'You're great at talking to people.'

'I'm not great at talking bullshit. I don't know. I want to get this book out, that's my goal at the moment and I want to see it through. But who knows what I'll do after that.' He strokes the side of my face tenderly. 'Maybe it might be nice to spend more time here. Cook at The Barn, keep it small and simple, live the French dream.'

My breath hitches. 'With me? You want to be with me or is this nothing to do with me?' The question hammers in my skull but I don't dare voice it. 'Maybe' is an awfully equivocal word. The moment is poignant, heavy with meaning, yet I still can't open my mouth and ask. I'm too afraid I'm being delusional, making too much of this.

Like before.

Like with Aiden.

Instead I rest my head on his chest.

'Sounds good,' is all I can say, my heart thumping so fiercely I'm afraid he might notice.

* * *

I wake from a nightmare drenched in sweat, heart pounding, feeling utterly overwhelmed. It takes a few minutes for my pulse to slow to a reasonable rate and for me to remember that the nightmare isn't really happening. Aiden was in the dream, filming me with Cal and saying how the footage was going to make me famous again. Then there were loads of reporters and paparazzi all shoving their way into my bedroom, jostling to get the best shot of me. And I was naked, of course . . .

It felt so real. So gut-wrenchingly, achingly real. All the emotions I experienced when I found out about the sex tape come flooding back.

Fuck.

I get up quietly so as not to wake Cal, go to the bathroom and splash cold water over my face. I can't do this. No way can I willingly put myself into the spotlight again. Maybe I'll have to keep my distance from Cal if I want to avoid being dragged into the media circus again.

Back in the bedroom my heart contracts as I look at Cal still asleep in bed. How can I bear to keep my distance from him? He's given me hope of a different future, a life in which I might actually be happy and confident enough to hold my head up high.

But . . . the emotions of the nightmare linger. I don't know what to do. I'm not sure I can be brave enough to face this head on, head up . . .

I crawl into bed next to him. I'll tell him in the morning that I really need time to think about things, to work out if I can even still do this with him. For one more night I can pretend that everything is normal. That the bubbles of hope I've been experiencing recently haven't been burst, bumping me back down to earth. I'm still feeling a bit shaky from the nightmare but as I snuggle into Callum's side, resting my head on his chest, I feel my heartbeat gradually go back to normal. I can't sleep though. My mind is racing.

Would staying away from Cal mean I'd have to stay away from Les Coquelicots as well? After the video footage anyone can track me down to Mirepoix and after that it's no distance to St Quentin. The thought of losing my new life makes me feel sick. Where would Flump and I go?

But it's the thought of losing Cal that really twists my stomach. I don't want to give him up, I don't. I can't, but . . . The memories of the awfulness of those months after the media storm broke are still so painfully raw. I can't face that again either.

I just can't do it.

So . . . what do I do now? Neither choice feels palatable or possible. There's got to be another way. There must be. I toss and turn for the rest of the night and eventually watch the pale grey light of pre-dawn cast shadows in the room and lie awake until I feel Cal stirring next to me.

Eager to avoid any more difficult questions I slip out of bed to get my phone from where I'd left it charging. When I turn the 'do not disturb' off I find I've got six missed calls and a text from Annabel.

Sorry JoJo it's bad news – Gran had a heart attack last night and died before the ambulance could get her to hospital. When do you think you can get home?

xx

Chapter 14

'Where you grew up becomes a big part of who you are for the rest of your life. You can't run away from that. Well, sometimes the running away from it is what makes you who you are'

Helen Mirren

Lying in my old bedroom at Mum and Dad's the night before Gran's funeral I'm ashamed because I should be mourning her but instead I'm numb. Somehow it hasn't really hit me yet, it doesn't feel real. Instead all I can think about is Cal and how I could never give him up. And then about how I can't stay with him, simply can't face the attention again.

It's late but I text Cal anyway.

How's Flump? Did you get him to eat anything in the end?

A reply comes back almost instantly.

He's fine, asleep on my chest at the moment . . . I'm still awake because I had to roast a chicken for the little sod! I swear he's the most fussy customer I've cooked for! Are you okay? How's things at home?

I smile, thinking about Flump holding out for roast chicken. I think it's really sweet that Cal stayed up to roast him one; I think he's really getting quite fond of him. I'm sure the other dogs all stayed up and claimed severe hunger pangs too, despite having actually eaten their dinners.

Thanks so much for doing the chicken for him, I can stop fussing about him now. I'm okay-ish I suppose. I know I should be focusing on Gran but it's hard, I'm worrying about seeing everyone again. Or rather everyone seeing me.

I bite my lip as I cradle my phone, waiting for my lifeline to flash into action again. Just how did Cal come to mean so much to me in such a short space of time? It's a scary kind of wonderful. My phone beeps and I look at the screen.

You know people only have the power to hurt you if you give it to them.

Really? Great. He keeps coming out with all this life advice and I'm sure it's true but God, he makes it sound so easy. Like I can just decide not to care about all the vile things people have said.

You make it sound so easy!

I just about manage not to add an eye-rolling emoji.

I never said it was easy. Shame I can't be there with you for moral support.

My heart surges, a flare of warmth in response to his words. Though his presence would inevitably lead to more drama I still appreciate the thought. Is he really as okay about being linked to a disgraced reality star and her tawdry baggage as he seems?

I wish you were here too. But Flump needs his personal chef in attendance so my needs must come second! Night night xx

His reply is quick again.

Haha re my new job title.
Btw here are a couple of photos of Flump trying to hitch a ride on Maxi's blanket. Maxi was dragging it across the floor and Flump decided to jump on. Oh, and one of Pickwick with his dinosaur toy, staring up at me in that pleading, cute way he has of making you

do exactly what he wants. Hope they make you smile!
Night xx

I send back a smiling emoji and a heart emoji.

I do have a daft smile on my face in real life too. Cal is so sweet with the dogs. With the text conversation over I'm missing him already, which is just ridiculous. I want him so much it hurts. I keep getting flashes of memory accompanied by sharp erotic charges – his fingers stroking my skin, tangled in my hair, in between my legs . . . Then remembering how it felt to have him inside me, on top of me, under me . . . holding me in his arms after sex . . . The longing the memories stir in me is so visceral I can scarcely breathe.

I've never loved like this before, I didn't even know it was possible, and it's freaking me out. I'm vulnerable again, in spite of my best efforts. I'm at Cal's mercy. Maybe there is no true love, no intimacy without real vulnerability. That's how it is, and I just have to deal.

My mind turns again to my favourite of the memories, to lying in bed with Cal after sex. I would never have had him down as a cuddler but I've become addicted to those post-sex cuddles. The memories are so vivid I can practically feel Cal lying next to me in bed, our legs entwined and my soft curves curled snugly around his firmer body. The peace of those moments floods me as I recall them. Nothing bad can happen in this peaceful post-sex space. There is only Cal and I in this bubble; no one can hurt me, and I'm flooded with a deep contentment. If only I could stay there forever, never break the spell.

I can't give up Cal. I just can't.

I won't.

I stare at my old bookshelves, still piled with my childhood books, even though this room is now used as a guestroom. I don't want Cal to be relegated to just another piece of my past. I try to imagine a future without him, and . . . I can't bear it. Something inside me threatens to curl up and die if I take the no-Cal option.

I never knew it could be like this. That a wide smile could make me light up inside, whatever my mood. That love would make everything brighter, sharper, more joyful as it injected colour into my landscape. That its potential withdrawal threatens to drain the colour to grey, to dim the brightness and damp down joy.

I'm not sure that thinking this through is doing me any good. It hasn't got me anywhere. I can't be with Cal because his celebrity lifestyle comes with a price I can't bear to pay and I can't be without him either because, well, frankly I'd rather die.

In vain I struggle to find another, third option. There has to be one. There must be.

I lie awake, unable to get to sleep, staring out of the window at the sky above the neighbours' rooftops. It's nothing like the deep black of the night sky back home in rural France. If I close my eyes, I can picture the myriad stars of that night sky, both brighter and so much more plentiful than I've ever seen before. There the only constant night light source is the moon but here in the London commuter belt the sky is tinged by the faint orangey glow from lampposts and other light pollution.

Home. That's odd. I wonder at what point England stopped being 'home' for me. I know for sure that France and Les Coquelicots feel like home for me now. And Poppy and Leo feel like family, not to forget all the animals. Leo's parents, Madame and Monsieur Dubois, were so kind to me when the reporters came sniffing around last summer and they let me stay with them in their vast and scarily elegant château until it all blew over. I dare say if you grow up with it it's not intimidating but for a girl who grew up in a suburban semi in a road of identical houses it was pretty daunting. The Dubois put me at ease though and were so kind.

France is home, family and community. How can I even be considering leaving that?

So I can't leave Cal and I can't leave St Quentin . . . but . . . Being back home is bringing back the horror of last year, things I'd forgotten like Mum trying to get hot chocolate down me because I stopped eating. Seeing my parents again today helped me to see they hadn't been avoiding looking me in the eye because they were ashamed of me but because they couldn't bear to see me in so much pain. With Dad it was partly embarrassment because he couldn't deal with the sex tape, but I didn't give either of them enough credit. They were trying to deal with the situation, and with me in the best way they knew how. I shouldn't have left it a year to see them.

I wish they weren't so worried about me again, now there's all the media about being linked with Cal.

If I'd come back I would have seen Gran again, one last time.

By the time the sky outside has lightened to an orangey-grey dawn I'm no closer to reaching a firm conclusion. Except that I won't ask Cal to give up the *Sex in the Suburbs* special. I can't let his career suffer because of me.

And given that I can't bear to give him up I'll just have to cope with whatever price I have to pay for staying with him.

Yeah, right. I'll cope. Just like that.

I remember getting into my car last summer with just my handbag and an overnight bag and driving blindly with no clue where I was going except it had to be away or I was going to lose my mind. Away from everything and everyone.

On a whim I drove towards Folkestone and, at a motorway services pit stop, I booked a Eurotunnel crossing on my phone. Those first weeks, driving through the French countryside, staying at cheap hotels, I was a mess. I don't think my heart stopped pounding the whole time. I had a tightness in my chest that never went away, my emotional heart attack. The thought of the 'Disgraced Joanna Grant' being found dead in her car after fleeing the country depressed me so much, I booked into the next cheap hotel I could find.

After a while the wide open spaces of the French countryside and the anonymity of budget hotels helped me calm down. I'd go for long walks in the woods and grounds around the motorway service areas and then in my hotel room I practised all the breathing and relaxation exercises I could remember. Once I realised that here no one recognised me I managed to calm down into something resembling a normalish human being.

Maybe it will be easier this time round. After all I'll have Cal at my side. The glimmer of hope is tinged with fear of him seeing me at my emotionally messy worst.

My heart tells me that wouldn't scare Cal off . . . hopefully.

But things are different this time round. My feelings for Cal are deeper, stronger, more profound. What I felt for Aiden by comparison appears to be a hormone-induced crush. I never talked with Aiden like I talk with Cal. In fact, I don't think I ever really knew Aiden at all. He was a chameleon; he told me so many lies it became impossible to know what, if anything, was true.

I sigh and sit up in bed, wishing like crazy that Cal were here beside me and coming to the funeral with me. What I wouldn't give for a Cal cuddle right now.

I hug my knees to my chest and think of Gran. She never trusted Aiden and I wish I'd listened to her. When will it hit me that she's gone? I hate this numb nothingness. I run my eyes over my old bookshelves. Maybe I'll take my childhood books back to France so we can expand Les Coquelicots' guest library.

Then I catch sight of my box of treasures sitting on the bottom shelf and cross the room to fetch it. Going through it easily beats thinking in endless repetitive circles.

Sitting on my old childhood bed with its primrose-dotted duvet cover and duck-egg-blue eiderdown I feel like I've been transported back in time. My box of treasures is on the bed in front of me, covered with a patchwork of pretty wallpaper samples. I lift the lid and sift through the collections of flowery hair clips in tins and make-up bags filled with sparkly lip gloss to find my very first cookbook at the bottom of the bag. I got my love of cooking from Gran. I run my thumb over the cover thinking of the many times she touched this book, from when she first gave it to me to the cookery lesson she gave me in her kitchen after school, while Mum was still at work. It's like I'm hoping to still feel the touch of her hand as I stroke the cover, to connect with her in some way. How daft. I wipe away the tear that is sliding down my face.

Why did I take for granted that she would always be there? She was so active, going to keep fit classes at the village hall and always on her feet, bustling about, trying to feed someone whether they wanted to eat or not.

It was her way of showing love, cooking and feeding people. I think that rubbed off on me. For me food and love are intermingled. I suppose it's hardly surprising I fell for a chef!

On the front cover is a picture of biscuits with currants for eyes, standing up in little rows. We used to call them crumblies because the buttery shortbread would always crumble in your mouth. They were the very first thing I ever baked on my own, with Gran keeping a beady supervisory eye on me, of course. She was always very strict about clearing up as you went along. I used to love the whole ritual of washing hands and putting on the flowery apron Gran had made for me by hand to match hers. That should be in the box too. I dig to the bottom, pull it out and run my fingers over the fabric, thinking about the time she put into making it. Next in our ritual was the prepping of ingredients. There was always a sense of peace in Gran's kitchen, accompanied by the delicious aromas of freshly baked bread and cakes or a meaty casserole.

I open the book and read the inscription.

'To my darling JoJo, sous chef extraordinaire and baker in waiting. May this book bring you hours of joy.'

My eyes sting with tears again. Gran gave me my love of cooking, along with a large dose of unconditional love. It breaks my heart to think she died ashamed of me, and maybe disappointed in me for running away too. Was her love really as unconditional as I believed? I can't bear to think of her being questioned by reporters about my 'sexploits'. That was my fault. The guilt I feel won't be reasoned with even though I had no control over the situation. I'll always feel bad that she got caught up in something so . . . sordid.

I wrap my arms around my legs and hug them to my chest.

We never really talked before I left for France and now I wish so much I'd taken the time to talk to her properly. Instead we exchanged the odd pretty greetings card and said nothing of any substance at all.

Today, I have to face the mess I left behind and that knowledge weighs me down. I ran away and let my family face the press.

That's on me.

I remind myself I had to go. I wasn't coping and was just a few crying sessions away from total hysteria or a breakdown or whatever. I wanted to crawl into a deep black hole somewhere and disappear, never coming out again. I couldn't bear the slut-shaming, the trolls, the hatred, the shame, my broken heart or the betrayal of my best friend.

So, I had to run to survive but I'm always going to feel bad about the fallout.

I'm dreading the funeral. All those whispers and staring eyes . . . distracting me from saying goodbye to Gran. Making it doubly difficult to endure and detracting from the reason we're all there.

I'll just have to cope. I'll find the strength from somewhere.

Cal's words, 'No more shame', come into my mind along with the memory of his touch. Thinking of Cal gives me a much-needed boost of confidence. I can do this. Every time I'm tempted to run, I'll think of Cal's words and draw strength from him. I don't know how or if we can be together but whatever happens Cal has changed me. He's woken me up and given me a hunger to engage with life again.

I'll always be grateful to him for that.

Annabel stays by my side for the whole service, like my own personal bodyguard. My little sister, not so little any more, and so fiercely protective of me that few people approach to talk to me. Only back at the house does she relax her guard a little and I go to sit with Gran's next-door neighbour Mary. I need to talk to someone who cared about Gran far more than any stupid reality show. Mary's genuine smile lights up her face as I sit down and I relax a little.

'It's lovely to see you, love.' Mary makes extra room on the sofa for me.

'And you too. It's just all such a shock, given she wasn't ill, you know.' My voice catches a little and the tears I'd held back during the service start to slide down my cheeks.

'It's how she would've wanted it, slipping away without any fuss,' Mary says. 'She always hated fuss.'

'I know and when I think what I put her through . . . I feel really bad about it,' I admit. Mary was Gran's neighbour for fifteen years and they went to bingo together so I feel I can talk to her.

'She was proud of you, you know.' Mary pats my hand and gives me a tissue from her handbag.

Tears are streaming unchecked down my cheeks now.

'Really? Even with . . . you know, everything that happened?' My voice breaks. I see Annabel watching me from across the room, looking stricken, and I feel awful that she's worrying about me, today of all days. I am so sick of it being about me.

I don't want to be the subject of worry for anyone any more.

'Absolutely. She didn't give a fig for any of that nonsense. She was so proud of you for opening that café and she never lost faith in you.' Mary's tone is firm and no nonsense. 'When anyone said anything less than kind about you she gave them what for all right. She never stopped standing up for you. You should have seen her telling one reporter to get lost. She could be quite intimidating when she wanted to be.'

'She could, I know. Mary, thank you so much.' I manage a small smile. 'You have no idea how much I needed to hear that.'

I wipe away the tears. They are still falling but it's grief for Gran this time, not tears for myself. There's a peace creeping in I've been missing for a very long time. My relationship with Gran was precious. Her love was precious. The thought that what Aiden did might have ruined that had been tormenting me.

I smile to think of her telling reporters where to go. She would never have used bad language but would have remained dignified throughout. When she worked she was a primary school teacher and she never stopped teaching when she retired. Her teaching tone and her 'getting the class to settle down' voice were particularly effective. I saw her use them more than once on strangers she thought needed putting in their place.

I only have one more night at home because I need to get back to help with preparations for Poppy's wedding, and there's the hen weekend too. I spend the remaining time trying to convince my family I'm not broken and I'm doing okay. I don't know if I succeed and it's pretty exhausting. I also try to avoid all questions about Cal and brush off the video of me kissing him as nothing important, but I can see Mum and Dad and Annabel are afraid.

They're afraid I'm going to fall apart like last time.

I wish I could tell them that I'm afraid of that too, but it wouldn't be fair, not when I'm setting off for another country again. So we leave the important things unspoken, as usual, but all the time Cal's words, the seeds in my mind, are germinating and I'm wondering if there's a different, better way to deal with things.

It's only on the flight back to Carcassonne airport that I get the space to really process everything. Gran's defiance makes me wonder if maybe I do have it in me to be brave, to face this thing with Aiden and Sally head-on instead of hiding in the shadows. It's tempting.

Maybe I can. I think Gran would have wanted me to stand up for myself.

* * *

Parking back at the guesthouse I leave my overnight bag in the boot of the car and my heart thumps painfully in my chest, a moment of uncertainty making my stomach do the now familiar falling-lift lurch. Will Cal be as glad to see me as I am him? All the lies I've tried to tell myself about why I'm better off without him have vanished. Being without him for the past couple of days has clarified for me that I simply can't be without him. He gives my life energy and colour and I can finally believe in a future that isn't just about survival. He makes me want to live to my full potential and to love and be engaged in the world around me.

No more shame.

He gives me strength and my body craves him, states its allegiance and tells me again that it belongs to him. I've always believed sex is about connection, not possession, but now I'm having to rethink. My body says otherwise. Every cell, every atom in my body is drawn towards Cal with a magnetic pull I can't resist.

I am his. Pure and simple. As for all the rest . . . well, I'll just have to deal, or put my big girl's pants on, as Annabel would say. I'll find the courage to deal with the fallout from somewhere. I want to try to be the woman Cal believes I can be.

I find him on a bench behind the barn. He's sitting in the sun, eyes closed, but he must sense me watching him because suddenly he opens his eyes and a definite frisson passes between us. He tilts his head a little and raises an eyebrow in query. There's a gleam in his eye that tells me my big girl's pants might be about to be ripped off, albeit temporarily.

'Hi,' I say, feeling shy and inexplicably nervous. Why am I feeling jittery with Cal? I'm comfortable enough to be naked with him but still my nerve endings are doing a jig and sending messages to my brain that this is a huge deal. I close the distance between us.

'Hello, you. Everything okay?' He pulls me onto his lap, and I feel like I've come home.

'Yes, I'm okay.' I've no desire to go into everything that happened at home and anyway I'm okay now. Okay now that I'm back with Cal and back at my *real* home. I'm not sure when I made the switch from calling England home to calling France home. Or rather this particular corner of France. It's the people that make it home for me and Cal is now integral to that.

I wish I knew how long he was staying and how he feels but . . . as he would say, I need to focus on the moment. On this particularly perfect moment.

'Where's Flump?' I ask.

'He's on a long walk with Poppy, Leo and the rest of the pack,' Cal says. 'So we have a little time alone.'

'Oh, do we?' I smile but my heart is thumping away, my nerve endings super-sensitised.

He entwines the fingers of one of his hands in my hair. I can feel the tension in his grip, his barely concealed passion. Yet his lips on mine are soft, gently caressing me, his tongue slowly parting my lips. Cal's other hand is against the small of my back, pulling me against his firm body, and then I'm pressing every part of me against him, just as hungry as he is to celebrate being together again.

He must sense a shift in me, the absence of doubt from my mind, because his kisses become more passionate, claiming my mouth and then trailing along my jawline to my neck and earlobes, his teeth nipping on just the right side of pain. When his lips dip to my collarbone and down to the swell of my breasts the breath catches in my chest and I'm practically panting.

Cal's breath is ragged too as he gently strokes my breast through the layer of dress and lacy bra. After checking there is no one else around he tugs my neckline down a little to expose one lace-covered breast. He lowers his mouth and sucks my nipple hard through the sheer lace. I deliberately wore my sexiest underwear and the lace is practically see-through. From Cal's appreciative intake of breath as he traces the swell of my breasts with his fingers I know it was worth it.

I practically groan with disappointment as he pulls away and tugs me to my feet but that vanishes when he takes me into the barn and locks the door behind him.

Once inside he finds another chair and pulls me back down onto his lap, only this time I slip one leg either side of his hips so I'm straddling him, the skirt of my dress riding up my hips. I know it hasn't been long but it feels like it's been forever, and my body is delighting in reacquainting itself with Cal's, exploring joyfully, unable to believe its luck, that this amazing soul-searing joy wasn't an illusion or a one-off sensation never to be repeated. I honestly never believed it could be this good. That it could be so much more than a meeting of bodies. But there's an undeniable sense of energy mixing in the air between us, encircling us and carrying us up to dizzying heights.

Our bodies are just playing catch up to that fantastic phenomenon.

I lean forward so Cal's mouth can reach my breasts while his hands slide up beneath my skirt, cupping my sex and bottom and making me catch my breath again. My knickers are made of the same sheer lace as the matching bra so don't provide much of a barrier. If anything they increase the sensation.

I bite my lower lip, arousal pulsing between my thighs, urgent and powerful.

'I missed you.' I lean forward and kiss Cal's neck. 'I want you so much.'

'God, I missed you too,' Cal virtually growls. 'And as for wanting you I don't think you can have any doubt about that.'

He pulls one of my hands across to feel his extremely hard erection, straining against his shorts. I place my hand over it and squeeze, making Cal groan. He tugs at my knickers and I move my legs to facilitate their speedy removal. I'm so intensely aroused I honestly don't care what happens to them. When I straddle him again his fingers penetrate me and I can feel how wet I am, my arousal soaking his fingers.

I reach out for Cal's cock, desperate to have him inside me, fumbling with his fly and tugging at his trunks. Then I'm finally able to take his erection in my hands. I barely need to touch him to get him ready and within seconds I'm lowering myself down onto his cock and riding him. One of Cal's hands is beneath my bottom, the other on my opposite hip. With their grip he controls my pace and rhythm. It feels so good, so perfect to have him inside me again. As though I were made for him.

It's not just good sex. It's good everything. I'm at peace and this is coming home.

I was a fool to think staying away from him was an option, or that I could ever stop loving him.

I'll just have to find a way to cope with whatever is coming my way.

Chapter 15

'There is nothing better than a friend, unless it is a friend with chocolate'

Linda Grayson

From callum@callum'scook-off.com
To caitlino'connor85@hotmail.com
Subject: You won't believe it
Hey, how are things? You're never going to believe this but I'm actually going to be on a Sex in the Suburbs South of France special! I know, I know, after everything I said but my agent thinks it's a great opportunity, it will all help promote the French cookbook so it's time to swallow my pride. Maybe it's also penance for being so quick to judge. JoJo has got me thinking recently about a lot of things and let's just say I'm working on it . . .

And my plans for the future? I'm working on those too. Let's just say I've got a few ideas percolating . . . I'll let you know when they're brewed!

From annabelgrant@thestickybun.co.uk
To joannagrant@thestickybun.co.uk
Subject: Go for it!
I think you should go for it, JoJo. I know what I said before but if Cal wasn't on the level he wouldn't have offered to turn down the Sex in the Suburbs gig at the Château would he? He seems like a nice guy, if you can tell from the telly! He's certainly hot and I think all things considered you should give him the benefit of the doubt. That's my sisterly advice FWIW!

Hugs,
Annabel xx

When I planned Poppy's hen weekend via email with Michelle, Poppy's friend from the UK, I hadn't anticipated being eaten up with a personal dilemma. Though the distraction of the hen weekend activities is very welcome and might be just what I need. I still have absolutely no idea what the fallout has been from the video of my kissing Cal at Mirepoix market. I'm itching to look, just so I can know what's being said about me, but Cal has convinced me the way to rise above it all is to simply not look at it. Well, virtually convinced me anyway.

I'm sure there will be people out there who are sure we were deliberately putting on a show but honestly, I was so caught up in the moment, so distracted, that being watched couldn't have been further from my mind.

'Are you okay?' Poppy asks, frowning a little as we drive

into the village to pick up Sophie on the way to Carcassonne airport where we'll be meeting Michelle.

'Yes, I'm fine.' I put on a bright smile and try to stay focused on the details.

Flump, Peanut, Treacle and Pickwick are also in the car, completely overexcited, picking up on the unusual activity at home. The guesthouse is empty, ready for Michelle and other guests who are staying for the wedding.

There will only be four hens for this stage of the proceedings as Sarah, Leo's old veterinary practice partner in Paris, can't fly out until tomorrow and Angeline is needed at the veterinary clinic in St Quentin today.

'Are you sure that you are okay to do this so soon after your gran's funeral?' Poppy asks me for the second time this morning.

'Of course. It's all right, Poppy. I've just got a few things on my mind.'

Like how to wipe the floor with my ex-boyfriend and ex-best friend, how to do it while taking the moral high ground, getting closure and making a new statement to the world about who I am. All while ignoring the temptation to scour the internet for every new mention or bad picture of me.

Cal says I have to change the narrative, that I need to refuse to let anyone else label me. That it's up to me how I define myself. Action and not reaction. That's the idea anyway. I know in my gut it's the right thing to do. My self-preservation instinct told me to run away last year and

I think, given the fragile emotional state I was in, that it was the right thing to do. Yet something about not fighting back with every atom of my being meant the darkness ended up being turned inwards. I have a feeling standing up for myself now, while utterly terrifying, will be ultimately far less depressing.

I haven't told Poppy yet about Cal's idea that I use the *Sex in the Suburbs* Château dinner to do all of that. It's so close to the wedding I think she might really freak out if she adds worrying about me to her already extensive list.

It might be impossible to keep quiet though. Maybe I'll tell her and Sophie this weekend. It might depend on how many cocktails are consumed.

Once we've picked up Sophie, I let her take over the conversation with Poppy. It gives me space to mull things over. By the time we've picked up Michelle from Carcassonne I'm satisfied that Poppy is no longer suspicious and fretting over my odd mood. She's far too busy catching up with Michelle.

We then head to Castelnaudry where we're hiring a boat for a chilled-out afternoon on the Canal du Midi. That's the plan anyway.

At first everything goes as planned. The dogs are all on leads so they can't go for impromptu swims. Sophie seems to know what she's doing with the boat so that means I can relax, at least for a bit.

We have prosecco which we mix with crême de cassis to make Kir Royales. We'll have proper Kir Royales with champagne later on and plenty of cocktails tomorrow. I'm being stingy with the alcohol, aware that booze and boats aren't a good mix, plus I need to drive home. Poppy is convinced that something disastrous is going to happen during the hen weekend or when the stags go off hiking and camping in the Pyrenees tomorrow.

It is true that things often tend to happen around her. The psychotic goat incident is legendary in the village and the time the marauding donkeys tried to wreck the village inspection day last year springs to mind. I plan to show her that being really organised means we can avoid unnecessary drama.

There's not a cloud in the sky and it's a shade of blue I'm not sure I've ever seen back in England. Light dances on the still surface of the water and a gentle breeze ruffles the silvery green boughs of the willows on the towpath. I watch the people we pass on the towpath and the other boats and wonder what problems they are dealing with, beneath the calm surface. If there's one thing I've learnt it's that beneath the surface we all have our hidden depths.

'How are things with you, JoJo?' Michelle is having a Flump cuddle. He has the softest fur and absolutely loves being cuddled. He is snuggling his head into her chest asking for more scratches. 'This is one super cute puppy you have here.'

'Isn't he just?' I beam.

I know I've caught the dog parent bug big time and I'm as dotty about and doting on Flump as Poppy is with her dogs. I still love her rescue mutts, especially Pickwick, but the bond that Flump and I have is something truly special.

'And how is your love life?' Michelle's tone is a bit too casual.

'Poppy's already told you all the gory details, hasn't she?' I roll my eyes.

'She has told me also,' Sophie calls across. 'But we also saw the kiss, you know, on the internet.'

Poppy's face blooms a pretty pink.

'Sorry, JoJo, I'm just so happy for you. Cal is a lovely guy and I'm thrilled for both of you. You know Sophie and Michelle would never talk to the press, don't you?'

She bites her lip, anxiety plain in her expression.

'It's fine,' I say, because it's her hen weekend and I know she honestly didn't mean any harm by it.

'That was some kiss. Is he really as hot in the flesh as he seems on the telly?' Michelle hands me back Flump because he's wriggling to see the ducks in the water.

We've seen the odd jogger and a few dog walkers along the towpath, which has got our canine crew excited, but mostly it's peaceful. I feel like I can finally take a breath.

'*Absolument*.' Sophie replies, an emphatic 'absolutely', at the same time as Poppy says, 'God, yes.'

Yes, my boyfriend is sinfully sexy. Is he actually my boyfriend though? I wish I knew for sure that this isn't just a casual fuckbuddy thing or a summer romance that's just convenient before he goes back to England. What if

I'm reading too much into our relationship? I hate that I have become this person.

'JoJo?' Michelle says my name with an air of expectancy. I've clearly missed part of the conversation.

'I think she's day dreaming about Cal,' Poppy teases me.

'Sort of.' I feel heat creeping up my neck in spite of the gentle breeze keeping it from being too hot today. I take another sip of my drink. I love the rich blackcurrant taste of the cassis combined with the bubbles. Poppy is the one who got me into drinking this and now Kir Royale is my favourite drink.

'What's up?' Michelle's frank gaze unnerves me. I'd forgotten how direct she is. When she visited last summer, I was staying with Poppy incognito, hiding in St Quentin. It was Michelle who broke the news of my identity to a clueless Poppy.

Actually, Michelle is someone whose advice I would appreciate, given she gets how the celebrity world works a bit better than Poppy. Maybe now would be a better time to talk to them than tomorrow when Sarah and Angeline are with us. I've nothing against those two; I just don't know them as well.

'I think we're at that stage where you don't really know where you stand, you know?' I say. 'Even if I know how I feel, how do I know that the label I'm applying to the relationship is the same as Cal's label? Are we friends with benefits, or a summer romance that will end when Cal goes back the UK? Or are we boyfriend and girlfriend?

And then there's the question of whether we are exclusive or not . . .'

'Hey, take a breath,' Michelle says. 'A nice deep breath.'

I do as she says, and I feel a little better.

'I can't know whether his label matches with my label unless I ask him and I just . . . can't do that.' I take another deep breath 'He still hasn't said the L word, well, except in the bedroom and that doesn't really count, does it? As far as I know this is just a summer fling for him and he won't look back when he heads back to London in the autumn.'

'Ahh, okay. So that's it.' Michelle seems satisfied that we've got to the bottom of it.

I know I'm sounding overwhelmingly insecure and vulnerable. I don't like the sensation but it's too late, I'm there now . . . The words are out there.

'Yes, that's it. I'm in love and I'm afraid to be the one who says, 'I love you' first just in case I'm being delusional.' I attempt a smile, but it slips. 'I know it's pathetic but after Aiden I don't feel like I can trust my judgement, not totally. I mean maybe he is just in lust with me?'

I deftly scoop Flump up and stop him from leaning too far over the edge of the boat.

'No way,' Poppy protests. 'Absolutely no way. I've seen the way he looks at you. It's easy to solve, just tell him you love him, get it out there.'

Easy? Ha ha.

'There is something else, it's sort of related . . . well, it could be . . . *Sex in the Suburbs* is coming to Carcassonne. They've rented a château for a summer special.'

I tell them all about the plans for Cal to cook for them, his cookbook deal and his suggestion that I use this opportunity to confront Aiden and Sally on my terms.

'You're not going to, are you?' Poppy's eyes widen anxiously, just as I predicted. I really shouldn't have said anything.

I feel a twinge of guilt. This is supposed to be a special fun day out for Poppy.

'It'll be fine, honestly, don't worry,' I reassure her. 'I am not going to go off the rails, not when we've got the final prep to do for your wedding day. I'm not going to let you down.'

'That isn't what I'm worried about.' Poppy stares down at her glass.

'So, are you worried about Cal's motives?' Michelle asks, fixing a shrewd gaze on me.

I knew that Michelle would get that aspect of it in a way that Poppy can't because she always sees the best in people. Michelle reads the gossip magazines and the celebrity news online. She would be aware of the benefits of extra publicity for Cal, especially with the whole Aiden–Sally saga potentially reigniting. I know Cal well enough to know that this isn't necessarily the kind of publicity he would choose but . . . well, publicity is publicity and his agent obviously thinks it's a good idea.

'I don't know.' I shrug helplessly.

'I'm sure that his motives are only to look out for you, JoJo.' Poppy frowns. As predicted she always sees the best in people, which is a nice quality but . . .

'Do you trust him?' Michelle asks.

'I think I do,' I say. 'I'm just second-guessing myself.'

'So, what does your gut instinct, your intuition tell you?' Michelle asks. 'Your head says you could be being manipulated and you need to be careful but your heart says . . .'

I consider for a minute and try to get in touch with my gut instinct, or what she means by my heart. The same gut instinct that had its reservations about Aiden, but I was too dazzled to listen to it. I don't want to make the mistake of ignoring it again.

I consider for a minute.

'It says to trust him and to go with it,' I say, relaxing properly for the first time today.

It's at that moment I hear a splash and realise that Flump's lead is no longer in my hand.

Ten exhausting and very scary minutes later Flump and I are both back on the boat, soaking wet, dripping puddles onto the deck.

Thankfully I thought to hand Poppy my phone before I dived in.

I pat at my shorts pocket and suddenly realise. The car key isn't in it. My car key is in the canal. Oh, fuckity fuck . . .

I agree to half a glass of Kir Royale in the end as it doesn't seem very likely I'll be driving any time soon.

It's Cal who comes to pick us up because both Leo and Angeline are needed in surgery.

He raises an eyebrow when he sees me.

'So you're the reason I'm bringing towels?' He gets one out of the car and wraps one around me, wrapping me up in his arms at the same time. He kisses my neck and then presses his lips to my ear. 'You need to be careful when I'm not around to protect you.'

I suppose I should be glad there's no one around filming this. Michelle is watching though and gives me a discreet thumbs-up signal once his back is turned. He hands me another towel to wrap up Flump.

I know it's hopeless. The car is going to smell of wet dog and canal for days.

'I couldn't find your spare car key. I'm sorry,' Cal apologises.

'Really?' I groan. 'It looks like I'm going to be up late looking for it tonight then. We'll have to come back and get the car in the morning.'

Flump and I both sit on towels all the way back to the guesthouse. At least the others seem to be having a good time. I am . . . disturbed would be the right word, I suppose. How could I be so caught up in thinking about Cal that I stopped paying attention to Flump? I know how quickly he can get into trouble and I feel wretched. To be fair he is extremely quick and also possesses Houdini-like escape skills but even so . . . It frightens me to be so consumed by a man.

Cal's sway over me is potent and mesmerising. I don't want to pull away, I'm not sure that I could. If I did then the firm cord between us would just tug me straight back onto his lap where I would inevitably end up kissing him. He really is the best kisser. How often do you find that – a man who kisses perfectly?

I want to be there and yet I am still afraid . . . of the depth of my love for him and the awful potential to be catastrophically hurt.

Cal follows me into my bathroom where he helps me undress. I know he is dying to make a joke about the fact he is getting me out of my wet clothes but the energy between us feels too serious for jokes. It's both intense and intimate.

Flump is outside drying off in the sunshine underneath the watchful eyes of Poppy so I can relax.

Cal strips off too and turns on the shower, stepping into it with me. I lean back against him with a sigh and he massages my neck and shoulders. Then he puts shower gel onto his hands, soaps them up and runs them down over my collarbone to my breasts. He soaps and fondles them, squeezing my nipples in a way he knows always makes me moan.

I lean back against him with a satisfied sigh, feeling his growing erection pressing against my buttocks. His hands massage my tummy and then travel down between my legs. He nudges my legs apart with his knee and stands between my thighs, bending a little as he slides his hard cock along the length of my slit to my very wet entrance. Then he straightens up and enters me in one hard thrust.

It takes my breath away but in a good way. I press my hands and face up against the tiles, warm water coursing down over my body as Cal fucks every last bit of stress out of me. It's a delicious quickie.

Cal is delicious, addictive and infinitely moreish.

I am in trouble.

The next day involves a lie-in, which makes a nice change, and then we have a nice afternoon on a chocolate and wine tasting tour in Carcassonne, followed by dinner and cocktails at the Hotel de la Cité. At least things go to plan: no one gets wet and the worst that happens is a slightly twisted ankle for Sarah, a casualty of wearing high heels on cobbled streets. Poppy enjoys the chocolate tasting at artisanal chocolate shops. As she's not so keen on wine we wanted to find something a bit different for her to do. I actually manage to forget all about my dilemma and Aiden coming to the area, and stop angsting for a bit.

I miss Cal when we get back to the guesthouse though. He's off with the other stags, hiking and camping, and my bed feels really empty without him. When Poppy suggested driving up into the mountains on early Sunday morning to surprise the boys I readily agree. Partly because I always love walking in the Pyrenees but mostly because I miss Cal. It's ridiculous. He's only been out of cell reception for about twenty-four hours but I'm already getting withdrawal symptoms.

Ridiculous or not, it's true.

Sophie says she wants a lie-in, and Angeline has to be on call for emergencies as Leo is out of mobile range, but Sarah says her ankle is fine and she and Michelle are both keen to make the trip up into the Pyrenees.

Poppy offers to drive today and I'm happy to accept. After the all too brief alcohol- and chocolate-induced respite, my mind is full of the coming week . . . My stomach churns at the thought of seeing Aiden and Sally again. I can't believe I ever thought Sally was my friend. Anyone who has experienced it will know that getting your heart broken at the same time as you lose your best friend is like getting it broken twice over. To say it feels like a double bereavement isn't that extreme.

I've been tasked with map reading as our destination isn't an address the car satnav can help us with. I glance over at Poppy. She is nothing like Sally and I know without a doubt that she would never betray me. She just couldn't. It's not in her DNA. I think trusting again, loving again, being open to connect with people instead of hiding away forever has to be the best way forward for me. If I want to be happy, that is.

If I want to live, not just survive.

What good is safe if safe is miserable? It's not actually living. It's ticking the days off in the calendar until death, sighing with relief with every tick, grateful that nothing terrible happened that day.

That way of living isn't for me any more. I like connecting with people. I am affectionate and loving. Suppressing that would only end up suffocating me.

As for the second love of my life, Flump is strapped in with the other dogs, totally overexcited again, not daunted by his dunking on Friday. Today I brought my jogging lead with me so that means he'll be attached to my waist with a long zero-shock lead at all times. I am not taking any chances today.

'We need to head south towards Andorra,' I tell Poppy. 'The hot springs they're camping at are near the village of Mérens-les-Vals.'

Obviously, I have been to the baths at Ax-les-Thermes with Poppy but I hadn't realised there were natural hot springs in the area where you could bathe for free. It makes sense, I suppose, that there would be plenty of hot springs that have not been developed because they're in inaccessible places. Inaccessible for anyone except hikers, that is.

We park in the lower part of Nabre valley. The walk up to where are the boys are camping is challenging for Michelle, who admits that she is out of shape. Sarah is a gym bunny and has strapped her ankle so she's fine. Poppy might loathe jogging and has never understood why I love to run but she does however do a lot of hill walking and yoga so she's quite fit. She's also been here with Leo before and recognises the path once we get onto it.

We hear them before we see them. There is the sound of splashing and conversation. Pickwick lets out a little woof but we manage to keep the other dogs quiet and held back and we are hidden by the trees and rocks as we approach. At least Pickwick's woof sounds a lot more like pigeon than dog. Poppy is in the lead and she stops suddenly, her face going pink.

'Maybe we shouldn't surprise them,' she whispers.

'Why not?' asks Michelle, leaning forward to see round her. 'Oh, I see . . .'

Then of course Sarah and I have to push forward to see what they're talking about.

The men are all naked and their clothes are lying on a nearby rock. I have accidentally seen Leo naked once, due to a dodgy bathroom lock, and obviously I've seen Cal but the other two I've only ever seen fully clothed. I can't help leaning forward to get a better look. It's so wrong but really . . .

I'm not the only one looking and despite Poppy's initial suggestion not one of us suggests actually turning back.

'I have an idea.' Sarah's face lights up, her eyes bright with mischievous gleam. 'Let's steal their clothes!'

I smile and look at Poppy. 'What do you think? I mean a naked groom is traditional on an English stag do . . .'

'Let's do it,' she agrees with a hint of wickedness in her smile. There is definitely a bad girl inside the good girl, and I can't resist encouraging it out whenever I get a chance.

Michelle and Sarah nip forwards to take the clothes while Poppy and I hide behind the rocks with the dogs. Once the clothes are safely hidden, we arrive, making a lot of noise as we approach the hot spring pools. There is a moment of confusion as they see us, try to cover themselves and look around for their absent clothes.

Leo rolls his eyes good-naturedly and stays seated. Cal however stands up and walks towards me, not seeming at all embarrassed at being naked and making no attempt to cover himself up.

Figures. But then it's not like he has anything to be embarrassed about.

He unclips Flump's lead from my waist and hands it to Poppy. Then he scoops me up in his arms and takes me towards the pool with him. I'm still fully clothed.

'Cal . . .' I try to protest.

'Stop struggling or I'll strip you naked first,' he says sternly.

I believe him as well. He's quite capable of carrying out his threat.

'My phone and my keys . . .' I can't believe I'm going to get unintentionally wet for the second time in one weekend.

Cal frees one hand and finds my phone and keys which he then drops onto a clump of grass before stepping into the hot springs pool with me. I'm only wearing shorts and a low-cut white t-shirt which instantly reveals my lacy bra once wet. He lowers himself down so I'm sitting sideways on his lap.

'I'll punish you properly later, when we are alone,' he whispers in my ear as one of his hands massages my bottom.

I can feel his growing erection beneath me and have to admit his words are making me wet in a way that has nothing to do with the water. My nerve endings tingle where he touches me. I suspect his method of 'punishing' me will involve teasing me until I'm begging him to make me come, so I'm not too worried. I wriggle on his lap, pretending to be innocent of the effect it is having on him and unconcerned by the dire threats of extra punishment he's whispering in my ear.

Poppy has caved and fetched the men's clothes but Cal has to wait until the others have moved off before he can get out of the water because of my not so innocent wriggling.

'Oh, you are definitely going to be punished later,' he says. 'First for the clothes and also for making me so hard when I can't do anything about it.'

'I missed you again,' I whisper into Cal's ear and he pulls me in tighter. There is a pause and I'm afraid I'm being too full on. Should I have stayed away and let him have his time alone with the stags?

'I missed you too,' he replies and gives me a sharp nip on my ear lobe with his teeth that makes me squirm again.

I sigh in relief. I hope this anxiety will pass. It's exhausting. It's a stressful week though, what with *Sex in the Suburbs* coming next week, and getting everything ready for the wedding next weekend.

Once he has dried off and changed, I take his hand. I have dried as best I can. I refused his offer to strip me and dry me properly because I'm already as turned on as he is and it's a bit too public here. I'll just have to dry in the sun and be glad my shorts aren't see-through too. At least

I'm wearing one of my good bras. I suppose it's no worse than me wearing a bikini.

At least that's what I tell myself when we join the others and I catch one of the guys staring at my chest. He looks away quickly though, when Cal glares at him.

We join the men at their camp for a breakfast of bacon and sausage rolls cooked on the metal barbecue trays out in the open air. The dogs do quite well out of the meal. I think Cal's last roll was mostly bread by the time Flump was done with him. Flump is admittedly very good at begging. He sits quietly looking soulful and hungry and if that doesn't work, he tries a gentle paw tap and tilt of the head. I have to admire his technique.

Once everyone has eaten, both girls and small dogs head back home and leave the stags in peace for the rest of the day. Michelle walks next to me on the way back to the car.

'I don't think you have anything to worry about,' she says. 'He seems nuts about you.'

'What if it's just a sex thing?' I bite my lip anxiously.

'Then enjoy it, see if it turns into something else. But if not, well . . . enjoy it anyway, I say. You're bloody lucky!'

But wearing one of the good ones I suppose it's no worse than me wearing a hat.

At least that's what I tell myself when [illegible] and I catch one of the dogs sniffing at my chest. He looks away quickly, as if [illegible].

We join the [illegible] at their [illegible] for a [illegible] of bacon and sausage [illegible] cooked for the [illegible] of the [illegible]. [illegible] one of the [illegible] Cal [illegible] last [illegible] was mostly [illegible]. By the time [illegible] was done with [illegible] Thump [illegible] at [illegible] a [illegible] and [illegible] the [illegible] and [illegible] of the head [illegible] its tongue.

[illegible] we [illegible] have eaten [illegible] and [illegible] back home and [illegible] the [illegible] for the rest of the day. [illegible] on the way back to the [illegible].

'I don't think you have anything to worry about,' she says. '[illegible] about you.'

'What? [illegible] a few [illegible]?' [illegible] my [illegible].

'[illegible] [illegible] something else [illegible] not [illegible] I saw [illegible] like a [illegible].'

Chapter 16

'You have to stop crying, and you have to go kick some ass'

Lady Gaga

The plate slips from my fingers and smashes on the old flagstone floor.

I'm on the floor clearing up the pieces when Poppy enters the kitchen.

'Are you okay?'

'Just got things on my mind . . .' I say. 'Seeing Aiden and Sally again tomorrow, you know?'

'Have you got cold feet?' she asks.

'Distinctly chilly,' I reply. 'But I'm still going into the water. Rather an appropriate analogy given my dunkings last weekend.'

'You think you've got problems. I accidentally sent a sexy text to my mother instead of Leo.' Poppy grimaces.

'Seriously? How did you manage that?'

'Sleep-deprived,' she replies shortly. 'I've got a lot on my mind. Mum is kicking up all sorts of fuss that I am not accommodating all of our relations. Actually, she's just kicking up a fuss full stop. Although she has gone distinctly quiet since I sent her the sex text, so you know, silver linings and all that.'

I burst out laughing and Poppy joins in. She scoops down to pick up a shard of plate that I missed. There is a distinct tinge of hysteria to our laughter.

'Are you really sure you want to do this thing with Aiden?' she asks, once we've stopped laughing. 'You could pull out.'

I pause and give her question due consideration.

'I don't want to do it. I *need* to do it,' I say firmly, realising it's true. 'What's the alternative? Do I seethe in silence for the rest of my life? Let my official label every time I am mentioned in conjunction with Cal be "disgraced Joanna Grant"? No way.'

'You want to choose your own label and tear up your old one. You know, that might give me an idea,' Poppy says thoughtfully. 'It's very brave of you.'

'Hmmm.' I don't reply properly. I'm really not feeling all that brave today.

'We should do a social media campaign.' Poppy's eyes light up.

'Erm, what now?' I can't help the concern creeping into my voice. I haven't been on social media since shortly after my life imploded so publicly for all of the social media world to comment on. I've been resisting checking to see what people are saying about me and Cal.

'We'll call it #rewritethelabel or #rewritingthelabel.' Poppy touches my arm. 'It'll be brilliant. I've got a great idea for a short video clip. You can rip up a card sign in front of you saying "disgraced reality TV star" and then hold up a different one saying, well . . . whatever you want it to. I've got it. You should say "real life star". Because you are to me. You've been a total star the whole time you've been here. The kind of star that really matters.'

I give her a hug, my eyes pricking with unexpected tears.

'It's a great idea. I'm just not sure I can do the whole social media thing again.'

'You post once, on the evening of the event, which is what, tomorrow? We will tag the *Sex in the Suburbs* people and then you can bow out. We can do it straight after you get back from the Château and then I can repost everything for you when the *South of France* special is aired on TV. In fact, I can do all of the posting for you if you give me your passwords.'

'You would do that for me?' I ask. 'But you're so busy with your wedding.'

'Nonsense, look at how much you're doing for me. Of course I can find time. If you trust me with your passwords, that is.'

'Without a single doubt.' I hug her again, my feet now not feeling quite so cold as they did earlier. I'm fairly sure that life without trust would be pretty cold. There's such a thing as too much caution.

That evening, after we've cleared away the dinner dishes, I change into a dress and make sure I look presentable. I change out of my first choice when Michelle and Poppy veto it and insist I show a bit of cleavage, saying it's important I look fabulous so I can stick two fingers up to Aiden, but in a dignified, moral-high-ground kind of way.

Right . . . Okay. Dignified but desirable. I can do that. I swallow hard.

'Are you ready to do this?' Poppy asks, holding up her phone so she can film me.

'Okay, I'm ready.'

I take a deep breath and hold the card in front of my chest that reads DISGRACED REALITY STAR. I tear it up and let it fall to the ground to display a second card behind it that reads RESPECTED REAL-LIFE STAR. I don't even have to remember to smile because tearing up my former 'label' feels really good, very therapeutic.

'Okay, that looks good. Here, have a look.' Poppy studies her phone for a minute then passes it to me to watch the clip. 'Do you know what you want to say? Do we have any text? Not that you need to say much, I think the images are powerful enough. So we've got the video and we've also got the two photos of you holding each card so we can do a two-picture collage separate to the video. You could put a cross in the corner of the first photo or a line through it or something.'

I appreciate Poppy's creative vision. I'm not sure I would have thought this up on my own.

'I've already got what I want to say written. It's short but powerful, I hope. Here, I'll send it to you in a text so you can copy and paste it into the posts. Let's see if anyone on social media is interested.'

'Are you kidding?' Michelle laughs. 'They will eat this up. You look fabulous and whoever's in charge of social media for the show will make sure it gets traction. The best thing is that it's got a powerful message too. Wouldn't it be great if we could get "rewriting the label" trending?'

'It would be wonderful,' I admit. 'Not worth going through everything I've been through, but amazing nonetheless.'

I don't sleep very well, in spite of Cal's comforting presence in my bed. I'm feeling too sick to eat when I go down to the kitchen, so I get a bottle of water to take out to the garden. We've still got a little while before we leave, and saying I need to calm down would be an understatement. I'm so tense it feels like my jaws are glued together and my shoulders are up by my ears. I grab one of the yoga mats we keep for guests and head for the terrace.

After a few sun salutations and breathing exercises I'm feeling much better. Ideally, I prefer to go for a run to get rid of nervous energy but it's a hot day already. The last thing I want is to get all hot and sweaty and I've actually got quite fond of yoga since Poppy has been teaching me. It's calming and balancing in some way I can't ascribe purely to the physical exercises.

I'm in the down dog position and frantically running through the moral-high-ground script I've been rehearsing for Aiden and Sally. I do know it's not in the spirit of yoga but I'm only human. I really don't want to mess up today. Then I hear Cal's voice from behind the hedge.

'No, Vanessa, I told you I'm not prepared to use JoJo like that.' Cal sounds irritated. I imagine him running his hands through his messy hair like he always does when he's exasperated.

Vanessa, Vanessa . . . Is that his agent? Using me like what? My mind boggles and my pose wobbles a little as my attention meanders. I try to work out what Vanessa is saying at the other end of the conversation.

'I don't care if it will get more book pre-orders. Joanna has been through enough. I'm not asking her to do a joint interview with me.' There's steel in his tone. 'You persuaded me this would be a great idea and I've agreed to do it but that's as far as it goes. My relationship with JoJo isn't entertainment. It's real. Not reality.'

Real. Warmth creeps through my body. Warmth to do with feeling loved and protected. Warmth that joins with my growing excitement at finally shedding the weight of shame that has been dragging me under for too long.

It feels like when I'm with Cal I rise to the surface. I am more me when I'm with him.

I knew I was right to trust Cal. I knew it deep down but still it's oh so nice to have it confirmed.

I hear Cal end his call and his footsteps approaching

so I quickly resume my pose, pretending to be in a deep meditation state and therefore utterly incapable of eaves-dropping.

'Well, that's a sight for sore eyes.' Cal's tone is warmer now.

I jump when he places a hand on the back of my thigh and slides it up to my rear.

'Hey, I was trying to relax,' I protest a little feebly because the usual reaction has kicked in with his touch. In other words, my insides feel like molten chocolat chaud whenever he touches me.

Every single time.

'I'm trying to de-stress before we leave,' I say but there's no conviction in my voice. Cal has me and he knows it.

'I could help you with that.' His fingers brush the waist-band of my yoga pants and the strip of exposed bare flesh where my T-shirt has ridden up.

With a sharp intake of breath, I lose my pose and slide down onto the mat.

'I suppose I could be persuaded.' I meet Cal's gaze. 'I need time after to do a proper job of my make-up and hair.'

Living in rural southern France I've let my standards fall and my regime usually involves putting my hair up in a ponytail and using a good moisturiser. Maybe a slick of lip gloss if I'm going somewhere I might be recognised. The thought of putting foundation and powder on is a little like putting armour on. At the very least it will boost my confidence.

'You're gorgeous, you've got nothing to worry about.'

Nothing to worry about? I love his confident assertion. As far as I can see I've got everything to worry about but there are better things to do with our time than argue.

'I'll feel better arriving made up.' I shrug and take Cal's hand.

In the privacy of my room he takes control, stripping me of my clothing piece by piece and then laying me down on his bed. I keep my gaze fixed on his oh so familiar piercing blue eyes. The sensations he's stirring as he tenderly strokes me are doing a very good job of distracting me, particularly when his hands skim my breasts and between my legs.

'Remember what I said.' Cal nuzzles my neck and nips at my earlobe. 'You have absolutely nothing to be ashamed of.'

His fingers are inside me now and warmth spreads through me, not just from the sexual contact but another kind of warmth to do with not feeling so alone any more, to do with feeling loved. Whether he says the L word or not really shouldn't matter given Cal shows me love on a daily basis.

I've felt alone for so long, in spite of Poppy's kindness, that the emotion almost overwhelms me. It is so very lovely to know that someone properly sees me, likes what they see and wants to be there for me. Cal's touch is tender, gentle and sensuous.

'You're lovely, JoJo, and you're not disgraced. Promise me

you'll remember that today.' He props himself up and his intense gaze rakes me as though searching for any lingering doubts to be captured and dealt with.

'Okay, I promise,' I say obediently, half automatically but as the words leave my lips it strikes me that I really do believe him now, finally. It's taken some time but eventually I got there.

There's a peaceful, contented joy radiating through my body as Cal makes love to me, also a sense of being whole again, of being wholly myself at long last. The joy isn't Cal completing me but Cal helping me to find the missing part of myself. Cal waking me up to remember who I am, to wake from my stupor, step out of the shadows and live again. Because one thing he's taught me is that living isn't just about breathing, just about surviving from day to day, but about embracing life fully and being fully alive. Otherwise what's the point?

It's definitely time to stop hiding.

And if I'm seeing Aiden again it's not going to hurt that I've got a post-orgasmic glow to my cheeks. I might be ready to move on but I'm also happy to show Aiden what he's missing.

Thankfully the combination of the tan I've acquired living in the South of France for the past year and the post-sex glow means I don't actually need too much make-up to feel confident I'm looking my best. My hair is blonder and what with running, yoga and the outdoor lifestyle I'm in better shape than ever. The shortish plum-coloured summer dress, one I would never have dared wear before Cal, shows all this off to best advantage. I'm glad now that Poppy persuaded me into a shopping trip with Michelle.

'You look amazing.' Cal grins, putting his arms around my waist and nuzzling my neck. 'Are you ready to show the world you're not hiding any more and there's absolutely no reason in the world why you should be?'

'Yes, let's go.' I nod. I think that was a rhetorical question. Cal seems quite fond of them. It's just one of the quirks that I love about him, like his interest in science and his zest for life in general. There are no half measures with him. 'I want to get this over with.'

My stomach muscles clench and its sparse contents feel like they're on a washing machine spin cycle. I'm glad I've not had much to eat now. I feel sick at the thought of being filmed. Cal has persuaded me it's for the best, that I need to show the world at large that the image they have of me and the labels they've assigned me are wrong. Not because the opinions of faceless strangers actually matter but because it matters to me that the world sees there's more to me than my assigned storyline. I have to show them who I really am, that I'm more than those stories they printed. To show the world my story didn't end in tears and scandal; that was just a black moment, only one part of the story, and one I've overcome.

This isn't just about Aiden and Sally. I've been hurt by many more people than just the two of them. The others who hurt me are, for the most part, nameless and faceless. They don't know me, they just think they do. Some of them are trolls but not all; some are just mostly decent people who enjoyed the show and the drama that continued off screen. When they commented on social media and the show's fan website they forgot I was a girl just like them, with real feelings and a heart that could be broken. The majority of them would never have said the things to me face to face that they were happy to type from the anonymity of their own homes. They didn't have to look me in the eye and see my pain or see the impact on my family.

They never knew me.

They never knew the facts.

Yet they considered themselves entitled to sit in judgement over me.

Cal is right, I know. This way I get to write my own storyline, to change the outcome from tragedy to triumph, a tribute to girl power everywhere.

I want to do this for all those other women and girls whose stories I read online, who were filmed without their consent or filmed and photographed with consent on the assumption it would remain private. I'm doing this in memory of those who tragically took their lives and for those who are still living with it and feeling alone and ashamed. I want them to know that they aren't alone. Strength in numbers maybe?

The seeds of ideas he planted in my subconscious have definitely taken root and are flourishing.

The thought that I'm doing this for those other women, the ones who never got to fight back, gives me the strength I need. It stiffens my spine and makes me eager to go tell Aiden just what sort of worm he really is. Ahem, I mean take the moral high ground and look poised and elegant, of course. Any name-calling must be in my head only.

'Thanks, Cal.' I squeeze his hand and turn and look into his piercing blue eyes. I swear I see his belief in me, see his . . . love. Yes, I am looking into his soul and what I see sends a frisson of pure pleasure travelling through my body like a wave.

It hasn't always been comfortable, this fierce connection between us. He stripped me bare emotionally and saw straight through my defences. Most of all he made me face the truth. Where would I be if he hadn't woken me up? Hadn't made me face everything I ran from?

I really don't know if I believe in fate, but I know I needed him and he came. This isn't me being delusional. This is human interaction at its most raw and sexual love at its most powerfully vulnerable. I know what I get from our relationship but I'm still not sure what I do for him. Have I shown him a taste of what life could be outside of the celebrity world? Or is it that he likes fixing people and once I'm fixed he'll move on?

Maybe he just loves me for me, loves the depth of our connection.

Maybe.

'You're welcome.' He squeezes my hand back, his firm grip reassuring me.

My phone beeps with a text from Annabel.

Go and give them Hell JoJo. I suppose a bitch slap is out of the question? I would soooo love to see that :-)

I laugh and text my reply:

Definitely out of the question, however tempting it might be. Moral high ground remember? I'm going for cool, calm and collected! xx

A reply pings back almost instantly;

Good luck with that ;-) A xx
P.S. A bitch slap would be much more fun!

The drive to the Château is a tense one. Normally I'd be captivated by the endless fields of sunflowers and pretty villages, but I can't stop fidgeting. Thankfully Cal is driving.

'So they definitely are expecting me to arrive with you?' I ask him as we get close.

'For the third time, yes, they are definitely expecting us both. It's fine, JoJo. It's all going to be fine.'

'Sorry.' My fingers are knotted together in my lap and he reaches out and puts a hand on top of them, lightly squeezing.

'Take a deep breath or five.'

I take his advice and do more yoga square breathing, feeling a little better afterwards.

'Just remember to breathe when you're there,' he reminds me.

'Good advice. Breathe.' I roll my eyes. 'Got any more?'

He ignores the snark in my tone and answers seriously. 'Yes, keep the moral high ground. No matter how much they try to provoke you or get you off of whatever script you've decided you want to keep to today.'

'So they really think I've come to play nice and make up, because I want another fifteen minutes of fame?'

'That's pretty much the gist. They were definitely happy you were coming today.'

'I don't know how they believe that so readily. Do they not know me at all?'

'I think they can't compute the idea of somebody not wanting to be famous. After all it's the business they're in, the business of being famous. Being famous for what, though, I don't know. Isn't Aiden famous for being a dick?'

'At least you are famous for your cooking,' I say. 'You have an actual skill, that's completely different from the kind of thing you're talking about.'

'I thought I was famous for my dazzling good looks and my Irish charm.' Cal flashes me a grin.

'Get over yourself.' I roll my eyes. 'Well, okay, maybe a bit.'

Cal snorts with laughter.

'So, are you looking forward to today?' I deliberately change the subject.

'To teaching blonde bimbos how to cook?' He pulls a face. 'Can't wait.'

'Hey, enough with the blonde-bashing.'

'I don't mean you, obviously.'

'Hmm.' I stare out of the window and get a glimpse of the Château *Sex in the Suburbs* have rented for the next week.

My stomach churns and I try to ignore it; instead I run through the strategy I prepared with Poppy in my head. I need to remember that I have done nothing wrong. If anyone has anything to be ashamed of it's them.

The Château is elegantly traditional with lots of turrets and, unlike Château St Quentin, has been renovated to an incredible degree to make it into a chic boutique hotel. I think I prefer the aged feel of Château St Quentin; it feels more honest, more authentic somehow. This place is just a bit too perfect, too showy. Maybe a bit like a Disney princess castle. I'm sure that Sally feels quite at home. I try to rein in my inner bitch. I hate the fact they're practically on my doorstep. I'll only properly relax when they are all safely back in the UK again.

I've done nothing wrong. No more shame. I repeat the mantra in my mind and keep up the yoga breathing unobtrusively. So, I can look both Sally and Aiden in the eye and thank them for setting me free to discover true friendship with Poppy and true love with Cal. Though . . . I'm still not sure exactly how I'm going to express that last part. I do love Cal but saying it today, in public, might place unfair pressure on him to reciprocate before he's ready to. Maybe I can phrase it differently.

There's a decidedly weird atmosphere when we arrive. There is much fawning over Cal, but they don't seem to know what to make of me. The behaviour of the crew and cast towards me is tinged with embarrassment mixed with curiosity. There's no sign of Aiden or Sally yet.

I get the feeling they hoped I would look like a broken woman. I'm not in the least bit sorry to disappoint them.

My initial plan was to try to do this privately but Aiden and Sally had no interest in an off-camera meeting, for all their professed desire to move on from the past and sit down to talk to me so we can sort things out. No, instead they want to leverage some drama out of it, as I expected.

I did consider turning up incognito as Cal's assistant or PA or something and confronting them, but only for about five minutes. I realise I might be edited to look like a deranged stalker trying to get close to Aiden again – or at least I'm sure that's how they would want to portray me.

To arrive as Cal's girlfriend and out in the open felt like the best approach. Poppy helped convince me the best way to handle this is to behave as though Aiden and Sally are insignificant to me. The line is that obviously I was hurt but I've moved on and isn't my new boyfriend Cal fantastic by the way . . .? That kind of thing.

I haven't really discussed that part of my plan with Cal. It's been so hectic the past few days, what with the hen weekend, wedding guests turning up and all the wedding prep. Yet Cal seems to sense his role in the proceedings and is demonstratively affectionate, his hand resting proprietorially on me, on my elbow, the small of my back, holding my hand at every opportunity he gets.

I had wondered if Cal had told his agent our relationship was off limits because he doesn't want to be too closely associated with me or be tainted by my sordid scandal. Yet here he is demonstratively proving he's happy to be seen with me.

As soon as I set eyes on Aiden and Sally, I can tell they are miffed to see me looking great and coupled up with Cal. I think Sally was planning to play a seemingly sympathetic but overtly superior role in the proceedings and she seems a little thrown by my demeanour. Aiden seems shorter than I remember. After so long of them both looming so large in my thoughts, they are surprisingly insignificant in the flesh.

'I'm so pleased to see you finally moving on,' Sally says, once I've been forced to endure the charade of air-kissing her.

I ignore the 'finally' barb in her sentence. I also can't help noticing that Aiden doesn't look at all happy that I have moved on. From the way he's running his eyes over me and the dark looks he is shooting at Cal it's kind of obvious.

'Oh, I've been enjoying my new life in France for quite a while now,' I say breezily. 'It's been great meeting new people. I've got some really fantastic friends here and of course a lovely new boyfriend.'

I finally meet Aiden's eye properly.

I've wondered so many times how I would feel, finally meeting Aiden again, but I feel . . . nothing at all. His gaze travelling over my body is having zero effect on me. The rose-tinted filter I used to apply to him is well and truly switched off from my worldview finder. All I see is a handsome but petulant man, in love with himself and pissed off because I'm not pining for him.

Aiden is nothing next to Cal, he is a boy compared to a man. I don't even fancy him any more, as though my body sees itself as belonging to Cal, my body chemistry remaining loyal to him.

Sure, sex with Aiden was nice and he knew what he was doing but . . . somehow I was always worrying about pleasing him, afraid I was so far out of his league that I had to make up the deficit by being extra good in bed. An awful lot of people, I don't even want to know how many, have watched the video of me going down on Aiden but there is no footage of him going down on me.

Because he never did.

Cal, however, is always super concerned about my pleasure. He isn't at all selfish in bed.

He isn't Aiden.

And that means I'm not repeating history. It's taken seeing the two of them together today for me to finally get it. The close proximity has given me a much-needed perspective: what I had with Aiden is nothing like what I have with Cal.

And that is such a relief.

'I know it's been so hard for Aiden, the whole sex-tape business,' Sally says.

For a minute I am speechless, the moral high ground approach is forgotten, to be replaced with a bizarre moment of mental what-the-fuckery.

'Hard for him?' I ask, wondering what alternative reality I've wandered into. I try to catch Aiden's eye, but he won't meet my gaze. 'But Sally, it was Aiden who . . . Sorry, you did say hard for *him*, right?'

'Of course.' Sally stares at me like I'm the one who is mad. 'He had his privacy invaded just as much as you did. Didn't you, babe?'

I just stare. The silence opening up between Aiden and me morphs into a palpable tension in the air.

'Sure, he admits he shouldn't have shot the video without telling you,' Sally carries on, blithely regardless of the atmosphere.

Surely no one can be this oblivious? Then I remember how easily I bent my version of reality to fit my love story with Aiden. I simply ignored any uncomfortable truths and silenced any nagging niggles. I didn't listen to my intuition and I suffered for it. Sally is doing the same thing. I almost feel sorry for her.

Almost.

'He meant it to be a nice surprise for you, didn't you, Aiden darling?' his appointed spokeswoman asks.

'Did you really, Aiden?' I ask, my voice strained. My cheek muscles ache from the effort of smiling.

'Yes,' Aiden mutters, clears his throat and then falls silent again, all the while looking down as though fascinated by something on the ground.

That is clearly all I'm getting. So, this is it. The rewriting of history. The Aiden and JoJo story retold to not make Aiden look like a total shit. Except Aiden appears to have forgotten his lies.

'It was just dreadful that hackers stole the clip and leaked it on the internet. We were both so upset to see you looking so . . . dreadful. I mean dreadfully sad.' Sally reaches over to clasp Aiden's hand proprietorially.

There's a slightly manic quality to her expression, as though she alone has remembered the lines to the play and she is having to perform it all single-handedly because all the other actors have frozen and forgotten their lines.

There are no words. I simply don't care. Let her flounder.

I'm having my say, I'm sticking to my own narrative and then I'm walking out.

'Well, it's all worked out okay in the end, so, you know, no worries.' I smile, actually enjoying myself. I thought I would have to fake it, but I am genuinely amused by the bafflement in Sally eyes. I'm not playing by her script. From now on I'm not playing by anyone's script except my own.

'No worries?' She blinks, her false eyelashes making her look like she's being attacked by spiders. Surely I'm allowed to be a teensy bit bitchy today of all days?

I shrug. It's time for me to take control of this.

'If it hadn't happened the way it did, I never would've moved to France. I wouldn't have got together with Callum. I wouldn't have found a really great man and I guess I've got you both to thank for that. So, you know, I suppose I should say thanks.' I smile and even manage to keep my tone sarcasm-free. I had to practise that bit with Poppy. 'I'm doing great now so it's all worked out. Everyone is happy, right?'

Aiden chooses that moment to look up and catch my eye. Mixed in with the confusion I think I catch the tiniest bit of respect. I craved that respect once, I would've done anything to get his approval.

Now I simply don't give a fuck and Aiden doesn't seem remotely happy about it.

[illegible] together. She [illegible] her false [illegible] the mail together [illegible] and [illegible] figured by [illegible], which I [illegible] allowed [illegible] at [illegible] all [illegible].

Things [illegible] time to take control of this.

[illegible] hadn't happened the way it did, I never would [illegible] I would have [illegible] together with [illegible] how I found really great [illegible] you both [illegible] back [illegible] you know [illegible] [illegible] [illegible] happened.

[illegible] you [illegible] and catch [illegible] with the [illegible] while I [illegible] respect [illegible] and that respect [illegible] would have done anything [illegible].

Now I [illegible] and [illegible] completely happy about it.

Chapter 17

'You make a new life by making new choices'

Sean Stephenson

'How did that feel?' Cal asks as he gets into the car. We agreed I'd come back to pick him up; that way I didn't have to stay at the Château for a second longer than I wanted to, but he could stay and do his bit.

'Good,' I say. I don't really want to tell him that I went off to park on a track in the middle of the forest and had a bloody good cry. He can probably tell by my pink eyes anyway. I don't want him to think that I'm crying for Aiden. It was more about a general kind of loss, a letting go. I lost a friend, I lost a man I thought I loved, and I lost a part of myself as well. Today was about making my peace with all that.

'I know it was tough, but I think you did great.' Cal grins. 'Aiden and Sally were in such a grump after you left.'

'Well, that's something.' I smile. I really am trying to wish them well but mostly I'm just wishing them well away from me.

'So, is everything set for your "write your own label" campaign?' he asks.

'It's not really a campaign.' I shrug. 'Poppy's running it really. I got a text from her to say she's already posted. This way I can get ahead of anything they plan to say on social media. The show will be pleased because it will generate publicity for the episode when it's aired.'

'So are you planning to get involved on social media again?' Cal asks, concern in his tone, like I'm an addict about to dive headlong into the bad stuff after a successful yearlong detox. I never really cared that much about it. I used to enjoy keeping up with friends on Facebook but really, I text the people I care about and I haven't felt like I'm missing out.

'No way. Don't worry, I'm not getting sucked back in.' I manage a laugh, the tension of the day seeping away from me now the Château is well behind us. 'Poppy is acting as my social media buffer. She and my sister Annabel will tell me if there's anything I need to know. I don't think I could do it without her acting as a shield for me. I know that there are still Aiden fans out there who would love to eviscerate me with their fake fingernails for even daring to suggest he is anything less than perfect. And there will always be trolls who want to slag me off for things like my hairstyle or my supposed cellulite or my fashion sense . . . You name it, you know what it can be like.' I pause for breath. 'I'm afraid haters are going to hate whatever we do, and I don't need that in my life any more. I'm making my statement and then I'm moving on. Hopefully I'll be allowed to.'

'I think you're very brave,' Cal says. 'I'm proud of you.'

My cheeks heat up. I am ridiculously pleased to hear him say that.

'You were right. I needed to do it,' I say, appreciating the fields of sunflowers more now I'm relaxed. 'Now I can stop hiding. I don't want to be a part of the celebrity world any more. But I don't mind being on the edge of it, you know . . . I don't mind us being seen together.'

I flounder. God, this is so hard. I wish I could just say it, be upfront and say it, ask him if he wants me to be a part of his life and what exactly are his plans for the future, by the way? But I can't do it. I can't make myself form the words. Why am I so bad at this? I can't help wondering if everyone else goes around having mature adult conversations about their feelings and if I'm the only one who is this inept.

I'm not thrilled at the thought of having to go to celebrity events with Cal. But if he wants me to I will. I managed today after all and at least this time when they write about me hopefully they'll have something more positive to write. Cal is the one staying in the spotlight, not me. I'm just his plus one.

Plus he is worth it. Worth the effort. Worth the possible exposure.

He doesn't say anything and the silence seems to stretch out between us.

Relationships can be such potential minefields. I have to be honest but be careful not to overshare. I can love but I'd better not express it verbally because it's too soon, like I might jinx it or something. It's a tricky path to tread between authentic, real communication and social convention based on common sense. I never used to find it this hard.

I grip the steering wheel. Seeing Aiden today has helped me move on, but it's also unsettled me. I remember who I was when I was around him. I was always so worried about making him happy. Then I was worried about keeping him happy. There was always the anxiety about being attractive enough for him, because he got so many offers.

You name it, I worried about it. I'd almost forgotten about that aspect of our relationship.

I take a deep breath and try to lay the ghosts of the past to rest.

'You look fantastic today, JoJo.' Cal's voice cuts through my thoughts.

'Oh, thanks,' I reply.

'I think you look just as great with no make-up and naked in my bed though.'

I can hear the smile in his voice, and I smile too but keep my eyes on the road.

'Sorry, I forgot to ask how it went, teaching the cast how

to cook French cuisine.' I do my best to get out of my head. Today wasn't just about me. 'Was it okay?'

'It was about how you'd expect it to be really.' I can hear the resignation in his tone.

'But think about all the people watching,' I say. 'Some of them will appreciate your enthusiasm. I'm sure you'll inspire people.'

'Thanks, JoJo.' Cal pats my leg. 'You always know what to say.'

I almost laugh out loud. If only he knew. I haven't got a frigging clue.

* * *

The next few days are a flurry of arrangements and to-do lists. Cal is as busy as I am making sure the barn is ready. There are also lots of beds that need making and airport runs, not to mention arranging the decoration of the barn and field, plus the walkway from the Château where the blessing is to take place.

Because Leo is from the village it is expected that the entire village should be invited for an aperitif, or drinks at the Château before the main reception, and this adds to all the work we already have to do.

Because Cal and I are both so busy we haven't really had time to talk properly about what happened with Aiden and Sally and I never got an answer to all the questions that have been going round and round in my head. Cal thinks I'm brave but when it comes to talking to him about love I'm the biggest coward around.

I'm a little worried that maybe he misinterpreted my red eyes after the showdown and thinks I still have a thing for Aiden. I should have explained to him that I cried because I was finally letting go of the last of the hurt and the betrayal. It was more about emotional release than a current attachment.

It's the evening before the wedding when we're preparing the barn and stringing up the lights in the trees before Cal broaches the subject.

'So, are you still glad that you went to see Aiden?' he asks carefully as he takes a string of lights from me, not meeting my eyes. 'It didn't stir things up for you too much?'

He's normally so direct but now I'm not quite sure what he's after. Could it be that he's feeling as insecure as I am? Surely not.

I've still got all the cupcakes to ice and decorate for Poppy's cupcake tower wedding cake. She's having two cakes: I'm responsible for the English-rose-themed one and Cal is handling the Croquembouche – thankfully, given an intricate tower of perfect profiteroles glazed with golden caramel is probably out of my skill set. The Croquembouche can't be made too far ahead of time so there's a lot of last-minute prep to do.

I have drafted in some extra help. Michelle, Sophie and Sarah are all coming over later and helping, lured with the promise of some of Cal's fresh fruit cocktails.

'Yes, definitely. It reminded me that he means absolutely nothing to me and that what I thought was love wasn't. Oh, also it reminded me what a total twat he is.' I say and watch Cal. The corners of his lips twitch.

'Seriously, it was good, I think I let go of a lot of things,' I say. 'I feel free, I suppose. No longer looking backwards but forwards. It's also made me appreciate everything I have – good friends, true friends I can trust, a lovely home and a community that I could put roots down into, like your tree communities.'

'Could or will?' Cal asks.

I haven't a clue what the right answer is. I still have no idea when he is planning to go back to the UK; he hasn't said. This summer was only supposed to be a temporary arrangement. Also I still have no idea how he views our relationship. Maybe this is just a summer fling to him, something that he plans on ending when he goes back.

My chest is tight. I wish I could just come out with it, tell him just how much he means to me, that I love him now more than ever. That seeing Aiden just brought into focus how much I love Cal and that this time it's the real deal. That I never knew it was possible to love someone this much. But the part of me that wants to stay safe, already having conniptions because I ignored it and went to the Château to confront Aiden, won't let me open up fully in case he says that for him it is only about sex. Only casual. Nothing more.

I still don't know how it could be possible for it to be

one-sided when the chemistry is crackling like this, but I could be wrong. If that does happen, however kindly he expresses it, and I know he would be kind, I will be totally and utterly crushed.

Heartbroken, but properly this time.

'Could, I suppose is the answer. I'm fairly sure that I want to stay here,' I say eventually. 'I'm happy here and I asked Poppy about investing in the guesthouse or The Barn like you suggested. I think she and Leo are thinking about it. They realise that no matter how many times they say it's my home, if I actually part-own the business it will make it so much more secure for me. I know it will be better for me, working for something that is partly mine again.'

'That's great,' Cal says, bending down to check one of the lanterns going into the trees.

And you, Cal? What's happening with us? What do I mean to you? My head feels too full, like all the questions are crowding in, filling me up and causing a mental traffic jam, but I can't let them go. I can't let the words leave my lips. My chest and throat feel tight. This conversation feels a hundred times more difficult than facing up to Aiden and Sally did. I suppose it's because this really matters, far more than that did.

Frustration nags at me. I have to say something, I have to end this mental turmoil one way or the other. Just rip the sticking plaster off in one go.

'And you, Cal?' I clear my throat, which is now incredibly dry. 'Do you know how long you'll be staying?'

My heart thumps wildly in my chest, so loud to me that I'm sure he must hear it too.

I pick up a string of fairy lights and try to look casual.

Yeah, right. I'm sure I'm fooling no one. The lights have become knotted, and I try to unravel them but end up dropping them on the ground.

'That's something I've been thinking about,' Cal says. 'There is a lot to consider but I've been so busy with The Barn and the SIS thing this week, it's been hard to get the space to think. Maybe after tomorrow, once the wedding is over, we can sit down and have a talk about it. I'd like your opinion.'

What the fuck does that mean?

'Um, okay,' I say instead. I want to ask him to elaborate, like right now, please, but the night before Poppy's wedding is really not the time to have a big emotional conversation with potentially huge implications.

I need to focus on the wedding. It's just as well I've got lots to keep me busy.

I put Michelle and Sarah onto making more buttercream icing. Sophie, it turns out, has a very delicate, artistic touch so I can trust her with the more fragile edible roses and sugar leaves that are going on some of the cupcakes.

To go with the overall wedding colour scheme I have lots of white and pale green in the mix but also some pale pinks and creamy yellows. The vintage teacups that the cupcakes will be displayed in were a great find at a *brocante*, and I hope they will make Poppy's vision of a very English high tea wedding cake come to life.

I've left Cal in the barn and I have taken over the guest-house kitchen. Poppy is with her family, something she is none too pleased about. Her mum hasn't been happy since she arrived, finding fault with virtually all of Poppy's arrangements.

I've made quite a few extra cupcakes with the promise that we can all eat them, along with a second Kir Royale, when we have finished. I have been very mean and won't let them have a second drink until we finish. This matters too much to have it messed up because we are tipsy.

Finally it *is* finished, and the result does look a lot like English high tea perfection, assuming cake is your priority. The cupcakes look like tea roses growing inside delicately patterned china cups.

I sit down with a sigh of release and relax. Michelle pours a Kir Royale and thrusts it into my hand. I drink gratefully. Then I take a bite of one of the spare cupcakes and they are totally scrummy if I do say so myself. I have also kept back some extra spares just in case there are any accidents, so I know that we can eat these without any guilt. As I eat I realise exactly how hungry I am. I'm not sure I can remember the last time I ate. It's been a warm day as well which always curbs my appetite, but I've also been so preoccupied, thinking about what might be happening with Cal, that food for myself has been the last thing on my mind.

'Have you all seen that hashtag "write your own label" is trending on Twitter?' Michelle asks, taking a cake for herself.

'Really? No, I've been too busy. And what have they . . .' I stop myself from asking the question. I don't want to know what the *Sex in the Suburbs* crowd are saying about me on Twitter. There is a very good reason why I'm keeping my distance. My sanity depends on it.

'Do you mean what have Aiden and Sally said?' Michelle guesses what I was asking.

'Don't tell me if it's going to wind me up.' I take another gulp of my drink. 'I've got too much wedding stuff in my head. There is no room for any Aiden crap.'

Really it's the conversation that I'm going to be having with Cal after the wedding that has got me stressed but I don't want to say that because some of them are bound to give me false assurances that everything will be okay. It's their way of being kind, I know; they just want to make me feel better. But I'm not sure I need that.

What I need is the truth, but only Cal can give me that.

'It's just some lame tweets about how they are glad you have finally moved on,' Michelle says.

'Finally?' I roll my eyes. 'There has always got to be a barb in there somewhere, hasn't there?'

'Don't worry, you came across brilliantly and there is so much support for you on Twitter, on Facebook too,' she says enthusiastically. 'Other people have been posting their own videos, ripping up their old labels, it's great.'

'I think what you did was really brave,' Sarah says, hiding a yawn behind her hand.

'Me also,' Sophie adds emphatically. 'It is something I do not think I could do.'

I notice that Sophie's French accent becomes more pronounced when she's drinking, and her English more stilted. It's still miles better than my French though.

'Cal persuaded me it would help me to move on and he's right,' I say. 'I shouldn't have let other people label me. Even worse, I didn't have to go and believe them.'

'It is a very positive thing. To . . . write your own label.' Sophie says the words slowly, as though memorising a new phrase.

'Do we really want labels at all though?' Sarah asks thoughtfully.

'I think it's more that it's an easy way to say, "You don't get to define me. I get to choose who I am and how the world sees me. Me and no one else." It's shorthand for saying all that.' I feel a surge of emotion in my chest and I'm not quite sure where it's come from or what it means. It's a strong, positive emotion though and for some reason the warrior yoga pose comes to mind.

I am stronger now. Even if, God forbid, Cal leaves me never to return here again he will have left me stronger and happier. He woke me up, and he stopped me sleep-walking through life.

He made me want more. More out of life.

He has made me want more of him too. I think he might

be the loveliest, best man I have ever met. Infuriating at times but even when he is infuriating me, I still love him with every fibre of my being.

All I need now is the courage to tell him.

The morning of the wedding I am up with the sunrise, rushing around checking all the last-minute arrangements are in place. I still can't help wondering – well, worrying really – what Cal is planning to talk to me about. Wanting my opinion doesn't sound like breaking up with me but . . .

The dogs are all attending the wedding, naturally, and it's one of my jobs to make sure they behave. Ha! Confusingly it is also my job to make sure that Flump doesn't behave. I have to make sure he runs off with the veil so Poppy can get married with flowery combs in her hair instead.

As though sensing I'm thinking of him Flump suddenly appears and I see a streak of blonde dog pass me in a chaotic, joyful flurry, heading out into the garden.

A shriek comes from further inside the house and the next thing I know Sarah runs into the room.

'I was sure that I had closed my bedroom door. He has run off with my . . .' Sarah's cheeks grow uncharacteristically pink and her mouth opens and closes.

'Sorry, he is a thieving little sod. What has he got?' I ask with a twinge of familiar guilt. 'I'll get it back off of him. He doesn't actually chew what he steals any more.'

'Actually, don't worry,' she says abruptly, her cheeks going even redder. 'I don't want it back, you can throw it away.'

Bemused I go off to find Flump and discover he has a bright pink vibrator in his mouth. I fight back a laugh and do my best to tell him off. It's difficult because he's looking particularly cute, his head tilted to one side as though trying to compute why I am upset. He is very fond of running off with the other dogs' favourite toys in order to get them to chase him. I think that's what he's trying to do when he steals our stuff too. He just wants to play.

Also, I have to hold back from telling him off, given my plan to get him to steal to order later with the veil. I don't want to unduly confuse him and as Poppy can't face yet more conflict with her mother, I feel I need to make good on my promise to help her out with the veil.

As it happens the look of outrage on Poppy's mother's face and the smile on Poppy's face make the effort of getting Flump to steal the veil all worth it. I had to play with it for ages first, to pretend it was an item of great value to me, then leave it on the ground with my back turned and the patio doors opening up near the flowerbeds.

Poppy mouths a thank you and I turn away to hide my smile.

'Poppy, you look gorgeous. You're an absolute knockout.' I smile properly when I see her ready to go, looking lovely, both elegant and very pretty. The less conventional dress suits her and flows out into a silky ivory puddle around her feet. Hang on. 'Have you forgotten to put your shoes on?'

'Oh yes, I thought I was missing something,' Poppy answers vaguely and looks around.

I spot the shoes before she does, and bring them over. Only Poppy could forget something so obvious. But then her brain sees the world differently from mine. I'm mostly practical and she is mostly creative so we complement each other as friends.

With her shoes on the ivory silk is more of a ripple around her ankles than a puddle on the floor.

'It's very sad about my veil.' Poppy smiles and pats gently at the combs in her hair with gypsophila and tiny white flowers on them.

'Your mum is out for my blood, and I will have to hide Flump until she goes,' I say. 'You owe me one.'

'I owe you far more than one, JoJo. I meant what I said about you being a real-life star.' Poppy reaches out and takes my hand. 'You know, I should wait until later, but Leo and I have a gift for you.'

'You do?'

'Yes, it's a share in the guesthouse. And you can then buy extra shares in the guesthouse or invest in The Barn if you like, once your café money comes through. I'm not sure quite how it will work; we will have to sit down with Leo's lawyer. I just want you to know that this really is your home. It always has been your home, but I know that you want more security than that.'

'That is so kind of you.' I squeeze her hand and have to stop myself from hugging her. I don't want to mess up her make-up or hair. I'm blinking back tears so that I don't mess up my own make-up.

The wedding itself is a blur of behind the scenes tasks to make sure everything goes well. I barely seem to sit still. I remember the wedding in snapshots – Flump running away with the veil earlier, Poppy's look of total bliss after the blessing ceremony, Monsieur and Madame Dubois tearfully hugging her and welcoming her to the family . . .

And then the whole party making its way down to the barn, oohing and ahhing over the decorations. The food is also rapturously welcomed. I'm too busy to eat except for when Cal firmly takes hold of me, tells me to open my mouth and puts some food into it, like I'm a baby bird. It's nice, and surely it's a good sign that he isn't planning to dump me? Bah. I wish he would just tell me now and get it over with.

I only get to relax once the sun has sunk down behind the Pyrenean mountaintops, streaking the sky with hues of pink and amber. The candles, lanterns and fairy lights are all lit, turning the barn, field and trees into a truly magical setting. The lavender in the copper planters scents the air and the setting is pretty much perfect. I'm pleased with how it has all turned out.

I eventually get to sit and have a drink with Cal, but the dogs get restless; it's way past their usual bedtime and they've had a long day. I know how they feel! I offer to take them back to the guesthouse. I want to check on Barney, who stayed behind, anyway.

'Don't be too long,' Cal says, distracted as Poppy's mother ambushes him for a conversation.

Once the dogs are back in the house, I make my way back to the barn. It's dark and when someone grabs my wrist I jerk back in surprise. I turn around to see Aiden, unsmiling and unshaven, just about visible in the moonlight now he's on the path. He must have been waiting for me in the shadows. I shiver.

'What—what on earth are you doing here?' I can't imagine either Poppy or Leo invited him to their wedding, and I would've noticed him earlier, surely, if he'd come with another reception guest?

'I came to see you. You could at least try to look pleased that I came all this way.' Aiden still hasn't let go of my wrist and there's an unpleasant glint in his eye I really don't like the look of.

I take a deep breath. I need to placate him. Just like I used to all those times when we were going out together and he would sulk until he felt I'd suffered enough or had made it up to him enough or whatever the hell used to go through his head. Then he would change again, be sweet and loving and make it up to me.

The fake smile I try to summon won't come though. As far as I'm concerned I'm done with Aiden. I honestly haven't given him another moment's thought since the day I saw him at the Château. Why would I when I have Cal? I was a fool to ever imagine myself in love with him.

'I don't think there's anything left to be said, Aiden.' My tone is cool, and I think I sound composed. It's just as well he can't hear the rapid beating of my heart.

'I still have something to say.' Aiden's grip on my wrist doesn't lessen even when I try to tug it away.

'Funny, you didn't have much to say when I saw you the other day.' I purse my lips. 'Fine, go ahead then.'

The sooner he says what he needs to, the sooner I can get this charade over and done with and get back to Cal.

'When I saw you again I realised I'd made a big mistake, JoJo. You were always the one for me.' Aiden grabs hold of my other arm and pulls me closer towards him.

Every muscle in my body tenses. This feels a whole world of wrong. It should be Cal's hands on my body. Only Cal's. I can't even imagine wanting any man's hands on me except his.

How can someone who used to turn me on now repulse me so much? I try to shake him off, to pull away, but Aiden has tight hold of me, and I feel the first stirrings of genuine fear. The music from the barn is too loud for anyone inside to hear me scream. Have I been gone long enough for Cal to come looking for me? I try to bring my knee up between his legs, but he has me backed against the wall, pinning me in so I can't move.

'What do you see in that prat Callum O'Connor

anyway?' Aiden's eyes bore into me. Now his mouth is closer I can smell the unmistakeable fumes of alcohol on his breath. 'I bet you've been missing having a real man between your legs.'

I struggle in earnest, trying to break free from his grasp, but I'm simply not strong enough.

'You always did like it rough, didn't you?' he murmurs into my ear, his stubble scratching my cheek.

'No, I bloody didn't,' I all but snarl at him. 'I'm saying no, Aiden. Got it? That's "no" spelt f-u-c-k-y-o-u.'

'Who are you to say no to me?' His eyes glitter with a mixture of lust and anger. 'You were nothing until I asked you out. You were a nobody then and you're a nobody now. I'm offering to make you a somebody again. What do you think? You can be back on the show again. I could make that happen for you if you're a good girl and do exactly what I tell you.'

'Seriously?' Despite everything I start to laugh. There's a tinge of hysteria to it; after all, this seems so stupidly unreal and I can't believe how deluded Aiden is to actually think . . . But then he's surrounded by people telling him how wonderful he is, and he honestly believes that fame is the absolute pinnacle of anything anyone could ever want.

At least Cal has a passion for food and cooking. He's never been out to be famous for its own sake. I can't believe how long it took for me to see how pathetic Aiden is. Was I really ever infatuated with this man?

'What do you think you're laughing at?' Aiden presses against me and I can feel his erection pressing into my abdomen. Surely, he wouldn't . . . not here . . . Someone is bound to come . . . How can he think he'd get away with it?

Except Aiden has been getting away with things, one way or another, all his life.

My laughter dries in my throat. Didn't I learn the hard way to not, on any account, make Aiden angry? I take a deep breath. It might be a bit late for that now and I simply can't bring myself to grovel.

'I feel sorry for you, Aiden.' I meet his gaze levelly. 'If you actually think being famous for looking good is what everyone wants out of life. Because one day you're not going to look so good and who are you going to be then?'

'You're just the same as me,' he scoffs. 'Why else agree to be on the show?'

'Because I stupidly imagined myself in love with you and I would've done anything you asked. Past tense. I am never ever going to have sex with you again and I don't want to be back on some crappy reality show pretending to be what I thought you wanted me to be. Ow . . .'

His fingers are really digging into me now and I renew my effort to break free.

'Past tense?' he scoffs. 'You don't get to say no to me, darling. I didn't come all this way to not get what I came for. Who on earth is going to believe you're over me anyway? And I can't imagine you'd want anything going to court, not when you don't know what else I might have recorded.'

I force myself to breathe slowly and calm down. He's not really going to rape me.

A chill runs along my skin, raising goosebumps, like the stirring of air on the lake before a summer storm. He's just trying to frighten me. And succeeding, but I'm not going to let him see that.

Then a tiny flash of movement catches my eye and Aiden yelps, letting go of one of my wrists to rub his ankle.

'Ow, that little rat bit me. Get it off of me,' he snarls.

'Pickwick is not a rat, he's a miniature Yorkie.'

There's another flash of movement and Flump attaches himself to Aiden's other leg, tugging with all his might at his jeans. Normally he gets told off for playing tug of war with people's clothing so he's having a great time.

'Get them off me, JoJo, or I'll kick them.'

I believe him and reluctantly reach down to detach Pickwick and Flump. Then the rest of the dogs come running and I have to say they sound pretty ferocious. Barney growls a low, menacing growl, his hackles up. I've never even heard him growl before. He might be blind but he's not going to let that stop him piling in. Peanut and Treacle are doing their best to yap and sound menacing but I suspect it's probably the low-throated growl of Max, the Pyrenean mountain dog, that persuades Aiden he'd be best off on the other side of the gate.

'Call them off, JoJo.' Aiden's voice is an octave higher than normal as he backs towards the gate.

'But Aiden, I thought you liked it rough?' I can't help

the snort of relief and laughter that escapes my mouth. 'Anyway Max isn't my dog. I don't think he'll listen to me.'

Aiden makes it out through the gate and then turns to glare at me.

'Bitch.' His snarl almost equals Max's.

'Barney and Max are boy dogs actually, not bitches.' The smile on my face grows even wider at the thought that Aiden might actually be walking out of my life forever. Thank God and good riddance.

'You'll regret this. You needn't think I'll give you another chance when you come crawling back to me.'

'That's a risk I'm happy to take.' I turn my back on him and pick Flump up to give him a cuddle.

'Hello, gorgeous. Did you see the nasty man off for me? Well done.' I kiss the tops of his soft ears and then bend down to make a fuss of the other dogs. The Chihuahuas are intent on making a racket until Aiden actually gets into a car and drives off. I hope he gets caught drunk driving; I'm sure he's over the limit.

'You called me?' Cal's voice comes from the side of the house and he comes into view.

'Huh, actually I was talking to Flump, one of my furry heroes.' I narrow my eyes at Cal. How long was he there?

'Who do you think let the dogs out?' Cal rolls his eyes. 'I came over to find out what was keeping you and when you weren't at the house I spotted Aiden. I was trying to give you some space to get rid of him. I thought you might enjoy putting him in his place but I didn't like how long it was taking or how close to you he was standing so I gave the canine contingent the pleasure of seeing him off the premises. If that hadn't worked, I'd have given myself the pleasure of ejecting him myself.'

'Okay, you can be my human hero.' I put my arm around Cal and include him in the cuddle I'm giving Flump.

'Dogs can be a good judge of character, you know,' Cal murmurs into my ear. 'Scientists have proved dogs can recognise when someone is a total gobshite.'

'That was the actual wording of the findings, was it?'

'Something like that.' Cal gently detaches Flump and pulls me into a proper hug. 'Have you noticed how fond the dogs are of me? Like I said, definitely good judges of character.'

'Funny, that.' I roll my eyes and rest my head against his chest. 'But in this instance I'd have to say I think they got it right.'

I lean into Cal's hug, standing cheek to cheek as I place my hand over his heart, feeling the steady thump of his heartbeat. I think about what he taught me about the heart's electrical field and imagine his heart talking to mine, our heart rates syncing. I feel in sync with him, a peace radiating through me and joy lifting me up. It's like our energies are merging and creating something magical. It feels wonderful and so, so lovely.

He's the first man I've ever known to truly touch my heart and mind, as well as my body. I can't believe how lucky I am. I hug him tighter, wanting this hug to go on forever. I never want to let him go. Was I really planning to leave him because I couldn't face standing up to my past or because I couldn't cope with the opinions of nameless, faceless people I'm never going to meet and who really, really don't matter?

I want him so much it's ridiculous. I never wanted to be this vulnerable to another human being again but anyone who says love is a choice is talking about a different type of love. Romantic love is like a tsunami, crashing into your world when you least expect it and disrupting your nicely ordered life. It doesn't take any notice of whether you want to be in love or not, it just happens. It's a force of nature. I once read somewhere that love has a capacity for endless self-humiliation. Thankfully I've fallen in love with a kind man. I can't see Cal ever taking advantage of my peculiar vulnerability to him.

Intimacy, trust, vulnerability and desire are all strands of my love for Cal. They're woven together with love and respect into a band that's as strong as steel, unbreakable. Unshakeable. This is definitely not just about sex, although the sex is incredible. I love Cal's mind, his humour and intelligence. I love his infectious vitality for life that stirs me and has woken me up, made me want to live and engage with life instead of hiding away from the world.

Joanna Grant is no longer disgraced and no longer in hiding. No more shame. Ever again. And I owe so much to Cal for helping me rewrite my narrative.

'I love you so much, Cal,' I say, the words rising up naturally inside of me. Now that I've said them it feels ridiculous that I spent so long worrying about saying them. I know that whatever Cal replies I'm glad I've told him the truth.

Cal exhales deeply. I feel his chest rise and fall and the ensuing relaxation of his muscles. Did he honestly think I'd ever choose Aiden over him? That I still had a thing for him?

'I love you too, JoJo.' Cal pulls me tightly against him and lowers his mouth to mine in a warm and sensual kiss. His exploration of my mouth is tender, passionate and simply wonderful.

'What were you going to get my opinion on?' I ask once the kiss ends.

'I'm thinking about staying on here a bit longer.' Cal eyes me seriously. 'Getting back to the roots of what I am passionate about – food not fame. It's been on my mind for a while. It's partly why I wanted to take some time off down here, to think. I'm contracted for the book and that happens to be a project I care about, and I'm contracted for one more series of the show so I need to make a few trips back to the UK, but that will mostly be in winter. I've been thinking about experiencing life in France, actually being the head chef at The Barn when it opens to the public. Staying here . . . with you. What do you think about that?'

'I think that sounds wonderful.' I lean forward for

another kiss and imagine I'm putting down roots into the earth, next to Cal's, entwining with his. Peace washes through me.

I'm not a lone tree any more.

Epilogue

Poppy's Daydream blog

Hi, it's JoJo here again, guest blogging for Poppy while she's away on her honeymoon in Florence.

Some of you might have seen me on social media in the past few days and wondered why I'm back after an absence of over a year.

A very good, very wise friend persuaded me that I was letting other people label and define me. I was 'disgraced reality star Joanna Grant'. How many times did you read that about me? My friend persuaded me I had nothing to be ashamed of. I had sex with my boyfriend and I liked it.

Big deal.

Enjoying sex doesn't make me a slut. It makes me human.

Guys – some of you need to drop the double standards. You know who you are!

Girls – stop the slut shaming, it isn't nice, and it

isn't clever. It's especially self defeating when you're slut shaming yourself. Take it from one who knows.

We all have the choice, to decide who we want to be. Not everyone has been publicly shamed and labelled in the way I have, I know, but I'm writing this post because lots of people are still wearing the labels given to them by someone else – parents, teachers, school bullies, ex boyfriends or girlfriends . . .

This post is for you, if you've ever been told you're not enough and believed it. It's not true. You are enough. You matter and you're amazing!

If this post helps any of you out there then it will mean something good came out of all the bad things that happened to me.

Only you get to choose who you are. Write your own label. If you don't like the one you're wearing then rewrite it and change the narrative. This is your story, you get to choose.

#ReWriteTheLabel #ReWritingTheLabel #ChangeTheNarrative #YouAreEnough

Pass it on.

If you were wondering, the 'good friend' who inspired me was Callum O'Connor and we're in love, it's officially official! You can pass that on too if you like!

On a lighter note – for those of you following the exploits of my puppy Flump aka The Artful Dodger, his latest 'acquired items' tally since I last posted here includes:

Three silver photo frames
My favourite ballet pumps
A large living room rug (rolled up and dragged!)
Two toothbrushes
A dressing gown
A birthday card
A cushion
An antique lace pillowcase
An owl doorstop
A flowerpot
A book about the Languedoc
My iPhone (yes, really! His teeth got a grip on the case and he took it under my bed where I couldn't reach him)
A pink vibrator
And a wedding veil

P.S. For any of you who were wondering the wedding veil was dry-cleaned and returned to its original owner, none the worse for its Flump adventures. Thankfully he's out of his chewing phase, even if his thieving phase is still going strong!

THE END

Acknowledgements

I'd like to offer special thanks to the extremely talented Tom Sleigh, chef at the Abbeye Chateau de Camon, for giving up his time to answer all of my questions, and also to the owners of Château Camon for allowing me access.

The Selected Stories

of

Rhys Davies

PARTHIAN

LIBRARY OF WALES

Rhys Davies (1901-78) was among the most dedicated, prolific and accomplished of Welsh prose writers, in both the short story and the novel form. Davies wrote approximately one hundred short stories, as well as twenty novels, three novellas, two books about Wales and an autobiography. Born in the Rhondda, Davies spent most of his life in London, although much of his writing is set in Wales, typically either in a fictionalised Rhondda or further west in his rural stories. Davies was awarded an OBE in 1968.

Parthian, Cardigan SA43 1ED
www.parthianbooks.com wwwthelibraryofwales.com
The Library of Wales is a Welsh Government initiative which highlights and celebrates Wales' literary heritage in the English language.
Published with the support of the Welsh Books Council.
Series Editor Dai Smith
First published 2017

ISBN 9781912109784
Cover Design Rob Harries
Cover Image Vera Bassett *Gossip*
Typeset by Alison Evans
Printed by Pulsio

CONTENTS

Foreword

Tongues wag incessantly in the stories of Rhys Davies. Talk is everywhere, even though many of the characters live lives of intense isolation and loneliness. While disconnection or exclusion are experiences common to several of the individuals who populate Davies's stories, there is something undeniably loquacious – chatty – about his writing. For Oscar Wilde the only thing in life worse than being talked about was not being talked about; for Rhys Davies, similarly, the only thing worse than a gossip is the absence of something to gossip about. News spreads, but with it goes hearsay, speculation, conjecture. The origin and indignity of Rowland Canute's nickname follows him, inescapably, from his former village 'to his new home in the Cwm Mardy valley' ('*Canute*'). In '*The Benefit Concert*' the return of the fabulous soloist Madame Sarah Watkins, whose voice 'was legendary and a tale told by firesides', is the talk of Twlldu. News of the death of Griff, in '*Period Piece*', spreads unbidden and almost instantaneously around the houses upon discovery of his body. The magnificent Mrs Mitchell, the eponymous Fashion Plate in the story of that title, is said to have lobster for breakfast and to have had her photograph taken in a studio – lying down! (Another quasi-mythical and recumbent female – Velásquez's Rokeby Venus on display at the National Gallery – is the subject of plenty of debate and conversation among the male day-trippers to London in '*Canute*'.) What is rumoured is often as telling as what is known.

Recent critics and biographers have identified in Davies's work the outsider-figures and experiences of separation or disconnect. In his 2013 biography *Rhys Davies: A Writer's Life*, Meic Stephens remarks on how Davies 'cultivated detachment as if by not fully belonging to any one place, or by not wholly identifying with any coterie, he could preserve something of himself, something secret, his inviolable self, which he prized above all else'. Tensions between belonging and not belonging were acutely felt by Davies from a young age; liminality, marginality and a sense of being on the periphery of a wider social world are states which Davies's stories speak about and emerge from. In another recent book Huw Osborne sees Davies as a border-crosser in more ways than one. Rhys Davies was born in Blaenclydach in 1901, the fourth child of Thomas Rees Davies and Sarah Ann Davies; they kept a grocer's shop, the Royal Stores. In social and economic terms, Davies, as the son of shopkeepers, received an upbringing of relative comfort in a community where economic hardship was the more common and prevailing condition. As Osborne puts it, Davies was someone who 'was part of a community of working people, but was also at one remove from it (Rhys Davies, in the '*Writers of Wales*' series, 2009). Davies's own acknowledgement of this comes in his 1969 autobiography *Print of a Hare's Foot*, when he recalls how his father would extend and further extend lines of credit to his customers during hard economic times. Growing up in the rooms above and behind the Royal Stores may have contributed to the sense of disconnect between the Davies family and the working people of the town, but it also sharpened Davies's ear for gossip. As Huw Osborne notes, 'the shop was a meeting-place for many of the people of the village, and the affairs and lives of Blaenclydach were shared between the shop's customers'.

Alongside and coterminous with this sense of class separation, Davies's homosexuality within a heavily, oppressively, masculine society brought with it another inflection of separation and disconnect; while his departure for London – where he lived and worked for the rest of his life – may have eased somewhat the pressure felt on this aspect of his identity, both Osborne and Stephens have noted that the position of the outsider remained, with Osborne arguing that the life of a writer enabled Davies to negotiate the tensions and prevailing norms which set him apart. Secrecy, concealment, the unsayable; deviancy, scandal and taboo: these are all things worth gossiping about. And they are present, abundantly, in this collection of stories.

Davies was a tremendously single-minded and prolific writer, so much so that he was able to make a long career living almost entirely by his pen. He wrote twenty novels (two of which, *The Withered Root* and *A Time to Laugh*, have recently reappeared in the Library of Wales), three novellas, two books about Wales and a memoir. In spite of the richness of these other works it is likely to be as a writer of short stories that Davies will be best remembered. He wrote over a hundred; a short story competition bears his name today. The present volume which you hold in your hands is intended to bring into renewed focus Davies's talents as one of the foremost practitioners of the form among Welsh writers, and indeed beyond Wales. (As well as the present collection, a further selection of his short stories is included in the Library of Wales's two-volume anthology, *Story*).

That Davies should be both a supreme exponent of the short story and also Wales's supreme author of gossip is no coincidence. Frank O'Connor's still influential study of the short story characterises it as the literary mode of the 'lonely voice': this is the genre of the outsider, the malcontent, the misfit – again, there is no shortage of these in Davies's fiction. Taken together, the population of the south Wales valleys of Davies's stories may – as the critic Tony Brown has argued – constitute one of O'Connor's 'submerged population groups' so frequently explored and expressed through the short story. In Davies's fiction, even the lonely voices talk.

Indeed, in these stories, there is much to talk about. In '*The Dilemma of Catherine Fuschias*', for instance, it is Catherine's reputation which is under the scrutiny of the folk of the village, who must decide whether to accept her version of the events surrounding the untimely death of Lewis the Chandler. While Catherine is faced with a tricky dilemma in her attempt to cover over scandal and preserve her good name against the suspicions of the widowed Mrs Lewis, it becomes apparent that the entire situation is something of a dilemma for the people of Banog. After all, 'a Jezebel, for the common good and the protection of men, must not be allowed to flourish unpunished!' Deciding who to believe, and why, is indeed a dilemma. Typically for Davies, the solution to this social conundrum must be found through talk – and through gossip in particular. We learn that 'the matter was observed from several loquacious angles', a phrase which captures the important function of talking and gossiping within these stories: the truth may be a matter of fact, but it may also (for better or worse) be a matter of common consensus. There is no single, final, definitive point of view, but rather a variety of perspectives. In many words, gossip is not merely idle talk but is the very way by which a community may come to know itself and know about itself – particularly if that community is marginalised or not often written or spoken about elsewhere.

These tensions – between intimacy and alienation, belonging and not belonging – are inherent to gossip as a form of speech. Originally denoting a relative or sibling in god ('gossip' from godsibb; god + sibb, a relative), the word came to refer to a familiar acquaintance, or a friend: a 'gossip' is a particular person with whom select or secret information is shared. But gossip can also take other forms, namely as a person, often a woman, who delights in tittle-tattle and chit-chat. There are gossips and there is gossiping aplenty. What is learned via gossip is a particularly intimate kind of knowledge; it is a way of knowing and a way of being. In this collection the story which most strikingly explores the double-edged nature of gossip as public speech is '*The Fashion Plate*', a text which begins – 'The Fashion Plate's coming –' – with the curtain-twitching whispers of the townspeople beholding the magnificent Mrs Mitchell sailing grandly in her furs down the main road. The first section of this wonderful story, as well as introducing Mrs Mitchell, is a kind of exposition on the function of gossip within this community in response to this spectacular woman: furniture is moved from the window to enable the inhabitants to catch a glimpse of her twice-weekly promenade; agog, people ask how she can afford such splendid array: 'Their eyes admired but their comments did not'. Yet Davies is a keen enough observer to note that 'within the criticism was homage', and within the scandalised responses triggered by Mrs Mitchell there is among the women of the village a 'vicarious triumph of themselves' as a woman dares to explode the humdrum and the mundane by cultivating a persona dripping with ostentatious luxury. However outrageous to the public gaze, there is nevertheless a triumph to be gained by adding a splash of lavish colour to the otherwise monochromatic Rhondda grey.

'*Nightgown*' dramatizes the erosive and stultifying effect on ordinary people, especially women, of living in the coal-mining communities of south Wales. The significantly-unnamed Welsh Mam of this story is ground down by her 'obstreperously male' household to the extent that 'she began to lose all feminine attributes'. Her gamble at the end of the story is played for high stakes, and can be read as an attempt to recover or recoup the femininity which has been eroded by years of being keeper of such a masculine house, within a masculine culture. Hers is a lonely voice; her only real confidante is Mrs Lewis next door; their only conversations are conducted over the back wall. Yet, tellingly, crucially, there is an intimacy which emerges from their garden-fence gossiping which means that Mrs Lewis knows exactly what to do at the moment the story reaches its powerful conclusion.

Rhys Davies's own trip to London was to some extent a one-way journey: he never returned to live again in Wales. In another sense, however, Davies was continually pulled back to Wales in his work. The source of his alienation, his disconnection and his outsider status nonetheless exerted upon his work a strong, almost gravitational pull; little wonder that the name of one of his fictional valley villages is Twlldu – Black Hole. Davies's spaces and places, his individuals and his communities, are both attractive and repulsive; they are sites of vociferous talk, communal voice and desperate loneliness; they are places of ridiculous farce as well as common feeling. And there are also surprises. Davies has the gift for writing the surprising sentence, the sentence that makes the reader sit up. In the present collection the first sentence of '*Resurrection*' must surely be the most surprising: a sentence in which Meg herself sits up, and speaks. Against all odds, despite expectations and in the face of the scandal it will surely cause, there is more to say; there is one more loquacious angle.

Tomos Owen

Nightgown

She had married Walt after a summer courtship during which they had walked together in a silence like aversion.

Coming of a family of colliers too, the smell of the hulking young man tramping to her when she stepped out of an evening was the sole smell of men. He would have the faintly scowling look which presently she, too, acquired. He half resented having to go about this business, but still his feet impelled him to her street corner and made him wait until, closed-faced and glancing sideways threateningly, she came out of her father's house. They walked wordless on the grit beside the railway track, his mouth open as though in a perpetual yawn. For courting she had always worn a new lilac dress out of a proper draper's shop. This dress was her last fling in that line.

She got married in it, and they took one of the seven-and-six-penny slices of the long blocks of concreted stone whipping round a slope and called it *Bryn Hyfryd*, that is, Pleasant Hill. Like her father, Walt was a pub collier, not chapel.

The big sons had arrived with unchanged regularity, each of the same heavy poundage. When the sex of the fifth was told her, she turned her face sullenly to the wall and did not look at him for some time. And he was her last. She was to have no companionable daughter after all, to dote on when the men were in the pit. As the sons grew, the house became so obstreperously male that she began to lose nearly all feminine attributes and was apt to wear a man's cap and her sons' shoes, socks, and mufflers to run out to the shop. Her expression became tight as a fist, her jaw jutted out like her men's, and like them she only used her voice when it was necessary, though sometimes she would clang out at them with a criticism they did not understand. They would only scowl the family scowl.

For a while she had turned in her shut-up way to Trevor, her last-born. She wanted him to be small and delicate – she had imagined he was of different mould from his brothers – and she had dim ideas of his putting his hand to something more elegant than a pick in the pits. He grew into the tall, gruff image of his brothers. Yet still, when the time came for him to leave school at fourteen, she had bestirred herself, cornering him and speaking in her sullen way:

'Trevor, you don't want to go to that dirty old pit, do you? Plenty of other things to do. One white face let me have coming home to me now.'

He had set up a hostile bellow at once. 'I'm going to the pit. Dad's going to ask his haulier for me.' He stared at her in fear. 'To the pits I'm going. You let me alone.' He dreaded her hard but seeking approaches; his brothers would poke jeering fun at him, asking him if his napkins were pinned on all right, it was as if they tried to destroy her need of him, snatching him away.

She had even attempted to wring help from her husband: 'Walt, why can't Trevor be something else? What do I want with six men in the pit? One collier's more work in the house than four clean-job men.'

'Give me a shilling, 'ooman,' he said, crossing his red-spotted white muffler, 'and don't talk daft.' And off he went to the Miskin Arms.

So one bitter January morning she had seen her last-born leave the house with her other men, pit trousers on his lengthening legs and a gleaming new jack and food tin under his arm. From that day he had ranged up inextricably with his brothers, sitting down with them at four o'clock to bacon and potatoes, even the same quantity of everything, and never derided by them again. She accepted his loss, as she was bound to do, though her jutting jaw seemed more bony, thrust out like a lonely hand into the world's air.

They were all on the day shift in the pits, and in a way she had good luck, for not one met with any accidents to speak of, they worked regular, and had no fancies to stay at home because of a pain in big toe or ear lobe, like some lazybones. So there ought to have been good money in the house. But there wasn't.

They ate most of it, with the rest for drinking. Bacon was their chief passion, and it must be of the best cut. In the shop, where she was never free of debt, nearly every day she would ask for three pounds of thick rashers when others would ask for one, and if Mr. Griffiths would drop a hint, looking significantly at his thick ledger, saying: 'Three pounds, Mrs. Rees, again?' her reply was always: 'I've got big men to feed.' As if that was sufficient explanation for all debt and she could do nothing about it; there were big, strapping men in the world and they had to be fed.

Except with one neighbour, she made no kind of real contact with anyone outside her home. And not much inside it. Of the middle height and bonily skimped of body, she seemed extinguished by the assembly of big males she had put into the world off her big husband. Peering out surly from under the poke of her man's cap, she never went beyond the main street of the vale, though as a child she had been once to the seaside, in a buff straw hat ringed with daisies.

Gathered in their pit-dirt for the important four o'clock meal, with bath pans and hot foods steaming in the fireplace, the little kitchen was crowded as the Black Hole of Calcutta. None of the sons, not even the eldest, looked like marrying, though sometimes, like a shoving parent bird, she would try to push them out of the nest. One or two of them set up brief associations with girls which never seemed to come properly to anything. They were of the kind that never marry until the entertainments of youth, such as football, whippet-racing, and beer, have palled at last. She would complain to her next-door-up neighbour that she had no room to put down even a thimble.

This neighbour, Mrs. Lewis – the other neighbours set her bristling – was her only friend in the place, though the two never entered each other's house. In low voices they conversed over the back wall, exchanging all the eternal woes of women in words of cold, knowledgeable judgment that God Himself could have learnt from. To Mrs. Lewis's remark that Trevor, her last, going to work in the pits ought to set her on her feet now, she said automatically, but sighing for once: 'I've got big men to feed.' That fact was the core of her world. Trevor's money, even when he began to earn a man's wage, was of no advantage. Still she was in debt in the shop. The six men were profitless; the demands of their insides made them white elephants.

So now, at fifty, still she could not sit down soft for an hour and dream of a day by the seaside with herself in a clean new dress at last and a draper's-shop hat, fresh as a rose.

But often in the morning she skulked to London House, the draper's on the corner of the main road, and stopped for a moment to peer sideways into the window where two wax women, one fair and one dark, stood dressed in all the latest and smiling a pink, healthy smile. Looking beautiful beyond compare, these two ladies were now more living to her than her old dream of a loving daughter. They had no big men to feed and, poised in their eternal shade, smiled leisurely above their furs and silk blouses. It was her treat to see them, as she stood glancing out from under Enoch's thrown-away cap, her toe-sprouting shoes unlaced and her skirt of drab flannel hanging scarecrow. Every other week they wore something new. The days when Mr. Roberts the draper changed their outfits, the sight of the new wonders remained in her eyes until the men arrived home from the pit.

Then one morning she was startled to find the fair wax lady attired in a wonderful white silk nightgown, flowing down over the legs most richly and trimmed with lace at bosom and cuffs. That anyone could wear such luxuriance in bed struck her at first like a blow in the face. Besides, it was a shock to see the grand lady standing there undressed, as you might say, in public. But, staring into the window, she was suddenly thrilled.

She went home feeling this new luxury round her like a sweet, clean silence. Where no men were.

At four o'clock they all clattered in, Walt and her five swart sons, flinging down food tins and jacks. The piled heaps of bacon and potatoes were ready. On the scrubbed table were six large plates, cutlery, mugs, and a loaf, a handful of lumpy salt chucked down in the middle. They ate their meal before washing, in their pit-dirt, and the six black faces, red mouths and white eyes gleaming, could be differentiated only by a mother.

Jaw stuck out, she worked about the table, shifting on to each plate four thick slices of bacon, a stream of sizzling fat, ladles of potatoes and tinned tomatoes. They poked their knives into the heap of salt, scattered it over the plate, and began. Lap of tongue around food was their only noise for a while. She poured the thick black tea out of a battered enamel pot big enough for a palace or a workhouse.

At last a football match was mentioned, and what somebody said last night in the Miskin taproom about that little whippet. She got the tarts ready, full-sized plates of them, and they slogged at these; the six plates were left naked in a trice. Oddments followed: cheese, cake, and jams. They only stopped eating when she stopped producing.

She said, unexpectedly: 'Shouldn't be surprised if you'd all sit there till doomsday, 'long as I went on bringing food without stoppage.'

'Aye,' said Ivor. 'What about a tin of peaches?'

Yet not one of them, not even her middle-aged husband, had a protuberant belly or any other signs of large eating. Work in the pit kept them sinewy and their sizes as nature intended. Similarly, they could have drunk beer from buckets, like horses, without looking it. Everything three or four times the nice quantities eaten by most people, but no luxuries except that the sons never spread jam thinly on bread like millionaires' sons but in fat dabs, and sometimes they demanded pineapple chunks for breakfast as if they were kings or something. She wondered sometimes that they did not grind up the jam pots, too, in their strong white shiny teeth; but Trevor, the youngest, had the rights to lick the pots, and thrust down his tongue almost to the bottom.

At once, after the meal, the table was shoved back. She dragged in the wooden tub before the fire. The pans were simmering on hobs and fire. Her husband always washed first, taking the clean water. He slung his pit clothes to the corner, belched, and stepped into the tub. He did not seem in a hurry this afternoon. He stood and rubbed up his curls – still black and crisp after fifty years – and bulged the muscle of his black right arm. 'Look there,' he said, 'you pups, if a muscle like that you got at my age, men you can call yourselves.'

Ranged about the kitchen, waiting for their bath turn with cigarette stuck to red-licked lower lip, the five sons looked variously derisive, secure in their own bone and muscle. But they said nothing; the father had a certain power, lordly in his maturity. He stood there naked, handsome, and well-endowed; he stood musing for a bit, liking the hot water round his feet and calves. But his wife, out and in with towels, shirts, and buckets, had heard his remark. With the impatience that had seemed to writhe about her ever since they had clattered in, she cried:

'What are you standing there for showing off, you big ram! Wash yourself, man, and get away with you.'

He took no notice. One after the other the sons stripped; after the third bath the water was changed, being then thick and heavy as mud. They washed each other's backs, and she scuttled in and out, like a dark, irritated crab this afternoon, her angry voice nipping at them. When Ieuan, the eldest and six foot two, from where he was standing in the tub spat across into a pan of fresh water on the fire, in a sudden fury she snatched up the dirty coal-shovel and gave him a ringing smack on his washed behind. Yet the water was only intended for the dirt-crusted tub. He scowled; she shouted:

'You blackguard, you keep your spit for public-house floors.'

After she had gone into the scullery, Trevor, waiting his turn, grunted:

'What's the matter with the old woman today?' Ieuan stepped out of the tub. The shovel blow might have been the tickle of a feather. But Trevor advised him:

'Better wash your best face again; that shovel's left marks.'

From six o'clock onwards one by one they left the house, all, including Walt, in a navy-blue serge suit, muffler, cap, and yellowish-brown shoes, their faces glistening pale from soap.

They strutted away on their long, easy legs to their various entertainments, though with their heads somehow down in a kind of ducking. Their tallness made it a bit awkward for themselves in some of the places down in the pits.

Left alone with the piles of crusted pit clothes, all waiting to be washed or dried of their sweat, she stood taking a cup of tea and nibbling a piece of bread, looking out of the window. Except on Sundays her men seldom saw her take a meal, though even on Sunday she never ate bacon. There was a month or two of summer when she appeared to enjoy a real plate of something, for she liked kidney beans and would eat a whole plateful, standing with her back to the room and looking out of the window towards the distant mountain brows under the sky, as if she was thinking of Heaven. Her fourth son Emlyn said to her once:

'Your Sunday feed lasts you all the week, does it? Or a good guzzle you have when we're in the pit?'

She stood thinking till her head hurt. The day died on the mountain tops. Where was the money coming from, with them everlastingly pushing expensive bacon into their red mouths? The clock ticked.

Suddenly, taking a coin from a secret place and pulling on a cap, she hurried out. A spot burning in her cheeks, she shot into the corner draper's just as he was about to close, and, putting out her jaw, panted to old Roberts:

'What's the price of that silk nightgown on the lady in the window?'

After a glance at the collier's wife in man's cap and skirt rough as an old mat, Roberts said crossly: 'A price you can't afford, so there!' But when she seemed to mean business he told her it was seventy bob and elevenpence and he hoped that the pit manager's wife or the doctor's would fancy it.

She said defiantly: 'You sell it to me. A bob or more a week I'll pay you, and you keep it till I've finished the amount. Take it out of the window now at once and lay it by. Go on now, fetch it out.'

'What's the matter with you!' he shouted testily, as though he was enraged as well as astonished at her wanting a silk nightgown. 'What d'you want it for?'

'Fetch it out,' she threatened, 'or my husband Walt Rees I'll send to you quick.' The family of big, fighting males was well known in the streets. After some more palaver Roberts agreed to accept her instalments and, appeased, she insisted on waiting until he had undraped the wax lady in the window. With a bony, trembling finger she felt the soft white silk for a second and hurried out of the shop.

How she managed to pay for the nightgown in less than a year was a mystery, for she had never a penny to spare, and a silver coin in the house in the middle of the week was rare as a Christian in England. But regularly she shot into the draper's and opened her grey fist to Roberts. Sometimes she demanded to see the nightgown, frightened that he might have sold it for quick money to someone else, though Roberts would shout at her: 'What's the matter with you? Packed up safe it is.'

One day she braved his wrath and asked if she could take it away, promising faithful to keep up the payments. But he exclaimed: 'Be off! Enough tradesmen here been ruined by credit. Buying silk nightgowns indeed! What next?'

She wanted the nightgown in the house; she was fearful it would never be hers in time. Her instinct told her to be swift. So she hastened, robbing still further her own stomach and in tiny lots even trying to rob the men's, though they would scowl and grumble if even the rind was off their bacon. But at last, when

March winds blew down off the mountains so that she had to wrap round her scraggy chest the gaunt shawl in which her five lusty babies had been nursed, she paid the last instalment. Her chin and cheeks blue in excitement, she took the parcel home when the men were in the pit.

Locking the door, she washed her hands, opened the parcel, and sat with the silk delicately in her hands, sitting quiet for half an hour at last, her eyes come out in a gleam from her dark face, brilliant. Then she hid the parcel down under household things in a drawer which the men never used.

A week or two later, when she was asking for the usual three pounds of bacon at the shop, Mr. Griffith said to her, stern: 'What about the old debts, now then? Pity you don't pay up, instead of buying silk nightgowns. Cotton is good enough for my missus to sleep in, and you lolling in silk, and don't pay for all your bacon and other things. Pineapple chunks every day. Hoo!' And he glared.

'Nightgown isn't for my back,' she snapped. 'A wedding present for a relation it is.' But she was a bit winded that the draper had betrayed her secret to his fellow tradesman.

He grumbled: 'Don't know what you do with all you take out of my shop. Bacon every day enough to feed a funeral, and tins of fruit and salmon by the dozen. Eat for fun, do you?'

'I've got big men to feed.' She scowled, as usual.

Yet she seemed less saturnine as she sweated over the fireplace and now never once exclaimed in irritation at some clumsiness of the men. Even when, nearly at Easter, she began to go bad, no complaint came from her, and of course the men did not notice, for still their bacon was always ready and the tarts as many, their bath water hot, and evening shirts ironed.

On Easter Bank Holiday, when she stopped working for a

while because the men had gone to whippet races over in Maerdy Valley, she had time to think of her pains. She felt as if the wheels of several coal wagons had gone over her body, though there was no feeling at all in her legs. When the men arrived home at midnight, boozed up, there were hot faggots for them, basting pans savoury full, and their pit clothes were all ready for the morning. She attended on them in a slower fashion, her face closed and her body shorter, because her legs had gone bowed. But they never noticed, jabbering of the whippets.

Mrs. Lewis next door said she ought to stay in bed for a week. She replied that the men had to be fed.

A fortnight later, just before they arrived home from the pit and the kitchen was hot as a furnace, her legs kicked themselves in the air, the full frying-pan in her hand went flying, and when they came in they found her black-faced on the floor with the rashers of bacon all about her. She died in the night as the district nurse was wetting her lips with water. Walt, who was sleeping in a chair downstairs, went up too late to say farewell.

Because the house was upside down as a result, with the men not fed properly, none of them went to work in the morning. At nine o'clock Mrs. Lewis next door, for the first time after thirty years back-wall friendship with the deceased, stepped momentously into the house. But she had received her instructions weeks ago. After a while she called down from upstairs to the men sitting uneasy in the kitchen: 'Come up; she is ready now.'

They slunk up in procession, six big men, with their heads ducked, disturbed out of the rhythm of their daily life of work, food, and pub. And entering the room for the last view, they stared in surprise.

A stranger lay on the bed ready for her coffin. A splendid, shiny, white silk nightgown flowing down over her feet, with rich lace frilling bosom and hands, she lay like a lady taking a rest, clean and comfortable. So much they stared, it might have been an angel shining there. But her face jutted stern, bidding no approach to the contented peace she had found.

The father said, cocking his head respectfully: 'There's a fine 'ooman she looks. Better than when I married her!'

'A grand nightshirt,' mumbled Enoch. 'That nurse brought it in her bag?'

'A shroud they call it,' said Emlyn.

'In with the medical benefits it is,' said his father soberly. 'Don't they dock us enough every week from our wages?'

After gazing for a minute longer at the white apparition, lying there so majestically unknown, they filed downstairs. There Mrs. Lewis awaited them. 'Haven't you got no 'ooman relation to come in and look after you?' she demanded.

The father shook his head, scowling in effort to concentrate on a new problem. Big, black-curled, and still vigorous, he sat among his five strapping sons who, like him, smelt of the warm, dark energy of life. He said: 'A new missus I shall have to be looking for. Who is there about, Mrs. Lewis, that is respectable and can cook for us and see to our washings? My boys I got to think about. A nice little widow or something you know of that would marry a steady working chap? A good home is waiting for her by here, though a long day it'll be before I find one that can feed and clean us like the one above; she worked regular as a clock, fair play to her.'

'I don't know as I would recommend any 'ooman,' said Mrs. Lewis with rising colour.

'Pity you're not a widow! Ah well, I must ask the landlady of the Miskin if she knows of one,' he said, concentrated.

The Last Struggle

Grief for the newly dead is natural in the living and thought of legacies and insurance money to be drawn from them comes second in most persons. Megan Pugh, wife of Sam Two Fingers, thought of the insurance on her husband first, that day when the pit undermanager came to her in person and sat in her kitchen telling her that all hope of rescuing Sam and the other two entombed miners had been abandoned. Megan managed to pull a face. But already her mind was wandering in speculation. A pity she would have to wear black for a time. There was a cerise dress in the window of Lewis Paris House that she madly coveted.

'The water it is,' mourned Mr. Rowlands, 'they must have been drowned.' He avoided even thinking that the three men were very likely more horribly obliterated; drowning sounded ordinary. 'Can't get at them,' he mumbled, 'for weeks, p'raps never. Blocks of stone nearly as big as a house and water running under all the time; might cause a flood of the mine if we blast the stone.' There had been a big collapse of roof four days before; four days the men had been entombed.

Fifty pounds Sam was insured for, with the Globe and Atlas people, whose New Year gift calendar was on the wall; and of course there would be the compensation money from the pit too. She could go to the seaside; she could even live away from the valley at last. And why should she wear black! Black made her look sallow.

Perhaps, in a way, it was only natural that Megan should be so unnatural. Sam had always kept her short of money; you couldn't hold him off the dogs, though much of a drinker he was not and he had never hit her. He was known as Sam Two Fingers because after a previous accident in the pit one hand was left with the other fingers gone. The strange thing was those two fingers developed a peculiar iron grip.

Only a few months after she had married him – a couple of years ago it was they had hurried to the chapel – she felt it was a mistake; a false alarm the wedding had been. As a courter he had strutted cockily at her side and she took it as pleasure in being in her company. As a married man he had got bossy at once and, when she complained that he was never in the house, answered: 'You can't bring a dog race to the house, can you? Don't I sleep tidy at home every night? What more you want?'

She wanted to be taken about by him, she wanted clothes and train journeys; she did not want to become like the dumpy women of the valley, who only left their doors to go to the shops and the chapel. They had quarrelled like hell. But even in those two years she had been defeated. The valley was a man's valley, with pubs, clubs, dog tracks and football grounds for men only. Perhaps this would change if women went down to work in the pits. But not yet.

'The Company will give you compensation, I dare say,' Mr. Rowlands mumbled in embarrassment, thinking her far-away look meant shock or worry.

'How much?' she asked.

Mr. Rowlands shook his head. 'An inquest and an enquiry there'll have to be before anything is settled.' He was tired and grey from the worry, but tough from long experience of these incidents. Thank goodness, though, Sam Two Fingers's wife didn't make a scene, as some wives did, especially the young ones. He heaved himself up to make the other two calls with the sad news. In their black tomb the men were lying beyond the fret of the living, sealed away for ever from the numerous details and costs of this world. Megan Pugh had sense. She did not cry out for the remains to be found and re-buried in a proper funeral.

Megan locked her front door after him. She did not want neighbours coming in to condole. There were many things to plan. She was tied in no way. Not a child to delay her. The empty days were over. Next morning she was up early and by half past nine was sitting in a tram-car which linked the districts, colliery by colliery, of the long crab-coloured valley. The July sun shone. It would be nice by the sea if this weather kept.

At the valley's end, in a cottage overlooking the railway, she knocked at a door. It belonged to her Uncle Dai, a greaser on the railway and a private bookie. Dai was no fool with his money but could be persuaded. His wife made a cup of tea when she heard the news and, taking her cue from Megan's lack of tearful display, asked: 'What your plans now?' For Megan still had a gloss on her, knew how to wear a hat, and was a good-looker with skin and teeth still fresh as daisies.

'A little rest straight away,' Megan replied; 'a little rest by myself in Weston-super-Mare, to think things out.'

'Get married more careful next time,' Dai's wife said shrewdly.

'I've been locked up!' Megan said with violence.

'Aye, a regular old Tory your Sam was. A wife was set final for him and couldn't be broke away.'

Dai came in for his dinner at twelve. He made more money as a quiet bookie than as a greaser and did not dislike his niece. Megan produced the insurance book out of her bag and all the weekly payments for Sam were down regular.

'And there's the compensation from the pit too,' she added. 'Mrs. Bevan near me had a couple of hundred pounds when her Emlyn got killed.'

She was asking her uncle for an immediate loan of fifty pounds, since very likely, what with inquests and fusses, it would be a week or more before the insurance people paid out. For this favour she was willing to pay him two pounds interest. He could keep the insurance book for security and she would see the insurance agent and tell him that her Uncle Dai was handling her affairs. She wanted to go to Weston-super-Mare without delay; her nerves were upset from the shock.

The chance of making a couple of pounds on such a certain deal made even Dai joke: 'A fancy piece of goods in trousers you got in Weston-super-Mare, Megan? Well, well—'

So, bad though it looked, she skulked off the next day. She took train to the seaside town the other side of the Bristol Channel, did not jib at the high charge in a boarding-house, and then went at once to the drapers' shops and spent ten pounds in an hour. Her most daring purchases, owing to their colour, were a scarlet frock with handbag to match. For three days she lived in the shops and began to believe in happiness again. It was not until the Sunday that she felt appeased and, examining the beach and pier, began to wonder if she had come to the English town to look at men who did not work down under. For she would never marry another miner, coming home black and bellicose from dirty pits.

Weston-super-Mare, in the season, is bright. She sat eating striped ice-cream and one afternoon she went to Cheddar to visit the famous caves. She kept herself to herself but noticed a man looking at her instead of at the crystal grottoes and stalactites. And in the coach going back there he was sitting next to her!

They got talking. He said he was from Birmingham, but he belittled the caves and said there were much finer ones in India.

A quiet-looking chap he was, chatting quite sedate. Malaria had sent him back from India. He was an electrician and had a job in a Birmingham factory now. His lean, lonely appearance was of one who wants looking after, but he ushered her out of the high plush coach with polite confidence. She accepted his invitation to take a glass of something in the lounge of a hotel on the front.

At the end of the second week she told him, grandly: 'I am a widow. Husband killed in the pits at home. But I got a bit of property. Independent.' She wished to be respected and she sounded short.

'Well,' Ted Cricks said, 'that's fine. Look here, I got to go back on Monday. But I dare say I could do a weekend soon as you get home, if asked. Is there a pub I could stay at there?'

She got a bit flustered, thinking of the neighbours. But, sitting on a golden beach with the sky blue and music coming from the pier, the world seemed easy. The tide was rolling in, moving with dark but careless force. She gave him her address and invited him for a weekend. He could sleep at her Uncle Dai's. He said he would wire her from Birmingham.

'Back soon, lovely weather,' was all she had said on the post-card she had sent to Uncle Dai. Forty pounds had been spent and her new suitcase was full. She stayed a few more days. After all, there was the compensation money to come, and she had a houseful of furniture, to say nothing of a promising courter from Birmingham.

On the way back she stopped in Cardiff for an hour and drank three ruby ports in farewell of the triumphant holiday. Wearing the red dress she arrived in the valley at dusk with three pounds in the handbag. But she tossed her head at the valley and admired herself for the flaunting display she was making. It was time some woman showed a respect for her own wants in this place. She did not care what the neighbours, stern guardians of the inexorable laws of the hearth, would think of the gay clothes. Sam wasn't worth mourning, the way he had treated her. She had a good mind to march into a pub there and then and scandalise those entirely male haunts.

As it happened there was no one about in her street. Preened and sunburnt, she unlocked her door. In the dusky passageway she paused just behind the door. Was that the sound of mice? Then her head hung forward and she dropped her red handbag.

The kitchen door at the end of the passage was slowly opening. A two-fingered hand came round it. She could see it distinctly in the twilight. But she could not scream. Her knees like water, she went squatting to the floor. But her face was stretched up, stiffly gazing. The door had been pushed wide open and the ghost of Sam, grey and silent, stood looking at her.

Just the same as when he sat before the fire for a while after his evening bath, before going off to the dogs, he wore trousers and sleeve-rolled shirt, a loose belt round his middle. But his cheeks were hollow and his eyes burned. It was Sam and it wasn't. And from the look of those smouldering eyes she could not move. They stood looking at each other for an age. Suddenly the ghost breathed, far away:

'You get up from there!'

'Sam...' she whimpered at last.

'I'll Sam you!' he panted now. 'I'll give you Weston-super-Mare...' But she had fainted.

To her dying day Megan thought she would never forget those two fingers coming round the door. It had burned into her mind. She found herself lying on the kitchen sofa. The strange thing was that he did not attack her either with tongue or hand. He only looked at her now and again. But for her it was a dead man looking at her. He was still grey from his burial, and thinner, and in his eyes lurked that stagnant glow of one not yet fully back in the world.

'You...' she whispered, 'you were rescued?'

'Aye, I was rescued,' he replied, stern. 'The only one.'

For, when the cracks had sounded in the roofing, he had leapt to a manhole in the facing, a pick-axe in his hand. Two huge blocks of stone from the falling roof had sealed him in there neatly as in an upright coffin. He heard the rush of water and waited to be choked. But the water found a channel away from the manhole and it had faded to a trickling sound. And then time too had faded. The pick's wooden handle had been caught by the edge of the stone and he could not budge it in the narrow space. He had gnawed it through with his teeth, but how long this had taken he did not knew, for he had slept, waking again and again to resume the gnawing. He swallowed the chewed-off wood. On the floor was a puddle of gritty water which he managed to scoop up with his hand. At last he could wrench away a stump of the handle. He had thumped with it against the stone for hours, for days, waking from sleep. The miracle had happened at last: they heard the ghostly tapping. By the time they reached him he was unconscious. But after attention he came to with a grunt. Sam Two Fingers was tough as a mule.

She did not ask for the history of his return. She only whimpered from the sofa: 'I want to go to bed.'

'Aye,' he said briefly, 'go on.'

She rose, swayed, but huddled herself to the door. He stood, looking taller in his leanness, and watched her from those resurrected eyes.

'A red dress!' was all he said. 'No mourning for me!'

He lay at her side in bed like a stranger, not moving. Even his breathing was different; soft it was, as a cat breathes. If only he would touch her she thought her fear would break; once more he would be an alive man. Yet she dreaded that he would touch her with that two-fingered hand. She forced her tongue to say: 'You are sleeping?' He did not answer but she knew he was awake. That night she went down to the last depths of the world. She slept at last and woke to find him gone from her side. And the house felt empty, as a house from which a dead person has been removed.

Yet he was downstairs and she smelt something burning. She went down in her nightgown. He had kindled the kitchen fire and was burning her red dress. Under his arm was the handbag. She whispered: 'There's three pound notes in that bag.'

'Not now,' he said. 'Three pounds towards the fifty you got to save.' And he thrust the bag into the fire's core.

Her new suitcase would come up with the station lorry that morning. She went pale. Thought of the suitcase brought that Birmingham man back to her mind. What was his name? Had that holiday been? She ran upstairs and threw herself on the bed in fright. She did not know his address. But perhaps he would not come, perhaps he had only been playing with her, like they did on holiday. Very likely he was married.

She crept about the house, mechanical at tasks. Sam took very little notice of her, calm in his new power. His only move from the house was to the back lane, where he gossiped with such night-shift men as were hanging about. She had to go to the shops. Women looked at her curiously but no one spoke to her; she kept her eyes down. When she arrived back he was smashing up her suitcase, a look of calm but terrible deliberation in his face.

'Well,' she panted, 'there's foolish!'

'You shut up,' he said. He glanced at her shopping basket. 'You better start saving. Fifty quid you owe your uncle.'

Three days passed just the same, Sam silent but watching her like a cat that seems not to be watching. He never touched her, day or night. Was it that, though physically he was not harmed by his entombment, the shock had unhinged his mind? From him came that new shut-in strength. He had always been bossy and a talkative strutter, but now a deeper and more tenacious power surrounded him so that she felt he was following her even when she went out alone. She wanted to run away, to plead for sanctuary at her Uncle Dai's, screaming that Sam was contemplating some awful punishment, perhaps murder. He showed no signs of returning to work and sat reading a newspaper or book for hours. If only he went to a dog race!

Several times she walked as far as the tram-car stop but always turned back. And there he was still, grey by the fireside, his thick neck bent over a newspaper. If she said something he told her to shut up. But once again he warned her to start saving; he wasn't going to have her beholden to her tyke of an uncle.

'How can I save all that?' she whimpered, but a bit rebellious too.

'Starve yourself,' he barked. 'And if you buy any clothes I'll knock you into the middle of next week.'

Bad luck follows the damned. Sam it was who, when she was out, took in the telegram and opened it. She found the slip of paper on the kitchen table – 'Arriving tomorrow afternoon. Ted.' Sam sat laboriously reading the book of Dickens lent him by a neighbour. He said nothing and she knew by his shoulders that no word could be dragged out of him. She went upstairs and lay on the bed; her stomach was plunging. But presently a new thought came to her and she sat up with a vindictive expression. Now was her chance!

Next day she dressed herself carefully, made up her face, and took several aspirins. She told Sam: 'I've got a visitor coming to tea.'

'Aye,' he said, 'I'll be here.' And turned a page of that maddening book.

'When are you going back to work?' she forced herself to ask.

'You'll know when... But I'm not working for you to bloody well pay your uncle fifty quid, see! You got to pay him off your own belly and back, if it takes you ten years.'

'You... you devil!' she breathed. But her inside was plunging again. He read on calmly.

There was only one train in the afternoon. She could have met it. But, her face set, she stayed in the house. She did not want Ted to turn back at the station. The kettle was beginning to boil on the fire when the knocker went. Sam still read, sitting in old trousers and shirt sleeves rolled up; with him a book had to be finished once begun. Her neck throbbing, she closed the kitchen door behind her. Ted stood on the front step with an attache case, a new soft hat, and a raincoat neatly folded over his arm. Quite smartly dressed he was, and a man who would make such a long journey to see a holiday pick-up is clearly much attracted. Her confidence grew.

'Hello, Megan,' he said with a kind of nervous jauntiness. 'You never thought I'd come, I bet?'

She smiled gently and quiveringly, the whole appeal of an ill-used woman in it. Her eyes had both hurt and begging. And in the passage she clutched his arm, whimpered a little against his shoulder and let him smell her hair, shampooed that morning. He said, unsteadily: 'Why, what's the matter? ... There, there now. Have you missed me?'

'Something has happened,' she whispered. 'My husband is here.'

He stiffened. 'But you told me he was dead.'

'It was a mistake. He was rescued after being buried a whole week in the pit... Oh, Ted, so cruel he's been to me. I've been going mad. I can't stand it any longer, no indeed I can't.' She clung to his arm.

A call made to a man's gallantry – unless he is of exceptional quality – is rarely left unanswered. Though still bewildered, Ted's face became stern. Having travelled to India he looked upon himself as a man of the world. This dour, ugly coal-mining valley with its harsh look and frowning mountains had depressed him as he walked up from the station. And here was a dainty, tragical little woman chained in it by some ruffian of a husband who was ill-treating her.

All the same, he mumbled cautiously enough: 'Well, do you want me to see him?'

'Yes,' she whispered, in a weak little voice.

'And you want to come away with me?' he asked, a trifle uneasily.

Again she laid her head in trust on his shoulder and breathed: 'Yes.'

Sam looked up from his book when they walked in. The table was laid for tea, very bright and clean, though there was not much food. Sam looked thick, squat and working man beside Ted's slim but half-wavering height. Megan, standing with her eyes suddenly flashing, said to her husband, who had nodded briefly to the stranger: 'A friend that I met in Weston-super-

Mare.'

'Your fancy man, you mean,' Sam grunted, and gave Ted another hard but not dangerous look.

'Will you sit down, Ted?' she asked in an ignoring way, and went to pour water into the teapot.

'You stop that!' barked Sam to her. 'There's no fancy man of my wife going to drink tea in my house.'

'Don't be so silly,' she said unsteadily, and went on pouring water.

He lifted his foot and neatly kicked the pot out of her hand. It smashed on the hearth. Ted involuntarily jumped up, his hat falling from his knee. Megan began whimpering; perhaps her hand was scalded.

'Here!' exclaimed Ted in a peculiar way.

Sam sat back in his chair and looked at him squarely. 'What you going to do about it?' he asked, but quite polite.

'He's taking me away!' shouted Megan, enraged. Her face had become twisted and mottled, lips thin as a viper's, eyes hard and menacing. But only for a moment – for she had caught Ted's glance at her. She threw herself whimpering into the sofa, her head lolling woebegone.

Sam, quite calm, told Ted to sit down again. He then addressed the visitor exclusively and with concentration, paying no attention to Megan's sobs: 'Look here now, Mr. What's-your-name, you listen to me... You're welcome to her, if you like. She's a bitch but got good points and only wants training – ever had anything to do with greyhounds?' Ted, pale at the gills, shook his head. 'Well,' Sam resumed, 'you don't know how they got to be trained, then, and what I'm meaning is that everybody's got to be trained in the same way. Everybody's got to knuckle under some way or another. I got to knuckle under to a lot of sods in the pits, and as I see it a woman's got to knuckle under to a boss of a husband... She,' he jerked a thumb towards Megan, 'don't want to and thinks she can break this bloody world's rules and go kicking around with no respect for anything... Know what she did soon as she thought I wasn't coming out of that pit alive? Raised fifty quid on my insurance and ran off to Weston-super-Mare without as much as buying a black blouse in mourning of me! That's the sort of woman she is. The 'ole blooming place is talking about it. Why did she do it? All because I go off to the dogs when I've had a day's bellyful of the pits and don't hang around her neck of evenings like a suckling pig.' His eyes seemed to shoot together in a righteous ferocity. 'She's one of those women that want to make a chap go wobbly at the knees before her, see? Or treat him like a concertina ready for her to play a tune on when she feels like it. She's got to be cured of it, and that's my warning to you.' He slewed a cunning little eye over the startled visitor. 'All the same, she's married to me and I'm not divorcing her, see! But if you want her, there she is and you won't be hearing from me any more.'

Ted had listened to this recital with astonishment and perhaps a bit of fear in his narrow, orderly face. He opened his mouth but closed it again. It was the decisive moment. Suddenly Megan jumped wildly off the sofa.

'You're a bully and a brute,' she flared at Sam. Her fists doubled, she heaved towards him. 'If I was a man I'd knock you down. I don't care if he takes me away or not. I'm going to leave you.' Glitteringly she advanced a step further towards him. He looked at her unswervingly but his eyes began to dance. 'You've never been anything else but a mean ruffian, and I hate you. I wish you were rotting now in the pit!' Their gaze was entwined like two flames. She screamed: 'I'm going, I'm going now.'

As if to ward off a blow, he lifted his hand. It was the stumpy two-fingered hand. And she stared at those fingers like someone gone daft. The shadow of a little grin seemed to lurk on his face. But all he said, coolly, was: 'Don't forget your Uncle Dai wants fifty quid off you, and if I know the tyke he'll track you down to the end of the earth for fifty bob!'

Shrinking back, she broke into sobbing and fell once more on to the sofa. 'Why wasn't you killed, why wasn't you killed!' she wept.

Sam turned to the visitor: 'Well, what you going to do? Make up your mind, man. Women don't like mild guts. If you want her, she's there.'

Ted shifted his new hat uneasily from one knee to the other. But he mumbled: 'It can't be done if you won't divorce her.'

'I see you got a respect for the wedding ring,' Sam said approvingly. He added largely: 'Seeing that you thought I was dead I'm not blaming you for chasing a skirt to where you got no business... Well,' he raised his voice to the still sobbing Megan, 'seems that your fancy bloke don't want you. Perhaps he thinks you'd do him in for the sake of insurance on him. So you're left on the seashore properly, eh?'

Megan wept: 'I won't be bandied about. Devils of men. I'll kill myself—' She jumped up again.

'You've brought it on your own head,' Sam barked, very severe. 'What about me, coming back after seven days in my grave and finding my wife gallivanting to the seaside on the insurance money? Expect me to sit down and eat a pork pie as if nothing had happened? By Christ, what about me! I been dead and come alive again and I find the world gone rotten because a woman haven't got even the bit of decency to pull down the blinds and sit wearing a bit of black for me.'

She gazed at him in fear. But for the first time since her return he looked more the old Sam, more alive, as if he was smashing his way through from wherever he had been, that place of stern and ghostly silence. Yet there was something new in him too, something less cocky and more mature. She shrank back from him, and at the same time her body slackened. Her face looked dwindled and older. She leaned against the dresser, hanging her head.

The visitor rose awkwardly. The room had suddenly filled with a new private tension in which he was cancelled out. He did not know what to say. Sam helped him. 'They'll give you a meal in the Tuberville Arms. Beer there is all right. So long.' Ted went out with a quick sidling movement; even his slim hips, going round the door, looked relieved.

'Done for proper, aren't you!' Sam remarked. 'Fancy man gone, fifty quid in debt, and a cruel husband back from the grave. Well, there's the door. It's a free country.'

'He wasn't ever my fancy man,' she burst out. 'Everything was respectful. We were only interested in each other... How was I to know they'd rescue you,' she wailed, 'after Mr. Rowlands told me there wasn't any hope!'

'You should have stayed here and gone into mourning properly,' he insisted, severe as a chapel minister. 'Coming back here dressed up in red like a Christmas doll...' His voice began to boil again.

She leaned her head on the dresser shelf and wept again. Hearing him approach she lifted her head and cried out in hysteria, a long irritating howl. It was her last struggle. He gave her a crack on the jaw, not heavy but sufficient to send her against the wall, where she slumped down more in submission than because of the blow. She stopped howling. She saw him not as Sam but as some huge force not to be escaped. He picked her up. His two fingers dug into her back. His mouth caught hers like flame obliterating a piece of paper. She writhed and twisted for a few moments. But she went under, and came to life again.

The Dilemma of Catherine Fuchsias

Puffed up by his success as a ship-chandler in the port forty miles away, where he had gone from the village of Banog when the new town was rising to its heyday as the commercial capital of Wales, Lewis had retired to the old place heavy with gold and fat. With him was the bitter English wife he had married for her money, and he built the pink-washed villas overlooking Banog's pretty trout stream. And later he had set up a secret association with an unmarried woman of forty who was usually called Catherine Fuchsias, this affair – she received him most Sunday evenings after chapel in her outlying cottage – eluding public notice for two years. Until on one of those evenings, Lewis, who for some weeks had been complaining of a 'feeling of fullness', expired in her arms on the bed.

In every village there is a Jezebel or the makings of one, though sometimes these descend virtuous to their graves because of lack of opportunity or courage, fear of gossip or ostracism. Lewis the Chandler was Catherine Fuchsias' first real lover, so that for her to lose him like that not only dreadfully shocked her but, it will be agreed, placed her in a serious dilemma. She was not a born bad lot and, as a girl, she had been left in the lurch by a sweetheart who had gone prospecting to Australia and never fulfilled his promise to call her there. Thereafter she had kept house for her father, a farm worker, until he had followed her mother into the burial ground surrounding Horeb chapel, which she cleaned for five shillings a week; in addition she had a job three days a week in the little wool factory a mile beyond Banog. It was in Horeb chapel during service that Lewis first studied her and admired her egg-brown face, thick haunches and air of abundant health. Her cottage stood concealed on a bushy slope outside the village, and she had a great liking for fuchsias, which grew wonderfully in the rich lap of the cottage.

When her paramour died on her bed she at first refused to believe it, so pertinacious and active was he and so unlike her idea of a man of sixty-four. Nevertheless, she ran howling downstairs. There she madly poked the fire, flung the night cloth over the canary's cage, ran into the kitchen and swilled a plate or two in a bowl, straightened a mat, and tidied her hair. In the mirror there was her face, Miss Catherine Bowen's face, looking no different, a solid unharmed fact with its brown speckles. The autumn dusk beginning to arrive at the window was quiet and natural as the chirp of the bird winging past the pane. For a moment she listened to the grandfather clock ticking away the silence. Then, with a bustling haste, she filled the kettle, lit the oil cooker, took an apple tart out of a zinc safe, looked at it, and put it back. She stood still again. And groaned. She crept half-way up the stairs and called:

'Mr Lewis... Mr Lewis, here I am! Just put the kettle on. Time's going, boy. Come down straight away... Mr Lewis!' She raised her voice. 'Lewis, stir yourself, boy. Come on now!' Only the clock replied. She sat on the stairs and groaned. 'Lewis,' she whispered, 'there's a trick you are playing on me! Don't you come here again, I am offended... Yes, offended I am. I'll go for a walk, that's what I'll do. And don't you be here when I'm back.' She tramped noisily down the stairs, unlocked the front door, and slammed it behind her.

Bats were flying round the cottage. The sunflowers were

hanging their half-asleep heads, and the old deep well among the luxuriant chrysanthemum bushes at the bottom of the garden, on which her eye rested for a dazed but speculative minute, stood in secret blue shadow. But she hurried out of the garden by the side gate where a path led into a coppice of dwarf trees and bushes. 'I'll go and pick mushrooms in Banner's fields, that's what I'll do,' she assured herself. 'Gone he'll be by the time I'm back.' But she did not descend the slope to the farm's fields. She scrambled into a ring of bushes and hid herself there on a patch of damp grass. One eye remained open in palpitating awareness, the other was half closed, as if she was in profound thought.

A bad shock can work wonders with a person's sensibility. Buried talents can be whisked up into activity, a primitive cunning reign again in its shady empire of old instincts. Or such a shock can create – women especially being given to escape into this – a fantasy of bellicose truth, a performance of the imagination that has nothing to do with hypocrisy but is the terrified soul backing away from reality. Catherine sprang up and hurried back to her whitewashed cottage. Already in the long dusky vale and the distant village a few lights shone out. She shot into the cottage and ran upstairs.

'Well, Mr Lewis,' she exclaimed loudly, 'better you are after your rest?' She went close to the bed and peered down at the stout dusky figure lying on the patchwork quilt. 'Well now, I am not liking the look of you at all,' she addressed it, half scoldingly. 'What have you taken your jacket off for? Hot you were? Dear me, quite bad you look. Best for me to fetch your wife and the doctor. But you mustn't be there with your coat off or a cold you will catch.' Volubly tut-tutting, she lit a candle and set about the task. Already in the hour that had elapsed, he had begun to stiffen somewhat. She perspired and groaned, alternately blanching and going red. He was heavily cumbersome as a big sack of turnips: she was obliged to prop up his back with a small chair wedged against the bedsteads. Luckily he had removed only his jacket, but (since of late he had got stouter) this, which was of chapel-black vicuna, fitted tight as the skin of a bladder of lard. Downstairs, the grandfather clock ticked loud and hurried. Finally, buttoned up complete, he rested tidy, and she staggered back sweating. To lay out her father she had got the assistance of the blacksmith's wife.

For a minute she stood in contemplation of her work, then ran downstairs to fetch up his hat, umbrella, and hymn book. She dropped the umbrella beside the bed, placed the hat on the bedside table, and laid the hymn book on the quilt as though it had fallen from his hand. And all the time she uttered clamorous remarks of distress at his condition – 'Oh, Mr Lewis, you didn't ought to have taken a walk unwell like you are. Climbing! Lucky I saw you leaning over my gate. Dropped dead in the road you might have, and stayed there all night and got bitten by the stoats! You rest quiet now, and I won't be long.' At another thought she placed a glass of water by the bedside. Then, giving her own person a quick look-over, she put on a raincoat and a flowered hat, blew out the candle, and hastened from the cottage. It was past nine o'clock and quite dark, and she never rode her bicycle in the dark.

Half an hour later she banged at the costly oaken door of the pink villa, calling excitedly: 'Mrs Lewis, Mrs Lewis, come to your husband!' Milly Jones, the servant, opened the door, and Catherine violently pushed her inside. 'Where's Mrs Lewis? Let me see her, quick.' But Mrs Lewis was already standing, stiff as a poker, in the hall.

'Catherine Fuchsias it is!' exclaimed Milly Jones, who was a native of Banog. 'Why, what's the matter with you?'

Catherine seemed to totter. 'Come to your husband, Mrs Lewis, crying out for you he is! Oh dear,' she groaned, 'run all the way I have, fast as a hare.' She gulped, sat on a chair, and panted: 'Put your hat on quick, Mrs Lewis, and tell Milly Jones to go to Dr Watkins.'

Mrs Lewis, who had the English reserve, never attended chapel, and also unlikably minded her own business, stared hard.

'My husband has met with an accident?' she asked, precise and cold.

'Wandering outside my gate I found him just now!' cried Catherine. 'Fetching water from my well I was, and saw him swaying about and staring at me white as cheese. "Oh, Mr Lewis," I said, "what is the matter with you, ill you are? Not your way home from chapel is this!" ... "Let me rest in your cottage for a minute," he said to me, "and give me a glass of water, my heart is jumping like a toad." ... so I helped him in and he began to grunt awful, and I said: "Best to go and lie down on my poor father's bed, Mr Lewis, and I will run at once and tell Mrs Lewis to fetch Dr Watkins." ... Bring the doctor to him quick, Mrs Lewis! Frightened me he has and no one to leave with him, me watering my chrysanthemums and just going to lock up for the night and seeing a man hanging sick over my gate— ' She panted and dabbed her face.

Milly Jones was already holding a coat for her mistress, who frowned impatiently as Catherine went on babbling of the fright she had sustained. Never a talkative person, the Englishwoman only said, abrupt: 'Take me to your house... Milly, go for the doctor and tell him what you've just heard.' And she did not say very much as she stalked along beside Catherine, who still poured out a repeating wealth of words.

Arrived at the dark cottage, Catherine bawled comfortingly on the stairs: 'Come now, Mr Lewis, here we are. Not long I've been, have I?'

'You ought to have left a light for him,' remarked Mrs Lewis on the landing.

'What if he had tumbled and set the bed on fire?' said Catherinely. In the heavily silent room she struck a match and lit the candle. 'Oh!' she shrieked.

Mrs Lewis stood staring through her glasses. And then, in a strangely fallen voice, said: 'John! John!' Catherine covered her face with her hands, crying in dramatic woe. 'Hush, woman... hush,' said Mrs Lewis sternly.

Catherine moved her hands from her face and glared. Woman, indeed! In her own house! When she had been so kind! But all she said was: 'Well, Mrs Lewis, enough it is to upset anyone with a soft heart when a stranger dies in her house... Why,' she began insidiously, 'was he wandering in the lanes all by himself in his bad state? Poor man, why is it he didn't go home after chapel? Wandering lost outside my gate like a lonely orphan child!'

Mrs Lewis, as though she were examining someone applying for a place in her villa kitchen, gave her a long, glimmering look. 'Here is the doctor,' she said.

'Yes indeed,' Catherine exclaimed, 'and I am hoping he can take Mr Lewis away with him in his motor.' The glance she directed at the corpse was now charged with hostility. 'He is a visitor that has taken advantage of my poor little cottage.' And was there a hint of malice in her manner as she swung her hips past Mrs Lewis, went to the landing, and called down the stairs:

'Come up, Dr Watkins. But behind time you are.'

Having verified the death and listened to Catherine's profuse particulars of how she had found him at the gate and strained herself helping him up the stairs, Dr. Watkins, who was of local birth and a cheerful man, said: 'Well, well, only this evening it was I saw him singing full strength in chapel, his chest out like a robin's. Pity he never would be a patient of mine. "You mind that heart of yours, John Lewis," I told him once, free of charge, "and don't you smoke, drink, or sing." Angina he had, sure as a tree got knots.'

'He liked to sing at the top of his voice,' agreed Mrs Lewis. She took up the hymn book from the quilt, turned quickly to Catherine, and demanded: 'Did he take this with him to bed, ill as he was?'

'No!' Catherine's voice rang. With Dr Watkins present, the familiar local boy, she looked even more powerful. 'After I had helped him there and he laid a minute and went a better colour, I said: "Now, Mr Lewis, you read a hymn or two while I run off, strength they will give you."'

'But you put the candle out!' pounced Mrs Lewis. 'It must have been getting quite dark by then.'

'There,' Catherine pointed a dramatic finger, 'is the box of matches, with the glass of water I gave him.' She stood aggressive, while Dr Watkins's ears moved. 'Candles can be lit.'

'This,' proceeded Mrs Lewis, her eyes gazing around and resting in turn on a petticoat hanging on a peg and the women's articles on the dressing table, 'this was your father's room?'

'Yes,' Catherine said, defiant; 'where he died and laid till they took him to Horeb. But when the warm weather comes, in here I move from the back; cooler it is and the view in summer same as on the postcards that the visitors buy, except for the old Trout Bridge... What are you so inquisitive about?' She began to bridle.

'Tidy it is here, and no dust. You would like to look under the bed? In the chest?'

Mrs Lewis, cold of face, turned to the doctor. 'Could you say how long my husband has been dead?'

He made show of moving the corpse's eyelids, pinching a cheek, swinging an arm. 'A good two hours or more,' he said with downright assurance.

'Then,' said Mrs Lewis, 'he must have been dead when he walked up those stairs! It takes only half an hour to reach my house from here.' She turned stern to Catherine: 'You said you came running to me as soon as you helped him up here to your father's room.'

'A law of the land there is!' Catherine's voice rang. 'Slander and malice is this, and jealous spite!' She took on renewed power and, like an actress towering and swelling into rage, looked twice her size. 'See,' she cried to Dr Watkins, 'how it is that kind acts are rewarded, and nipped by a serpent is the hand of charity stretched out to lay the dying stranger on a bed! Better if I had let him fall dead outside my gate like a workhouse tramp and turned my back on him to water my Michaelmas daisies. Forty years I have lived in Banog, girl and woman, and not a stain small as a farthing on my character.' With her two hands she pushed up her inflated breasts as though they hurt her. 'Take him out of my house,' she sang in crescendo, 'my poor dead visitor that can't rise up and tell the holy truth for me. No husband, father, or brother have I to fight for my name. Take him!'

'Not possible tonight,' said Dr Watkins, bewildered but appreciative of Catherine's tirade. 'Late and a Sunday it is, and the undertaker many miles away.'

'The lady by there,' said Catherine, pointing a quivering finger, 'can hire the farm cart of Peter the Watercress, if he can't go in your motor.'

'I,' said Mrs Lewis, 'have no intention of allowing my husband to remain in this house tonight.' The tone in which she pronounced 'this house' demolished the abode to an evil shambles.

'Oh, oh,' wailed Catherine, beginning again, and moving to the bedside. 'John Lewis!' she called to the corpse, 'John Lewis, rise up and tell the truth! Swim back across Jordan for a short minute and make dumb the bitter tongue that you married! Miss Catherine Bowen, that took you innocent into her little clean cottage, is calling to you, and— '

Dr Watkins, who had twice taken up his bag and laid it down again, interfered decisively at last, for he had been called out by Milly Jones just as he was sitting down to some slices of cold duck. 'Hush now,' he said to both women, a man and stern, 'hush now. Show respect for the passed away... A cart and horse you would like hired?' he asked Mrs Lewis. 'I will drive you to Llewellyn's farm and ask them to oblige you.'

'And oblige me too!' Catherine had the last word, swinging her hips out of the room. The corpse, though not much liked owing to its bragging when alive, was of local origin, and Llewellyn the Farmer agreed readily enough to disturb his stallion, light candles in the cart lanterns, and collect two village men to help carry the heavy man down Catherine Fuchsias' stairs. Already the village itself had been willingly disturbed out of its Sabbath night quiet, for Milly Jones, after calling at the doctor's, was not going to deprive her own people of the high news that rich Mr Lewis had mysteriously been taken ill in Catherine's cottage. So when the farm cart stopped to collect the two men, news of the death was half expected. Everybody was left agog and expectant of the new week being a full one. What had Mr Lewis been doing wandering round Catherine's cottage up there after

Chapel? Strange it was. Married men didn't go for walks and airings after chapel.

On Monday morning, before the dew was off her flowers, Catherine's acquaintance, Mrs Morgans, who lived next door to the Post Office, bustled into the cottage. 'Catherine, dear,' she exclaimed, peering at her hard. 'What is this, a man dying on your bed!'

'My father's bed,' corrected Catherine. And at once her body began to swell. 'Oh, Jinny Morgans, my place in Heaven I have earned. I have strained myself,' she moaned, placing her hands round her lower middle, 'helping him up the stairs after I found him whining like an old dog outside my gate. A crick I have got in my side too. So stout he was, and crying to lay down on a bed. I thought he had eaten a toadstool for a mushroom in the dark.'

'What was he doing, walking about up here whatever?' Mrs Morgans breathed.

'Once before I saw him going by when I was in my garden. He stopped to make compliments about my fuchsias. Oh—' she groaned, clasping her stomach, 'the strain is cutting me shocking.'

'Your fuchsias—' egged on Mrs Morgans.

'Very big they hung this year. And he said to me, 'When I was a boy I used to come round here to look for tadpoles in the ponds.' Ah!' she groaned again.

'Tadpoles,' Mrs Morgans nodded, still staring fixed and full on her friend, and sitting tense with every pore open. As is well known, women hearken to words but rely more on the secret information obtained by the sense that has no language.

Catherine, recognising that an ambassador had arrived, made a sudden dive into the middle of the matter, her hands flying away from her stomach and waving threatening. And again she went twice her size and beat her breast. 'That jealous Mrs Lewis,' she shouted, 'came here and went smelling round the room nasty as a cat. This and that she hinted, with Dr Watkins there for witness! A law of slander there is,' she shot a baleful glance at her visitor, 'and let one more word be said against my character and I will go off straight to Vaughan Solicitor and get a letter of warning sent.'

'Ha!' said Mrs Morgans, suddenly relaxing her great intentness. 'Ha!' Her tone, like her nod, was obscure of meaning, and on the whole she seemed to be reserving judgment.

Indeed, what real proof was there of unhealthy proceedings having been transacted in Catherine's cottage? Mrs Morgans went back to the village with her report and that day everybody sat on it in cautious meditation. In Catherine's advantage was the general dislike of proud Mrs Lewis, but, on the other hand, a Jezebel, for the common good and protection of men, must not be allowed to flourish unpunished! All day in the post office, in the Glyndwr Arms that evening, and in every cottage and farmhouse, the matter was observed from several loquacious angles.

On Wednesday afternoon Mr Maldwyn Davies, B.A., the minister of Horeb, climbed to the cottage, and was received by his member and chapel cleaner with a vigorous flurry of welcome. Needlessly dusting a chair, scurrying for a cushion, shouting to the canary, that at the minister's entrance began to chirp and swing his perch madly, to be quiet, Catherine fussily settled him before running to put the kettle on. In the kitchen she remembered her condition and returned slow and clasping herself. 'Ah,' she moaned, 'my pain has come back! Suffering chronic I've been off and on, since Sunday night. So heavy was poor Mr Lewis to take up my stairs. But what was I to be doing with a member of Horeb whining outside my gate for a bed? Shut my door on him as if he was a scamp or a member of the Church of England?'

'Strange,' said Mr Davies, his concertina neck, that could give forth such sweet music in the pulpit, closing down into his collar, 'strange that he climbed up here so far, feeling unwell.' He stared at the canary as if the bird held the explanation.

'Delirious and lighted up he was!' she cried. 'And no wonder. Did he want to go to his cold home after the sermon and singing in chapel? No! Two times and more I have seen him wandering round here looking full up with thoughts. One time he stopped at my gate and had praises for my dahlias, for I was watering them. "Oh, Mr Lewis," I said to him, "what are you doing walking up here?" and he said, "I am thinking over the grand sermon Mr Davies gave us just now, and I would climb big mountains if mountains there were!" Angry with myself I am now that I didn't ask him in for a cup of tea, so lonely was he looking. "Miss Bowen," he said to me, "when I was a boy I used to come rabbiting up here."'

'Your dahlias,' remarked Mr Davies, still meditatively gazing at the canary, 'are prize ones, and the rabbits a pest.'

'Oh,' groaned Catherine, placing her hand round her lower middle, 'grumbling I am not, but there's a payment I am having for my kindness last Sunday! Hush,' she bawled threateningly to the canary, 'hush, or no more seed today.'

Mr Davies, oddly, seemed unable to say much. Perhaps he, too, was trying to sniff the truth out of the air. But he looked serious. The reputation of two of his flock was in jeopardy, two who had been nourished by his sermons, and it was unfortunate that one of them lay beyond examination.

'Your kettle is boiling over,' he reminded her, since in her exalted state she seemed unable to hear such things.

She darted with a shriek into the kitchen, and when she came back with a loaded tray, which she had no difficulty in carrying, she asked: 'When are you burying him?'

'Thursday, two o'clock. It is a public funeral... You will go to it?' he asked delicately.

This time she replied, sharp and rebuking: 'What, indeed, me – me that's got to stay at home because of my strain and can only eat custards? Flat on my back in bed I ought to be this minute... Besides,' she said, beginning to bridle again, 'Mrs Lewis, the lady, is a nasty!' She paused to take a long breath and to hand him a buttered muffin.

'Her people are not our people,' he conceded, and pursed his lips.

Fluffing herself up important, and not eating anything herself, Catherine declared: 'Soon as I am well I am off to Vaughan Solicitor, to have advice.' Black passion began to scald her voice; she pointed a trembling finger ceilingwards. 'Up there she stood in the room of my respected father, with Dr. Watkins for witness, and her own poor husband not gone cold and his eyes on us shiny as buttons, and her spiteful tongue made remarks. Hints and sarcastic! Nearly dropped dead I did myself... The hand stretched out in charity was bitten by a viper!' She began to swell still more. 'Forty years I have lived in Banog, clean as a whistle, and left an orphan to do battle alone. Swear I would before the King of England and all the judges of the world that Mr John Lewis was unwell when he went on the bed up there! Swear I would that my inside was strained by his weight! A heathen gypsy would have taken him into her caravan! Comfort I gave him in his last hour. The glass of water by the bed, and a stitch in my side racing to fetch his wife, that came here stringy and black-natured as a bunch of dry old seaweed and made evil remarks for thanks... Oh!' she clasped her breasts as if they would explode, 'If justice there is, all the true tongues of Banog must rise against her and drive the bad-speaking stranger away from us over the old bridge. Our honest village is to be made nasty as a sty, is it? No!'

Not for nothing had she sat all these years in close attention to Mr Davies's famous sermons, which drew persons from remote farms even in winter. And, as she rocked on her thick haunches and her voice passed from the throbbing of harps to the roll of drums, Mr Davies sat at last in admiration, the rare admiration that one artist gives to another. She spoke with such passion that, when she stopped, her below-the-waist pains came back and, rubbing her hands on the affected parts, she moaned in anguish, rolling up her big moist eyes.

'There now,' he said, a compassionate and relenting note in his voice, 'there now, take comfort.' And as he pronounced: 'There must be no scandal in Banog!' she knew her battle was won.

'Put your hands by here,' she cried, 'and you will feel the aches and cricks jumping from my strain.'

But Mr Davies, a fastidious look hesitating for a moment across his face, accepted her word. He took a slice of apple tart and ate it, nodding in meditation. A woman fighting to preserve the virtue of what, it is said, is the most priceless treasure of her sex is a woman to be admired and respected. Especially if she is a Banog one. And it was natural that he was unwilling to accept that two of his members could have forgotten themselves so scandalously. Nevertheless, as Catherine coiled herself down from her exalted though aching state and at last sipped a little strong tea, he coughed and remarked: 'It is said that nearly every Sunday night for two years or more Mr Lewis never arrived home from chapel till ten o'clock, and no trace is there of his occupation in these hours. 'A walk,' he used to tell in his home, 'a Sunday-night walk I take to think over the sermon.' That is what the servant Milly Jones has told in Banog, and also that in strong doubt was Mrs Lewis concerning those walks in winter and summer.'

'Then a policeman she ought to have set spying behind him,' said Catherine, blowing on a fresh cup of tea with wonderful assurance. 'Oh, a shame it is that the dead man can't rise up and speak. Oh, wicked it is that a dead man not buried yet is turned into a goat.' Calm now, and the more impressive for it, she added: 'Proofs they must bring out, strict proofs. Let Milly Jones go babbling more, and two letters from Vaughan Solicitor I will have sent.'

'Come now,' said Mr Davies hastily, 'come now, the name of Banog must not be bandied about outside and talked of in the market. Come now, the matter must be put away. Wind blows and wind goes.' He rose, gave a kind nod to the canary, and left her.

He would speak the decisive word to silence offensive tongues. But, as a protest, she still stayed retreated in the cottage; serve them right in the village that she withheld herself from the inquisitive eyes down there. On Friday morning the milkman told her that Mr Lewis had had a tidy-sized funeral the previous day. She was relieved to hear he was safely in the earth, which was the home of forgetfulness and which, in due course, turned even the most disagreeable things sweet. After the milkman had gone she mixed herself a cake of festival richness, and so victorious did she feel that she decided to put an end to her haughty exile on Sunday evening and go to chapel as usual; dropping yet another egg in the bowl, she saw herself arriving at the last minute and marching to her pew in the front with head held high in rescued virtue.

On Saturday morning the postman, arriving late at her out-of-the-way cottage, threw a letter inside her door. A quarter of an hour later, agitated of face, she flew from the cottage on her bicycle. The village saw her speeding through without a look from her bent-over head. She shot past the post office, Horeb chapel, the inn, the row of cottages where the nobodies lived, past the house of Wmffre, the triple-crowned bard whose lays of local lore deserved to be better known, past the houses of Mr Davies, B.A., and Mrs Williams Flannel, who had spoken on the radio about flannel-weaving, past the cottage of Evans the Harpist and Chicago Jenkins, who had been in jail in that place, and, ringing her bell furious, spun in greased haste over the cross-roads where, in easier times, they hanged men for sheep stealing. She got out on to the main road without molestation.

'Judging,' remarked Mrs Harpist Evans in the post office, 'by the way her legs were going on that bike the strain in her inside has repaired quite well.'

It was nine miles to the market town where Vaughan the solicitor had his office, which on Saturday closed at midday. She stamped up the stairs, burst into an outer room, and demanded of a frightened youth that Mr Vaughan attend to her at once. So distraught was she that the youth skedaddled behind a partition of frosted glass, came back, and took her into the privacy where Mr Vaughan, who was thin as a wasp and had a black hat on his head, hissed: 'What are you wanting? Closing time it is.' Catherine, heaving and choking, threw down the letter on his desk and, after looking at it, he said, flat: 'Well, you can't have it yet. Not till after probate. You go back home and sit quiet for a few weeks.' Accustomed to the hysteria of legatees, and indeed of non-legatees, he turned his back on her and put a bunch of keys in his pocket.

She panted and perspired. And, pushing down her breasts, she drew out her voice, such as it was, 'Oh, Mr Vaughan,' she whimpered, 'it is not the money I want. Come I have to ask you to let this little business be shut up close as a grave.' A poor misused woman in mortal distress, she wiped sweat and tears off her healthy country-red cheeks.

'What are you meaning?' He whisked about impatient, for at twelve-five, in the bar-parlour of the Blue Boar, he always met the manager of the bank for conference over people's private business.

She hung her head ashamed-looking as she moaned: 'A little favourite of Mr Lewis I was, me always giving him flowers and vegetables and what-not free of charge. But bad tongues there are in Banog, and they will move quick if news of this money will go about.'

'Well,' he said, flat again, 'too late you are. There is Mrs Lewis herself knowing about your legacy since Thursday evening, and—'

Catherine burst out: 'But she will keep quiet for sure! She won't be wanting it talked that her husband went and left me three hundred pounds, no indeed! For I can say things that poor Mr Lewis told me, such a nasty she was! It is of Horeb chapel I am worrying – for you not to tell Mr Davies our minister or anyone else that I have been left this money.' She peeped up at him humble.

'Well,' he said, even flatter than before and, as was only proper, not sympathetic, 'too late you are again. Same time that I wrote to you I sent a letter to Mr Davies that the chapel is left money for a new organ and Miss Catherine Bowen the cleaner left a legacy too: the letter is with him this morning. In the codicil dealing with you, Mr Lewis said it was a legacy because your cleaning wage was so small and you a good worker.'

The excuse would have served nice but for that unlucky death on her bed. She groaned aloud. And as she collapsed on the solicitor's hard chair she cried out in anguish, entreating aid of him in this disaster. Pay him well she would if he preserved her good name, pounds and pounds.

'A miracle,' he said, 'I cannot perform.'

Truth, when it is important, is not mocked for long, even in a solicitor's office. The legatee went down the stairs with the gait of one whipped sore. She cycled back to her cottage as though using one leg, and, to avoid the village, she took a circuitous way, pushing the cycle up stony paths. At the cottage, after sitting in a trance for a while, she walked whimpering to the well among the chrysanthemums, removed the cover, and sat on the edge in further trance. An hour passed, for her thoughts hung like lead. She went into the dark night of the soul. But she couldn't bring herself to urge her body into the round black hole which pierced the earth so deep.

Then, on the horizon of the dark night, shone a ray of bright light. For the first time since the postman's arrival the solid untrimmed fact struck her that three hundred pounds of good money was hers. She could go to Aberystwyth and set up in partnership with her friend Sally Thomas who, already working there as a cook, wanted to start lodgings for the college students. The legacy, surprising because Mr Lewis had always been prudent of pocket – and she had approved of this respect for cash, believing, with him, that the best things in life are free – the legacy would take her into a new life. She rose from the well. And in the cottage, shaking herself finally out of her black dream, she decided that Mr Lewis had left her the money as a smack to his wife the nasty one.

No one came to see her. She did not go to chapel on the Sunday. Three days later she received a letter from Mr Davies, B.A., inviting her to call at his house. She knew what it meant. The minister had sat with his deacons in special conclave on her matter, and he was going to tell her that she was to be cast out from membership of Horeb. She wrote declining the invitation and said she was soon to leave Banog to live at the seaside in quiet; she wrote to Sally Thomas at the same time. But she had to go down to the post office for stamps.

She entered the shop with, at first, the mien of an heiress. Two women members of Horeb were inside, and Lizzie Postmistress was slicing bacon. Catherine stood waiting at the post office counter in the corner. No one greeted her or took notice, but one of the customers slipped out and in a few minutes returned with three more women. All of them turned their backs on Catherine. They talked brisk and loud, while Catherine waited drawn up. Lizzie Postmistress sang: 'Fancy Lewis the Chandler leaving money for a new organ for Horeb!'

'The deacons,' declared the wife of Peter the Watercress, 'ought to say "No" to it.'

'Yes, indeed,' nodded the cobbler's wife; 'every time it is played members will be reminded.'

'Well,' said single Jane the Dressmaker, who had a tapemeasure round her neck, 'not the fault of the organ will that be.'

They clustered before the bacon-cutting postmistress. On a tin of biscuits, listening complacent, sat a cat. The postmistress stopped slicing, waved her long knife, and cried: 'Never would I use such an organ – no, not even with gloves on; and *I* for one won't like singing hymns to it.'

'A full members' meeting about all the business there ought to be! Deacons are men. Men go walking to look at dahlias and fuchsias—'

'And,' dared the cobbler's wife, 'drop dead at sight of a prize dahlia.'

Catherine rapped on the counter and shouted: 'Stamps!'

The postmistress craned her head over the others and exclaimed: 'Why now, there's Catherine Fuchsias! ... Your inside is better from the strain?' she enquired. The others turned and stared in unison.

'Stamps,' said Catherine, who under the united scrutiny suddenly took on a meek demeanour.

'Where for?' asked the postmistress, coming over to the post office corner, and snatching up the two letters Catherine had laid on the counter. 'Ho, one to Mr Davies, B.A., and one to Aberystwyth!'

'I am going to live in Aberystwyth,' said Catherine grandly.

'Retiring you are on your means?' asked Jane the Dressmaker.

'Plenty of college professors and well-offs in Aberystwyth!' commented Peter's wife.

'Well,' frowned the postmistress, as if in doubt about her right to sell stamps to such a person, 'I don't know indeed... What you wasting a stamp on this one for,' she rasped out, 'with Mr Davies living just up the road? Too much money you've got?'

'Ten shillings,' complained unmarried Jane the dressmaker, 'I get for making up a dress, working honest on it for three days or more. Never will *I* retire to Aberystwyth and sit on the front winking at the sea.'

'What you going there so quick for?' asked the cobbler's wife, her eyes travelling sharp from Catherine's face to below and resting there suspicious.

'Two stamps.' The postmistress flung them down grudgingly at last, and took up Catherine's coin as if she was picking up a rotten mouse by the tail. 'Wishing I am you'd buy your stamps somewhere else.'

Catherine, after licking and sticking them, seemed to regain strength as she walked to the door, remarking haughtily: 'There's wicked jealousy when a person is left money! Jealous you are not in my shoes, now *and* before.'

But, rightly, the postmistress had the last word: 'A cousin I have in Aberystwyth. Wife of a busy minister that is knowing everybody there. A letter *I* must write to Aberystwyth too.'

CANUTE

As the great Saturday grew nearer most men asked each other: 'Going up for the International?' You had the impression that the place would be denuded of its entire male population, as in some archaic tribal war. Of course a few women too intended taking advantage, for other purposes, of the cheap excursion trains, though these hardy souls were not treated seriously, but rather as intruders in an entirely masculine rite. It was to be the eternal England versus Wales battle, the object now under dispute being a stitched leather egg containing an air-inflated bladder.

The special trains began to leave round about Friday midnight, and thereafter, all through the night and until Saturday noon, these quaking, immensely long vehicles feverishly rushed back and forth between Wales and London. In black mining valleys, on rustic heights, in market towns and calm villages myriads of house doors opened during the course of the night and a man issued from an oblong of yellow light, a railway ticket replacing the old spear.

The contingent from Pleasant Row, a respectable road of houses leading up to a three-shafted coal-mine, came out from their dwellings into the gas-lit winter midnight more or less simultaneously. Wives stood in worried farewells in the doorways. Their men were setting out in the dead of night to an alien land, far away from this safe valley where little Twlldu nestled about its colliery and usually minded its own business.

'Now be careful you don't lose your head, Rowland!' fretted his wife on their doorstep. 'You take things quiet and behave yourself. Remember your trouble.' The 'trouble' was a hernia, the result of Rowland rescuing his neighbour, Dicky Corner House, from a fall of roof in the pit.

Rowland, grunting a repudiation of this anxiety, scuttled after a group of men in caps. 'Jawl,' shouted one, 'is that the whistle of the 'scursion train? Come on!' Out of the corner house ran Dicky, tying a white muffler round his neck. Weighted though they all were with bottles for the long journey, they shot forward dramatically, though the train was still well up the long valley.

The night was clear and crisp. Thousands of stars briskly gazed down, sleepless as the excited eyes of the excursion hordes thronging all the valley's little stations. Stopping every few minutes, the train slid past mines deserted by their workers and rows of houses where, mostly, only women and children remained. It was already full when it stopped at Twlldu, and, before it left, the smallest men were lying in the luggage racks and sitting on the floor, placing their bottles safe. Some notorious passengers, clubbing together, had brought crates of flagons.

Dicky Corner House, who was squat and sturdy, kept close to Rowland, offering him cigarettes, or a swig out of his bottle and a beef sandwich. Ever since Rowland had rescued him he had felt bound to him in some way, especially as Rowland, who was not a hefty chap, had that hernia as a result. But Rowland felt no particular interest in Dicky; he had only done his duty by him in the pit. 'Got my own bottle and sandwiches,' he grunted. And: 'No, I am not feeling a draught.' The train rocked and groaned through the historic night. Some parts of it howled with song; in other parts bets were laid, cards played, and tales told of former internationals.

Somewhere, perhaps guarded by armed warriors, the sacred egg lay waiting for the morrow. In its worship these myriads had left home and loved ones to brave the dangers of a foreign city. Situated in a grimy parish of that city, and going by the name of Paddington, the railway terminus began to receive the first drafts at about 4 a.m. Their arrival was welcomed by their own shouts, whistles and cries. From one compartment next to the Pleasant Row contingent a man had to be dragged out with his legs trailing limply behind him.

'Darro,' Rowland mumbled with some severity, 'he's started early. Disgrace! Gives the 'scursionists a bad name.'

'Hi!' Dicky Corner House tried to hail a vanishing porter, 'where's the nearest public house in London?'

'Pubs in London opened already, then?' asked Shoni Matt in wonder and respect, gazing at 4.30 on the station clock.

'Don't be daft, man,' Ivor snarled, surly from lack of sleep. 'We got about seven hours to wait on our behinds.'

A pitchy black shrouded the great station. Many braved the strange dark and wandered out into it, but in warily peering groups. A watery dawn found their numbers increased in the main thoroughfares; early workers saw them reconnoitering like invaders sniffing out a strange land.

'Well, well,' said Rowland at ten o'clock, following his nose up the length of Nelson's column, 'how did they get that man up there? And what for?'

'A fancy kind of chimney stack it is,' Dicky declared. 'A big bakehouse is under us.' He asked yet another policeman – the fourth – what time the public houses opened, but the answer was the same.

'Now, Dicky,' said Rowland, in a severe canting voice like a preacher, 'you go on behaving like that and very sorry I'll be that

I rescued you that time. We have come here,' he added austerely, 'to see the International, not to drink. Plenty of beer in Wales.'

'I'm cold,' bleated Shoni Matt; 'I'm hungry; I'm sleepy.'

'Let's go in there!' said Gwyn Short Leg, and they all entered the National Gallery, seeing that admission was free.

It was the Velasquez 'Venus' that arrested their full attention. 'The artist,' observed Emlyn Chrysanthemums – he was called that because he was a prize grower of them in a homemade glasshouse – 'was clever to make her turn her back on us. A bloke that knew what was tidy.'

'Still,' said Rowland, 'he ought to have thrown a towel or something across her, just by here—'

'Looking so alive it is,' Ivor breathed in admiration, 'you could smack it, just there—'

An attendant said: 'Do not touch the paintings.'

'What's the time?' Dicky Comer House asked the attendant. 'Are the pubs open yet?'

'A disgrace he is,' said Rowland sharply as the contingent went out. 'He ought to have stayed home.'

By then the streets were still more crowded with gazing strangers. Scotland had sent tam-o'-shantered men, the North and Midlands their crowds of tall and short men in caps, bowlers, with umbrellas and striped scarves, concertinas and whistles. There were ghostly looking men who looked as if they had just risen from hospital beds; others were unshaven and still bore the aspect of running late for the train. Many women accompanied the English contingents, for the Englishman never escapes this. By noon the invaders seemed to have taken possession of the metropolis and, scenting their powerful majority, they became noisy and obstreperous, unlike the first furtive groups which had arrived before dawn. And for a short while, a million beer taps flowed ceaselessly. But few of the visitors loitered to drink overmuch before the match. The evening was to come, when one could sit back released from the tremendous event.

At two-thirty, into a grey misty field surrounded by huge walls of buzzing insects stickily massed together, fifteen red beetles and fifteen white beetles ambled forward on springy legs. To a great cry the sacred egg appeared. A whistle blew. The beetles wove a sharp pattern of movement, pursuing the egg with swift bounds and trim dance evolutions. Sometimes they became knotted over it as though in prayer. They worshipped the egg and yet they did not want it: as if it contained the secret of happiness, they pursued it, got it, and then threw it away. The sticky imprisoning walls heaved and roared; myriads of pin-point faces passed through agonies of horror and ecstasies of bliss. And from a great quantity of these faces came frenzied cries and urgings in a strange primitive language that no doubt gave added strength to the fifteen beetles who understood that language. It was not only the thirty below the walls who fought the battle.

The big clock's pallid face, which said it was a quarter to midnight, stared over the station like an amazed moon. Directly under it was a group of women who had arranged to meet their men there for the journey back. They looked worried and frightened.

And well they might. For surely they were standing in a gigantic hospital base adjacent to a bloody battlefield where a crushing defeat had been sustained. On the platforms casualties lay groaning or silently dazed; benches were packed with huddled men, limbs twitching, heads laid on neighbours' shoulders or clasped in hands between knees. Trolleys were heaped with what looked like the dead. Now and again an ambulance train crawled out packed to the doors. But still more men kept staggering into the station from the maw of an underground cavern and from the black foggy streets. Most of them looked exhausted, if not positively wounded, as from tremendous strife.

But not all of them. Despite groans of the incapacitated, grunting heaves of the sick, long solemn stares of the bemused helplessly waiting for some ministering angel to conduct them to a train, there was a singing. Valiant groups of men put their heads doggedly together and burst into heroic song. They belonged to a race that, whatever the cause, never ceases to sing, and those competent to judge declare this singing something to be greatly admired. Tonight, in this melancholy place at the low hour of midnight, these melodious cries made the spirit of man seem undefeated. Stricken figures on floors, benches and trolleys stirred a little, and far-gone faces flickered into momentary awareness. Others who still retained their faculties sufficiently to recognise home acquaintances shouted, embraced, hit each other, made excited turkey-cock enquiries as to the activities of the evening.

A youngish woman with parcels picked a zigzag way to under the clock and greeted another there. 'Seen my Glynne, have you?' she asked anxiously, 'I've been out to Cricklewood to visit my auntie... Who won the match?' she asked, glancing about her in fear.

'You can tell by the state of them, can't you!' frowned the other.

Another woman, with a heave of hostility, said: 'Though even if Wales had lost they'd drink just the same, to drown the disappointment, the old beasts... Look out!' The women scattered hastily from a figure who became detached from a knot of swaying men, made a blind plunge in their direction, and was sick.

'Where's the porters?' wailed one woman. 'There's no porters to be seen anywhere; they've all run home... Serve us right, we shouldn't have come with the men's 'scursion... I'm feeling ill, nowhere to sit, only men everywhere.'

Cap pushed back from his blue-marked miner's face, Matt Griffiths of Gelli bellowed a way up No. 1 platform. He was gallantly pulling a trolley heaped with bodies like immense dead cods. 'Where's the backwards 'scursion train for Gelli?' he shouted. 'Out of the way there! We got to go on the night shift tomorrow.'

'The wonder is,' said a woman, fretful, 'that they can find their way to the station at all. But there, they're like dogs pointing their snouts towards home.'

Two theological students, solemn-clothed as crows, passed under the clock. They were in fierce converse and gesticulated dangerously with their flappy umbrellas. Yet they seemed oblivious of the carnal scenes around them; no doubt they were occupied with some knotty biblical matter. The huddled women looked at them with relief; here was safety. 'We'd better get in the same compartment as them,' one of them said to her friend, 'come on, Gwen, let's follow them. I expect they've been up for a conference or an exam.' Soon the two young preachers-to-be were being followed by quite a band of women though they remained unconscious of this flattering retinue.

'That reverse pass of Williams!' one of the students suddenly burst out, unable to contain himself, and prancing forward in intoxicated delight. 'All the matches I've been to I've never seen anything like it! Makes you want to grab someone and dance ring-a-ring-o'-roses.'

Elsewhere, an entwined group of young men sang 'Mochyn

Du' with an orderly sweetness in striking contrast to their mien; a flavour of pure green hills and neat little farmhouses was in their song about a black pig. On adjacent platforms other groups in that victorious concourse sang 'Sospan Fach' and even a hymn. As someone said, if you shut your eyes you could fancy yourself in an eisteddfod.

But in the Gentlemen's Convenience under No. 1 platform no one would have fancied this. There an unusual thing had occurred – the drains had clogged. Men kept on descending the flight of steps only to find a sheet of water flooding the floor to a depth of several inches. They had to make do with standing on the bottom steps, behind them an impatient block of others dangerously swaying.

And this was not all. Far within the deserted convenience one man was marooned over that sheet of water. He sat on the shoe-shine throne which, resting on its dais, was raised safely – up to the present – above the water. With head lolling on his shoulder he sat fast asleep, at peace, comfortable in the full-sized armchair. Astonished remarks from the steps failed to reach him.

'Darro me,' exclaimed one man with a stare of respect across the waters, 'how did he get there? No sign of a boat.'

'Hoy,' another bawled over, 'what train you want to catch? You can't stay there all night.'

'Who does he think he is,' someone else exclaimed in an English voice – 'King Canute?'

The figure did not hear, though the head dreamily lolled forward an inch. Impatient men waiting on the crowded steps bawled to those in front to hurry up and make room. Soon the rumour that King Canute was sitting below passed among a lot of people on No. 1 platform. It was not long before someone – Sam Recitations it was, the Smoking Concert Elocutionist – arrived at the bottom step and recognised that the figure enthroned above the water was not King Canute at all.

'I'm hanged if it isn't Rowland from Pleasant Row!' he blew in astonishment. 'That's where he's got! ... Rowland,' his chest rose as in a recitation, 'wake up, man, wake up! Train is due out in ten minutes. Number 2 platform...'

Rowland did not hear even this well-known Twlldu voice. Sam, himself not in full possession of his faculties, gazed stupidly at the sheet of water. It looked deep; up to your calves. A chap would have soaking wet socks and shoes all the way back to Wales. And he was appearing at a club concert on Tuesday, reciting four ballads; couldn't afford to catch a cold. Suddenly he pushed his way through the exclaiming mob behind him, hastened recklessly through the platform mobs, reached No. 2 platform and began searching for the Pleasant Row contingent.

They were sitting against a kiosk plunged in torpid thought. Sam had to shake two or three of them. 'I've seen him!' he rolled. 'Your Rowland! He isn't lost – he's down in the men's place under Number 1, and can't budge him. People calling him King Canute—'

They had lost him round about nine o'clock in crowded Trafalgar Square. There the visiting mob had got so obstreperous that, as someone related later at a club in Twlldu, four roaring lions had been let loose and stood lashing their tails in fury against these invaders whose nation had won the match; and someone else said that for the first time in his life he had seen a policeman who wore spectacles. While singing was going on, and two or three cases of assault brewing, Rowland had vanished. From time to time the others had missed him, and Dicky Comer House asked many policemen if they had seen Rowland of Twlldu.

Sam Recitations kept on urging them now. 'King Canute?' repeated Shoni Matt in a stupor. 'You shut up, Sam,' he added crossly; 'no time for recitations now.'

'He's down in the Gents under Number 1,' Sam howled despairingly. 'English strangers poking fun at him and water rising up! He'll be drowned same as when the Cambrian pit was flooded!' He beat his chest as if he was giving a ballad in a concert. 'Ten minutes and the train will be in! And poor Rowland sitting helpless and the water rising round him like on the sands of Dee!'

Far off a whistle blew. Someone nearby was singing *Cwm Rhondda* in a bass that must have won medals in its time. They shook themselves up from the platform, staring penetratingly at Sam, who was repeating information with wild emphasis. Six of them, all from Pleasant Row. Awareness seemed to flood them simultaneously, for suddenly they all surged away.

By dint of pushing and threatening cries they got down all together to the lower steps of the convenience. Rowland had not moved in the shoe-shine throne. Still his head lolled in slumber as if he was sitting cosy by his fireside at home after a heavy shift in the pit, while the waters lapped the dais and a yellow light beat down on the isolated figure indifferent to its danger. They stared fearfully at the sheet of water.

'Shocking it is,' said Gwyn Short Leg, scandalised. 'All the Railway Company gone home, have they, and left the place like this?'

'In London too!' criticised Ivor, gazing below him in owlish distaste.

Then in one accord they bellowed: 'Hoy, Rowland, hoy!'

He did not stir. Not an eyelid. It was then that Shoni Matt turned to Dicky Corner House and just looked at him, like a judge. His gaze asked, 'Whose life had been saved by Rowland when that bit of roof had fallen in the pit?' Dicky, though he shivered, understood the long solemn look. 'Time to pay back now, Dicky,' the look added soberly.

Whimpering, Dicky tried to reach his shoelaces, on the crowded steps. But the others urged excitedly: 'No time to take your shoes off. Hark, the train's coming in! Go on, boy. No swimming to do.'

Dicky, with a sudden dramatic cry, leapt into the water, foolishly splashing it up all round his legs. A pit-butty needed to be rescued! And with oblivious steps, encouraged by the applause of the others, he plunged across to the throne. He stepped on the dais and, being hefty, lifted Rowland across his shoulders without much bother. He staggered a bit as he stepped off the dais into the cruelly wet water.

'Careful now,' shouted Emlyn Chrysanthemums, 'don't drop him into the champagne.'

It was an heroic act that afterwards, in the club evenings, took precedence over tales of far more difficult rescues in the pits. Dicky reached the willing arms of the others without mishap. They took Rowland and bore him by his four limbs up the steps, down the platform and up the other, just as the incoming train was coming to a frightened standstill. After a battle they got into a compartment. Dicky took off his shoes, hung up his socks over the edge of the rack and wiped his feet and calves in the white muffler that had crossed his throat.

'Wet feet bad for the chest,' he said fussily.

All the returning trains reached the arms of Wales safely, and she folded the passengers into her fragrant breast with a pleased sigh of 'Well done, my sons'. The victory over her ancient enemy – it was six points to four – was a matter of great Sunday celebration when the men's clubs opened in the evening, these having a seven-day licence, whereas the ordinary public houses, owing to the need to appease old dim gods, were not allowed to open on Sundays.

The members of the Pleasant Row contingent, like most others, stayed in bed all the morning. When they got up they related to their wives and children many of the sights and marvels of London. But some weeks had passed before Rowland's wife, a tidy woman who starched her aprons and was a great chapel-goer, said to him in perplexity: 'Why is it people are calling you Rowland Canute now?'

Only that evening, Gwyn Short Leg, stumping to the door on his way to the club, had bawled innocently into the passage: 'Coming down, Rowland Canute?' Up to lately Rowland had been one of those who, because he seemed to have no peculiarity, had never earned a nickname.

'Oh,' Rowland told his wife, vaguely offhand, 'some fancy name or other it is they've begun calling me.'

'But a reason there must be for it,' she said inquisitively. 'Canute! Wasn't that some old king who sat on his throne beside the sea and dared the tide to come over him? A funny name to call you.'

'What you got in the oven for my supper?' he asked, scowling at the news in the evening paper.

She knew better than to proceed with the matter just then. But of course she did not let it rest. It was the wife of Emlyn Chrysanthemums, living three doors up, who, in the deprecating way of women versus the ways of men, told her the reason. There are nicknames which are earned respectably and naturally, and indeed such nicknames are essential to identify persons in a land where there are only twenty or so proper baptised names for everybody. But, on hearing how Rowland earned Canute, his wife pursed in her lips like a pale tulip, opening them hours later to shout as Rowland tramped in from the pit:

'Ah, Canute is it! ... Sitting there in that London place,' she screamed, 'and all those men—' She whipped about like a hailstorm. 'You think I'm going to stay in Twlldu to be called Mrs. Rowland Canute, do you? We'll have to move from here – you begin looking for work in one of the other valleys at once.'

And such a dance she led him that in a couple of months they had left Pleasant Row. Rowland got taken on at the Powell pit in the Cwm Mardy valley, several stout mountains lying between that and Twlldu.

Yet give a dog a bad name, says the proverb, and it will stick. Who would have thought that Sam Recitations, growing in fame, would visit a club in faraway Cwm Mardy to give selections from his repertoire at a Smoking Concert? And almost the first man he saw when he entered the bar-room was Rowland. 'Why now,' his voice rolled in delight, 'if it isn't Rowland Canute! Ha, ha' And not noticing Rowland's dropped jaw of dismay, he turned and told all the clustering men what had happened under Paddington platform that time after the famous International – just as the history of the rescue had been told in all the clubs in the valley away over the mountains.

FEAR

As soon as the boy got into the compartment he felt there was something queer in it. The only other occupant was a slight, dusky man who sat in a corner with that air of propriety and unassertiveness which his race – he looked like an Indian – tend to display in England. There was also a faint sickly scent. For years afterwards, whenever he smelled that musk odour again, the terror of this afternoon came back to him.

He went to the other end of the compartment, sat in the opposite comer. There were no corridors in these local trains.

The man looked at him and smiled friendlily. The boy returned the smile briefly, not quite knowing what he was thinking, only aware of a deep, vague unease. But it would look so silly to jump out of the compartment now. The train gave a jerk and began to move.

Then, immediately with the jerk, the man began to utter a low humming chant, slow but with a definite rhythm. His lips did not open or even move, yet the hum penetrated above the noise of the train's wheels. It was in a sort of dreamy rhythm, enticing, lonely and antique; it suggested monotonous deserts, an eternal patience, a soothing wisdom. It went on and on. It was the kind of archaic chant that brings to the mind images of slowly swaying bodies in some endless ceremony in a barbaric temple.

Startled, and very alive to this proof of there being something odd in the compartment, the boy turned from staring out of the window – already the train was deep in the country among lonely fields and dark wooded slopes – and forced himself to glance at the man.

The man was looking at him. They faced each other across the compartment's length. Something coiled up in the boy. It was as if his soul took primitive fear and crouched to hide. The man's brown lips became stretched in a mysterious smile, though that humming chant continued, wordlessly swaying out of his mouth. His eyes, dark and unfathomable, never moved from the boy. The musk scent was stronger.

Yet this was not all. The boy could not imagine what other fearful thing lurked in the compartment. But he seemed to sense a secret power of something evilly antipathetic. Did it come from the man's long pinky-brown hands, the sinewy but fleshless hands of a sun-scorched race? Long tribal hands like claws. Or only from the fact that the man was of a far country whose ways were utterly alien to ours? And he continued to smile. A faint and subtle smile, while his eyes surveyed the boy as if he contemplated action. Something had flickered in and out of those shadowy eyes, like a dancing malice.

The boy sat stiffly. Somehow he could not return to his staring out of the window. But he tried not to look at the man again. The humming did not stop. And suddenly it took a higher note, like an unhurried wail, yet keeping within its strict and narrow compass. A liquid exultance wavered in and out of the wail. The noise of the train, the flying fields and woods, even the walls of the compartment, had vanished. There was only this chant, the man who was uttering it, and himself. He did not know that now he could not move his eyes from those of the man.

Abruptly the compartment was plunged into blackness. There was a shrieking rush of air. The train had entered a tunnel. With a sudden jerk the boy crouched down. He coiled into the seat's corner, shuddering, yet with every sense electrically alive now.

Then, above the roar of the air and the hurling grind of the train, that hum rose, dominantly establishing its insidious power. It called, it unhurriedly exhorted obedience, it soothed. Again it seemed to obliterate the louder, harsher noises. Spent and defeated, helplessly awaiting whatever menace lay in the darkness, the boy crouched. He knew the man's eyes were gazing towards him; he thought he saw their gleam triumphantly piercing the darkness. What was this strange presence of evil in the air, stronger now in the dark?

Suddenly crashing into the compartment, the hard blue and white daylight was like a blow. The train had gained speed in the tunnel and now hurled on through the light with the same agonising impetus, as if it would rush on for ever. Spent in the dread which had almost cancelled out his senses, the boy stared dully at the man. Still he seemed to hear the humming, though actually it had ceased. He saw the man's lips part in a full, enticing smile, he saw teeth dazzlingly white between the dusky lips.

'You not like dark tunnel?' The smile continued seductively; once more the flecks of light danced wickedly in his eyes. 'Come!' He beckoned with a long wrinkled finger.

The boy did not move.

'You like pomegranates?' He rose and took from the luggage rack a brown wicker basket. It was the kind of basket in which a large cat would be sent on a journey. 'Come!' he smiled friendlily and, as the boy still did not move, he crossed over and sat down beside him, but leaving a polite distance.

The staring boy did not flinch.

'Pomegranates from the East! English boy like, eh?' There seemed a collaboration in his intimate voice; he too was a boy going to share fruit with his friend. 'Nice pomegranates,' he smiled with good humour. There was also something stupid in his manner, a fatuous mysteriousness.

The basket lay on his knees. He began to hum again. The boy watched, still without movement, cold and abstract in his non-apprehension of this friendliness. But he was aware of the sickly perfume beside him and, more pronounced than ever, of an insidious presence that was utterly alien. That evil power lay in his immediate vicinity. The man looked at him again and, still humming, drew a rod and lifted the basket's lid.

There was no glow of magically gleaming fruits, no yellow-and-rose-tinted rinds enclosing honeycombs of luscious seeds. But from the basket's depth rose the head of a snake. It rose slowly to the enchantment of the hum. It rose from its sleepy coil, rearing its long brownish-gold throat dreamily, the head swaying out in languor towards the man's lips. Its eyes seemed to look blindly at nothing. It was a cobra.

Something happened to the boy. An old warning of the muscles and the vulnerable flesh. He leapt and flung himself headlong across the compartment. He was not aware that he gave a sharp shriek. He curled against the opposite seat's back, his knees pressing into the cushion. But, half turning, his eyes could not tear themselves from that reared head.

And it was with other senses that he knew most deeply he had evoked rage. The cobra was writhing in disturbed anger, shooting its head in his direction. He saw wakened pin-point eyes of black malice. More fearful was the dilation of the throat, its skin swelling evilly into a hood in which shone two palpitating sparks. In some cell of his being he knew that the hood was swelling in destructive fury. He became very still.

The man did not stop humming. But now his narrowed eyes

were focused in glittering concentration on the snake. And into that hum had crept a new note of tenacious decision. It was a pitting of subtle power against the snake's wishes and it was also an appeasement. A man was addressing a snake. He was offering a snake tribute and acknowledgment of its right to anger; he was honeyed and soothing. At the same time he did not relax an announcement of being master. There was courtesy towards one of the supreme powers of the animal kingdom, but also there was the ancient pride of man's supremacy.

And the snake was pacified. Its strange reared collar of skin sank back into its neck; its head ceased to lunge towards the boy. The humming slackened into a dreamy lullaby. Narrowly intent now, the man's eyes did not move. The length of tawny body slowly sank back. Its skin had a dull glisten, the glisten of an unhealthy torpidity. Now the snake looked effete, shorn of its venomous power. The drugged head sank. Unhurriedly the man closed the basket and slipped its rod secure.

He turned angrily to the boy; he made a contemptuous sound, like a hiss. 'I show you cobra and you jump and shout, heh! Make him angry!' There was more rebuke than real rage in his exclamations. But also his brown face was puckered in a kind of childish stupidity; he might have been another boy of twelve. 'I give you free performance with cobra, and you jump and scream like little girl.' The indignation died out of his eyes; they became focused in a more adult perception. 'I sing to keep cobra quiet in train,' he explained. 'Cobra not like train.'

The boy had not stirred. 'You not like cobra?' the man asked in injured surprise. 'Nice snake now, no poison! But not liking you jump and shout.'

There was no reply or movement; centuries and continents lay between him and the boy's still repudiation. The man gazed at him in silence and added worriedly: 'You going to fair in Newport? You see me? Ali the Snake Charmer. You come in free and see me make cobra dance.'

But the train was drawing into the station. It was not the boy's station. He made a sudden blind leap away from the man, opened the door, saw it was not on the platform side, but jumped. There was a shout from someone. He ran up the track, he dived under some wire railings. He ran with amazingly quick short leaps up a field – like a hare that knows its life is precarious among the colossal dangers of the open world and has suddenly sensed one of them.

I will keep her company

When he achieved the feat of getting down the stairs to the icy living room, it was the peculiar silence there that impressed him. It had not been so noticeable upstairs, where all night he had had company, of a kind. Down in this room, the familiar morning sounds he had known for sixty years – all the crockery, pots and pans, and fire-grate noises of married life at break of day, his wife's brisk soprano not least among them – were abolished as though they had never existed.

It was the snow had brought this silence, of course. How many days had it been falling – four or five? He couldn't remember. Still dazed and stiff from his long vigil in a chair upstairs, he hobbled slowly to the window. Sight of the magnificent white spread brought, as always, astonishment. Who would have thought such a vast quantity waited above? Almighty in its power to obliterate the known works of man, especially his carefully mapped highways and byways, the weight of odourless substance was like a reminder that he was of no more account than an ant. But only a few last flakes were falling now, the small aster shapes drifting with dry languor on the hefty waves covering the long front garden.

'They'll be here today,' he said aloud, wakened a little more by the dazzle. The sound of his voice was strange to him, like an echo of it coming back from a chasm. His head turning automatically towards the open door leading to the hallway, he broke the silence again, unwilling to let it settle. 'Been snowing again all night, Maria. But it's stopping now. They'll come today. The roads have been blocked. Hasn't been a fall like it for years.'

His frosting breath plumed the air. He turned back to the window and continued to peer out for a while. A drift swelled to above the sill and there was no imprint of the robins and tits that regularly landed before the window in the morning, for breakfast crumbs. Neither was there a sign of the garden gate into the lane, nor a glimpse of the village, two miles distant down the valley, which could be seen from this height on green days. But the mountains, ramparts against howling Atlantic gales, were visible in glitteringly bleached outline against a pale-blue sky. Savage guardians of interior Wales, even their lowering black clouds and whipping rains were vanquished today. They looked innocent in their unbroken white.

His mind woke still more. The manacled landscape gave him, for the moment, a feeling of security. This snow was a protection, not a catastrophe. He did not want the overdue visitors to arrive, did not want to exercise himself again in resistance to their arguments for his future welfare. Not yet. He thought of his six damson trees which he had introduced into the orchard a few years before and reared with such care. Last summer, there had been a nice little profit from the baskets of downy fruit. Was he to be forced away from his grown-up darlings now? Just one more season of gathering, and, afterwards, he would be ready to decide about the future...

Then, remembering something else, he lamented, 'They'll come, they'll come!' They had such a special reason for making the journey. And this marooning snow would give even more urgency to their arguments regarding himself. He strained his keen old countryman's eyes down the anonymous white distances. Could they come? Could anyone break a way through those miles of deep snow, where nothing shuffled, crawled, or even flew? The whole world had halted. They would not come today. There would be one more day of peace.

Mesmerized at the window, he recalled another supreme time of snow, long ago, before he was married. He and two other farm workers had gone in search of Ambrose Owen's sheep. An old ram was found in a drift, stiff and upright on his legs, glassy eyes staring at nothing, curls of wool turned to a cockleshell hardness that could be chipped from the fleece. Farther away in the drift, nine wise ewes lay huddled against each other, and these were carried upside down by the legs to the farmhouse kitchen, where they thawed into life. But Ambrose, like that man in the Bible with a prodigal son, had broken down and shed tears over his lost ram that had foolishly wandered from the herd. The elderly farmer was in a low condition himself at the time, refusing to be taken to hospital, wanting to kick the bucket not only in his own home but downstairs in his fireside chair. Quite right too.

He returned from the window at last, drew a crimson flannel shawl from his sparsely haired head, and rearranged it carefully over his narrow shoulders. He wore two cardigans and trousers of thick home-spun, but the cold penetrated to his bones. Still unwilling to begin the day's ritual of living down in this room, he stood gazing vaguely from the cinder-strewn fireplace to the furniture, his eyes lingering on the beautifully polished rosewood table at which, with seldom a cross word exchanged (so it seemed now), he had shared good breakfasts for a lifetime. Was it because of the unnatural silence, with not the whir of a single bird outside, that all the familiar contents of the room seemed withdrawn from ownership. They looked stranded.

Remembrance came to him of the room having this same hush of unbelonging when he and Maria had first walked into it, with the idea of buying the place, a freehold stone cottage and its four acres, for ninety-five sovereigns, cash down. They were courting at the time, and the property was cheap because of its isolation; no one had lived there for years. The orchard, still well-stocked, had decided him, and Maria, who could depend on herself and a husband for all the talking she needed, agreed because of the tremendous views of mountain range and sky from this closed end of the valley. What a walker she had been! Never wanted even a bike, did not want to keep livestock, and was content with the one child that came very soon after the rushed purchase of the cottage. But, disregarding gossip, she had liked to go down to church in the village, where she sang psalms louder than any other woman there.

He had huddled closer into the shawl. Since he would not be staying long down here, was it worthwhile lighting a fire? Then he realized that if the visitors found means of coming, it would be prudent to let them see he could cope with the household jobs. First, the grate to be raked, and a fire laid; wood and coal to be fetched from outside, but he couldn't hurry. His scalp was beginning to prickle and contract, and he drew the shawl over his head again. Feeling was already gone from his feet when he reached the shadowy kitchen lying off the living room, fumblingly pulled the back door open, and faced a wall of pure white.

The entire door space was blocked, sealing access to the shed in which, besides wood and coal, oil for the cooking stove was stored. He had forgotten that the wall had been there the day before. Snow had drifted down the mountain slope and piled as far as the back window upstairs even then; it came back to him that he had drawn the kitchen window curtains to hide that weight of tombstone white against the panes. 'Marble,' he said now, curiously running a finger over the crisply hardened surface. He shut the door, relieved that one item in the morning jobs was settled; it would be impossible to reach the shed from the front of the cottage.

Pondering in the dowdy light of the kitchen, he looked at the empty glass oil-feeder of the cooking stove, at the empty kettle, at an earthenware pitcher which he knew was empty too. He remembered that the water butt against the outside front wall had been frozen solid for days before the snow began. And even if he had the strength to dig a path to the well in the orchard, very likely that would be frozen. Would snow melt inside the house? But a little water remained in a ewer upstairs. And wasn't there still some of the milk that the district nurse had brought? He found the jug in the slate-shelved larder, and tilted it; the inch-deep, semi-congealed liquid moved. He replaced the jug with a wrinkling nose, and peered at the three tins of soup that also had been brought by Nurse Baldock.

Sight of the tins gave him a feeling of nausea. The last time the nurse had come – which day was it? – a smell like ammonia had hung about her. And her pink rubber gloves, her apron with its row of safety pins and a tape measure dangling over it, had badly depressed him. A kind woman, though, except for her deciding what was the best way for a man to live. The sort that treated all men as little boys. She had a voice that wouldn't let go of a person but, being a woman, a soft wheedling could come into it when she chose. Thank God the snow had bogged her down.

He reached for a flat box, opened it, and saw a few biscuits. Maria always liked the lid picture of Caernarfon Castle, which they'd visited one summer day; he looked at it now with a reminiscent chuckle. His movements became automatically exact, yet vague and random. He found a tin tray inscribed

'Ringer's Tobacco' and placed on it the box, a plate and, forgetting there was no milk left upstairs, a clean cup and saucer. This done, he suddenly sat down on a hard chair and closed his eyes.

He did not know how long he remained there. Tapping sounds roused him; he jerked from the chair with galvanized strength. Agitation gave his shouts an unreasonable cantankerousness as he reached the living room. 'They've come! Open the door, can't you? It's not locked.'

He opened the front door. There was nobody. The snow reached up to his waist, and the stretch of it down the garden slope bore not a mark. Only an elephant could come to this door. Had he dreamed the arrival? Or had a starving bird tapped its beak on the window? The dread eased. He shut the door with both his shaking hands, and stood listening in the small hallway. 'They haven't come!' he shouted up the stairs, wanting to hear his voice smashing the silence. 'But they will, they will! They are bringing my pension money from the post office. Dr Howells took my book with him.' Self-reminder of this ordinary matter helped to banish the dread, and the pain in his chest dwindled.

Pausing in the living room, he remembered that it was actually Nurse Baldock who had taken his book and put it in that important black bag of hers. She had arrived that day with Dr Howells in his car, instead of on her bike. The snow had begun to fall, but she said it wouldn't be much – only a sprinkling. And Dr Howells had told him not to worry and that everything would be put in hand. But even the doctor, who should have had a man's understanding, had argued about the future, and coaxed like Nurse Baldock. Then she had said she'd bring Vicar Pryce on her next visit. People hissing! But he couldn't lock the door against them yet. It was necessary for them to come just once again. He would pretend to listen to them, especially the vicar, and when they had gone he would lock the door, light a fire, and sit down to think of the future in his own way.

His eyes strayed about the room again. He looked at the table with its green-shaded oil lamp, at the dresser with its display of brilliant plates and lustre jugs, at the comfortable low chairs, the bright rugs, the scroll-backed sofa from which Maria had directed his activities for the week before she was obliged to take to her bed at last. After the shock of the fancied arrival, the objects in the room no longer seemed withdrawn from ownership. They would yield him security and ease, for a long while yet. And the cooking stove in the kitchen, the pans, brooms and brushes – they had belonged solely to Maria's energetic hands, but after a lifetime with her he knew exactly how she dealt with them. Any man with three penn'orth of sense could live here independently as a lord. Resolve lay tucked away in his mind. Today, with this cold stunning his senses, not much could be done. He must wait. His eyes reached the mantelpiece clock; lifting the shawl from his ears, he stared closer at the age-yellowed face. That was why the silence had been so strange! Was even a clock affected by the cold? Surely he had wound it last night, as usual; surely he had come downstairs? The old-fashioned clopping sound, steady as horse hooves ambling on a quiet country road, had never stopped before. The defection bothering him more than the lack of means for a fire and oil for the stove, he reached for the mahogany-framed clock, his numb fingers moving over it to take a firm grip. It fell into the stoneflagged hearth. There was a tinkle of broken glass.

'Ah,' he shouted guiltily, 'the clock's broken, Maria! Slipped out of my hand!'

He gazed at it in a stupor. But the accident finally decided him. Down in this room the last bits of feeling were ebbing from him. There was warmth and company upstairs. He stumbled into the kitchen, lifted the tin tray in both hands without feeling its substance, and reached the hallway. Negotiation of the stairs took even more time than his descent had. As in the kitchen, it was the propulsion of old habit that got him up the flight he had climbed thousands of times. The tray fell out of his hands when he reached a squeaking stair just below the landing. This did not matter; he even liked the lively explosion of noise. 'It's only that advertisement tray the shop gave you one Christmas!' he called out, not mentioning the crocks and biscuit box which had crashed to the bottom. He did not attempt to retrieve anything. All he wanted was warmth.

In the clear white light of a front room he stood for some moments looking intently at the weather-browned face of the small woman lying on a four-poster bed. Her eyes were compactly shut. Yet her face bore an expression of prim vigour; still she looked alert in her withdrawal. No harsh glitter of light from the window reached her, but he drew a stiff fold of the gay-patterned linen bed curtains that, as if in readiness for this immurement, had been washed, starched and ironed by her three weeks before. Then he set about his own task. The crimson shawl still bonneted his head.

His hands plucked at the flannel blankets and larger shawls lying scattered on the floor around a wheelbacked armchair close to the bed. Forcing grip into his fingers, he draped these coverings methodically over the sides and back of the chair, sat down, and swathed his legs and body in the overlapping folds. It all took a long time, and for a while it brought back the pain in his chest, compelling him to stop. Finally, he succeeded in drawing portions of two other shawls over his head and shoulders, so that he was completely encased in draperies. There had been good warmth in this cocoon last night. The everlasting flannel was woven in a mill down the valley, from the prized wool of local mountain sheep. Properly washed in rain water, it yielded warmth for a hundred years or more. There were old valley people who had been born and had gone in the same pair of handed-down family blankets.

Secure in the shelter, he waited patiently for warmth to come. When it began to arrive, and the pain went, his mind flickered into activity again. It was of the prancing mountain ponies he thought first, the wild auburn ponies that were so resentful of capture. He had always admired them. But what did their lucky freedom mean now? They had no roof over their head, and where could they find victuals? Had they lost their bearings up in their fastnesses? Were they charging in demented panic through the endless snow, plunging into crevices, starvation robbing them of instinct and sense? Then there were the foxes. He remembered hearing during that drastic time of snow when he rescued Ambrose Owen's sheep, a maddened fox had dashed into the vicarage kitchen when a servant opened the back door. It snatched in its teeth a valuable Abyssinian cat lying fast asleep on the hearth rug, and streaked out before the petrified woman could scream.

A little more warmth came. He crouched into it with a sigh. Soon it brought a sense of summer pleasures. A long meadow dotted with buttercups and daisies shimmered before him, and a golden-haired boy ran excitedly over the bright grass to a young white goat tied to an iron stake. Part of the meadow was filled with booths of striped canvas, and a roundabout of painted horses galloped to barrel organ music. It was that Whitsuntide fete when he had won the raffled goat on a sixpenny ticket – the only time he had won anything all his life. Maria had no feeling for goats, especially rams, but she had let their boy lead the snowy-haired beast home. Richard had looked after it all its sturdy years and, at its hiring, got for himself the fees of its natural purpose in life – five shillings a time, in those far-off days.

The father chuckled. He relaxed further in the dark chair. His hands resting lightly on his knees, he prepared for sleep. It was slow in taking him, and when, drowsily, he heard a whirring sound he gave it no particular attention. But he stirred slightly and opened his eyes. The noise approached closer. It began to circle, now faint, then loud, now dwindling. He did not recognize it. It made him think of a swarm of chirping grasshoppers, then of the harsh clonking of roused geese. Neutral towards all disturbance from outside, he nestled deeper into the warmth bred of the last thin heat of his blood, and when a louder noise shattered the peace of his cocoon he still did not move, though his eyes jerked wide open once more.

The helicopter circled twice above the half-buried cottage. Its clacking sounded more urgent as it descended and began to pass as low as the upstairs windows at the front and back. The noise became a rasp of impatience, as if the machine were annoyed that no reply came to this equivalent of a knocking on the door, that no attention was paid to the victory of this arrival. A face peered down from a curved grey pane; the head of another figure dodged behind, moving to both the side panels.

Indecision seemed to govern this hovering above the massed billows of snow. After the cottage had been circled three times, the machine edged nearer the front wall, and a square box wrapped in orange-coloured oilskin tumbled out, fell accurately before the door, and lay visible in a hole of snow. The machine rose; its rotor blades whirled for seconds above the cottage before it mounted higher. It diminished into the pale afternoon light, flying down from the valley towards immaculate mountains that had never known a visit from such a strange bird.

Evening brought an unearthly blue to the sculptured distances. Night scarcely thickened the darkness; the whiteness could be seen for miles. Only the flashing of clear-cut stars broke the long stillness of the valley. No more snow fell. But the cold hardened during the low hours, and at dawn, though a red glow lay in the sun's disc on Moelwyn's crest, light came with grudging slowness, and there was no promise of thaw all morning. But, soon after the sun had passed the zenith, another noise smashed into the keep of silence at the valley's closed end.

Grinding and snorting, a vehicle slowly burrowed into the snow. It left in its wake, like a gigantic horned snail, a silvery track, on which crawled a plain grey motor van. Ahead, the climbing plough was not once defeated by its pioneering work, thrusting past shrouded hedges on either side of it, its grunting front mechanism churning up the snow and shooting it out of a curved-over horn on to bushes at the left. The attendant grey van stopped now and then, allowing a measure of distance to accumulate on the smooth track.

The van had three occupants. Two of them, sitting on the driver's cushioned bench, were philosophically patient of this laborious journeying. The third, who was Nurse Baldock, squatted on the floor inside the small van, her legs stretched towards the driver's seat and her shoulders against the back door. She was a substantial woman, and the ungainly fur coat she wore gave her the dimensions of a mature bear. She tried not to be restless. But as the instigator of this rescuing operation, she kept looking at her watch, and she failed to curb herself all the time. The two men in front had not been disposed for talk.

'I hope that thing up there won't break down,' she said presently. 'It's a Canadian snowplough – so I was told on the phone. The Council bought it only last year.'

'It took them a deuce of a time to get one after we had that nasty snowfall in 1947,' remarked the driver, a middle-aged man in a sombre vicuna overcoat and a bowler hat. 'A chap and his young lady were found buried in their car halfway up Moelwyn when we had that lot – been there a week, if you remember, Vicar. Thank God these bad falls don't come often.'

'Councils seldom look far outside their town hall chamber after election,' mumbled Vicar Pryce, who had been picked up in Ogwen village twenty minutes earlier. Under his round black hat only his eyes and bleak nose were visible from wrappings of scarves. It was very cold in the utilitarian van, lent for this emergency expedition by a tradesman of the market town at the valley's mouth; the road from there to Ogwen had been cleared the day before.

'Well, our Council has got hold of a helicopter this time, too,' Nurse Baldock reminded them, not approving of criticism of her employers from anyone. 'Soon as I heard they had hired one to drop bundles of hay to stranded cattle and mountain ponies, I said to myself, "Man first, then the beasts," and flew to my phone. I'm fond of old John Evans, though he's so wilful. I arranged to have tins of food, fruit juice, milk, a small bottle of brandy, fresh pork sausages, and bread put in the box, besides a plastic container of cooker oil and a message from me.'

'Couldn't you have gone in the helicopter?' the driver asked, rather inattentively.

'What, and got dropped out into the snow with the box?' The nurse's bulk wobbled with impatience. 'If the machine couldn't land anywhere on those deep slopes of snow, how could I get down, I ask you?'

'I thought they could drop a person on a rope.' The driver sounded propitiatory now. For him, as for most people, the district nurse was less a woman than a portent of inescapable forces lying in wait for everybody.

'Delivery of necessities was the point,' she said dismissingly, and, really for Vicar Pryce's wrapped ears, continued, 'After getting the helicopter man's report yesterday, I was on the phone to the Town Hall for half an hour. I insisted that they let me have the snowplough today – I fought for it. It was booked for this and that, they said, but I had my way in the end.'

'Last night was bitter,' Vicar Pryce said, following a silence, 'I got up at 3 a.m. and piled a sheepskin floor rug on my bed.'

'Bitter it wr,' agreed Nurse Baldock. 'We single people feel it the more.' Neither of the men offered a comment, and, with another look at her watch, she pursued, 'Of course, the helicopter man's report needn't mean a lot. Who could blame Evans if he stayed snuggled in bed all day? And at his age, he could sleep through any noise.'

'One would think a helicopter's clatter would bring him out of any sleep, Nurse,' the Vicar remarked.

'I think he's a bit deaf,' she replied, rejecting the doubt. 'In any case, I don't suppose he'd know what the noise meant.' The van stopped, and she decided, 'We'll have our coffee now.'

She managed to spread quite a picnic snack on the flat top of a long, calico-covered object lying beside her, on which she wouldn't sit. There were cheese and egg sandwiches, pieces of sultana cake, plates, mugs, sugar and a large Thermos flask. A heavy can of paraffin propped her back, and, in addition to the satchel of picnic stuff, she had brought her official leather bag, well known in the valley. Nurse Baldock's thoroughness was as dreaded by many as was sight of her black bag. After determined efforts over several years, she had recently been awarded a social science diploma, and now, at forty-five, she hoped for a more important position than that of a bicycle-borne district nurse. This rescuing mission today would help prove her mettle, and Vicar Pryce, to whom she had insisted on yielding the seat in front, would be a valuable witness of her zeal.

'I'll keep enough for the young man in the snowplough,' she said, pouring coffee. 'He ought not to stop now. The quicker we get there the better.'

'Makes one think of places on the moon,' the driver remarked, gazing out at the waxen countryside.

Sipping coffee, she resumed, 'I have eight patients in Ogwen just now, and I really ought not to be spending all this time on a man who's got nothing the matter with him except old age and obstinacy. Two confinements due any day now.' The men drank and ate, and she added, 'What a time for births! There's Mavis Thomas, for instance – she's not exactly entitled to one, is she, Vicar? But at least that man she lives with keeps her house on Sheep's Gap warm, and her water hasn't frozen.'

'Nobody except a choirboy turned up for matins last Sunday,' the meditative vicar said. 'So I cancelled all services that day.'

Nurse Baldock finished a piece of cake. 'I heard yesterday that a married woman living up on Sheep's Gap was chased by two starving ponies that found a way down from the mountains. You know how they won't go near human beings as a rule, but when this woman came out of her farmhouse in her gumboots they stampeded from behind a barn; with their teeth grinding and eyes flaring. She ran back screaming into the house just in time.'

'Perhaps she was carrying a bucket of pig feed and they smelt it,' the driver suggested, handing back his mug.

Undeterred, Nurse Baldock gave a feminine shiver. 'I keep an eye open for them on my rounds. We might be back in the days of wolves.' The van resumed its amble on the pearly track as she proceeded. 'But these are modern times. Old Evans would never dream he would get a helicopter for his benefit, to say nothing of that great ugly thing in front, and us. There's real Christianity for you! This affair will cost the Council quite a sum. It will go on the rates, of course.'

'John and Maria Evans,' Vicar Pryce said, rewrapping his ears in the scarves, 'were always faithful parishioners of mine when they were able to get down to the village. I remember their son Richard, too. A good tenor in the choir. Emigrated to New Zealand and has children of his own there, I understand.'

'Well, Vicar,' Nurse Baldock said, packing the crocks into the satchel between her knees, 'I hope you'll do your very best to persuade Evans to leave with us today and go to Pistyll Mawr Home. Heaven knows, I did all I could to coax him when I was at the cottage with Dr. Howells the other day.'

'It will be a business,' he mumbled.

She pursed her lips. 'He told me it was healthy up there in his cottage, and that he and his wife had always liked the views. "Views!" I said, "Views won't feed and nurse you if you fall ill. Come now, facts must be faced." Then he said something about his damson trees. I told him Pistyll Mawr had fruit trees in plenty.'

The driver, who lived in the market town, spoke. 'Don't the new cases take offence at being forced to have a bath as soon as they enter the doors of Pistyll Mawr?'

'So you've heard that one, have you? Why, what's wrong with a bath? Is it a crime?' Nurse Baldock had bridled. 'I am able to tell you there's a woman in Pistyll Mawr who brags about her baths there – says that for the first time in her life she feels like a well-off lady, with a maid to sponge her back and hand her a towel. You're out of date, sir, with your "take offence".'

'Aren't there separate quarters for men and women, even if they're married?' he persisted.

'As if very elderly people are bothered by what you mean! Besides, they can flirt in the garden if they want. But old people have too much dignity for such nonsense.'

'I dare say there are one or two exceptions.'

'Ah, I agree there.' Nurse Baldock pulled gauntlet gloves over her mittens. 'The aged! They're our biggest problem. The things that come my way from some of them! One has to have nerves of iron, and it doesn't do to let one's eyes fill. Why must people trouble themselves so much about the young? My blood boils when I see all the rubbishy fuss made about the youngsters by newspapers and busybodies of the lay public. Sight of the word "teenagers" makes me want to throw up. Leave the young alone, I say! They've got all the treasures of the world on their backs, and once they're out of school they don't put much expense on the rates.'

After this tirade no one spoke for a time. As the van crawled nearer the valley's majestic closure, Nurse Baldock herself seemed to become oppressed by the solemn desolation outside. Not a boulder or streak of path showed on Moelwyn's swollen heights. Yet, close at hand, there were charming snow effects. The van rounded a turn of the lane, and breaks in the hedges on either side revealed birch glades, their spectral depths glittering as though from the light of ceremonial chandeliers. All the crystal-line birches were struck into eternal stillness – fragile, rime-heavy boughs sweeping downward, white hairs of mourning. Not a bird, rabbit, or beetle could stir in those frozen grottoes, and the blue harebell or the pink convolvulus never ring out in them again.

'Up here doesn't seem to belong to us,' Vicar Pryce said, when the van halted again. 'It's the white. If only we could see just one little robin hopping about the branches! The last time I came this way, I saw pheasants crossing the roads and then they rose. Such colour! It was soon after Easter, and the windflowers and primroses were out.'

'We might be travelling in a wheelbarrow,' sighed Nurse Baldock, as the van moved. She looked at her watch, then into her official bag, and said, 'I've got Evans's old-age-pension money. Because of his wife's taking to her bed, he worried about not being able to leave the cottage. I told him, "You're lucky you've got someone like me to look after you, but it's not my bounden task to collect your pension money, Council-employed though I am. Things can't go on like this, my dear sir, come now."'

'You've been kind to him,' the Vicar acknowledged at last.

'It's the State that is kind,' she said stoutly. 'We can say there's no such thing as neglect or old-fashioned poverty for the elderly now. But in my opinion the lay public has begun to take our welfare schemes too much for granted. The other day, I was able to get a wig free of charge for a certain madam living not a hundred miles from this spot, and when I turned up with it on my bike she complained it wasn't the right brown shade and she couldn't wear it – a woman who is not able to step outside her door and is seventy-eight!'

'The aged tend to cling to their little cussednesses,' Vicar Pryce mumbled, in a lacklustre way.

'Yes, indeed.' They were nearing their destination now, and Nurse Baldock, tenacity unabated, seized her last opportunity. 'But do press the real advantages of Pistyll Mawr Home to Evans,

Vicar. We are grateful when the Church does its share in these cases. After all, my concern is with the body.' This earned no reply, and she said, 'Germs! It's too icy for them to be active just now, but with the thaw there'll be a fine crop of bronchials and influenzas, mark my words! And I don't relish coming all this way to attend to Evans if he's struck down, probably through not taking proper nourishment.' There was a further silence, and she added, 'On the other hand, these outlying cases ought to convince the Health Department that I must be given a car – don't you agree, Vicar?'

'I wonder you have not had one already. Dr. Howells should—'

A few yards ahead, the plough had stopped. Its driver leaned out of his cabin and yelled, 'Can't see a gate!'

'I'll find it,' Nurse Baldock declared.

The vicar and van driver helped to ease her out of the back doors. She shook her glut of warm skirts down, and clumped forward in her gumboots. A snow-caked roof and chimney could be seen above a billowing white slope. Scanning the contours of a buried hedge, the nurse pointed. 'The gate is there. I used to lean my bike against that tree.' It was another lamenting birch, the crystal-entwined branches drooped to the snow.

The plough driver, an amiable-looking young man in an elegant alpine sweater, brought out three shovels. Nurse Baldock scolded him for not having four. Valiantly, when he stopped for coffee and sandwiches, she did a stint, and also used the vicar's shovel while he rested. They had shouted towards the cottage. There was no response and, gradually, they ceased to talk. It took them half an hour to clear a way up the garden. They saw the oilskin wrapped box as they neared the door. The nurse, her square face professionally rid of comment now, had already fetched her bag.

It was even colder in the stone house than outside. Nurse Baldock, the first to enter, returned from a swift trot into the living room and kitchen to the men clustered in the little hallway. She stepped to the staircase. All-seeing as an investigating policewoman, she was nevertheless respecting the social decencies. Also, despite the sight of broken crockery, a biscuit box, and a tray scattered below the stairs, she was refusing to face defeat yet. 'John Ormond Evans,' she called up, 'are you there?' Her voice had the challenging ring sometimes used for encouraging the declining back to the world of health, and after a moment of silence, she added, with an unexpected note of entreaty, 'The vicar is here!' The three men, like awkward intruders in a private place, stood listening. Nurse Baldock braced herself. 'Come up with me,' she whispered.

Even the plough driver followed her. But when the flannel wrappings were stripped away, John Ormond Evans sat gazing out at them from his chair as though in mild surprise at this intrusion into his comfortable retreat. His deep-sunk blue eyes were frostily clear under arched white brows. He looked like one awakened from restorative slumber, an expression of judicious independence fixed on his spare face. His hands rested on his knees, like a Pharaoh's.

Nurse Baldock caught in her breath with a hissing sound. The two older men, who had remained hatted and gloved in the icy room, stood dumbly arrested. It was the ruddy-cheeked young man who suddenly put out a bare, instinctive hand and, with a movement of extraordinary delicacy, tried to close the blue eyes. He failed.

'I closed my father's eyes,' he stammered, drawing away in bashful apology for his strange temerity.

'Frozen,' pronounced Vicar Pryce, removing his round black

hat. He seemed about to offer a few valedictory words.

Nurse Baldock pulled herself together. She swallowed, and said, 'Lack of nourishment, too!' She took off a gauntlet glove, thrust fingers round one of the thin wrists for a token feel, and then stepped back. 'Well, here's a problem! Are we to take him back with us?'

Vicar Pryce turned to look at the woman lying on the curtain-hung bed. Perhaps because his senses were blurred by the cold, he murmured, 'She's very small – smaller than I remember her. Couldn't he go in the coffin with her for the journey back?'

'No,' said Nurse Baldock promptly. 'He couldn't be straightened here.'

The van driver, an auxiliary assistant in busy times to Messrs Eccles, the market-town undertakers, confirmed, 'Set, set.'

'As he was in his ways!' burst from Nurse Baldock in her chagrin. 'This needn't have happened if he had come with me, as I wanted six days ago! Did he sit there all night deliberately?'

It was decided to take him. The coffin, three days late in delivery, was fetched from the van by the driver and the young man. Maria Evans, aged eighty-three, and prepared for this journey by the nurse six days before, by no means filled its depth and length. Gone naturally, of old age, and kept fresh by the cold, she looked ready to rise punctiliously to meet the face of the Almighty with the same hale energy as she had met each washing day on earth. Her shawl-draped husband, almost equally small, was borne out after her in his sitting posture. Nurse Baldock, with the vicar for witness, locked up the house. Already it had an air of not belonging to anyone. 'We must tell the police we found the clock lying broken in the hearth,' she said. 'There'll be an inquest, of course.'

John Evans, head resting against the van's side, travelled

sitting on his wife's coffin; Vicar Pryce considered it unseemly for him to be laid on the floor. The helicopter box of necessities and the heavy can of oil, placed on either side of him, held him secure. Nurse Baldock chose to travel with the young man in the draughty cabin of his plough. Huddled in her fur coat, and looking badly in need of her own hearth, she remained sunk in morose silence now.

The plough, no longer spouting snow, trundled in the van's rear. 'Pretty in there!' the driver ventured to say, in due course. They were passing the spectral birch glades. A bluish shade had come to the depths.

Nurse Baldock stirred. Peering out, she all but spat. 'Damned, damned snow! All my work wasted! Arguments on the phone, a helicopter, and this plough! The cost! I shall have to appear before the Health Committee.'

'I expect they'll give you credit for all you've done for the old fellow,' said the driver, also a Council employee.

She was beyond comforting just then. 'Old people won't listen'. When I said to him six days ago, "Come with me, there's nothing you can do for her now," he answered, "Not yet. I will keep her company." I could have taken him at once to Pistyll Mawr Home. It was plain he couldn't look after himself. One of those unwise men who let themselves be spoilt by their wives.'

'Well, they're not parted now,' the young man said.

'The point is, if he had come with me he would be enjoying a round of buttered toast in Pistyll Mawr at this very moment. I blame myself for not trying hard enough. But how was I to know all this damn snow was coming?'

'A lot of old people don't like going into Pistyll Mawr Home, do they?'

'What's wrong with Pistyll Mawr? Hetty Jarvis, the matron,

has a heart of gold. What's more, now I've got my social science diploma, I'm applying for her position when she retires next year.'

'Good luck to you.' The driver blew on his hands. Already, the speedier van had disappeared into the whiteness.

'The lay public,' Nurse Baldock sighed, looking mollified, 'will cling to its prejudices.' And half to herself, she went on, 'Hetty Jarvis complained to me that she hasn't got anything like enough inmates to keep her staff occupied. "Baldock," she said to me, "I'm depending on you,' and I phoned her only this week to say I had found someone for her, a sober and clean man I would gamble had many years before him if he was properly cared for.'

'Ah,' murmured the driver. He lit a cigarette, at which his preoccupied passenger – after all, they were in a kind of funeral – frowned.

'People should see the beeswaxed parquet floors in Pistyll Mawr,' she pursued. 'When the hydrangeas are in bloom along the drive, our Queen herself couldn't wish for a better approach to her home. The bishop called it a noble sanctuary in his opening-day speech. And so it is!'

'I've heard the Kingdom of Heaven is like that,' the young man remarked idly. 'People have got to be pushed in.'

Nurse Baldock turned to look at his round face, to which had come, perhaps because of the day's rigours, the faint purple hue of a ripening fig. 'You might think differently later on, my boy,' she commented in a measured way. 'I can tell you there comes a time when few of us are able to stand alone. You saw today what resulted for one who made the wrong choice.'

'Oh, I don't know. I expect he knew what he was doing, down inside him.'

She sighed again, apparently patient of ignorance and

youthful lack of feeling. 'I was fond of old Evans,' she said.

'Anyone can see it,' he allowed.

She remained silent for a long while. The costly defeat continued to weigh on her until the plough had lumbered on to the flat of the valley's bed. There, she looked at her watch and began to bustle up from melancholy. 'Five hours on this one case!' she fidgeted. 'I ought to have gone back in the van. I'm due at a case up on Sheep's Gap.'

'Another old one?'

'No, thank God. An illegitimate maternity. Not the first one for her either! And I've got another in the row of cottages down by the little waterfall – a legitimate.' The satisfaction of a life-giving smack on the bottom seemed to resound in her perked-up voice. 'We need them more than ever in nasty times like these, don't we? Providing a house is warm and well stocked for the welcome. Can't you make this thing go faster?'

'I'm at top speed. It's not built for maternities of any kind.'

Nurse Baldock sniffed. She sat more benevolently, however, and offered from the official black bag a packet of barley sugar sweets. The village lay less than a mile distant. But it was some time before there was a sign of natural life out in the white purity. The smudged outline of a church tower and clustering houses had come into view when the delighted young man exclaimed, 'Look!' Arriving from nowhere, a hare had jumped on to the smooth track. His jump lacked a hare's usual celerity. He seemed bewildered, and sat up for an instant, ears tensed to the noise breaking the silence of these chaotic acres, a palpitating eye cast back in assessment of the oncoming plough. Then his forepaws gave a quick play of movement, like shadowboxing, and he sprang forward on the track with renewed vitality. Twice he stopped to look as though in need of affiliation with the plough's motion. But, beyond a bridge over the frozen rivers he took a flying leap and, paws barely touching the hardened snow and, scut whisking, escaped out of sight.

BLODWEN

'Pugh Jibbons is at the back door,' cried Blodwen's mother from upstairs. 'Go and get four pounds of peas.'

A sulky look came to Blodwen's face for a moment. She hated going out to Pugh Jibbons to buy vegetables, she couldn't bear his insolent looks. Nevertheless, after glancing in the kitchen mirror, she walked down the little back garden and opened the door that led into the wasteland behind the row of houses.

A small cart, with a donkey in the shafts, stood there piled high with vegetables. Pugh Jibbons – the son of old Pugh Jibbons, so called because he always declared that jibbons (that being the local name for spring onions) cured every common ailment in man – leaned against the cart waiting for her. This was almost a daily occurrence.

He did not greet her. He looked at her steadily, as she stood under the lintel of the door, a slight flush in her cheeks, and ordered, in a harsh voice of contempt:

'Four pounds of peas!'

Pugh Jibbons grinned. He was a funny-looking fellow. A funny fellow. Perhaps there was a gipsy strain in him. He was of the Welsh who have not submitted to industrialism, Nonconformity or imitation of the English. He looked as though he had issued from a cave in the mountains. He was swarthy and thick-set, with rounded, powerful limbs and strong dark tufts of hair everywhere. Winter and summer he bathed in the river and lived in a tiny house away up on the mountainside, near to the lower slope where his allotment of vegetables was. His father, with whom he lived, was now old and vague and useless; the jibbons had not kept him his senses; and his mother was dead. They had always lived a semi-wild life on the mountainside, earning a bit of money selling their vegetables, which were good and healthy, in the valley below.

'Fourpence a pound they are today,' he informed Blodwen. And all his browny-red face went on grinning. He looked right down into her eyes. His were dark and clear and mocking, hers were dark blue and inflamed with anger.

She shrugged her shoulders, though she was indignant at the doubling of the price since yesterday.

'Coming to an end they are now,' he said, weighing the peas, but keeping his eye on her, which he winked whenever her disdainful glance came round to him. But she would look into the distance beyond him.

There was usually a box of flowers on the cart. Today there were bunches of pinks in it. He took one out. She held out her apron for the peas and he shovelled them into it, placing the bunch of pinks on the top.

'But I'll chuck those in for the price,' he said.

Though nearly always he would thrust a bunch of flowers on her. Usually she took them. But today she didn't want to. She wanted to tell him something. She said:

'Take those flowers back.' Her colour came up, she arched her beautiful thick neck, her eyes blazed out on him. 'And if you keep on following me about the streets at night I'll set the police on you, I warn you. Where's your decency, man?' And then she wanted to slam the door in his face and hurry away. But she waited, looking at him menacingly.

His mouth remained open for a moment or two after

her outburst, comically, his eyes looking at her with startled examination. Then he pushed his cap to the back of his head, thrust out his head aggressively, and demanded:

'Is that bloke that goes about with you your fellow, then?'

Her disdainful face lifted, she rapped out, 'Something unpleasant to say to you that fellow will have if you don't watch out, you rude lout.'

Then he became mocking and teasing again, his eyes sharp with wickedness. 'He's not a bloke for you, well you know that,' he said daringly. 'Toff as he is and tall and elegant, he's not a bloke for you. I know him and I know the family out of what he comes. There's no guts to any of his lot. Haw-haw and behave politely and freeze yourself all up. There's no juice and no seed and no marrow and no bones to him. Oswald Vaughan! Haw-haw.' And screwing up his face to a caricature of a toff's expression, he stood before her undismayed and mocking, his short thick legs apart and almost bandy.

'You...' she muttered, raging, 'you wait. You'll be sorry for this.' She slammed the door and hurried to the kitchen.

The unspeakable ruffian! What right had he to talk of Oswald like that. And 'He's not a bloke for you, well you know that!' Impudence. Pugh Jibbons, someone they bought vegetables from! Why, however had it happened? To have a ruffian of a stranger talk of her affairs like that.

She threw the peas out of her apron on to the table. The bunch of pinks was among them. She trembled with anger. She had intended throwing them back at him. She ought never to have accepted flowers from him before. He was always shoving a bunch of flowers in her hands or sticking them among the vegetables. Never again. She'd throw his flowers back at him. These pinks she had a good mind to put in the fire.

But they smelled so sweet and they were so delicate, she couldn't throw them away. She lifted her arm for a vase. Her shape was splendid. She was a fine, handsome young woman of twenty-five, all her body graceful and well-jointed, with fine movements, unconsciously proud and vehement. Her face, when she was silent and alone, was often sullen. But always it had a glow. She was a virgin. Her sister was married, her father was checkweight man in the colliery, her mother was always urging her to wed.

Oswald Vaughan, the son of the local solicitor, had been courting her for some months now. He was in his father's office. His family was one of the most respected in the place, big chapel people. Mrs. Vaughan had been put away in an asylum at one time. Even now there was a strange dead look about her. But Oswald was quite normal, he was all right and all there. He was the smartest man in the valley, with his London clothes and little knick-knacks. Both father and son read big books, and indeed they were very clever, in their minds. Very brainy.

Oswald courted Blodwen with great devotion. He came to her as though to a meal. He himself said he was hungry for women. He would sit with her in the parlour of her home and hold her hands tightly or hug her shoulders with a lingering pressure. He respected her and, believing her to be intelligent, he brought books on verse and read her Wordsworth and Tennyson, especially the latter's *In Memoriam*, of which he had a profound admiration. When he left her he was refreshed and walked home in an ecstasy. Blodwen would go to the kitchen for supper and, oddly enough, something would be sure to irritate her, always, either something wrong with the food or she took offence at some observation of her mother or father. She was a difficult girl, really.

Her anger against Pugh Jibbons persisted as she went about the duties of the day, fuming continually not only in her mind but in her blood. If there had been a stick near as he had mocked at her that morning she would have laid it about him. It was the only way to treat a man of his kind. She was quite capable of giving him a good sound beating with a strong stick. The low-down ruffian. And her anger had not abated even by the time Oswald called that evening. She went into the parlour, her eyes glittering with bad temper.

Oswald sat opposite her and laid his clean yellow gloves on his knee. His face was pale and narrow, with a frugal nose and pale, steady eyes. Dull his face was, Blodwen suddenly decided, looking at him with a new gaze, dull and unredeemed by any exceptional expression. And what he said, as he neatly pulled up his fine creased trousers at the knees and then sat back with his hands clasped in an attitude of prayer, made her want to slap him.

'You're looking very wicked and naughty this evening, my dear. That's no way to receive your young man.'

Her face became inscrutable: she stared through the window. He went on:

'You know, I always think a woman should never be anything but bright and happy when her menfolk are about. That's her duty in life.' He leant towards her and took her hand. 'When you're my wife, my dear—'

'Let's go out,' Blodwen suddenly interjected. 'I feel I must have some fresh air this evening. I've been in all day.' Her voice had become even and calm.

He drew back, a bit stiffly. He sighed. But he was submissive, much as he wanted to stay in the parlour and caress her. He began to draw on his gloves.

‘We’ll go to the pictures if you like,’ he said. He was very fond of going to the cinema with her. Nothing he liked better than sitting in the warm, florid atmosphere of the cinema, pressing Blodwen’s hand and watching a love film.

‘I’d rather go for a walk,’ she answered, turning her sparkling eyes on him fully.

‘There’s so few walks about here,’ he sighed.

‘There’s the mountains,’ she said.

She liked going up the mountains. He didn’t. Not many people climbed the mountains: they had been there all their lives and seemed not of much account, and dull to walk on. Great bare flanks of hills.

‘All right,’ he said, getting up and looking in the mirror over the mantel to put his tie straight. Blodwen went out to put on her hat.

As they went down the street the neighbours looked at them appraisingly. Everybody said what a picture they looked, the picture of a happy couple. He with his tall, slim elegance and she with her healthy, wholesome-looking body, her well-coloured face, they seemed so suitably matched to wed. His fine superiority and breeding wed to her wild fecund strength. They looked such a picture walking down the street, it did the heart good to see it.

They crossed the brook that ran, black with coal dust, beneath some grubby unkempt alders, and climbed a straggling path at the rocky base of the hills. Presently Oswald remarked:

‘You’re very quiet this evening.’

Then there came to her eyes a little malicious gleam. He had taken her arm and was gazing down at her fondly – even though, as the path became steeper, he began to breathe heavily, almost in a snort. She said:

'I've been upset today.'

'Oh! What was it?'

'You know that man called Pugh Jibbons, the son of old Jibbons, who sells vegetables in a donkey cart?'

'Yes, of course. Everybody knows him. They're a fine rough lot, that family. Half-wild.'

'Well, he molests me.'

'Molests you!' Oswald exclaimed. 'He has attacked you, you mean?' His mouth remained open in astonishment and horror.

'Oh no. Not attacked me. But he bothers me and follows me about. And this morning I was buying vegetables from him at our back door and he said – oh, he said some rude things.'

'Does he follow you about in the streets, make himself a nuisance to you?' Oswald demanded alertly, the young solicitor.

'Yes, he does,' she said angrily.

'Then,' said Oswald, 'we'll send him a warning letter. I can't have you being bothered like this. The rapscallion. I'll put a stop to him. I'll have a letter sent him tomorrow.'

'Will you?' she said mechanically, looking up to the hills.

'Of course. That's where I come in useful for you. A solicitor's letter will frighten him, you'll see.'

'Perhaps,' she said after a moment or two, 'you'd better leave it for a time. Nothing serious is there to complain of. And I told him myself this morning, I warned him. So we'll wait perhaps.'

She persuaded him, after some debate, that it would be better to postpone the sending of the letter: but as he argued she became angrier and nearly lost her temper. Then he became very gentle with her, endeavouring to soothe her, realising she had had a trying day. But her eyes remained hard.

Not until they got to the mountain top did she seem to regain her good spirits. She loved the swift open spaces of the mountain tops. They sat beneath a huge grey stone that crouched like an elephant in a dip of the uplands, which billowed out beneath them in long, lithe declivities. They could see all the far-flung valley between the massive different hills. Some of those hills were tall and suave and immaculate, having escaped the desecration of the coal mines, others were rounded and squat like the wind-blown skirt of a gigantic woman, some were shapeless with great excrescences of the mines, heaps of waste matter piled up black and forbidding, others were small and young and helpless, crouching between their bulked brothers. Blodwen felt eased, gazing at the massed hills stretched along the fourteen miles of the valley. She felt eased and almost at peace again. Oswald glanced at her and saw she wanted to be quiet, though the storm had left her brow. He sat back against the rock and musingly fingered his heavy gold ring. He did not care for the mountain tops himself. It was dull up there: and he seemed to be lost in the ample space.

He couldn't bear the silence for very long. He had to say something. He couldn't bear her looking away so entranced in some world of her own.

'A penny for them,' he said, touching her shoulder lightly.

She gave a sudden start and turned wondering eyes to him. And her eyes were strange to him, as though she did not know him. They were blue and deep as the sea, and old and heavy, as though with the memory of lost countries. She did not speak, only looked at him in startled wonder. One would have thought a stranger had touched her and spoken.

'Why d'you look at me like that?' he said at last, uneasy and hating her staring.

Her expression changed. She almost became his familiar Blodwen again. She smiled a little.

'You're a funny little woman,' he said, sliding his arm round her waist.

'It's fine up here,' she said.

But still she was different and not the human Blodwen that he knew in the parlour or the cinema. He couldn't warm himself with her at all. Her body seemed rigid and unyielding in his caress. She was hard and profitless as these mountain tops. Almost he began to dislike her, and something inside him stirred in dark anger against her. But all the time his manner and tactics became gentler and more coaxing and more submissive to her whim. His face was appealing and submissive. But she persisted in her odd aloof withdrawal, and at last he decided she couldn't be well, that she was suffering from some esoteric feminine complaint that he must not intrude upon. So he abandoned his love-making and sat back against the rock and became deliberately meditative himself. He did not see the shade of impatience that crossed her face.

He considered the evening wasted and a failure as they descended the mountain in the grey-blue light. And something had happened to Blodwen, something curious and beyond his understanding. Yet for all his secret dissatisfaction he became more anxious in his behaviour towards her, more gentle and tremulous in his approaches. But she spoke to him and treated him as though she were another man: they might have been men together instead of lovers. He was hungry to hold her, to feel the strong living substance of her body. But somehow he could not penetrate the subtle atmosphere of aloofness that she wrapped herself in. He kept on sighing, in the hope that she would notice it. Women were very funny.

She did not ask him into the house, but lifted her lips to him, her eyes shut, inside the gateway of the garden. In a sudden spurt of anger he pecked quickly at her mouth and withdrew. She opened her eyes and they seemed unfathomable as the night sky. They both waited in silence for a few moments and then, lowering her head, she said calmly:

'Good night, Oswald.'

'Good night, Blodwen.'

He lifted his bowler hat and turned resolutely away.

She went in, slowly and meditatively. Her face was calm and thoughtful now. But she was aware of Oswald and his dissatisfaction. She couldn't help it. There were times now and again when his limp and clumsy love-making affronted her, as there were times when it amused her and when it roused her to gentle tenderness. After all, he was young: only twenty-five. Married, she would soon change him and mould him, surely she would? She wondered. Married, things would be different. She'd have to settle down. Surely Oswald was the ideal husband to settle down with. She would have a well-ordered life with no worries of money or work. Oswald would have his father's practice and become a moderately wealthy man: and his family had position. Had always been of the best class in the place. Different from her family, for her grandfather had been an ordinary collier and even now they were neither working- nor upper-class. Her mother was so proud of the step up marriage to Oswald would mean: she had already bought several things on the strength of it – a new parlour set of furniture, a fur coat and odd things like a coffee set and silver napkin rings and encyclopaedias and leather books of poetry. It would be a lovely showy wedding too.

But she wished she didn't have that curious empty feeling in her when she thought of it all, sometimes. Not always. Sometimes she realised Oswald's virtues and deeply respected him for them: good manners, breeding, smartness, a knowledge of international affairs and languages, a liking for verse. Yet she knew and feared that void of emptiness in her when she thought of all that marriage with him implied.

When she went to bed a little perplexed frown had gathered on her brow. She rose early in the morning feeling very discontented and melancholy. She had a cold bath. In a kind of anguish of bliss she shuddered in the water, sluicing it between her pink-white breasts so that it rippled down her fine length like a quick, cool hand. Her wild fair hair glistening as though with dew, her limbs tautened by the cold bath, she strode downstairs and ate a good breakfast of bacon and eggs, stewed apples, toast and tea. Then she felt somewhat better, though she was far from being content.

She remembered Pugh Jibbons and how angry she had been with him yesterday. What he wanted now was a good rude snub and she'd give it him that morning. And thinking of him, her blood began to run faster again. She'd never heard of such impudence. Anybody would think she had encouraged him at some time or other. That riff-raff!

When she heard his shout in the back lane she asked her mother what vegetables they wanted and sauntered up the garden to the door.

'Morning,' said Pugh, looking at her with just a suspicion of mockery in his face. 'And how's the world using you today, then?'

Statuesque, with that insulting ignoring of a person that a woman can assume, she did not hear his greeting and ordered peremptorily:

'Three pounds of beans and six of potatoes.'

'Proud we are this morning,' he observed.

He stood before her and looked at her directly, unmoving. She began to flush and arch her neck; she looked beyond him, to the right, to the left, and then her glance came back to him. His smile was subtle and profound, the light in his gleaming dark eyes was shrewd. She wanted to turn and hurry away, slam the door on him. But she didn't. His swarthy face, with its dark gipsy strain, was full of a knowledge that she sensed rather than saw. His head rested deliberately and aggressively on his powerful neck.

Suddenly she ejaculated furiously:

'Don't stare at me like that! D'you hear! Where's your manners? What right have you to stand there staring at me!'

'You know what right I have,' he answered slowly. And the smile had left his face and given way completely to the hard determination of desire.

She hadn't expected all this, she had meant to coldly snub him and depart. And how strange she had gone, how still and waiting her body, as though absorbed in expectant fear for what would happen next. And she was amazed, when she answered, unable to bear the silence, that her voice faltered in her beating throat:

'I know, do I? I warn you, Pugh Jibbons, not to molest me.'

'Suppose,' he answered, a thin, wiry grin coming to his face, 'that Oswald Vaughan would have something to say and do about it?'

Her anger flowed up again. 'What right have you,' she demanded again, 'to interfere with me? Never have I encouraged you. Haven't you any decency, man? You're nothing to me.' And then she was angry with herself for submitting to his advances to the point of discussion, instead of maintaining a haughty aloofness. She couldn't understand why she had given way to him so easily.

He looked at her. All his body and face seemed tense, gathered up to impose themselves on her.

'I figure it out,' he said, 'that I've got a right to try and have you. Because I want you. You're a woman for me. And I think I'm a man for you. That's what I think. I could do for you what you want and I want. That's what I feel.'

She stared at him. She had got control of herself. But she couldn't snub him in the harsh final way she had intended. She said haughtily:

'I don't want to hear any more about this. Give me the beans and potatoes, please.'

Pugh Jibbons came a step nearer to her, and she became acutely conscious of his body and face.

'You come to me one evening,' he said. 'You come to me one evening and a talk we'll have over this. I promise to respect you. I've got more to tell you about yourself than you think.'

She drew back. 'Ha,' she exclaimed with fine derision, 'what a hope you've got! Are you going to give me the beans and potatoes or not?'

He looked her over and then immediately became the vegetable man. He weighed out the beans and potatoes. Aloofly she watched him, her face stern. Today there were bunches of wide flat marguerites in the flower box at the front of the cart. He took out a bunch.

'I don't want the flowers, thank you,' she said coldly.

'Nay,' he said, 'you must take them. You're one of my best regular customers.'

'I don't want the flowers,' she repeated, looking at him stonily.

He tossed the bunch back into the box.

'Silly wench,' he said.

'Don't you call me names!' she turtled up again.

'You deserve them,' he said. Then he looked her over with

desiring appreciation. 'But a handsome beauty you are, by God, a handsome beauty. Different from the chits of today. Pah, but your mind is stupid, because you won't be what you want to be.'

She quivered and her anger had become strange in her blood, rather like fear. She could find nothing to say to him; she turned, slammed the door and hurried with the vegetables to the kitchen. All her blood seemed to run cold, fear seemed to sink down in her body, and suddenly she felt desperately anxious. Desperately because something was withering within her being, some living thing she should have cherished. Beyond the anger and irritation of her mind she knew a fear and anxiety like a touch of icy death in her being.

The day became cold and drab to her. She went about the house shut in a sullen resentful silence. Her mother looked at her with ill-temper. The mother was a tall, vigorous woman. But her face had gone tart and charmless with the disillusion frequent in working women whose lives have been nothing but a process of mechanical toil and efforts to go one better than their neighbours. She, too, in her day had had her violences. But her strength had gone to sinew and hard muscle. Even now she cracked brazil nuts with her teeth, heaved a hundredweight of coal from cellar to kitchen and could tramp twenty miles over the hills on bank holidays. And now she distrusted the world and wanted security for herself and her daughters.

'What's the matter with you, girl?' she demanded irritably, as Blodwen sat silent over the midday meal. 'Shift that sulky look off your face.'

Blodwen did not answer. But her mouth sneered unpleasantly.

'You look at me like that, you shifty slut,' the mother exclaimed angrily, 'you'll leave this table.'

The daughter got up and swept out of the room. Her head was

turtled up fearless as an enraged turkey.

'Ha,' shouted the mother after her, 'don't you dare show that ugly face to me again, or, grown up or not, you'll feel the weight of my hand. Out with you.'

But Blodwen had dignity, sweeping out of the room, and her silence was powerful with contempt.

'Bringing a girl up,' muttered the mother to herself, 'to snarl and insult one, as though she's what-not or the Queen of England. Ach, that she was ten years younger. I'd give her what for on that b.t.m. of hers. The stuck-up insulting girl that she is.'

Blodwen stayed in her bedroom for the rest of the day, knitting. At six-thirty Oswald called. She came down to the parlour, still a little sulky. There was anxiety on Oswald's face as he greeted her. She had frightened him last night. And now he couldn't live without her: she was the sole reality in his life.

'My dear,' he murmured, pressing her hand, 'my own dear.'

She actually smiled up at him.

'Are you better?' he asked gently.

'I haven't been ill,' she said.

'Nothing physical, perhaps,' he said, primly, 'but out-of-sorts mentally, I should think.'

She sat beside him on the sofa.

'Oswald,' she said, 'when shall we get married?'

He started excitedly. Before, he had never been able to make her decide anything definite about their marriage. She had always dismissed the subject, declaring there was plenty of time yet. He wanted to get married quickly, so that he could proceed to entire happiness with this fine woman: he wanted it quickly.

'My darling,' he cried gratefully, 'my sweet, as soon as you like. I could be ready in a month. There's a house going on Salem Hill and I've got the money for furniture. We could begin buying at once. I saw a lovely walnut bedroom suite in a shop in Cardiff last week; I wanted to reserve it there and then. I'll phone for it tomorrow. And all the other things we could choose together. We'll go down to Cardiff tomorrow. I'll get the day off.' His face began to shine excitedly.

She looked at him.

'Not a month though,' she said slowly; 'perhaps we want more than a month to prepare.'

'Six weeks, then,' he said.

'Soon,' she said, in a curious kind of surging voice, 'Soon. Let it be soon. Six weeks, then. That will be soon enough.' Her hand crept up his arm. 'That will give us time to prepare and not too much time to change our minds. Six weeks. Oh, you do want to marry, don't you, Oswald?'

'My dear,' he cried in pain. 'How strange you are!'

But she put her face to his to be kissed. Their mouths met. She clung to him desperately.

She would not go out to buy vegetables off Pugh Jibbons again.

She told her mother how he molested her. The mother went to the back door and roundly denounced the young hawker. Pugh had laughed at her. And Oswald again offered to have a letter sent him.

The weeks went by: autumn came on. There were endless preparations for the wedding. Blodwen, it was true, took little interest in them. She allowed Oswald to arrange and buy everything. She was very calm; and her manner and behaviour changed. She lost her high-flown demeanour, she never lost her temper, and her face went a little wan. Now her dark blue eyes seemed deeper and more remote beneath her long brows, and her mouth was flower-soft, red as geranium, but drooped.

The week before the wedding there was a touch of winter in the air. Blodwen liked the winter. She was as strong as a bear amid the harsh winds and the wild snow and the whips of rain that winter brings to the vales of the hills. She took on added strength in the winter, like a bear.

One early evening as the wind lashed down through the serried rows of houses huddled in the vale she stood looking out at the hills from an upstairs window of her home. The grey sky was moving and violent over the brown mountains, and the light of evening was flung out. Her face was lifted like an eager white bird to the hills. She would have to go, she could not stay in the house any longer. She entirely forgot that Oswald was due in a few minutes.

She wound a heavy woollen scarf round her neck and, unknown to her mother and father, who were in the kitchen, she let herself out. And blindly, seeing no one and nothing in the streets, she went on towards the base of the lonely mountains. Slowly the light died into the early wintry evening, the heavens were misted and darkened, moved slower, though in the west a dim exultance of coppery light still loitered.

Her nostrils dilated in the sharp air, but her limbs thrilled with warmth. Her feet sank in the withering mignonette-coloured grass of the lower slopes, and she climbed lithely and easily the steep pathless little first hill. She was conscious of Pugh Jibbons' allotments surrounding his ramshackle stone house to the left, but she did not look at them. He, however, saw her, rising from his hoeing of potatoes.

The night would soon come. She cared nothing. She wanted to be on the dominant mountain tops, she wanted to see the distant hills ride like great horses through the darkening misty air. She quickened her steps and her breasts began to heave with the exertion. She had crossed the smaller first hill and was ascending the mountain behind it. She was quite alone on the hills.

The black jagged rocks jutting out on the brow of the mountains were like a menace. She began to laugh, shaking out her wild hair; she unwound her scarf and bared her throat to the sharp slap of the wind. She would like to dance on the mountain top, she would like to shake her limbs and breasts until they were hard and lusty as the wintry earth. She forgot her destination in the world below.

She had reached the top. Night was not yet, and out of the grey seas of mist the distant hills rode like horses. She saw thick, massive limbs, gigantic flanks and long ribbed sides of hills. She saw plunging heads with foam at their mouths. She saw the great bodies of the hills, and in her own body she knew them.

Oswald sat in the parlour with Blodwen's mother. The gas had been lit and a tiny fire burned in the paltry grate. Oswald looked distracted. He had been waiting for over an hour already. It was most strange. It had been a definite arrangement for him to see Blodwen that evening. There were important things to discuss for the wedding on Saturday. Her mother could offer no explanation but kept on repeating angrily:

'Why didn't she say she was going out! The provoking girl.'

'Can't you think where she has gone to?' Oswald asked more than once.

'No. Most secretive she's been lately. Secretive and funny. I've put it down to the fuss of preparing. A serious job it is for a girl to prepare for marriage. Some it makes hysterical, some silly and others secretive and funny, like Blodwen.' She tried her best to keep the conversation going with the distracted young man. Inside, she was fuming. She suspected that Blodwen had gone out with the deliberate intention of escaping Oswald. What madness! She'd give the girl a good talking-to when she returned.

'Have you noticed it too?' exclaimed Oswald. 'I've wondered what's the matter with her. But, as you say, it's such a big change for a girl to get married, she must lose her balance now and again.'

'Especially a highly strung girl like Blodwen,' said the mother. 'For highly strung she is, though in health as strong as a horse. No trouble of ailments have I had with her. From a baby she has trotted about frisky as can be.' And to try and soothe him she added gravely, 'Do you well she will, Oswald, a big satisfaction you'll have out of her. And in house matters she can work like a black and cook like a Frenchie, she can make quilts and eiderdowns and wine, and she can cure boils and gripe and other things by herbs as I have cured them in my own husband. Taught her all my knowledge I have. A girl she is such as you don't see often nowadays. Highly strung she might be, but, handled properly, docile enough she'll be.'

'I think we'll get on all right,' said Oswald nervously, 'though no doubt we'll have our ups and downs.'

'Aye,' said the mother.

The clock ticked away. Oswald kept on glancing at it mournfully, then at his watch, to make sure that was the time. The mother looked at him with a sort of admiring bliss in her eyes. He was such a toff and belonged to such a family. Fancy her Blodwen marrying into the Vaughan family! No wonder she was an envied mother and people were deferential to her now. She had been a cook at one time.

'Wherever can she be?' he repeated, sighing.

'I can't think at all,' said Blodwen's mother, sharpening her voice to sympathise with his agitation. 'But I'll tell her of this tonight, I'll tell her, never fear.'

'Oh, don't, please,' he begged. 'We must be gentle with her the next few days, we must put up with her whims.' He looked at her appealingly and added, 'No doubt she'll have a reasonable explanation when she arrives back.'

But Pugh Jibbons, in his old stony house on the hillside, was laying a flower on the white hillock of her belly, with tender exquisite touch a wide, flat, white marguerite flower, its stalk bitten off, his mouth pressing it into her rose-white belly, laughing.

The Fashion Plate

I

'The Fashion Plate's coming—' quickly the news would pass down the main road. Curtains twitched in front parlour windows, potted shrubs were moved or watered; some colliers' wives, hard-worked and canvas-aproned, came boldly out to the doorsteps to stare. In the dingy little shops, wedged here and there among the smart dwellings, customers craned together for the treat. Cleopatra setting out in the golden barge to meet Antony did not create more interest. There was no one else in the valley like her. Her hats! The fancy high-heeled shoes, the brilliantly elegant dresses in summer, the tweeds and the swirl of furs for the bitter days of that mountainous district! The different handbags, gay and sumptuous, the lacy gloves, the parasols and tasselled umbrellas! And how she knew how to wear these things! Graceful as a swan, clean as a flower, she dazzled the eye.

But, though a pleasure to see, she was also incongruous, there in that grim industrial retreat pushed up among the mountains, with the pits hurling out their clouds of grit, and clanking coal-wagons crossing the main road twice, and the miners coming off the shift black and primitive-looking. The women drew in their breaths as she passed. She looked as if she had never done a stroke of work in her life. Strange murmurs could be heard; she almost created a sense of fear, this vision of delicate indolence, wealth and taste assembled with exquisite tact in one person.

How could she do it? Their eyes admired but their comments did not.

Yet the work-driven women of this place, that had known long strikes, bitter poverty and a terrible pit disaster, could not entirely malign Mrs Mitchell. Something made them pause. Perhaps it was the absolute serenity of those twice-weekly afternoon walks that nothing except torrential rain or snow-bound roads could prevent. Or perhaps they saw a vicarious triumph of themselves, a dream become courageously real.

There remained the mystery of how she could afford all those fine clothes. For Mrs Mitchell was only the wife of the man in charge of the slaughterhouse. She was not the pit manager's wife (indeed, Mrs Edwards dressed in a totally different style, her never-varied hat shaped like an Eskimo's hut). Mr Mitchell's moderate salary was known, and in such a place no one could possess private means without it being exact knowledge. Moreover, he was no match to his wife. A rough and ready sort of man, glum and never mixing much in the life of the place, though down in the slaughterhouse, which served all the butcher shops for miles, he was respected as a responsible chap whose words and deed were to be trusted. Of words he had not many.

The women wished they could curl their tongues round something scandalous. Why was Mrs Mitchell always having her photograph taken buy Mr Burgess in his studio down an obscure yard where he worked entirely alone? But nobody felt that suspicion of Mr Burgess, a family man and a chapel deacon with a stark knobbly face above a high stiff collar, sat comfortably in the mind. The bit of talk about the two had started because one afternoon a mother calling at the studio to fix an appointment for her daughter's wedding party found Mrs Mitchell reclining on a sofa under a bust of Napoleon. She was hatless and, in a clinging dress ('tight on her as a snake skin') and her hand holding a bunch of artificial flowers, she looked like a woman undergoing the agonies of some awful confession. Mr. Burgess certainly had his head under the black drapery of his camera, so everything pointed to yet another photograph being taken. But to have one taken lying down? In the valley, in those days, to have a photo taken was a rare event attended by tremendous fuss. Accompanied by advising friends or relations, one stood up to the ordeal as if going before the Ultimate Judge, and one always came out on the card as if turned to stone or a pillar of salt.

The whispering began. Yet still everyone felt that the whispering was unfair to Mr Burgess. For thirty years he had photographed wedding parties, oratorio choirs and silver cup football teams in his studio, and nothing had ever been said against his conduct.

Mrs Mitchell, coming out of her bow-windowed little house as out of a palace, took her walks as if never a breath of scandal ever polluted her pearl earrings. Was she aware of the general criticism? If so, did she know that within the criticism was homage? – the homage that in bygone times would begin a dynasty of tribal queens? Was she aware of the fear too, the puritanic dread that such lavishness and extravagance could not be obtained but at some dire cost greater even than money?

II

This afternoon her excursion was no different from the hundreds of others. It was a fine autumn day. The tawny mountains glistened like the skins of lions. She wore a new fur, rich with the bluish-black tint of grapes, and flung with just the right expensive carelessness across her well-held shoulders: it would cause additional comment. With her apparently unaware look of repose she passed serenely down the long drab main road.

Down at the bottom of the valley the larger shops, offices, a music hall and a railway station (together with Mr Burgess's studio) clustered into the semblance of a town. She always walked as far as the railway station, situated down a hunchbacked turning, and, after appearing to be intent on its architecture for a moment, wheeled round and with a mysterious smile began the homeward journey. Often she made small domestic purchases – her clothes she obtained from the city twenty miles away – and as the ironmonger's wife once remarked: 'Only a rolling-pin she wanted, but one would think she was buying a grand piano.'

Today, outside the railway station, she happened to see her young friend Nicholas and, bending down to his ear, in her low sweet voice breathed his name. He was twelve, wore a school satchel strapped to his back, and he was absentmindedly paused before a poster depicting Windsor Castle. He gave a violent start and dropped a purple-whorled glass marble which rolled across the pavement, sped down the gutter and slid into a drain – 'It's gone!' he cried in poignant astonishment, 'I won it dinner time!'

'And all my fault.' Her bosom was perfumed with an evasive fragrance like closed flowers. 'Never mind, I have some marbles – will you come and get them this evening? You've been neglecting us lately, Nicholas.' She was neither arch nor patronising; he might have been a successful forty.

'I'll have to do my homework first,' he said with equal formality.

'Well, come in and do it with us. You shall have your own little table, and I'll be quiet as a mouse.'

They lived in the same street and though no particular

friendship existed between the two households, he had been on visiting terms with the Mitchells, who were childless, for a couple of years. The change from his own noisily warring brothers'-and-sisters' home to the Mitchells', where he was sole little king, nourished him. To his visits his mother took a wavering attitude of doubt, half criticism and compassion; before becoming decisive she was waiting for something concrete to happen in that house.

That evening Mrs Mitchell had six coloured glass marbles ready for him on a small table on which also, neatly set out, were a crystal ink well, a ruler, blotter and pencils and... yes! a bottle of lemonade with a tumbler. Very impressed by the bottle, which gave him a glimpse of easy luxury in a world hard with the snatching and blows of his brothers and sisters, he made little fuss of the glitteringly washed marbles, which he guessed she had bought in Watkins's shop after leaving him – and in any case they had not the value of those won from bragging opponents kneeling around a circle drawn in the earth.

'Is the chair high enough, would you like a cushion? ... You must work hard if you want to get near the top of your class, but you must enjoy working... There! Now I'll do my sewing and not say a word.'

Hers was not big industrious sewing, complete with bee-humming machine, as at home. She sat delicately edging a tiny handkerchief with a shred of lace, and on her face was a look of minutes strained to their utmost; she had the manner of one who never glances at a clock. The house was tidy, clean, respectably comfortable. But it was shabbier than his own home. And somehow without atmosphere, as if it was left alone to look after itself and no love or hate clashed within its shiny darkly papered walls. Occasionally this lack of something important vaguely bothered the boy. He would stand with his lip lifted, his nostrils dilated. He had never been upstairs, and he always wanted to penetrate its privacy. Was the thing he missed to be found there? Did they live up there and only come downstairs when there were visitors? Down here it was all parlour and Sunday silence, with for movement only the lonely goldfish eternally circling its bowl.

Mr Mitchell came in before the homework was finished. 'Good evening, sir,' he greeted Nicholas. 'Doing my accounts for me?' He seemed to look at the boy and yet not look at him. And he was not a jocular man. He had a full, dahlia-red, rather staring face of flabby contours, sagged in on its own solitude and the eyes did not seem to connect with the object they looked at. His face had affinities with the face of some floridly ponderous beast. He had a very thick neck. It was strange, and yet not at all strange, that his work had to do with cattle.

'Do you want a meal now,' Mrs Mitchell asked in the heavy silence, 'or can you wait?' Her voice was crisper; she stitched in calm withdrawal; she might have been an indifferent daughter. Though bent at the table, the boy sensed the change. There was a cold air of armistice in the room, of emptiness. Nervously he opened his bottle of lemonade. The explosion of the uncorking sounded very loud.

'I'll go upstairs,' Mr Mitchell said. 'Yes, I'll go upstairs. Call me down.'

'You'll hear the dishes,' she said concisely. The boy turned and saw her stitching away, like a queen in a book of tales. Mr Mitchell went out bulkily; his head lolled on the fleshy neck. It was as if he said 'Pah!' in a heavily angry way. His footsteps were ponderous on the staircase.

Had he come straight from the slaughterhouse and was weary?

Had he a short time ago been killing cattle? Nicholas, like all the boys of the place, was interested in the slaughterhouse, a squat building with pens and sties in a field down by the river. Once he had been allowed inside by an amiable young assistant who understood his curiosity, and he saw in a white-washed room hung with ropes and pulleys a freshly dead bullock strung up in the air by its legs; it swayed a little and looked startlingly foolish. Blood spattered the guttered floor and some still dripped from the bullock's mouth like a red icicle. In a yard another young man was rinsing offal in a tub filled with green slime. 'No, we're not killing pigs today,' he replied to Nicholas's enquiry. Because of the intelligent squeals and demented hysteria of these intuitive beasts as they were chased from the sties into the house of death, pig-killing was the prized spectacle among all the boys. But few had been fortunate enough to witness it; the slaughtermen usually drove them away from the fascinating precincts. Nicholas, an unassertive boy on the whole, had never liked to take advantage of his friendship with the Mitchells and ask to be taken to the place properly, an accredited visitor on a big day. He wondered if Mrs Mitchell went there herself sometimes. Could she get him a pig's bladder?

She did not bring in supper until he had finished the homework. 'There, haven't I been quiet?' she smiled. 'Did you work easily? I can see you're studious and like quiet. Do you like lobster too?'

'Lobster?' He looked at her vacantly.

She fetched from the kitchen an oval dish in which lay a fabulous scarlet beast. Cruel claws and quiveringly fine feelers sprang from it. At first he thought that Mr Mitchell must have brought it from the slaughterhouse, but when his excitement abated he remembered they came from the sea. 'How did you get it?' he asked, astonished.

'I have to ask Harris's fish shop to order one especially for me. I'm the only person here that wants them.'

'Do they cost a lot?'

Over the fiery beast she looked at him conspiratorially.

'Nothing you enjoy ever costs a lot,' she smiled mysteriously.

Mr Mitchell must have heard the dishes, but he came down looking more torpid than ever. 'Lobster again!' he said, sombrely. 'At night? There's stomachs of cast-iron in this world.'

Mrs Mitchell looked at him frigidly. 'If you encourage nightmares they'll come,' she said.

'You're not giving it to the boy?' he said.

'Why not? You'll have a little, Nicholas?' Of course he would.

'I have dreams,' said Mr Mitchell, his heavy dark-red face expressionless. 'Yes, I have dreams.'

'Do you?' Her husband might have been an acquaintance who had called at an inopportune time. 'A little salad, Nicholas? Shall I choose it for you?' In delightful performance she selected what seemed the best pieces in the bowl; with deft suggestions she showed him how to eat the lobster. He enjoyed extracting from inside a crimson scimitar shreds of rosily white meat. The evening became remarkable for him.

And it was because of it he added to the local legend of Mrs Mitchell. When he told them at home about the lobster there was at first a silence. His mother glanced up, his brothers and sisters were impressed. He felt superior. A couple of weeks later, while he waited to be served in Watkins's shop just after Mrs Mitchell had passed the window on her return from her walk, he heard a collier's wife say: 'Yes, and they say she has lobsters for breakfast nearly every day. No doubt her new hat she wears at breakfast too, to match them.' Despite his sense of guilt, he felt himself apart, an experienced being. No one else in the place was known to have dealings with the exotic fish.

'She'll be giving him champagne next,' he heard his father say to his mother. 'Mitchell, poor devil, will be properly in the soup some day.' And his mother said, troubled. 'Yes, I do wonder if Nick ought to go there—'

III

That winter Mrs. Mitchell won a £100 prize in a periodical which ran a competition every week. You had to make up a smart remark on a given phrase and send it in with a sixpenny postal order. A lot of people in the place did it; someone else had won £10, which set more members of both sexes running to the post office. It seemed quite in order that Mrs Mitchell, who dressed like no one else, should win a cracker of a prize, but everybody was agog the day the news got around.

'You'll be going to see her every day now,' Nicholas's eldest brother jeered, adding offensively: 'Take your money box with you.' And his father said to his mother, in that secret-knowledge way which roused an extra ear inside one: 'If she's got any feeling, she'll hand it to Mitchell straight away.' To this his mother said: 'Not she!'

A week later, with Christmas not far off, Mrs Mitchell took her afternoon walk in a new fur coat. It shone with an opulent gleam as if still alive and its owner walked with the composure of one who owns three hundred and sixty-five fur coats. It was treated to a companionable new hat into which a blue quill was stabbed cockily as a declaration of independence. Her red tasselled umbrella, exquisitely rolled, went before her with a hand attached lightly as a flower. The women watchers down the long bleak road gathered and stared with something like consternation. Surely such luxury couldn't proceed for ever! The God of Prudence, who had made his character known in abundant scriptures, must surely hurl one of his thunderbolts right in her path some day.

That same evening Nicholas visited the Mitchells' house. And he found Mrs Mitchell delicately shedding a few tears into a lacy wisp of the finest linen. He could not take this restrained sort of weeping seriously. Especially as she had just won a big prize. 'Have you got a headache?' he asked.

She blew her pretty nose and dried her tears. 'I'm glad you've come. It keeps Mr Mitchell quiet.' Pointing to the ceiling, she whispered dramatically: 'He's just gone up... Oh dear!' she sighed.

'What is he always doing upstairs?' It did not now take him long to adjust himself to being treated as a grown-up.

'Oh, only sleeping... He's a man that seems to need a great deal of sleep. He says he gets bad dreams, but I believe he likes them.' She smiled at him with dainty malice. 'Do you know what he wanted? ... My prize!' Nicholas looked thoughtful, like one privy to other knowledge. She went on: 'Week after week I worked so hard at those competitions, and he never helped me, it was all my own brains.' Her eyes shone with that refined malice. 'To tell you the truth, he isn't clever. Not like you and me.' She giggled. 'Oh dear, don't look so solemn, Nicholas; I've had a very trying day.'

'I have too,' he said.

'Have you, darling? Would you like a chocolate?' She jumped up and fetched a large ribboned box from the sideboard. They ate in release from the stress. But he could see her attention was on something else, and presently resumed: 'He found out today that I spent the prize on a fur coat. Oh good gracious, such a fuss!' She rummaged for other chocolates. 'An almond one this time? Nougat? I don't like the peppermint ones, do you? We'll keep them for Mr Mitchell... Of course, people do criticise me,' she said, wrinkling her nose. 'You must not repeat what I've said, Nicholas.'

'Oh no,' he said, decided but flushing. Memory of the lobster affair still obscurely troubled him.

'Gentlemen do not,' she said. 'As you know.'

'I'm going to visit my grandmother after Christmas,' he said awkwardly.

Suddenly footsteps sounded on the stairs, descending with pronounced deliberation. And Mrs Mitchell seemed to draw herself in, like a slow graceful snail into its shell. The door opened, and Mr Mitchell stood there in a bowler hat and overcoat, bulky and glowering. Even his ragged moustache looked as if it was alive with helpless anger – anger that would never really shoot out or even bristle. 'Am going out,' he said, in a low defeated growl. Of Nicholas he took no notice. 'Going out,' he repeated. 'Yes.'

'You are going out,' she murmured, remote in her shell. Her eyelids were down as if against some rude spectacle.

'Yes.' Something in his heavy neck throbbed, making it thicker. Yet there was nothing threatening in his mien. His slow, ox-coloured eyes travelled from his wife's face to the large pink box of chocolates on her knees. 'I hope,' he then said, 'you'll always be able to afford 'um.'

She asked faintly: 'What time will you be back? Supper will—'

'Going to the slaughterhouse,' he said sullenly. 'Got a job to do.'

'—will be ready at nine,' she said.

'Ha!' he said. He stared at her shut face. But the heavy gaze of his unlit eyes threw out no communication. The boy looked round. Feeling at a loss, he glanced uneasily at Mrs Mitchell and saw that a peculiar, almost dirty grey, tint blotched her face. 'Ha!' repeated Mr Mitchell. The large, sagged face hung down over his swollen neck. For a moment he looked vaguely menacing. Then he tramped into the hallway. The front door slammed.

Mrs Mitchell opened her eyes wide at the slam. 'Oh dear!' she wailed faintly. Her eyes were different, darker, almost black. 'He never says very much,' she fluttered, 'but he stands there looking... Good gracious!' She bit a chocolate mechanically and winced in chagrin as if it held a flavour she did not like. 'It seems he's having a very busy time in the slaughterhouse,' she went on erratically; 'Some sheep have come in... Ah, well!' She jumped up again. 'You haven't seen my new photographs.'

Once again they sat over the album: she inserted a copy of the new photograph. There she was in about thirty different representations, but whether she was sad or smiling, dreamy or vivacious, aloof or inviting, it was clear that the eye of Mr Burgess's camera found itself in concord with its elegant object. For nearly an hour she pored over the album with an exaggerated, detailed interest, demanding once more his opinion. Her voice was high, her manner hurried: 'Isn't this your favourite? Yes. It's mine too. Why do you like it so much?'

He thought carefully. 'You look as though you're just going for a holiday to the seaside,' he said finally.

'It's true I was happy that day. At the time I thought we were going to move to London... Then Mr Mitchell refused to take the job he was offered there.' Her voice sharpened remarkably. 'He refused... The fact is, he has no ambition.' Suddenly she snapped the album shut, rose with a bright restlessness. 'Will you come down to the slaughterhouse with me, Nicholas?'

At last the invitation! He agreed with alacrity and thought of the envy of the other boys.

'If you are with me, Mr Mitchell won't be so disagreeable.' She hurried upstairs and returned in her new fur coat and the coquettish toque. 'Come, I didn't realise we had sat here so long... I can't have him sulking and going without his supper,' she explained.

The starlit night was cold. There were few people in the streets. The secret mountains smelled grittily of winter. Somewhere a dog barked insistent, shut out from a house. The public house windows were clouded with yellow steam, and in a main street house a woman pulled down a blind on a lamplit front parlour where sat Mr Hopkins the insurance agent beside a potted fern. They crossed the main street and took a sloping road trailing away into wasteland. Odorous of violets and dark fur, Mrs Mitchell walked with a surprisingly quick glide; Nicholas was obliged to trot. They heard the icy cry of the river below, flinging itself unevenly among its stone-ragged banks. She said nothing now.

The slaughterhouse stood back in its field, an angular array of black shadows; no light showed there. Mrs Mitchell fumbled at the fence gate of the field. 'I've only been here once,' she said, 'when I brought down the telegraph saying his father had died.' She paused doubtfully. 'There's no light.' But the gate was unlocked.

'There are windows at the back,' Nicholas urged; 'there's a little office at the side.' But he himself was disappointed. It seemed unlikely that slaughtering was proceeding among those silent shadows.

They walked up the cobbled path. There was a double door leading into a stone-floored paddock; it swung loose. Inside, a huge sliding door led into the main slaughter chamber; this did not yield to their push. Then Nicholas remembered the smaller door at the side; he turned its knob, and they walked into a whitewashed passage lit at the end by a naked blue gas jet. 'The office is down there,' he said. He felt morose and not implicated; he remembered glancing into the office during his previous visit; it was no more than a large box with a table and chair and files and ledgers. They walked down the stone-flagged passage. She stopped. He heard her breathing.

'Go back,' she said.

Sharpened by her tone of command, he looked up at her. Her nostrils, blue in the gaslight, were quivering. He looked down quickly. From under a door a stream of dark thick liquid had crawled. It was congealing on the stone flag into the shape of a large root or a strand of seaweed. He looked at it, only distantly conscious of her further cry and her fingers pressing into his shoulders. 'Go back; go home,' she exclaimed. He did not move.

She stepped to the door as if oblivious of him. But she carefully avoided the liquid root. She turned the brass knob, slowly pushed back the door. Still the boy had not moved. He could not see inside the door. She gave a queer cry, not loud, a low hunted cry broken in her mouth. And Nicholas never forgot the gesture with which her hand went to her throat. He ran forward from the wall. At the same time his feet instinctively avoided the dark smears. 'Let me see!' he cried. But she pulled back the door. 'Let me see!' he cried. It was then he became conscious of another odour, a whiff from the closing door mingled with the perfume of fur and violets.

She violently pushed him back. 'Go home at once!' There was something like a terrible hiss in her voice. He looked up in confusion. Her face, blotched with a sickly pallor, was not the elegantly calm face he knew; the joints and muscles had loosened and were jerking convulsively. It was as if the static photograph of a pleasing face had in some nightmare way suddenly broken into ugly grimaces. For a moment he stared aghast at that face. Then he backed from her.

Her eyes seemed not to see him. 'Go!' she screamed, even more startlingly. Then he swiftly turned and ran.

IV

Three days later, carrying a large bunch of chrysanthemums from his mother, he walked down to the Mitchells' house. He went with a meek unwillingness, but not unconscious of the drama in which he was involved. All those three days the place had hummed with talk of the Mitchells. Within living memory there had been only one local suicide before.

Already there was pre-knowledge of the bailiffs who were only waiting for the coffin to leave the house before taking possession. The dead man's affairs were in shocking condition. Besides forcing him to mortgage his house several years ago, the Fashion Plate had bullied him into going to moneylenders... And no, she was not a nagging woman, but she got her way by slyly making him feel inferior to her. She had done him honour by marrying him and he must pay for what was necessary to her selfish happiness.

At first Nicholas's mother had said he must not visit the house again. Then that evening – the inquest had taken place the previous day – she told him to take the flowers. His unwillingness surprised her and, oddly enough, made her more decided that he should go on this compassionate errand. He frowned at the flowers but sheltered them from the wind. He wondered if it was true that the Mitchells' house was going to be sold up, and if so could he ask for the goldfish.

When Mrs Mitchell opened the door he looked at her with a furtive nervousness. But, except for the deep black of her shinily flowing new frock, she was no different. 'Oh, Nicholas darling!' she greeted him, with the same composed smile as before the event. And she accepted the flowers as if they were for an afternoon tea vase. She was alone in the house. But twice there was a caller who was taken privately into the front room for a short while.

'You haven't brought your homework with you?' she asked. He was a little shocked. Upstairs lay the dead man in his coffin. She sat making calculations and notes in a little book. A heap of black-edged stationery lay on the table. The pit hooter sounded. There were silences. He looked at the goldfish eternally circling its bowl – 'What do you feed it with?' he murmured at length.

'Black gloves—' she said inattentively, 'do you think I could find a decent pair in this hole of a place!'

Out of the corner of his eye he kept on glancing at her, furtively. Once she remarked: 'You are very distant this evening, Nicholas.' Then, as his silences did not abate, she asked suddenly: 'Well, haven't you forgiven me?' He looked confused, and she added: 'For pushing you away so rudely in the slaughterhouse.' The cloudy aloofness in his mind crystallised then, and he knew he indeed bore her a grudge. She had deprived him of something of high visual interest. In addition he was not yet reconciled to the revelation of how she had looked... 'Oh, it doesn't matter,' he mumbled, with hypocritical carelessness. He stared again at the goldfish. 'What do you feed the goldfish with?' he repeated.

'You must take that goldfish away with you tonight. Otherwise those dreadful men will stick a number on the bowl and get half a crown for it... Would you like to see Mr Mitchell now?' As he did not reply at once but still looked owlish, she said: 'Well, come along upstairs.' He rose and followed her, in half forgiveness. 'I don't like being depressed, it doesn't suit me,' she complained, 'I feel quite old.'

Her fresh poplin skirts hissed as she climbed. 'Poor Mr Mitchell,' she sighed, 'I do wish I could feel more sorry for him. But I'm afraid his nature made him melancholy, though I must say as a young man he wasn't so difficult... And he used to be quite handsome, in a footballer kind of way... Ah!' she said, shaking her head, 'These beefy sportsman types, they're often quite neurotic, just bundles of nerves... Oh, it's all been so unpleasant,' she went on, with a dainty squirm of repudiation, 'but I must own he had the decency to do it down there.'

Upstairs there were the same four rooms as in his own home. She took him into the end back room and turned on the light. It seemed to be the room where they had slept, there were brushes on the dressing table and a man's jacket was still flung across a chair. On the bed lay a coffin. It sank heavily into the mattress. The lid lay against a wall. 'You won't want to be here long,' she suggested, and left him to his curiosity. He saw her go across the landing to the main front room and put on the light there. She left both doors open.

He looked into the coffin. Mr Mitchell wore a crisp white shroud which somehow robbed him of the full powerfulness of being a man. And his face, with the dark red flabbiness drained out of it, was not his. He looked as if he had been ill in bed for a long time but was now secure in a cold sort of health. Round his throat a folded white napkin was tightly swathed. This linen muffler, together with the shroud, gave him an air of being at the mercy of apparel he would not himself have chosen. Nicholas' round eyes lingered on the napkin.

He left the room feeling subdued and obedient. The cold isolation of the dead man lying helpless in that strange clothing made him feel without further curiosity; there was nothing to astonish, and nothing to startle one into fearful pleasure.

Mrs Mitchell heard him come out and called: 'What do you think of this, Nicholas?' He went along the landing to the fully illuminated front room and saw at once it was where she slept. The room was perfumed and untidy with women's clothes strewn everywhere. Hadn't Mr and Mrs Mitchell used the same room, then, like other married people? He looked around with renewed inquisitiveness. A large cardboard hat box lay open on the bed. From it Mrs Mitchell was taking a spacious black hat on which the wings of a glossy blackbird were trimly spread in flight. Standing before the mirror she carefully put on the hat.

Even he could see it was an important hat. She turned and smiled with her old elegant brilliance. 'I'm wearing it to London as soon as Mr Mitchell is buried. My sister is married to a publican there... Do you like it?' she asked in that flattering way that had always nourished him and made him feel that he was a full-size man of opinions.

THE BENEFIT CONCERT

When it was decided to throw a benefit concert for Jenkin so that he could buy an artificial leg, no one thought this ordinary event would lead to such strife. But then no one suspected that the loss of his proper leg – it had gone gangrenous through neglect – had turned Jenkin into a megalomaniac. The affair not only divided the valley into bitterly opposed camps but it nearly caused a strike in the colliery. Imperfect mankind is addicted to warfare and a false leg is as good a pretext for liberating smouldering passions as greed for a continent.

To begin with, the colliery where Jenkin worked was not obliged to give him compensation. He had neglected a wound received in the pit, refusing medical attention, and it was not until some weeks had passed that the leg showed signs of protest. His blood was in bad condition (as the camp later opposed to his side repeated in another sense) and the leg had always been a twitchy one. Though he could have fought his case in the courts, this wasn't done, Jenkin having a horror of courts ever since that time he was accused – unfairly, though none the less he lost his case – of buying a concertina knowing it had been stolen. Well, now he had lost his leg, too, and not a penny in the bank.

He was still convalescent in the hospital when his butties in No. 2 pit decided to give him a benefit. A committee was formed and the valley's male voice choir, ever ready to open their melodious jaws, consented to give a selection from their repertoire including their famous 'Italian Salad'. This in itself would bring in sufficient money to cover the cost of a leg and the committee decided that two shillings was enough for top-price tickets. They approached the deacons of Horeb chapel for use of this big building; Jenkin, off and on, had been a member of Horeb, though he never had more than one leg – and that the twitchy one – in religion. The deacons, not liking their chapel to be taken out of their hands by a lot of more or less outsiders, said they would organise the concert themselves. The rough-and-ready committee readily agreed to this, glad to be rid of the work, and the deacons of Horeb then went into owlish conclave.

'Well, Jenkin' – one of his butties sat by the hospital bed – 'a present the boys will have ready for you after you come out. Tell that nurse by there to measure you and place the order for it at once.'

Jenkin showed one cunning eye from the bedclothes, for he liked his head covered in this draughty hospital. 'What's that, mun? Coffin is it to be, or a pair of homemade crutches?'

'Wind of it you've got already, I can see, Jenkin. Best-quality artificial leg you're going to have, the same as Samson the Fireman's got.' Samson, before wearing it, had proudly exhibited his leg for a week in his front parlour window, so that all passersby could see the marvel with its silver joints, leather flesh, and delicate screws.

'But what I'm going to do for work I don't know,' Jenkin grunted, however. 'A 'bacco shop I'd like to open.'

'The pit's sure to give you a job on top; in the lamp-room p'raps. Don't you worry now. You get well for the concert. On the platform you'll have to sit, and if the leg comes in time it can stand on a table to show everybody.'

Jenkin got better quickly after this and was out of the hospital long before the night of the concert. The leg had been ordered, but the date of delivery was unknown. But what did become known was that the deacons of Horeb had taken full advantage of this excuse for a concert and done things on a grand scale. They had solicited the charity of four vocalists, and of these four they had persuaded – great triumph – Madame Sarah Watkins to come out of her retirement and shed her lustre, gratis, on the event.

As soon as it became known that she was to appear all tickets were sold, and as top price for these was five shillings (for the deacons were business men), a sum would be raised far beyond the leg's cost. Sarah Watkins's voice was legendary and a tale told by firesides. Still more enticing, her life had been scandalous, though of course her voice covered a multitude of sins. Wife to four men (at different times), a heavy drinker (of whisky), a constant attendant at courts (for debt), notorious for tantrums (in her heyday, that is), a wearer of flashy clothes (all belonging to the era of plush pineapples and whole cygnets on hats), she was an explosion of female vitality to be reckoned with. Though now in her retirement she lived on the coast twenty miles away, Madame Watkins was a native of the valley, where her father had been one of the pioneering miners. And she had always declared, with a heave of her bosom, that she loved dear little Twlldu. Proof of this was now evident. She hadn't sung in public for fifteen years.

'Your leg it is, mun,' people said to Jenkin. 'Your leg it is that has given her a push out again.'

What the Jenkin crowd did not know was that it was the honeyed flattery, religious blandishments, and oratorical fervour of one of the Horeb deacons that had worked a spell on Sarah; he had called on her, claiming an acquaintance with her dead father. She didn't care a rap for Jenkin's leg. But, aged now, she had begun to turn an occasional eye to the religious things of her childhood; it was as well to be on the safe side. Yes, she would sing in a chapel, and not for money but for glory; and she had offered the deacon a whisky, which he at once declined.

Her name on the posters, with London, Milan, and Twlldu printed under it, created a sensation. The other three soloists were of local origin, too, though of course they were not to be compared. But, what with the choir as well, a huge success was assured. The deacons of Horeb informed the hospital that the bill for Mr Jenkin Morgans's leg was to be sent to them and same would be paid cash down. It was then that Jenkin began to wake up.

'How much the leg?' he mildly asked the hospital, going up there on crutches, and a sister who had taken a fancy to him promised to find out. 'Like to know, I do, how much money I am costing,' he explained, 'so that I can give thanks according.'

The day before the concert he called on one of the deacons in his home. 'Sit down by there,' said the deacon kindly, taking the crutches. 'Arrived has the leg in the hospital, then! Fixing it on you they'll be soon, no doubt.'

'Aye' – Jenkin blew straight, full of high stomach already because of all the talk about him – 'but what I am wanting to know, Mr Price-Harris, is what about the extra money?'

'Come now,' purred Mr Price-Harris, 'your leg you've got.'

'My benefit this concert is,' said Jenkin ominously. 'The talk is that more than a hundred pounds is left over.'

The deacon pronounced, stern at once: 'Work has been done by the deacons of Horeb, and Madame Sarah Watkins is singing out of love for the old chapel of her dead father. On the glory of Horeb the extra money will be spent. Dilapidations there are and a new coat of paint needed, and—'

Jenkin heaved himself up and took his crutches. 'Good day to you now,' he said meekly.

Half an hour before the concert's starting time the chapel was packed with women in all their beads, brooches, and furs, the men in Sunday dark and starch. A wooden platform had been erected under the pulpit; a piano, chairs, and a table stood on it.

In the gallery around the pipe organ behind the pulpit the male voice choir assembled in good time. But no one needed to hurry. Madame Watkins wasn't nearly ready. A turmoil was going on in the vestry behind. The diva, like an old warhorse taken out again too near the smell and roar of cannon, was behaving as in her heyday. The deacons were flustered. They couldn't be expected to know that such as Madame Watkins never got the inspiration to sing before they had torn a lion or two into pieces.

The car that had been hired to fetch her was an old decrepit one driven by the fishmonger's lout of a son. And he had taken it into his head to kill two birds on this trip by collecting a small cask of herrings from the coast; it was already beside him on the front seat when he called for Madame Watkins, who brought with her a large suitcase. Secondly, no one had remembered to welcome her arrival with flowers. Thirdly, no one had thought she would need, for changing into a concert dress, somewhere more private than a vestry filled with coming and going persons connected with tonight's affair. The other three soloists, neatly attired but of whom she had never heard, waited open-mouthed.

'Get me screens, then,' she bellowed, 'and a full-length mirror, and a dresser... Ach,' her body gave a great quake, 'I stink of fish... Violet scent too,' she screamed after people who were running out into the street in search of screens and mirrors. A deacon's wife went into the chapel to scan the tiers of people for someone known to be a dressmaker. Everything was procured in due time, though the mirror was only one taken down from someone's parlour wall. The concert began an hour late.

Yet no one would have guessed the diva's fury when at last she mounted the platform and, amid thunderous applause, gave a superb bow. She advanced like an old ruined queen majestically unaware of new fashions and systems, giving an expert kick to the billowing train of her dragon-coloured but tattered dress. At sight of her, and perhaps the train, a little hiss of awe seemed to come from the goggling women in the audience. The smile issuing from the clumps of fat, the ravines, and scarlet meadows of that face, was sweeter than Lucrezia Borgia's. An aigrette feather leaped from her auburn wig. There was a smell; a fierce perfume could be smelled even all round the gallery. It was as if Madame Watkins, a member of some mythical race, had risen through the parted earth amid the odours of flowers more gloriously ornate than were known above. The slim pianist seemed to wilt over the keys as he waited. Above, the male voice choir, which had already sung an opening chorus, slunk back in abeyance.

'Fancy,' a woman upstairs reminded her companion of the diva's last appearance, 'any council summonsing her for rates!'

'Oh, there's beautiful she is!' whispered the other in an aghast voice. 'And there's glad I am I've seen her. A pity for him, but if it wasn't for Jenkin's leg—'

But the erstwhile diva was launching into something out of *Carmen*. And soon it became plain that she had already given her performance. In her voice were gaping cracks through which wheezed a ghostly wind. No matter, no matter at all! For they were cracks in a temple of glorious style. A ruined temple far away in the mists of a lonely hilltop, but grander than anything of today.

Everyone felt sorry for the vocalist who followed Madame Watkins; she was still of coltish age, in full possession of her voice, very popular on the radio, and spick-and-span to look at as a new button. Madame Watkins refused to give an encore, but she was down to sing 'Home, Sweet Home', in the second half. Her exit had even more pomp than her entrance, and the applause (it was said afterwards) brought a rush of soot down the chimney of the house next door up Horeb.

Intermission said the programme, and everyone knew what that meant. Jenkin was going to go on the platform and give tidy public thanks for his artificial leg. Ah, there he was, clumping up on his crutches and followed by a pit butty who carried the leg. Sympathetic applause greeted him. The butty stood shyly holding the limb upright on the table. Those who had missed seeing Fireman Samson's leg in his window now had their opportunity. Necks were craned and approval seemed plain in the air. It was not known then that Jenkin's crutches and his thickset butty had forced their way to the platform through a wall of hostile deacons.

'No public speaker I am,' began Jenkin in a mild kind of way, 'and not yet properly back from my serious operation under chloroform. But things must be said. The leg by there is come and very thankful I am for it – and will be more after it is fitted on and got used to my ways.' He ran a cunningly assessing eye round all the chapel and curbed the aggressive note that had crept into his voice. 'But a dispute has arose, sorry to say. For my benefit this concert was made, as my butties in No. 2 pit can prove, and over a hundred pounds is lying in the chapel safe after the leg is paid for. A little 'bacco shop I want to open, and the hundred pounds just right! But no – the respected deacons of Horeb say, "No". For paint and varnish on Horeb they want the money. Well, permission I am asking to say just now that it is not right!' He nodded his head ominously and finished: 'No more now, then, thanking you one and all, and Mrs. Watkins, too, that don't know.' And nodding to the butty, who took the leg under his arm, he began to clump off the platform.

An awkward silence followed him. As far as could be judged, there were those who felt that a concert in a chapel was no place to make such a complaint. But also there were those who, ever ready to suspect ill-conduct in high places, followed Jenkin's exit with an approving eye. Then up to the platform walked dignified Mr J. T. Llewellyn, a deacon of long and admired standing. Sternly he said in the quiet:

'Respecting the matter mentioned just now by Mr Jenkin Morgans, the benefit that was asked by his friends of the pit is now fulfilled. A leg first-class is given to him. Success of this concert was business of Horeb's deacons and much interest in the needs of the chapel showed Madame Sarah Watkins when she remembered it was the chapel of her old father... Now,' he continued with an austere dismissal and looking at a copy of the programme, 'back to the concert! The choir will open again with a rendering of 'Italian Salad'. Ladies and gentlemen, 'Italian Salad'!' And with this flourish he swept away.

While Madame Watkins in the vestry – the screens around her – was taking a secret drink of whisky out of a medicine bottle, Mr J. T. Llewellyn thought it prudent to break into her privacy to mention the leg affair. Infuriated by (a) being caught red-handed drinking an intoxicant in a chapel vestry and (b) the deacon's tale of Jenkin's exhibition on the platform, the diva began to boil again. What, a surgical leg had been displayed on the platform a few minutes after her appearance! Her sense of style and what was fitting in a concert containing her was outraged. Amateurs, she taunted, bah! The deacon, flustered by this unaccustomed kind of high-mindedness, continued to mumble explanations uselessly. 'Interested in surgical legs I am not!' she stormed. 'Ring up that curtain, and let me get home.'

'No curtain there is here.' The deacon coughed. 'But a hot supper is waiting for you after the concert, along with the other soloists.'

'What! Who are these persons?' she blew. 'Do they sell cockles and mussels in the daytime?'

And she all but ran out to sing 'Home, Sweet Home'. Yet once more the smile that greeted the loving applause was of a piercing and all-embracing sweetness which made few shiver. And the cracked voice gave an added poignancy to the old song. Not many eyes remained quite dry, for was not the celebrated Madame Watkins singing this song in her true birthplace? The concert was considered, and rightly, a red-letter one.

But the matter of Jenkin's leg did not remain there. Many of the men in No. 2 pit took umbrage at the chapel's treatment of their one-time fellow workman. These, in any case, were always critical of chapels and their power over social pleasures. Fierce arguments developed in the pits, and the ancient question of whether there is an Almighty or not was yet again raised by the opposed forces. Continued in public places on top, the dispute caused some physical combats on Saturday nights. The men's families began to take sides, too, and many were the hostilities exchanged over back garden fences by wives pegging out washing; many were the schoolyard tumbles. After three weeks of this a meeting of miners was called in the Workmen's Hall. A strong faction of the men wanted to go on strike if Jenkin did not receive all profits from the concert.

The deacons of Horeb put on their armour. Some of them

were officials in the colliery; others hoped to be. They gave emphatic 'No' to this new blackmail by men whose infamy was worsened by their being of atheistic mind. They sat tight. Out in the valley a complication was added to the affair by Jenkin's decision not to use the artificial leg till his plea had been settled. He went about the place on his pathetic crutches, thus keeping quick his supporters' sympathy.

'No,' he would say, brave, 'all right I am. But set fire to me would that leg if I put it on. Just going down to the barber's I am to read the papers.' Too poor he was to buy papers, of course.

Well, the Miners' Federation, getting wind of this unofficial strike, forbade it. Jenkin's supporters became more haughty at this. Hadn't the men of Twlldu downed tools once because an unpopular policeman was carrying on with a married woman? Wasn't this robbery of Jenkin worse? Glittering words were used at a second Workmen's Hall meeting. Finally it was decided to give the deacons another fortnight to hand over the money. There had been no signs of painters and plasterers starting work on the chapel.

'No,' said Bryn Stop Tap, an extremist, 'nor won't be. But fur coats will be seen on the deacons' wives and the ginger beer van calling every day at their houses.'

Jenkin whimpered with devilish meekness: 'Stop the old fuss. Bad blood I am spreading.' But still he wouldn't use the leg, and his crutches and folded-up trouser were a standing reproach to everybody.

There was a nasty row in the fruit shop one Friday evening. Mrs Evans Fruit, a suspected supporter of the deacons' side, was accused by a pro-Jenkin woman of giving her nothing but damaged apples while only healthy ones had just gone into the basket of a customer also suspected to be on the other side. The shop was full of women.

'You get out of my shop, you liar!' shouted Mrs Evans.

Pointing at the fruiterer, another customer said two words: 'She's Horeb!'

As is known from the conduct of mobs in the French Revolution, a single accusing cry can batter down a palace and spread riot like a tornado. Soon the shop was in a very untidy state and several old insulting scandals had been referred to in the course of the row. Mrs Evans herself collapsed on to a basket of greengages, but by the time the policeman arrived order had been restored and everybody felt twice alive and that the world was worth living in after all. Jenkin heard, of course, of this battle on his behalf and once more called on the local reporter, trying to incite him to inform his paper. Meanwhile, he had also laboured over a long letter to Madame Sarah Watkins, soliciting her opinion. But he received no reply.

'Oh, don't you bother about me,' he whined in the Bracchi ice cream and coffee shop a week later, as everybody offered him a seat. 'Lean on my crutches I can. Only come in to pass the time I have. If I had my little 'bacco shop, busy enough I would be.'

But it was strange that no one offered him a cigarette that day, or refreshment.

A third Workmen's Hall meeting was held long after the fortnight had gone. The deacons had made no sign. But neither were the painters and ladders about Horeb. At the meeting there was a lot of high talk and everybody had a consoling word for Jenkin; the feeling was that soon as a painter's brush was put to Horeb the bomb would burst. But it was strange that the meeting got on quite soon to New Year fixtures for the Twlldu Eleven. Jenkin sat with his head on one side like a long-suffering bird.

'Waiting for the spring the deacons are,' someone told Jenkin outside the pub's closed door. 'Horeb will have a spring cleaning on your money. Better ask for a job on top of the pits, Jenkin.'

One January day Jenkin, giving vent to loud abuse, threw a crutch through a window of Horeb. But all that resulted was a summons and he had to pay the cost of the window. Feeling for and against him was revived for a day or two. Yet it was only talk and argument. Then at the end of February Mrs Roberts the Washing's house went up in flames. A poor widow who took in washing, her cottage wasn't insured. Though she was out during the fire and didn't have to be rescued, a long sigh of sorrow for her went right through the valley. It was plain what would have to be done in her aid.

'Ask Madame Sarah Watkins to come again,' several persons said. A committee was formed.

The day after the fire Jenkin's wife took out a long cardboard box from under the bed. She was a quiet little woman who rarely put a foot into the valley's doings. But she had good eyesight and ears clear of wax. Jenkin looked at her sulkily. 'A bit tired I am,' she said, 'of idleness and sloth. Put on your leg, Jenkin, and go up to the pits for work.' On the promise of the Horeb money coming she had been lent cash by her sister. 'Come on, Jenkin,' she coaxed. And she said cleverly: 'Put not your trust in princes and the people of this earth.'

Jenkin lifted his head. A religious light shone in his eyes. 'Aye,' he said in grand contempt, 'the bullseye you said there! Shall a man like me be lowered because all around him are low? Help me with my leg, Maria. The hospital said like this—'

In March men placed ladders against Horeb and, carrying cans of primrose paint, they went up them unmolested. But the concert for Mrs Roberts the Washing's benefit was not held there. And Madame Sarah Watkins did not appear for this; she wrote saying that her retirement was final unless her health improved. But she was in the papers again before March was out: a firm of licensed victuallers sued her for goods delivered. She told the court that she had been too goodhearted and lately had sung everywhere for nothing, in aid of this and that charity. After the painters had done the windows of Horeb they varnished the solid pews inside.

PERIOD PIECE

She swung open the tall rickety door of the shed and peered into the darkness within. It was a disused cart shed, used at one time by a tradesman now gone bankrupt: it stood at the end of the garden where grew frosty stunted cabbages and a few unwilling swedes. 'Griff?' she called. 'Griff, are you there?' He had gone out to the shed from the house an hour ago, before the dark had fallen; he used it as a place where he could occupy the many idle hours at tasks once welcomed as enjoyed hobbies.

For some reason she retreated from the shed door and ran back to the house, her feet skirmishing in heavy swiftness over the cindered garden path. The evening was very cold. She took up an oil lamp (they could no longer afford the electricity) from the kitchen table, and returned down the garden. The lamp's shaking flame revealed her broad, thick-skinned face clenched in apprehension.

Inside the shed, holding the lamp high, she stiffened, her flabby neck, with its promised goitre of the valley women, swelling. Hanging from a beam was the body of her husband. It swayed gently in the draught from the open door. A kicked-away pair of dwarf steps lay on its side beneath him. His head, the face bluish, lolled in defeated helplessness. The eyes were half open.

The entreating whimpers issuing from down her generous bosom were like an animal's. They soon ceased. She laid the lamp on a work table, which was covered with tools, a three-piece iron shoe last, tins of nails, a bottle holding a candle stub in its mouth, and a pair of her own shoes, cracked and limp, which he had been attempting to sole. 'No... Griff... no,' she entreated. Her head began to sway as though in unison with the body.

She had to believe it. She stared about her, then suddenly ran out of the shed, a big heavy woman with strong grey hair and sprawling breasts that seemed lifted now in fury. In the house she snatched up a shawl, threw it over her shoulders, and went out into the wintry street by the front door. It was the main street, gas-lit, with a few closed half derelict shops wedged among the dwellings: her own house, its front portion haphazardly adjusted, had once been a shop.

There were few people about tonight, and these did not loiter. She climbed a steep road leading out of the main street. It was bordered with pairs of better class houses, and it led to an eminence of villas which stood in pleasing contrast to the rough pioneering dwellings in the bed of the narrow valley. This removed little estate was the last attempt to modernise the district. People who had made money in the heyday, and who decided not to shake off the gritty dust of the place, dwelt retired up there; also the doctor, head schoolmaster and higher officials of the colliery.

She rang a bell at the shiny varnished door of a villa. A trim maidservant answered; the caller unceremoniously pushed past her without a word, trod across a hall and up a short stairway to a door with frosted glass panels displaying a yellow light within. She burst into this back room without a knock.

A tired-looking man of sixty, the general manager of the colliery, sat at a table on which papers and documents were scattered untidily. He looked up with a slight frown. The roused woman standing the other side of the table was the wife of a man who had been a friend of his youth, whom he had left far behind as he climbed to his exalted but not comfortable position.

'You must come with me, Hughes,' she said, loudly.

'What do you want?' he asked.

'Come with me,' she said.

He laid a pencil on the manuscript before him, but replied: 'I'm very busy at the moment. I expect you know I'm speaking at the two meetings tomorrow.' His tone was mechanical: he was accustomed to emotional people.

The colliery, which had not been working full time for years, ever since 'the depression' – had been completely closed for five months: the residue of employed men, perversely ungrateful that they were in jobs at all, had struck on the everlasting wages question. They now were ready to go back. But the owners were refusing to reopen the two pits on the men's amended terms – what was the use, there were no profits, no orders worth speaking of, it was not only a local question but a matter of blight affecting the whole... and so on. Hughes was to give the Company's reply and terms to the miners' committee in the morning, and this was to be followed by an afternoon mass meeting of the men, also to be addressed by him. On street corners the men already were saying that no real good would come of these meetings. The weather of failure, swollen clouds perpetually drifting over the mountains from the anonymous world beyond, had darkened the valley for too long a period: complete pessimism was rife.

'Yes, I know,' the woman said, 'I know about the meetings.'

'What do you want of me?' he repeated, with a half-kindly fretfulness now. He picked up the pencil and tapped it vaguely on the worrying manuscript.

'Come with me,' she begged, in such a strange manner that he looked at her again. 'Come, Hughes. It's Griff.'

'What's the matter?' he insisted.

The woman looked at him, her grey eyes shining with a kind of smothered anguish. He remembered her well enough. She had been a wild, rather rough local girl, and he had been surprised when Griff, a quiet chap with a liking for playing the piano at chapel concerts, had married her. That would be about sixteen or seventeen years ago, in the good times, when the war was on.

Occasionally, taking advantage of the fact that he had been born and bred in their midst, the work people would come to him with their private woes – an illness, a police court summons, a wayward son or daughter, the quibblings over a dead relative's property. Sighing, he laid the pencil down again. His face was lined, the cheeks slack; he looked in need of a holiday. He supposed that his one-time friend had been taken ill, and in fear wanted to ask something of him. The woman before him he judged to be not far from hysteria. He rose abruptly.

In overcoat and thick scarf, he accompanied the woman out of the house and down the hill. She said nothing and he remained preoccupied with his unfinished speech. Vaguely he noticed that they were hurrying. There was an obsessive sense of urgency about the woman. Her head swayed oddly. Her shawl hung loose, almost slipping off; she seemed unconscious of the bitter night.

The speech he had been preparing was giving him a great deal of trouble. His heart wasn't in it. But, in any case, hearts were out of place in such a speech. Hard facts only! With cold brevity he had written out the terms under which the Company was prepared to reopen the pits. He had stalked through so many conflicts that figures had become figures, terms merely terms. Only this time there was a stirring in his heart, like a nausea. Facts and figures were so easy to assemble, and he was weary of them. Perhaps he could work into the speech some real promise, a genuine gleam of hope, a looking up to a brighter future. But that nauseated him too, and, besides, he must be careful of such orator's tricks. Derisive hoots, ironical catcalls, would drown any attempt at uplift. No, what he wanted was to work into the speech a vision of a different nature. He wanted to express, courageously, the failure of a colossal structure, the crash of an intricate edifice built up through a long era, and, far from giving the men hope, to make them aware of a catastrophe much greater than this trivial closing-down of two holes in the local earth. But of course that would be mad and (even if he had the vocabulary necessary for such a vision) it was treacherous to the Company. He had become flabby. He needed a holiday; or at least a tonic.

The woman preceded him into her house. They passed through the unoccupied part that had been a shop in the prosperous days. The dwelling behind was rented cheaply to this miner, who was of those the colliery had not been able to employ, even on half-time, for years. A meagre fire warmed the living room. She opened a back door.

'This way. Out here, where he is.'

Sharpened, he peered at her. But in the open lean-to, hung with zinc baths and a wooden washing tub, it was too dark to see her face. He felt issuing from her a great anger, a thick physical hostility. For a moment he hesitated, in primitive caution. He had a few enemies; a few people had, of course, called him traitor to the class from which he had sprung. Once, during a strike in the old, more elementary days of pioneering disputes, the windows of his house had been stoned, and Judas tarred on his garden wall in letters a yard high.

A light could be seen shining through the open doorway of a shed at the end of the garden. The woman entered the shed with her head ducked forward. She lifted an arm with a strange unconscious gesture. As he advanced he saw her go through the shed and throw open the big double doors at the far end, which opened into a back lane used as a shortcut to the main road by people living in the rows beyond.

'He's dead,' she screamed.

So he was prepared for Griff hanging from the beam. The face was now a purplish black, the eyes staring down into the quiet light of the oil lamp. His own head slewed over for a moment. And then he jumped forward and acted swiftly, as he had acted swiftly in bloody accidents in the pits. Oblivious to her shrieks, he snatched a cobbler's knife from the table, picked up the thrown-over pair of steps and had already begun to mount them when the woman savagely pushed him away. He almost fell to the ground.

'Let him be,' she shouted.

'He must be taken down,' he gasped, oddly arrested by the power, unknown and chilling, emanating from her.

'Dead, you see he's dead! It's no use at all.'

Two faces now peered in from the dark lane; one vanished instantly. He struggled with her. But she was possessed of demoniac strength. He called to the man at the doorway, who was staring in with a peculiarly aloof distrust, his long bony face not human, its owner remaining perfectly still but watchful.

'Let them see,' she screamed, 'let them see!'

People crowded in then, six or seven of them, including the man who had vanished.

'Fetch a doctor,' panted Hughes, thrown off by the woman, 'someone fetch a doctor. And a policeman. At once.'

The woman strutted like a guardian before the corpse, which swung gently in the draught from the open doors. Her hands were fisted, her face was barbaric. Skeins of woolly drab grey hair pitched loose about her neck.

'There he is, people, you see him! Hanging like a bullock in the slaughterhouse. A good eyeful you can take of him.' She swerved on Hughes. 'And you, that was his friend, that was his friend,' she repeated balefully, 'take a good look at him, the damn coward, see him for the rat that he is.' She snatched up a garden rake which leant against the wall, and struck the corpse a violent blow, so that it swung out and back, out and back, several times. 'Coward!' she shouted. 'What's he done it for? Weary of life, then? – aye, tired of life. But what about me, and the three children? Answer me that!' She threw the rake to a corner. Her fists, clenched again into bluish knots of flesh, pounded against her thighs. But her face was wilting, its fury dying out, leaving the skin a slack greyish yellow. Her voice sank. 'What's he done it for?' she wailed. 'Leaving me alone!' At last she abandoned her awful dancing before the corpse. It all had seemed like an hour: it was only a minute or two. And each onlooker had been powerless to interfere.

Hughes, pale and stern, mounted the pair of steps. Quietly he bade two men hold the corpse. Still a hard silence wrapped the little crowd of people: they had been like figures in a dim photograph, grouped inside the tall oblong of doorway, the icy winter sky behind. As the corpse was lifted down, a policeman pushed his way in.

The policeman's appearance brought the proceedings down sharply to solid earth. The crowd lost its rigidity; a babel of voices broke out excitedly. Someone cleared the table of its objects, and the corpse was laid on it. Before this was done, Marged had trudged over to the table and picked up her old shoe, on which Griff had made his last poor effort to save a shilling or two. A woman neighbour went to her tentatively.

'Marged,' she whispered, 'Marged, come into the house now.'

She threw the shoe down and the fury surged out again. She cursed the heavens and the earth. Another woman assisted the neighbour, and Marged was urged out of the shed. In the garden she broke from their encircling arms, and ran into the house shouting something about burning it down. Presently she was got into the armchair in the living room. She began to sob in a normal way. 'He was never the same after his piano went,' she cried. And, a little more fiercely, 'It was always the piano first, then me and the children.'

'Hush, now,' soothed the neighbour, 'hush, now; you know he was a man respected by all of us. A good-living, hard-working chap.'

Her head lay on the neighbour's arm. 'There was a quarrel we had,' she whimpered, 'yesterday. Seeing that the piano went, I burned some of his music, lighting the fire with it, and when he knew what I'd done, his face went white as death... What was the use,' she wailed in appeal, 'of the old sheets of music and no piano to play them on?'

'Yes, yes,' coaxed the neighbour, 'no use at all. But it wasn't that made him do what he's done, Marged. You know how it's been with him, and with all of us, for years.'

'He said he could read the sheets,' Marged went on heedlessly. She sprang up and darted to a cupboard, threw out of it a few soiled and ragged music scores. 'Read them and hear them, he said. Without a piano! The music was always first with him! Me and the children afterwards.'

'It was not the music,' the neighbour repeated.

Marged wept over the music sheets. She knew Griff had been too gentle a chap altogether, and she could not forgive him that he had not her savage defiance.

*

They got her upstairs after a while. The women neighbours wanted her in bed before the children arrived home from the cinema. Dr Bowen, hearing of her plight, nipped back to his surgery and returned with a sedative. It was decided that the corpse should remain in the shed for the night. The onlookers had gone away. Hughes went back to his villa.

A. D. Jenkins, the schoolmaster (irate older pupils said it ought to be B. C. Jenkins), sat waiting in the villa study. For years he had scrutinised Hughes's speeches, mostly for faulty grammar, and he had already read the manuscript on the desk. 'No mistakes, so far,' he said, as Hughes sat down. 'But the style is flat, old chap, flat and anaemic – that is, in the circumstances,' he wheezed, coughing out acrid smoke from his evil pipe. 'Tomorrow is something of a crossroads, isn't it?'

Although such news as a suicide travelled instantaneously all over the place, Jenkins evidently had not heard it. For some reason, Hughes could not bring himself to speak of it. He only said, shortly: 'Well, my heart's not in the speech. I'm sick to death of speeches and mass meetings. What's the use of talking?'

'Would you prefer the men to repeat the rioting of 1910?' Jenkins asked. 'That generation had little education – and the little was of smaller use; their question mark was a tensed fist and arm.' He added: 'In 1935 they need respectful addressing, Hughes. Don't underestimate their intelligence or their temper, like our dear Prime Minister.'

'I'm rotting with inactivity as badly as the men – and with lack of belief.' Hughes fidgeted with the manuscript pages on the desk. 'I don't think their temper is on the boil at all. The whole climate of the times is one of hopelessness, and they sense it.

Change and decay in all around I see... We're not at a crossroads, but in a blind alley. That is what I ought to develop in my speech.'

'A funeral oration? Better stick to plain facts pertinent to a strike discussion – yes, pertinent to it,' Jenkins said, looking pleased as Punch.

'I'd like to be shot of the whole cursed coal business,' Hughes continued, morosely. 'It's been little else but a pain in the backside. I'd be glad if all the bloody mines were nationalised, as the Reds want.'

'That would be suicide for you,' Jenkins remarked, and did not notice Hughes wince. 'You belong too much to the old personal regime to become a nationalised puppet.'

'I should think it's coming,' Hughes brooded. 'Local catastrophes have gone on too long.'

'Do you think nationalisation will transform the souls of the men?' Jenkins asked, stretching his stout legs.

Hughes took up the manuscript more decisively. 'No, of course not. But souls are no business of mine or of the nation's.' Perplexing his visitor, he went on, 'If a man commits suicide, it's due to an inherent mental weakness—' He hesitated, but still found himself unable to tell Jenkins of the Griff affair: he still could feel the strange sensation of the lifeless body slipping through his hands to Griff's fellow workers waiting around the pair of steps. And a perverse undercurrent of respect for the woman Marged ran briefly through his mind.

He flicked through the manuscript and struck out an undeveloped sentence: We are at the end of an era and the fields on which we continue to stand like scarecrows are barren of grain. Stupid rhetoric! Politician's bilge! He also deleted, less readily, from another page: We must be careful we are not left with a legacy of bitterness that will sour our lives forever and destroy our faith in our country, our traditions, our faith in the ultimate goodness of life. That stuff wasn't his department. On the next page were some solid facts and figures from the Company's balance sheets for the past five years: also the gruesome announcement of the final loss of an important export order.

After Jenkins had gone, he continued to work on his speech. Facts and figures. For years he had been hardening himself, stifling all emotion. But he had a talent for drawing. As midnight approached, he found himself making a sketch of a hanging man on a margin of the manuscript – the face, however, not being Griff's but, moustached, more like his own, and looking tired.

*

Down in Marged's house the three children arrived home about ten o'clock. It had been their fortnightly treat at the cinema; from the front sixpenny benches they had stayed to see most of the programme through twice. Olwen, the eldest daughter, carried three pennyworth of hot chips, wrapped in a sheet of newspaper. She exclaimed bad-temperedly when she saw that the table wasn't laid for supper. The neighbour looked at them apprehensively, and told them to be quiet; their mother had been taken ill and was in bed. Through Olwen's mind flashed the suspicion that this was a repetition of what happened when her sister Maud, now placidly picking her eight-year-old nose, had joined the family as a baby.

'I brought some chips,' Olwen said, and threw the package sulkily on the bare table. She was a hard, penurious-looking girl of fifteen.

Gwen, the second girl, was pleasanter, rounder and plumper. 'Have you been to the Palace this week, Mrs. Roberts?' she asked. 'A very good picture there. *Champagne Bubbles*, it's called.' She was inclined to studiousness and, with lapses, had a philosophic attitude to all matters.

Mrs Roberts, her mind on the shed, replied, 'No', in a scared way, and helped with the supper. Olwen emptied the chips on to plates. Gwen rescued the newspaper wrapping and during supper read with absorbed attention a big advertisement for face cream: a titled woman swore that she never went to hunt balls – or, indeed, any other balls – without a pot; her complexion was admired everywhere in the county, so she said. Grease from the chips had spread over her photograph, making her skin look disgraceful now. But Gwen liked the description of the hunt ball, eating her chips enjoyably with her fingers. Maud sat prolonging this fortnightly treat of a late night by eating very slowly.

Gwen heaved a fat sigh. 'When you've been to the pictures,' she said, 'after coming out, things don't seem right at all.'

'What things?' asked Olwen, disagreeably concise.

'Why—?' said Gwen, and waved her hand largely, 'life.'

*

At the inquest, which was held in an upper room of The Golden Fleece, Marged sat wearing a borrowed black hat and looking as though she was not really under it. All the fury seemed drained out of her; she sat aloof but somehow hostile. She gave her evidence sullenly, in a low unwilling voice; she did not make a good impression. The coroner thought she was being obstinate.

'Had you and your husband been quarrelling?' he asked.

'Only about his music sheets,' she replied, oppressed by all this officiousness, 'that I lit the fire with.'

He got out of her how she had discovered the body and run for the colliery manager, and he said, quite sharply: 'But you might have saved your husband's life if you had cut him down at once! There is always a chance that life is not extinct in such cases.'

'He was dead,' she said.

'How did you know?'

'He was dead,' she repeated. Her eyes looked beyond the coroner into a world of her own where life was still to be dealt with, complete with three children.

When the coroner closed the inquest, he said: 'It is obvious that the home life of this poor man was not all it should have been. We have heard from the witnesses how his wife behaved on finding her husband. She did not attempt to cut him down, she even struck his body a blow with a rake. It is evident there were disagreements at home. Of course, the deceased had been out of work for some years, owing to the closing down of the pits, but that is no reason for a man to take his own life. In this and the surrounding valleys thousands of other men are, for the time being, in his position.'

He found that the man had committed suicide while of unsound mind, and, as he rose to go to luncheon in another room of the inn, he observed, to no one in particular: 'A deplorable story.'

A SPOT OF BOTHER

Ormond, upset by his favourite team losing the League match and, earlier in the day, a very raw shindy with his Mary Ann, so far forgot his principles as to go thoroughly astray in the city, that football Saturday. Sometimes sheepish, more often bellicose, he was a young married coal miner endeavouring to settle down, too soon, to life. Profligacy was not his natural bent, but exceptional circumstances can achieve an exceptional breakdown of discipline, and, in addition, he was not one to halt in the thought that eccentric conduct can bring perils pertinent to it.

As dusk fell, after the disastrous match, he uncharacteristically broke away from the bunch of faithful boys who had journeyed with him from Bylau, twenty railway miles away in the swart Welsh hills, and for a time he thrust his dejected jaw through back streets whilst a drizzle wetted his well-oiled mop of curls. Then, wandering into many by-path public houses, he drank far more than was normal with him. By ten o'clock he reached the docks district, reputed place of saturnalia, and there he picked up a harlot who seemed to his (by then) illumined eyes – perhaps because of the big amber beads she wore down her front – cheerful-looking as a string of Breton onions.

He met her in a crammed pub called 'The Fireman's Larder'. After sundry conventional courtesies had been exchanged she asked him if he was married.

'I am, see!' he replied. 'To the best little Mary Ann that ever trod on a man's toe.'

'I thought so; I can always tell the married ones.' The woman took out cosmetics and mirror from her bag and dabbed thickly at her face as though in logical comment. 'She's gone away for the weekend, I expect?'

'That's it!' Ormond said, enthusiastically recognising perception, but not mentioning that Mary Ann had torn off her thick-lensed glasses – always a bad sign – that morning and declared she was returning to her Aunt Maud's house 'for ever': she found his football excursions to the city objectionable and had not yet acclimatised herself to male isolations, though of course there were other seethings. 'She's gone by train!' he exclaimed, thumping the beer-soaked table. 'A puff-puff, see? Stops at a dozen stations before she put her lovely leg out and stares from her glasses to see who's meeting her. Short-sighted, see?'

'Sometimes they're well off, short-sighted,' the woman said, and swallowed at a gulp the single gin Ormond had bought her. He did not approve of women drinking, except a long-winded token one for sociability's sake. She told him her name was Patricia, and in return he took out his wallet and extracted several snapshots.

'There's me!' he pointed out, unnecessarily. There, indeed, he was: uniformed in the army; bare-kneed with the Bylau Football Club; standing in a meadow among whippets and daisies; proud before a pigeon cote in which meditated his racing birds; and one of him and Mary Ann twinly smiling a wide-open smile outside a chapel. Patricia made suitably attentive comments, and Ormond was encouraged to show, from among other documents in the wallet, the flattering character given to him by the C.O. of his regiment.

'Anyone would think,' she tittered, before excusing herself for five minutes, 'there isn't a wonky corner in you anywhere, sweetie.'

At closing time they sailed away from the wharves on a trolley bus brilliant as a ship lit up at night. When they got off they went up the portico steps of a tall gaunt house. Its peeling stucco was black-veined as a varicose leg. In the hallway a stately eighteenth century staircase stretched bereft not only of people but of carpet and the wash it had long needed. A naked electric bulb, spotted with fly dirt, hung forlorn in the strange locked-up silence. To Ormond, accustomed to the poky but bustling interiors of Bylau cottages, the proportions of everything were majestic, and Patricia's flat on the second floor palatial. A begrimed plaster bust of Socrates on the mantelpiece, although an empty beer bottle stood beside it, added to the splendour. 'Who is it?' he asked, gaping. 'Your dad?'

'No a Lord Mayor, I think.' Patricia, wheezing as she stooped, pulled off her mud-spotted shoes, which had buckles of the finest diamonds.

'Up in Bylau,' Ormond said, respectfully, eyeing the bust, 'we only have them in the cemetery, on high class graves.' Shortly afterwards he pulled her to him by her beads. She had switched on the wireless and a dance band started to croak.

'Oh, not yet!' Patricia said.

She had small eyes lolling far down in green sockets, and he admired, in solemn illumination, all that his own bared eyes saw: it was the same admiration that came from him in the cinema when actresses fabulous as mermaids waggled to and fro before their proud men. She lit a cigarette and seemed momentarily abstracted. The room was full of bulky furniture. A vast wardrobe of menacing black wood stood diagonally across a corner, near a door leading, presumably, to another room. The grand bedstead was of brass. Pink and blue articles of clothing hung over the top of a screen patched with floral wallpaper. Two windows were flimsily curtained. But the spacious room soon ceased to interest him. As is the way in drink, inquisitiveness had narrowed to a single obsessiveness. From outside came the hum of a passing trolley bus, and this reminder of journeying preoccupied him for only a second or two.

'Staying the whole night?' Patricia asked, suddenly eyeing him.

'If you please,' Ormond said bashfully. 'Owing to my last train being gone by now, even the one where you change at Pontypridd.'

He was undressing when a flashing explosion of light jumped through the room. 'What's that?' he called, above the wail of the dance band, trouser braces dangling in his arrested hand.

'The overhead bus wire does that sometimes,' declared Patricia. She was standing close to him. 'The flash comes through the curtains.'

'I thought it was lightning,' Ormond said, listening a moment as if for a growl of thunder.

'Perhaps it was lightning,' Patricia said indifferently. She unscrewed her pearl earrings, large and rosy as moons, which were almost her last coverings. 'I didn't hear a bus.' She ruffled his hair, sniffing. 'Nice hair, sweetie boy. Too much oil on it, though.'

His strong arm dotingly about her waist, he said: 'There's violets in it. Three-and-sixpence a bottle in Barney's Cash Chemists on the Square in Bylau.' Another flash of strange light tumbled through the room and, although engrossed in her charms, he mumbled, portentous: 'Storm brewing, right enough!' From the dance band came a jesting tune in welcome contrast to the previous wail.

'No, that one was a trolley bus,' Patricia said. 'I heard it passing. The reel gets jammed on the wire.' She jumped into bed quite briskly. 'Leave the light on, darling. I don't like the dark... No, don't turn off the wireless. I like a bit of dance music. It goes on 'til midnight.'

He went into a deep cave of sleep early, lulled by the siren's croon then oozing unhurried out of Patricia's wireless.

*

A knock on the door can mean anything, even in Bylau, or as in those places of the still older world where men believed that a stranger at the door is sent by the ever-watchful gods. Mary Ann answered the knock, peering from her thick glasses at the tall, thin man standing, politely enough, on the beautifully whitened steps.

Following his inquiry, she bawled down the short passage to the kitchen: 'Ormond! A fellow to see you.' When Ormond appeared, shirtsleeves rolled up, she retreated to the kitchen with a sniff. The breeze of her transit proclaimed that, in her judgement, the caller had to do with whippet racing, gambling, or other anti-home pursuits of the various male clubs in Bylau and thereabouts.

'Can I see you in private?' asked the caller. He wore a long black overcoat of flappingly thin material. His long thin nose was of startling, Caerphilly cheese whiteness, and it twitched whenever a vowel came into his words. 'Down the road, perhaps?' he invited, jerking his head towards the street of squat four-roomed dwellings, all alike and stuck together in well-kept solidity. A patch of waste ground, where children played, lay at the end.

'What for, down the road?' Ormond blew, sleepily astonished. He was not long home from the day shift, after a hot pithead bath, and he had just eaten one of Mary Ann's meat broths, full of root vegetables, and a milky rice and egg pudding. 'I've got a house of my own. Come in... No,' he warned, in sudden afterthought, 'I don't want any vacuum cleaners, electric washing machines, or encyclopaedias. The money in the pits won't allow them. No free samples, either.' Mary Ann closed the kitchen door with a concurring slam; she too disapproved of hire purchase goods and cheeky salesmen besieging orderly homes.

'It's a personal matter.' The caller's simple words came sliding out of the corner of his mouth. But his eyes gleamed with messages, to be revealed only in strict confidence: one moment they seemed probingly impudent, the next wooingly adulatory.

Ormond, yawning and scratching his curls, took him into the parlour. Languid tolerance lay in his flesh and muscles. Everybody had their living to earn. Perhaps this thin, black-overcoated chap wanted him to take out a life insurance on Mary Ann. Soon as a man got married, the insurance companies began to solicit him to think of burials.

The stuffy front parlour was seldom used. Its furnishings had belonged to Mary Ann's parents and included their bygone portraits in heavy golden frames. A mulberry plush cloth, thick as a carpet, covered a round table; on its centre lay a Family Bible of ornate leather and gilt clasps which had never been opened. Two china stallions of ferocious demeanour reared matched on the mantelpiece. The honeyed late afternoon light filtered in through foaming lace curtains kept clean as an angel's nightgown.

'Nor we don't want a television set,' Ormond added, absently. 'Owing to me being out a lot and Mary Ann's weak eyes.'

Standing by the round table, the caller showed sudden decision. A narrow hand of peculiarly swift pouncing whisked an envelope out of an inner pocket of the black overcoat. He drew three small limp cards from it and passed them across the table. Ormond gazed at each card in turn. Wonder slowly accumulated in his absorbed face.

'Well, well!' he remarked. He returned to the first card for further scrutiny, and said: 'Who's this? Not me, is it? Not with a pair of braces dangling from my hand!' He took the cards to the window, where the light was stronger.

The caller looked down his long white nose in deprecatory regret, though a smile of placating coyness went on and off his lips: he himself, saying: 'Excuse me,' had shut the parlour door, as if he feared draughts. 'It's you, plain enough, chum,' he now whispered. 'The one of you in bed is the best.'

It was. Ormond peered at it so concentratedly that his eyes squinted. There, solidly full-faced, was his head asleep on a white pillow, and, beside it, another head recognisable to the meanest intelligence as a woman's, complete with hair. 'Ay, it's the best,' he grunted, from down his throat. He spent quite a time in further study of the prints.

'Works of art!' the caller said, no censoriousness in his tone.

Ormond returned to the table and spread the three cards on Mary Ann's prized family plush. He pointed with a thick, strong forefinger. 'First class!' he agreed, congratulatingly. 'I'll have half a dozen of those two, postcard size... and an enlargement of that one, big enough to frame.'

The man, collecting the flaps of his long overcoat together with a wriggle of enjoyment, uttered a whinny of mirth. 'That's good, chum!' he jerked out, his manner still man-to-man. 'Negatives only for sale, though. Worth a lot, those negatives.

Sale to be completed on Saturday, if you can't manage it now.' He ended with accommodating comradeliness.

Ormond crossed to the door, opened it, and bawled into the passage: 'Mary Ann? Come here!'

She appeared with such rapidity that his call might have concealed some private bird-note understood by her ears alone. 'This chap wants to sell some photos of me,' Ormond announced, giving her an unnecessary push to the table. 'There they are!' The man drew his overcoat about him, blinked, but remained still.

Mary Ann, squarely short-bodied, fiery-coloured and altogether local-cast as her husband, but wearing a flowered voile frock, settled her glasses before taking up the cards for the important scrutiny due to any photographs of close relations or self. She, too, carried them to the window. Ormond followed her. 'I told him,' he said, pointing, 'six postcard-size of those two... and an enlargement of that one for framing.'

She peered at them with the suspicious intentness of the near-sighted, silent for long, long moments. Ormond stood waiting, hands on hips like an athlete poised for direction or assessing a distance. The caller had stepped back a yard from the table, towards the door: he had replaced the envelope in his pocket. But, upper lip lifted, he too waited.

'No,' Mary Ann decided at last, with mistress-of-the-home finality, 'not an enlargement of that one. It wouldn't frame well... not for the parlour or anywhere else, Ormond, dear.'

Ormond sprang. But the man, agilely black as an eel, was out, slithering down the passage before Ormond's raised foot could find relief. 'Ormond!' Mary Ann shouted, sprang too, and grabbed her husband by the waistband of his trousers seat. 'Think of the neighbours!' she hissed. The man escaped.

'Fetch my coat!' Ormond's snort was that of a boiling full-back cheated of the ball by a fouling opponent. Mary Ann, babbling, held on to her husband. He butted her backwards, so that she fell against the oak umbrella stand. Not more than a few seconds elapsed before he had put on his hairy Harris tweed jacket of myrtle green and, oblivious to Mary Ann's winded exhortations, streaked out of the house. The man was just disappearing round the corner at the end of the street.

Bylau is not of important dimensions; in fact, it is seldom spotted on maps. Under beetling hills rich with coal, it lies in uncaring sloth towards modern developments, though its little railway station functions, and buses ply in and out of it in haphazard easygoing. The natives know its every cranny, the various treads of its half-dozen police, and exactly what to do in time of trouble. Within three minutes Ormond had collected the following men: Goronwy Jones (from off the steps of the Miners' Institute), Wyn Davies (snatched out of the White Hart bar), Pennar Bevan (coming out of a convenience), and Aneirin Evans (standing in reverie before a Labour Party poster). All were miners and members of the Bylau Football Club.

Information was conveyed mostly by gesticulations, Ormond's only vocal explanation being: 'That bloke in the black overcoat has stolen something from me; it's in his pocket.' (For theft, of course, it was; dastardly theft of his good name and odour in Bylau.) The stranger, sliding round corners, jerking his head back, clutching his flapping overcoat about him, was kept securely in view all the time.

They headed him out of the shopping Square and away from the railway station, dribbled him through law-abiding Coronation Street and intersecting Pleasant Terrace. Neither pursuers nor pursued hurried now. Outside the colliery manager's villa, the group was joined by Reverend Meurig Morris, a useful inside-right in his day and still a standby for an occasional match. 'I've got to go to Miss Lloyd-Trealaw's house,' the Rev. declared. 'I can only give you ten minutes.' With his starched dog-collar and round clerical hat he lent the affair a suitable pomp.

Their non-committal progress became that of men enjoying a promenade among well-beloved nooks and haunts too familiar for discussion; silence hung about their prowl. The stranger, kept twenty yards ahead, seemed for a while to pretend that he too was lightly engrossed in a walk among quiet back streets which, however, did not lead him back into the Square with its traffic, plashing fountain, and dutiful policeman standing impartial. Soon three of the group sauntered up a steep street while the other three cut through an alley. Thus they manoeuvred the culprit into a shady cul-de-sac under the disused colliery coke ovens.

He cowered, spittle on his lips, against the padlocked door of a shed. But the half hour of plodding pursuit was his sole punishment, and in any case the Rev. would not have countenanced physical blows. Whilst the others stood in a semi-circle of thickset criticism, Ormond inserted his hand into the overcoat pocket, drew the envelope out, carefully looked in it, and stepped back with a mien of completion. 'Let him go, now,' he said graciously. Only the Rev., naturally a dab at recognising evil, had a word to say to the man. 'Better mend your ways, whatever you've done,' he pronounced; 'otherwise perdition will be your lot.' But the man's eyes had become unseeing slits refusing knowledge of anything.

They left him crouched into his overcoat like a bat closed on itself under a barn eave. 'Pickpocket!' Ormond mumbled to his friends, as they emerged from the cul-de-sac. 'Robbed me last Saturday when I was down in Cardiff for the match. No value in the envelope, except what's sentimental to me.' Tactful grunts came from the others, and they parted in the Square for their various evening pleasures. The noses of the cronies had sensed outrage against a son of clean Bylau, and it was enough.

*

His exalted shout, as he strutted down the passage, proclaimed that all was well. 'Mary Ann!' he bellowed, 'where are you? Let's go to the pictures. Best seats tonight!'

The kitchen door stood half open, and as he pranced round it something which seemed tremendous smacked him on the crown of his head. He staggered, stood still in shock, and another blow thumped on the same place; it was followed immediately by a shower of hard dried haricot beans. He gazed in stupor at the pallid stuff gushing around his feet. Above him, standing on a chair behind the door, stood a young Queen Boadicea upraised in powerful moral wrath. She had half-filled an artificial silk stocking with the beans and twisted the top, but this cudgel had split with the second blow.

Staring up at her, he experienced the impact of a stranger exploding into vengeful revelation, a secret enemy erupting into bitter truth. Mary Ann's glasses shone from a domain of dragons.

'What's the matter?' he growled, taking offence up to a point. They had fought innumerable verbal contests, but she had never assaulted him before. 'Beans!' he grunted, and stared down again at the floor, perhaps furtively. 'Try a bottle next time,' he said, attempting bravado. But as he stepped to the fireplace rug, crunching the beans, the strut was out of his gait.

Mary Ann did not dismount from the chair, though she gave the door a push, so that it slammed and left them enclosed from any neighbour rash enough to pop in just then. And from that dais she launched a tirade. Anciently hackneyed of theme, it sprang out in rhythmic congress with the heavings of her bosom. It placed his sex low in the structure of the universe. Nameless beasts crawling out of primeval slime, baboons of later date but scarcely more attractive, speaking but no-forehead creatures ambling out of dank caves with clubs in their hirsute hands – these, and marginal embroideries such as serpents, hog-pigs, toads and billy goats, haunted her abuse. Yet she did not snatch off her glasses with that ominous gesture her husband had learned to dread. The broken stocking waved from her hand as if she had enchanted it into a whip.

'A woman,' she shouted, apparently reaching crescendo, 'marries a man with two legs and finds he's got four like the dogs of the street!'

Ormond, twenty-five next birthday, stood on the rug with arms folded and eyelids stretched back as far as they'd go. Instinct informed him that it is always best, in such circumstances, to remain silent (but silent with an engrossed attention and not an insulting indifference). He continued to stare at her whilst she fulfilled herself in speech. When she stopped, he only remarked: 'You said last Saturday you were leaving me for your Auntie Maud's for ever. How was I to know you'd come bouncing back so quick the next day? I'm not God Almighty. I'm only a man.'

Still up on the chair, but looking as though she needed a glass of water, Mary Ann panted: 'Excuses! Being a man excuses everything?'

'That's how they are,' he said, even sombrely. He wanted to light a cigarette but somehow could not, as one can't in a solemn court of law. 'How would you like to be married to that crocodile in the black overcoat?' he inquired. 'Count your blessings, Mary

Ann.'

She jumped down from the chair, went to the table, and banged a pot or two about. Although the onslaughting fury had sunk, still she disclosed an identity new to him. 'There's a bit of that villain in every man,' she said rhetorically.

Ormond bridled. 'Here, that's a nasty insult!' In stern rebuke, he added: 'Not so insulting, though, as a married woman running away from her husband to her silly auntie's. A woman that won a scholarship in school, too... and top prize for good general conduct!' A certificate of these merits hung framed in the parlour: Mary Ann had a passion for framing everything framable.

'Ha!' She banged the lid on the casserole dish. 'A pity they don't give us girls lessons about men; we all leave school as big dunces about them.'

'Boys don't have lessons about women,' Ormond said, and, looking surprised himself at his ruminations, proceeded: 'That's proper enough; otherwise, we wouldn't have a champion time making big mistakes before settling down.'

She jabbed at the wilting dahlias in a pottery vase they had bought during a seaside holiday that summer. 'A pretty champion mistake you made last Saturday!' she exclaimed.

'And have dealt with it today in a champion way,' he retaliated, not without pride.

The dew was finally off the garden. They recognised it. Ormond crossed to her, took her shoulders, turned her round from the table. She had to be rediscovered. He gave her a shake. A bean fell out of his tight-knit curls and dropped into her bodice of flowered voile. Two pairs of tears also fell from behind her glasses.

'Let me find my bean,' he begged.

Later, tidily with handbrush and pan, he swept up all the beans from the floor. This was exceptional. In Bylau men are not much addicted to domestic jobs, and Ormond in particular, always out with the boys, was not partial to them. There was a vague aspect of compliant reformation about his figure as he stooped to the task.

RESURRECTION

Half a day before the lid was to be screwed down on her, Meg rose in her coffin and faintly asked for a glass of water. Her two sisters were bustling about the room, tidying and dusting and admiring the flowers, and both, after a few moments of terrified shock, looked at the recently deceased with a bitter anger. Once again she was doing something improper.

'Water!' stuttered Bertha. 'Go on with you now. What you want with water?' Gathering strength at the sound of her own voice, she went on sternly and as if speaking to a nuisance: 'Lie back thee, lie back. Dead you are.'

'Yes, indeed,' breathed Ellen, 'dead these four days, and the mourning ordered.'

Meg, nice in a new shiny white satin nightdress, trimmed with lace, stared back. But her gaze still had something of the marbled hardness of the dead. There seemed an awful weariness in the hang of her head. Her shoulders gave little clutching jumps. Suddenly she lay back in her coffin, sighing, and without further speech.

'Ha!' cried Bertha, in relief, 'a bit of life there was left in her nerves and made her body rise up like that. Funny thing! Just like some chickens run round the yard after you've chopped off their heads.' She sat down and her face was eased again. 'But a nasty turn it gave me, Ellen. Just like her it would have been, to do a trick on us, making us spend money on mourning and that five-guinea coffin.'

'Yes, indeed,' cried Ellen, her face still very grey from retreating hysteria, but relieved too, 'and eighty-five coming to the funeral tomorrow and an announcement in the newspaper.' She turned her head away from the coffin. 'A fine disgrace it would have been for us.'

And both sisters thought of the hours that must elapse before the undertaker arrived that afternoon safely to shut up the coffin. Meg might rise again and frighten them with a bit of secondhand life. Why, the next time something awful might happen – perhaps she would be jolted back entirely into the land of the living.

'He won't come till five o'clock,' said Bertha. 'He's busy burying Samson Lewis this afternoon.'

'Can't we screw the lid down ourselves?' Ellen quavered. 'Not right, is it, for us to have shocks like this. My heart's going pitapat.'

'Talk there might be if we shut her up before the time arranged,' Bertha answered, shaking her head. 'People will say we was in a hurry. You know,' she reminded her sister, 'that two or three are coming at tea-time to mourn with us while the job is being done.'

'Oh!' exclaimed Ellen, remembering at this, 'I didn't buy the cold ham at the shop this morning.'

'Sardines,' said Bertha definitely, reverting to a debate of that morning, 'will be enough, I tell you again. On toast. You can't give cold ham today and tomorrow.'

'When Ceinwen Roberts was buried,' Ellen, who was not quite so mean as Bertha, remarked, 'they had baron of beef, leg of pork, and veal pie. One meat is not enough for tomorrow, Bertha. Those there are who don't like cold ham.'

'Then the tinned salmon they must have,' Bertha grumbled.

'Haven't we spent enough on clothes! Twelve pound fifteen in the draper's. No one can say we've stinted decent burial for her.'

'Most of it,' said Ellen, with sudden sisterly sourness, 'on our backs.' Occasionally the sisters quarrelled.

'If we had died,' Bertha brooded, 'as cheap as possible she'd have put us away.'

'Well,' Ellen said, in the manner of one generously overlooking a fault, 'she was never a one to enjoy a funeral.'

'No,' continued Bertha, with a surprising depth of bitterness, 'men and whisky was her bent.'

'Hush, Bertha, hush. So many years ago that was.'

'Ha, craving she had for them always. If she hadn't been obliged to take to her bed and lie there helpless, she'd have been out in the world disgracing herself and us to her dying day.'

'Well,' soothed Ellen, 'safe she is now.'

But they both glanced apprehensively towards the coffin. Bleak and raddled and wintry, the sisters, who were in their fifties, pursed their lips. They were twins. Both wore a piled-up mass of coarse, dour hair in which were jabbed small combs and tortoise-shell prongs. Their faces were puckered in, secretive, and proud. In chapel and street they liked to swank: they liked people to think they were well off and to treat them with ceremony. They were daughters of a semi-successful builder, and in a hole behind some loose bricks in the cellar was the money he had made, for he had trusted no bank; his daughters thought likewise. A widower, he had died five years ago, and since then no event of importance had happened to the twins. But now the maladies of their younger sister Meg had culminated in a death too long delayed. They had looked on her as their cross. But they told themselves that they loved her, and indeed sometimes they had brought her a baked apple with clotted cream, her favourite, and showed affection. On the day she had lain back and stiffened, they thought it was for the best, all things considered. They began to fluff and preen themselves, for death is important and brings ceremony, display, and a great going out into public.

'She,' Ellen had wept at intervals, 'wasn't bad now and again, our poor Meg. After all, she didn't ought to have gone so young.'

'No,' agreed Bertha, who at intervals had been gloomy too, 'she didn't ought to have gone before she tried to tidy up her life a bit. But now it's happened—'

'Yes,' said Ellen, 'yes indeed.'

And after an hour or so of indulgence in the magic of grief they would bestir themselves, realising that a rare opportunity had come to them. Like royalty, they would ride in a procession for two miles to the cemetery, at every corner between the rows of houses knots of people gathered, craning their heads to see.

Then, again, it seemed they were to be thwarted. An hour or so later in that afternoon Meg sat up once more and peered round with dreadful stare, her white lips pulled back and showing her naked gums – for the sisters had removed her ten-guinea set of false teeth. And again she murmured for water. Ellen was alone in the room, Bertha having gone downstairs to prepare the food for the visitors; and realising this time that something remarkable had happened to the deceased, she tottered to the door and shrieked for her sister. Bertha came bustling upstairs, a half-cut loaf still clutched in her hand. 'What now, what now?' she, demanded, her suspicious fury ready.

'Come back again she has, asking for water,' moaned Ellen. And she added despairingly, 'Not dead at all is she.'

'Rubbish now, rubbish.' Bertha stood in the doorway like a snorting roused mare. 'Hasn't the doctor signed the certificate? Dead he said she was.' But there, undoubtedly, was the starkly upraised Meg, now looking round with vague and pathetic appeal. 'But if not dead she is,' breathed Bertha further, 'damages the doctor will have to pay us. Close on twenty pounds,' she suddenly screamed in shrill hysteria towards the menacing body, 'have we spent on you.'

The sisters advanced together towards the coffin, creeping, but angry now.

'Lie back,' Ellen also began shouting in the wrath of despair, 'lie back. Your funeral is tomorrow. At half-past two. Eighty-five are coming.'

Bertha laid her hand restrainingly on Ellen's bristling arm. She began to speak in a cunningly entreating voice, coaxing. 'Go you back, Meg, only half alive you'll be indeed if you don't. Not fit to live you are with your bladder and kidneys. And what if we go before you, who'll look after you then? The workhouse it'll be. Not worth living is life, Meg *fach*. A dirty business it is. Black is the future. Go you now, please, and follow soon we will, true enough. Better company in the other world than this.'

'Five guineas for your coffin alone!' Ellen took the coaxing cue from her sister, but added a whine to her voice. 'Look you how lovely it is. Polished oak. Die now, there's a nice girl, die now.'

But Meg's whitish eyes were fixed on the loaf of bread that was clutched in Bertha's hand; their dullness passed into a greedy gleam.

'Bread,' she mumbled, 'bread.' And with a pleased sigh she eagerly stretched forth her trembling hands.

Wholly convinced at last, the sisters cried out in fury and horror. The clamour brought neighbours running into the house. The foaming and stuttering twins were attended to by sympathetic women, while others stood in awe round the coffin. None attempted to lift the weak Meg out of her coffin or supply her with the refreshment she craved. Mrs. Williams, a strident and dominant woman, took charge and declared that a policeman must be informed before anything could be done. After some delay P.C. Johns appeared downstairs and in a stern, disapproving voice asked:

'What's this I hear about a corpse coming to life, Bertha Evans?'

'It's upstairs,' quavered Bertha. But at sight of the policeman she began to bounce back into energy, aware of the drama that was being offered her.

The policeman tramped heavily upstairs. Ellen had recovered some while before and was repeating over and over again how Meg had sat up twice. Exhausted with her futile demands for refreshment, Meg was now lying back amid the pleated mauve satin folds. There was no doubt, however, that life was flushing back into her features. The policeman gazed at her in the suspicious and convicting manner of his kind. At sight of him Meg gave a slight whimper, as if frightened. At one time in her young and gay days she had been arrested for drunkenness.

'A doctor must see her,' declared P. C. Johns, after ten minutes' cogitation. 'Nothing for me is there here.' And sullenly he went away.

After further delay and searching the doctor was found. It was now late evening and still Meg had not been removed from the coffin. As the news spread, people kept on trooping into the house from near and far. Bertha and Ellen, recovered, were the centre of much enquiry. Sympathy was lavished on them. What would be done with the black clothes now, and the coffin? And no ride to the cemetery tomorrow. Someone suggested that they should take a week at the seaside as recompense. Dr

Miskin himself, befuddled with whisky, as usual, glared at Meg so angrily that onlookers thought he was going to strike her. For a few moments he would not believe that she was living; he roughly pushed one of her already blinking eyelids up and down, prodded her, and spitefully gripped her limp wrist. Finally, he declared her living, told Bertha that in England such things often happened, and left instructions that Meg was to receive only milk and water for three days; he spoke as if she deserved such punishment. Bertha looked back at him malevolently.

'Dead you said she was and signed a certificate. Damages I ask you. What we've spent on mourning and the oak coffin. The food for the funeral tea tomorrow I leave out.'

The doctor spat and left the house. Bertha and Ellen began to weep in rage, several women loosened their tears, too, in sympathy. The undertaker, sweating in his haste, arrived and declared that contract had been made for the funeral tomorrow – he would keep it, and at two o'clock the hearse and carriages would be outside the house; no business of his was it if the corpse was not in the coffin. He was very agitated and spoke wildly; trade had been bad all winter. Bertha and Ellen, already incensed by the doctor, screamed and threatened until he went flying down the stairs. At the front door he turned and shouted back:

'On your hands the coffin will be, however. Made for you it was and I will not take it back now.'

Bertha and Ellen had to admit defeat. A neighbour consoled them by saying that the coffin could be kept under a bed until required and would make a good cupboard for blankets and such like.

Then once again Meg rose stark from her narrow bed and began whimpering.

'A bit of brandy,' she begged. 'And give me my teeth back, please, now.'

Bertha and Ellen looked at each other numbly. The teeth had already been sold to the pawnbroker, but this they did not want to admit before the neighbours. They went over to their sister and laid her back in the coffin.

'Hush now, Meg *fach*. Rest, be quiet, take time. The pump in your heart is not working proper yet. Soon it will be.'

'My teeth,' whispered Meg, 'give me my teeth—'

The twins were saved further explanation by the arrival of a reporter from the newspaper, Tommy Thomas, a frowning but brisk young man. After glancing at Meg, he took out his notebook and asked for particulars.

Bertha and Ellen began speaking together. Excitement shone from their eyes now. Never had they been in the newspapers. When Tommy asked for a photograph of Meg, Bertha declared flatly:

'No photo is there of her. But one of Ellen and myself I will give you, taken in Swansea.'

Tommy sucked his pencil. He asked the sisters if they had any special comment to make on the event. Bertha's sense of grievance again got the upper hand and she answered bitterly:

'Yes, indeed. This now. What she want to come back for? A fathead she was always. In life nightmares she was always having. Peace she had a chance of. Back she is now, the fool, where a lot of worries bit at her like a plague of evil rats. Fathead twice over. That put in your paper, young man, and let a bit of truth be told for once. Now then, Ellen, fetch the photo.'

In her coffin Meg still whimpered, as if in weary distress. When all the visitors had gone, weakly she managed to lift her head yet again. She asked to be taken out of the coffin. The twins pursed their lips; both, now that the excitement of the drama was over, felt flat, as if something had been filched from them. Ellen looked dangerously vexed. Bertha approached the coffin and said maliciously:

'What for you want to get out? Not many people is it get a chance to spend a night in a coffin. Comfortable it is surely? Clean and dry as the inside of a nut. You stay there, Meg. Stripped your bed is, and no sheets aired. And too weak you are to be shifted. Yes, indeed. Tomorrow we'll lift you out, yes, perhaps... Settle down now and rest...'

Tomos Owen is a lecturer, editor and writer. He has published on a range of Welsh writers, including Amy Dillwyn, Caradoc Evans, Arthur Machen and W.H. Davies.

Vera Bassett was born in Pontardulais in 1912. She held her first one-woman exhibition in the Hendy Urdd Centre in 1943, followed by others at the Mechanics Institute in the Bont in 1948 and the Glynn Vivian Art Gallery, Swansea, in 1949. Her work was considered by the critic Mervyn Levy "To express the very essence of the Welsh flair for interpreting aesthetic matters throughout the crystal flame of the lyrical, poetic eye." Her work reached an international platform with shows in New York and Paris. She died in 1997. A biography, *Vera Basset - a rare and endearing artist* by Donald Treharne was published in 2017.

The Rhys Davies Trust was set-up in 1990 through the support of his brother, Lewis Davies. It supports Welsh authors writing in the English language and sponsors the Rhys Davies Short Story competition, the winners of which include Leonora Brito, Lewis Davies, and Kate Hamer.

the RHYS DAVIES TRUST

LIBRARY OF WALES

The Library of Wales is a Welsh Government project designed to ensure that all of the rich and extensive literature of Wales which has been written in English will now be made available to readers in and beyond Wales. Sustaining this wider literary heritage is understood by the Welsh Government to be a key component in creating and disseminating an ongoing sense of modern Welsh cuture and history for the future Wales which is now emerging from contemporary society. Through these texts, until now unavailable or out of print or merely forgotten, the Library of Wales will bring back into play the voices and actions of the human experience that has made us, in all our complexity, a Welsh people.

The Library of Wales will include prose as well as poetry, essays as well as fiction, anthologies as well as memoirs, drama as well as journalism. It will complement the names and texts that are already in the public domain and seek to include the best of Welsh writing in English, as well as to showcase what has been unjustly neglected. No boundaries will limit the ambition of the Library of Wales to open up the borders that have denied some of our best writers a presence in a future Wales. The Library of Wales has been created with that Wales in mind: a young country not afraid to remember what it might yet become.

Dai Smith

LIBRARY OF WALES

FUNDED BY

CYNGOR LLYFRAU CYMRU
WELSH BOOKS COUNCIL

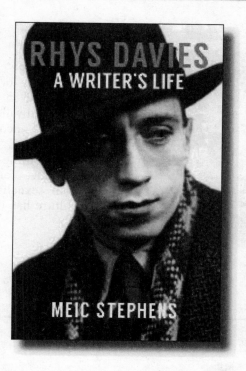

The Withered Root recounts the troubled life of Reuben Daniels. Reared in a South Wales industrial valley, in the bosom of the Nonconformist culture, revivalist passions constitute nothing but a perverse outlet for an all too human sexuality which chapel culture has otherwise repressed.

A Time to Laugh is set in a coal-mining valley on the eve of the 20th century against a background of industrial unrest and social change. The old certainties of pastoral Rhondda have given way to a new age of capital and steam, and life in the Valley has been transformed by strike, riot and gruelling poverty.

LIBRARY OF WALES

SERIES EDITOR: DAI SMITH

1	*So long, Hector Bebb*	Ron Berry
2	*Border Country*	Raymond Williams
3	*The Dark Philosophers*	Gwyn Thomas
4	*Cwmardy*	Lewis Jones
5	*Country Dance*	Margiad Evans
6	*A Man's Estate*	Emyr Humphreys
7	*Home to an Empty House*	Alun Richards
8	*In the Green Tree*	Alun Lewis
9	*Ash on a Young Man's Sleeve*	Dannie Abse
10	*Poetry 1900-2000*	Ed. Meic Stephens
11	Sport	Ed. Gareth Williams
12	*The Withered Root*	Rhys Davies
13	*Rhapsody*	Dorothy Edwards
14	*Jampot Smith*	Jeremy Brooks
15	*The Voices of the Children*	George Ewart Evans
16	*I Sent a Letter to my Love*	Bernice Rubens
17	*Congratulate the Devil*	Howell Davies
18	*The Heyday in the Blood*	Geraint Goodwin
19	*The Alone to the Alone*	Gwyn Thomas
20	*The Caves of the Alienation*	Stuart Evans
21	*A Rope of Vines*	Brenda Chamberlain
22	*Black Parade*	Jack Jones
23	*Dai Country*	Alun Richards
24	*The Valley, the City, the Village*	Glyn Jones
25	*The Great God Pan*	Arthur Machen
26	*The Hill of Dreams*	Arthur Machen
27	*The Battle to the Weak*	Hilda Vaughan
28	*Turf or Stone*	Margiad Evans
29	*Make Room for the Jester*	Stead Jones
30	*Goodbye Twentieth Century*	Dannie Abse
31	*All Things Betray Thee*	Gwyn Thomas
32	*The Volunteers*	Raymond Williams
33	*Flame and Slag*	Ron Berry
34	*The Water-castle*	Brenda Chamberlain
35	*A Kingdom*	James Hanley
36	*Autobiography of a Super-Tramp*	W.H.Davies
37	*Story I*	Ed. Dai Smith
38	*Story II*	Ed. Dai Smith
39	*A Time to Laugh*	Rhys Davies
40	*Young Emma*	W.H. Davies
41	*We Live*	Lewis Jones
42	*Carwyn*	Alun Richards
43	*Old Soldiers Never Die*	Frank Richards
44	*Old Soldier Sahib*	Frank Richards
45	*Farewell Innocence*	William Glynne-Jones
46	*Ride the White Stallion*	William Glynne-Jones
47	*Dat's Love*	Leonora Brito
48	*The Selected Stories of Rhys Davies*	Rhys Davies
49	*In and Out of the Goldfish Bowl*	Rachel Trezise

WWW.THELIBRARYOFWALES.COM